THE TROUBLEMAKERS

Books by Tamzin Merchant

THE HATMAKERS

THE MAPMAKERS

THE TROUBLEMAKERS

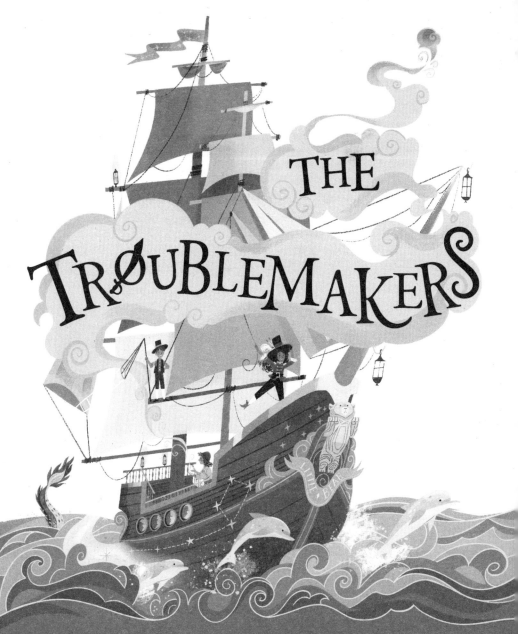

THE TROUBLEMAKERS

TAMZIN MERCHANT

Illustrated by PAOLA ESCOBAR

PUFFIN

PUFFIN BOOKS

UK | USA | Canada | Ireland | Australia
India | New Zealand | South Africa

Puffin Books is part of the Penguin Random House group of companies
whose addresses can be found at global.penguinrandomhouse.com.

www.penguin.co.uk
www.puffin.co.uk
www.ladybird.co.uk

First published 2024
001

Text copyright © Tamzin Merchant, 2024
Illustrations copyright © Paola Escobar, 2024

The moral right of the author and illustrator has been asserted

Set in 13.3/18 pt Bembo Book MT Pro
Typeset by Jouve (UK), Milton Keynes
Printed and bound in Great Britain by Clays Ltd, Elcograf S.p.A.

The authorized representative in the EEA is Penguin Random House Ireland,
Morrison Chambers, 32 Nassau Street, Dublin D02 YH68

A CIP catalogue record for this book is available from the British Library

HARDBACK ISBN: 978-0-241-61039-8
INTERNATIONAL PAPERBACK ISBN: 978-0-241-64871-1

All correspondence to:
Puffin Books
Penguin Random House Children's
One Embassy Gardens, 8 Viaduct Gardens, London SW11 7BW

For Katie, my favourite Troublemaker

List of Illustrations

The Troublemakers Island!

1. **The Belly Cave**
2. **Tumblerush Waterfall**
3. **Moonstruck Lagoon**
4. **The Soulhope Tree**
5. **Troublemaker Treeship**
6. **Tablecloth Glade**

Here be Dragons!

Prologue

It was a starless, moonless night.

A night dark enough for kidnapping . . .

A roaring October wind wailed around Gaunthead Towers, wrenching open windows and howling into rooms as the sea crashed on to the cliffs below.

Another kind of howl echoed down the cold stone corridors of the school:

'*PRUDENCE!*'

Urgent footsteps rang along one of the corridors. The dormitory door burst open, and frightened children sat up in their beds as a wild-eyed woman hurtled inside.

'*WHERE'S PRUDENCE?*' the woman screamed, charging to the bed at the end of the room.

The bed was empty, the covers pulled back.

'SHE'S GONE!' the woman cried, falling to her knees.

The open window banged in the wind and, across the bay, a ship with ragged sails lurched out to sea.

Lightning flashed through the dormitory, illuminating the wall between the window and the empty bed, where a single word was scrawled:

TROUBLEMAKERS

'The stars are full of stories, littlest Hatmaker. Following the stars will always lead you to great adventures.'

Cordelia Hatmaker gripped the ship's wheel, the deck of *Little Bear* solid beneath her feet. She could *smell* adventure in the spring wind; it smelled of salt and sky laced with a hint of fresh tar. Stars spangled the rigging, winking with the promise of exciting escapades to come.

Her father, Prospero Hatmaker, stood on the deck beside her.

'But every adventurer needs a compass,' he added. 'The *heart* is a compass. Follow your heart and you'll go wisely and wildly all your life.'

Cordelia put her hand to her heart. She could feel it beating, soft and steady in her chest – a living creature.

'Is that today's lesson, Father?' she asked.

Prospero grinned. 'Today's lesson is this: be careful of the ship's biscuit! It doesn't taste like biscuits at all!'

Cordelia grinned back.

They were not out at sea yet. All through autumn and winter, Cordelia had witnessed the ship being built and marvelled at the magic of making such a thing: a beast to ride the sea, made of wood and rope and canvas. She had climbed through the ribcage of its skeleton, been caught up in the criss-crossing sinews of rigging, and gaped at the baggy swags of sails that would fill, like lungs, with air. The ship was made of Fleetwood, which skimmed swiftly across water. The figurehead was a perfect little bear with fur carved into wind-blown ripples.

When the master shipwright, bobbing up from Greenwich on an important-looking barge, had come to inspect her, he had pronounced *Little Bear* 'the finest vessel of her kind' and had added, 'I'll wager she's the quickest too!' – causing Cordelia to glow with pride.

Tonight, *Little Bear* was quiet. After finishing the sticky job of tarring her hull, the shipbuilders had gone home, leaving Cordelia and her father listening to the lap and hush of the Thames just beyond the dry dock in which the ship had been built. In a few days, when the glistening tar had set, the dry dock would be flooded with water and *Little Bear* would float out on to the wide river.

'Then all that's left to do,' Cordelia said, 'is add *provisions*. Meaning food.'

'And water,' Prospero added.

'Yes,' Cordelia agreed. 'Water's very important for a sea voyage.'

The long-promised sea voyage! Now the spring tides were rising, it was nearly time to set off.

Cordelia and her father were going on a voyage to collect magical ingredients for the hats their family made. They were to sail to the Canary Islands, to search for the freckle-leafed Vim Shrub and Songstress Snails, whose pearly trails warbled with silvery music. From the Canaries, they would sail due east to the coast of Morocco, where they planned to rummage in the sands for the flashing whorls of Storm Nautilus Conches.

Soon there would be a much greater demand than usual for ingredients, because next week, for the first time in two hundred and fifty years, King George was to declare that making magical things would be unrestricted for everyone in Britain once again.

For the past two and a half centuries, only the six Maker families of London had been allowed to create clothes using magical ingredients. But in a few days' time *everyone* would be able to express themselves using magical ingredients, free from the fear of arrest.

Cordelia loved feeling the tingle in her fingertips when she was making something magical, whether it be a bonnet to give the wearer confidence or a bicorn to inspire daydreams. When she and her father returned from their voyage, the cargo hold of *Little Bear* would be bursting with magical ingredients to transform people's ordinary clothes into enchanted ones. Cordelia could not wait to set off.

However, one slight shadow was cast over the bright adventure: the rumours of a dangerous band of pirates calling themselves the Troublemakers.

First, these pirates had kidnapped the daughter of an important politician, snatching her from her boarding-school bed in the middle of the night, leaving nothing but their name scrawled across the wall as a sign that they'd been there.

Then there had been chaos at the Winter Ball, when several lords had suddenly been attacked by their own garments, shrieking and howling as their boots suddenly made them leap as though their feet were on fire. Moments later, their hats clamped themselves over their eyes and the wearers began bellowing swear words in multiple languages. A nest of Whistling Wasps had been thrown into their midst, and the air filled with the sinister whistle of thousands of wasps mingled with the sound of stampeding revellers fleeing the scene. In the ruckus, several ice sculptures – not to mention Lady Trundlemonk's nose – had been broken.

London had barely had time to recover from the Winter Ball (victims of the wasp stings were still whistling) when the Troublemakers struck again. Imp Eggs were crushed into the ink of a self-righteous magazine called *The Quarterly Scorn* and, rather than the usual articles sneering about the latest fashions, every single copy of the newest issue contained nothing but foul words and fart jokes from cover to cover.

Days later, the king's horses were somehow fed Craze-Hay, which led to neighing chaos in front of the palace. Riots broke out regularly at chocolate houses across the city, and strange orange caterpillars were placed on hundreds of paintings in the Royal Academy, so that very serious portraits of noble ladies and gentlemen all appeared to have bushy ginger moustaches. The caterpillars proved impossible to catch and several days later hatched into dazzling and distracting butterflies that caused three carriage accidents on Piccadilly, and Lady Clustertrunce to be tipped from her sedan chair into a large pile of horse poo.

All winter, the Troublemakers had gone on to create catastrophe and disaster throughout London, gloating about their actions in a morning newspaper called *The Rude Awakening*. Despite being the architects of some strange and spectacular acts of destruction, the Troublemakers had never actually been *sighted*. Rumours about them grew wilder in the dark. Some people claimed they were evil sorcerers, who wore the night like cloaks. Others insisted they transformed into ravens to flee the scenes of their crimes. One wild-eyed man was seen shouting at Speakers' Corner that the Troublemakers were 'the ghosts of traitors put to death in the Tower, risen from the dead for revenge'.

Although Prospero did not believe these feverish speculations, he became hesitant to take Cordelia on a voyage across seas that were infested with pirates. Cordelia, however, had endeavoured to persuade her father that the Trouble-makers were highly unlikely to cross their path, seeing as how the ocean was very large and ships were very small.

'Besides,' Cordelia had said persuasively, 'they're causing trouble in *London* – we'll be somewhere else!'

Prospero had pointed out that, although the trouble was being made in London, many of the magical ingredients being used to create the chaos were not commonly found in Great Britain.

'They must be finding them somewhere else,' he mused. 'And getting them into London somehow.'

Cordelia was not concerned by this small detail – so long as the Troublemakers did not stop her from going on the long-promised voyage with her father aboard *Little Bear*.

She had her own little cabin, with a bunk that swung gently from the ceiling on ropes to stop her from getting seasick as she slept, and a round porthole with rippled glass in it. She liked to look out of her porthole, imagining the sights she would soon see: perhaps a triumphant sunrise over the blue Atlantic or the coast of a whole new continent.

Her father's cabin, which had glittering windows that stretched the width of the ship, contained a collection of maps and instruments that he used to navigate the seas. The other cabins, pieced together within the ship like a neat puzzle, contained bunks for all twelve members of the crew – everyone from the first mate to the cabin boy. There was a galley for the ship's cook, complete with a brick stove, and a large store for the food and water they would need for the journey.

One of Cordelia's favourite nooks on *Little Bear* was the Weather Pantry, which had been stocked by her friend Win Fairweather, who brewed all kinds of weather and bottled it in glass jars. Weather-brewing was not officially legal yet, because it was a kind of ancient Maker magic that had been outlawed centuries ago, so the cabinet was cleverly concealed behind a wooden panel. The shelves hung on ropes so that the jars wouldn't be shaken about in stormy weather. In their secret cabinet, the Cumulus Bottles gleamed, the Wind Bags trembled on their pegs and the Breeze Strings danced.

'All you need do if you're stuck in the doldrums,' Win had told Cordelia, catching a piece of Breeze String as it wriggled away across the deck, 'is undo one of these knots. It will unleash the strand of wind caught within, then you'll be underway again. You should save the Wind Bags in case you ever become becalmed.'

When Cordelia put her hand on a Wind Bag, she felt a belly of air straining at the cloth. She was proud of the Weather Pantry; no other ship had a secret store of weather on board.

This evening, Cordelia decided to practise climbing the rigging once more before they went home for dinner. She was determined to climb it as fast as the cabin boy, Jack. He was as quick as a monkey, scampering up the ropes to the crow's nest. Cordelia climbed more slowly, hand over hand, up the nets. She had calluses forming on her palms from the rough ropes. She was very proud of her calluses.

She tucked her hatpin, with its ocean-blue stone, firmly into her hair and swung into the rigging, up, up into a complicated forest of ropes and masts. The deck grew smaller as she climbed; she saw her father beetling across it as he went to check the bowsprit ropes. Cordelia climbed high enough to see the haze of the marshes beyond London, almost lost in the blur of twilight. A ship was coming upriver towards them, a heavy shape low in the water, laden with goods it was bringing from some far-flung place.

'Must be a merchant ship,' Cordelia murmured.

Suddenly a *splash* tore through the quiet tapestry of evening river sounds.

A wooden crate had gone over the side of the merchant ship as it glided by. The crate bobbed in the water, but the ship sailed on, heedless of its lost goods.

Cordelia was drawing breath to call 'CARGO OVERBOARD!' when she heard a thread of voice twist along the river.

'*Double, double!*'

'Double, double!' came a hissed reply.

And, quick as an eel through the water, a rowing boat nipped out from the riverbank.

It was dangerous for a tiny boat to be out there among the hulking oceangoers. But the boat was nimble, the person rowing quick and strong, not hampered by the thick cloak that swaddled him.

As the merchant ship sailed onward, the rowing boat chased the crate left bobbing in its wake. Within moments, the boatman caught it and hauled it aboard, before slipping away into the shadows of the riverbank.

Cordelia was motionless in the rigging.

The river smoothed over as the whispers of 'Double, double!' dissolved in the air.

It had all happened in a few heartbeats, in that strange last light as the evening gave way to the oncoming night.

But Cordelia was sure she had seen . . .

'Smugglers!'

CHAPTER 2

'*D ouble, double?*' Goose Bootmaker frowned. 'What does that mean?'

'Maybe it's a code?' Sam Lightfinger suggested.

'Must be,' Cordelia agreed. 'Or a signal of some kind.'

It was the first good sunshine of spring. Daffodils gleamed in the grass of St James's Park as Cordelia and her friends Goose and Sam tramped across Pall Mall and down the Avenue, a long sweep of towering oaks.

The Avenue was every fashionable Londoner's favourite place to be seen. Many stylish (and some outlandish) outfits were on display today. There were ladies in hats adorned with Poetical Pears, wearing Ode-Ribboned Boots to complement them, and gentlemen in Frizzle Fern Cloaks offset with Fluttering Gloves to make their hands extra elegant.

But Cordelia, Goose and Sam hardly noticed these magical clothes. They were carrying a heavy bucket between them, which was almost overflowing with a glistering liquid that sparkled like diamonds. It bumped against their legs, splashing droplets on to the ground. Where they fell, tiny starlike flowers sprang up, bursting into rainbow blooms.

Hatmaker, Bootmaker and Lightfinger left a meandering trail of flowers down the Avenue. People picked the flowers, tucking them into buttonholes. They made everybody feel especially glad and springy. Somebody burst into song, while another danced a jig. The three friends were unaware of the frenzy of festivity left in their wake.

'Who was in the rowing boat yesterday evening?' Goose wondered.

'I couldn't see his face,' Cordelia said regretfully. 'He was wearing a cloak.'

At the end of the Avenue, they called cheery hellos to Master Ambrosius. The youthful sweetmaker often appeared in the park, selling delicious treats from his cart: gleaming toffee apples, strawberry nougat, iced coconut delights and clotted-cream cloudbuns so light they had to be kept in a box to stop them blowing away.

'My favourite Makers!' Master Ambrosius beamed as Cordelia, Sam and Goose passed by. 'Good morning!'

'We'll be back in a little while,' Cordelia told him, hauling the bucket along.

'I'll save you some Mint Cobwebs!' Master Ambrosius called after them as they trudged across the Great Lawn towards the shrubbery. 'They're very popular today.'

'Not – much – further!' Goose panted, stopping to wipe his forehead. He got a smear of the liquid on his face, dazzling a passer-by with sudden angelic looks.

The three friends wove through a pink flurry of ornamental cherry trees into a quiet corner of the park where a slender sapling grew.

'There's a flower on it!' Sam pointed. 'That's new!'

The sapling was all that was left of an orchard of magical golden apple trees that had been burned to the ground by an evil man named Lord Witloof. After Lord Witloof had been defeated, Cordelia had searched among the ashes of the ruined orchard and found a single golden apple that had survived the fire, lying in the blackened grass.

Cordelia, Goose and Sam had planted the apple, watering the spot frequently with buckets brimming with the Essence of Magic, the source of which they had discovered hidden in a secret well beneath the Makers' Guildhall.

The golden apples were said to have mysterious magical powers, and Cordelia and her friends carefully tended the spot, bringing magic and hope in equal measure, which is the best way to grow things. Eventually, in February, a green-gold twigling emerged from the earth. It had grown a little each day, venturing tender leaves at the beginning of March in answer to the strengthening sun.

It was now just taller than Goose. Today it offered a pale yellow blossom, like a hopeful question, on the end of its single branch. It was nothing like the grand orchard that had been destroyed; it was just a young tree with a single flower. But that was how every great orchard began.

'You'll be sure to look after it, won't you, Goose?' Cordelia asked. 'When we're —'

She stopped, catching sight of the sudden glum expression on Goose's face.

Goose's heart was set on joining the crew of *Little Bear*. He had earned his place on board the ship, spending hours learning the ropes with Jack, and he got so good at tying sailors' knots that it was impossible to tell the difference between the young bootmaker's and the cabin boy's. But now the subject of the voyage was a source of gloom whenever it was mentioned.

Several times, Goose had asked his mother's permission to take part in the voyage. The first time he asked, his mother said, 'No.' The second time, she said, 'No, *no*.' The third time, she replied with: 'No, *no*, NO!' At this point, Goose decided it would be wise to stop asking. He suspected his mother had an infinite supply of *no*'s, which she spat like darts at his adventurous ambitions and deflated them.

Although the Hatmaker and Bootmaker families had recently laid aside decades of enmity, Cordelia was still the *tiniest* bit nervous when Nigella Bootmaker smiled in her direction. She had not yet summoned the courage to knock on the tall door of Bootmaker Mansion to demand that Goose be allowed to go on *Little Bear*'s maiden voyage – much as she wanted to.

Thinking a change of subject might be helpful, Cordelia nodded to the watering can that they'd brought with them.

'Go on, maybe it'll grow a mind-changing apple?' she suggested. 'And we can put it as a decoration on your mother's hat!'

'That'd be good!' Goose enthused, filling the watering can from the bucket and carefully pouring the sparkling liquid around the tree's roots. 'D'you think that would work?'

Cordelia paused for a moment. 'Well, Aunt Ariadne did once tell me that trying to change someone's mind is Meddling Magic,' she admitted. 'Which is illegal.'

Before they could ponder the ethics of Meddling Magic, they were distracted by a puff of golden pollen that burst from the pale yellow flower, and a bumblebee landed on the blossom in a gentle embrace.

Heading back towards Master Ambrosius across the Great Lawn, the three children at last noticed the people wearing magical Maker hats and boots, with matching cloaks and gloves and watches. It was something they were only just becoming accustomed to seeing.

For three decades, the Maker families of London — Hatmakers, Bootmakers, Cloakmakers, Glovemakers, Watchmakers — had refused to speak to each other, let alone work together to create harmonious outfits. This refusal to co-operate meant that a customer would never dare to wear a Hatmaker hat at the same time as a pair of Bootmaker boots, for example, for fear that the magical ingredients would react strangely together. A Hot-Headed Hat worn with a pair of Louche Boots might result in the wearer's feet attempting to go in an entirely different direction from their head. A pair of Gladhand Gloves combined with a Doddle Watch would result in twitchy fingers.

At the end of last summer, Cordelia, Goose, Sam and the other Maker children had banded together to unite the Makers once more. Finally, after thirty years of exchanging nothing but scowls, the Makers had begun to exchange ideas again. Now Londoners were able to visit the Makers' Guild-hall and be fitted for an entire ensemble of clothes that worked together in perfect harmony.

'Look!' Goose pointed to a person dressed from head to toe in Mellifluent Silk, holding a slender cane carved from Buddleia wood, decorated with tiny jewelled flowers. At that very moment, a butterfly — the first the children had seen this spring — alighted on the cane.

'A Canemaker cane spotted out in the wild!' Cordelia whispered. 'Delilah will be delighted!'

While five of the Maker families had refused to work together for thirty years, the sixth and final family – the Canemakers – had been forbidden from doing so. Magical canes had been banned because many of them, encrusted with Fury Jewels, had contained treacherous hidden sword-sticks that led to hot-headedness, jealousy and sword fights in the streets. Those dangerous canes had been made by Solomon Canemaker, who had been found guilty of treason and expelled from the Makers' Guildhall. His daughter, Delilah, at first swore revenge, but had a change of heart when she was locked up in prison, realizing that it is a far greater deed to mend things than to break them apart.

Still, Londoners were slow to trust a Canemaker again. Though Delilah Canemaker created wondrous canes, wrapped with rainbows or decorated with Merrybird feathers, Cordelia had not yet seen one being used out and about in town. Today's was the first! And what a beauty it was.

As Cordelia, Sam and Goose reached Master Ambrosius (who was busy serving a crowd of ladies clamouring for sugared violets), they saw a procession of grey enter the bright spring green of the park.

Every fortnight, pupils from Miss Prim's Academy for the Improvement of Small Minds arrived in St James's Park to march up and down in solemn rows, led by the stately Miss Prim herself. These children, in their stiff, speckless clothes, displayed awe-inspiring politeness and serious deportment in a way that made Cordelia feel distinctly scruffy. Miss Prim was a paragon of perfect manners. She was neat and polished, and weaponized her smiles to let the recipient know she was judging them.

The grey procession turned neatly up the Avenue, leaving an awed silence in its wake. Even the herons, poised in the pond, looked sideways as Miss Prim and her pupils passed them by. Ladies paused, sugared violets forgotten in their mouths, to stare at the group. Everybody in the park felt a little more self-conscious, suddenly aware of having untidy hair or untied laces.

Before Cordelia had torn her eyes away from the impeccable headmistress and her gliding train of pupils, a strange bird call whooped through the trees – and Miss Prim twitched.

The headmistress turned to nod politely at the passing Lord Buncle, but suddenly jerked her head in a manner more befitting a sailor than a lady, and stuck out her tongue. Her neatly folded hands wrenched apart, splaying open in an extremely rude gesture that she waggled at the appalled lord.

There were gasps from the crowd of onlookers.

As Miss Prim's own mouth fell open in shock, an enormous belch came out.

Lord Buncle dropped his toffee apple.

The headmistress halted in the middle of the Avenue, and her pupils staggered into a crush behind her. She turned sharply to admonish them, and a sound erupted from her that Goose would later describe as being 'like the loudest trumpet in the orchestra'.

Someone snickered with laughter.

All of Miss Prim's composure evaporated and she stamped and yelled, swearing as she performed violent scissor kicks. She turned cartwheels, flashing her petticoats, and bowled over a doddering group of old men. She kicked horse poo at Lady Clustertrunce, pulled off a marquis's wig, and tore round in circles, barking like a dog.

Her pupils backed away fearfully as their headmistress began twisting on the spot, going faster and faster as though she was wearing a tornado instead of a cape.

'We'd better help!' Cordelia gasped, grabbing Goose and Sam. 'It's got to be the clothes – something's gone wrong!'

They hurried towards the howling blur that was Miss Prim.

'I'll get the shoes!' Goose declared gallantly.

'You take the cape, Sam!' Cordelia yelled. 'I'll get the hat!'

But it was the gloves that proved the first challenge for Cordelia; she had to fend off a two-pronged attempt from one of the lace-gloved hands to poke her in the eyes. Sam jerked Miss Prim to a stop, fumbling with her cape buttons, as Cordelia swerved and ducked, dodging a series of punches

All of Miss Prim's
composure evaporated . . .

and upper cuts. She finally managed to tear the gloves off, and threw them to the ground, where they flipped over and began grabbing at nearby ankles.

'Now for the bonnet!' she panted.

Miss Prim wailed, pulling grotesque faces that were more like the gurning of a gargoyle than the serenely superior expression she usually presented to the world.

Goose emerged from beneath the headmistress's dress, sporting a black eye and clutching one grey shoe. The other went flying over his head into the undergrowth.

Sam was still wrestling the cape, which appeared to be equally as difficult as wrangling a tornado. At last, she wrenched it loose and managed to throw herself to the ground, pinning the cape down.

Cordelia grabbed the straw bonnet and yanked it off.

At last, Miss Prim fell still. Her hair was a crazed haystack and her eyes were wild.

All around them, people stared in astonishment at the headmistress, who had just given the most spectacular display of bad behaviour ever seen in St James's Park.

'That was –' Cordelia began, but a tiny bird burst out of Miss Prim's pocket watch.

'*CUCKOO! CUCKOO!*'

'The watch too!' Cordelia yelped.

She grabbed at it but missed as Miss Prim took several jerky steps backwards.

'!ON' Miss Prim cried. '!WON EM FFO TI EKAT'

'*WHAT?*' cried Cordelia.

'!TARB DIPUTS UOY, EREHT DNATS TSUJ T'NOD'

Cordelia watched in horror as Miss Prim strode backwards across the grass, bawling, '*!CIGAM ETAH I*'

'Look out!' Cordelia shouted. 'The pond!'

But it was too late. Miss Prim sploshed backwards into the muddy shallows, slipped and sat down firmly in a green patch of weed.

A heron looked down its long bill at her disdainfully.

'We've got to tell them at the Guildhall!' Cordelia gasped, snatching up the cape and gloves while gingerly holding the bonnet, as Goose heaved Sam to her feet, trying not to drop Miss Prim's shoe. Together, they hurtled down the Avenue, leaving several of her pupils to pull Miss Prim out of the mud.

CHAPTER 3

'*Up a little!*'
'*A bit to the left!*'

Cordelia, Sam and Goose burst through the front door of the Guildhall and tumbled into the Great Chamber to find an array of Makers smiling fixedly at them from across the vast circular room. They skidded to a stop at the bottom of the sweeping staircase.

They could even see *themselves* standing in the unblinking group: Cordelia holding a filigree-feather hat, Goose posing with a silver-buckled boot, Sam smiling at a firefly on her fingertip.

'It's finally finished!' Goose whispered.

A life-sized portrait was being winched on to the wall. Beneath their painted selves, many real-life Makers milled about, admiring the artwork.

'Mrs Cloakmaker, you look positively regal!'

'Mr Watchmaker, you are mag*nan*imous!'

'Look at Violet picking her nose!' someone sniggered.

'That's not me; that's Vera!' protested Violet Glovemaker.

'Perfect!' a voice called. 'Just there!'

The painting came to a stop high above the Makers' heads. It was very wide, stretching between several tall stone pillars that lined the circular room. Every Maker belonging to the Guildhall — twenty-five in total — was depicted in the painting. Cordelia had to admire it: not only had the painting taken several weeks to complete, it had also meant that the Makers — sworn enemies until recently — had had to stand very close together and be polite to each other for hours on end.

Suddenly the painting disappeared from view and Cordelia was consumed by darkness.

'UUHUUHUUHUUH!' Cordelia heard her own voice juddering in her throat. She was lost in a grey tornado, spinning furiously. '*Help!*'

With a jolt, a scrap of light tore through the darkness and she was spun out of the whirlwind and across the Great Chamber, where she ended up sprawled on the floor. This time all the unblinking eyes looking down at her were real, not painted.

'Dilly!' Cordelia's aunt, Ariadne Hatmaker, exclaimed. 'What's happened?'

'In the park!' Cordelia gasped, pinning the lace gloves to the floor to stop them from poking her eyes. 'Miss Prim!'

'Maker clothes gone haywire!' Goose cried, holding up the headmistress's shoe. It bucked in his hands, trying to kick him.

'It was madness!' Sam added, dragging the cape away from Cordelia. It thrashed wildly, raring to ensnare its next victim. Makers gathered warily around it as Cordelia clambered to her feet, looking around for her father to show him the strange cloak.

She realized he wasn't there. He must have been at the shipbuilder's yard, overseeing the second tarring of *Little Bear*'s hull. But her uncle, Tiberius Hatmaker, stepped forward and poked the cape with his toe.

'What is this roguery?' he muttered. 'Looks like it's got bits of hurricane stitched in it.'

'That isn't ours!' Mr Cloakmaker cried. 'I've never seen such a naughty piece of clothing in my life!'

'And we certainly didn't make *this*!' Mrs Glovemaker declared, snatching a lace glove from the floor. It promptly slapped her in the face, and she dropped it. 'OUCH!'

'It's got a mind of its own!' Buster Glovemaker shrieked, chucking the glove across the room to start a violent game of catch with his twin, Bernard.

'That's not normal,' Aunt Ariadne muttered, watching the lace fingers making rude signs as the glove arced through the air.

Cordelia understood what her aunt meant: usually clothes woven with Maker magic only became animated when they were worn. But Miss Prim's clothes seethed with frenzied energy all on their own.

The glove began smacking Bernard round the head, and Cordelia rushed to his rescue.

Mrs Bootmaker examined the shoe. 'Look at this stitching!' she exclaimed. 'It's clearly been done by a lunatic!'

'Don't blame me, Mother,' Ignatius Bootmaker spluttered. 'I didn't make it.'

'None of us made *any* of these blasted things,' Uncle Tiberius growled, picking up the bonnet. He immediately threw himself across the floor in a series of forward rolls, bowling over the Watchmakers as if they were skittles.

'Tiberius, careful!' Aunt Ariadne yelped.

Uncle Tiberius collided with the wall, and the bonnet, thankfully, rolled away from him.

The young Watchmakers, Hop and Tick, levered their grandfather slowly to his feet, as though he was the hand of a clock striking twelve.

'I suspect this was the work of the Troublemakers,' Tyde Watchmaker announced gravely.

'They must be stopped!' Mr Bootmaker blustered. 'It's getting ridiculous! First the attack at the Winter Ball —'

'Bah!' Uncle Tiberius interrupted from the floor. 'The Sensible Party had that coming!'

The lords who had been tormented at the Winter Ball by Biting Boots and Whistling Wasps were a group of politicians called the Sensible Party. Their leader was a particularly pompous man named Sir Piers Oglethorne: the father of Prudence Oglethorne, who had been snatched from her bed by the Troublemakers in their very first act of mischief.

When Cordelia had found out that a collection of politicians was known as a 'party', she thought it a rather strange joke. The Sensible Party were quite the opposite of a party: they disapproved of fun and did not believe in dancing under any circumstances. Once, they had tried to cancel Christmas for being 'too frivolous'.

After the Winter Ball, Sir Piers had stood in the palace foyer, raging that the Makers had played a scandalous trick. It turned out that each member of the Sensible Party had received a parcel that afternoon, containing a pair of shiny shoes and a handsome new hat. Flattering handwritten notes had accompanied the parcels, urging each lord to wear the items to the ball that evening. Each one had been signed *From an Admirer*.

The Makers had stoutly denied they had created the clothes that had caused the politicians such embarrassment and had pointed out that the Troublemakers had in fact proudly claimed responsibility. But Sir Piers, who often railed against the Makers in Parliament for being 'fanciful', declared: 'You can't spell TROUBLEMAKER without MAKER!' and refused to believe the Guildhall Makers were innocent.

In the aftermath of the ball, Prospero had inspected the gentlemen's gifts, finding twitchy purple leaves tucked into the soles of every shoe, which explained the wild dancing. Wriggling strands of seaweed had been woven into the hatbands, and sinister frills of pulsing orange fungus had been discovered inside the hats.

'They're such rare ingredients that I don't recognize them,' Prospero had said, frowning. 'Something about these clothes is quite unhinged. They should go in the Menacing Cabinet.'

While more unrecognizable ingredients were detected in Miss Prim's clothing, Ignatius Bootmaker stood by and bellowed: 'The Sensible Party are right! The Troublemakers are DANGEROUS! They kidnapped a child OUT OF HER OWN BED!'

Mr Cloakmaker drew his two children closer, while Mrs Glovemaker clasped her daughters' hands and Hop Watchmaker's eyes grew round as clocks.

'The only reason the snivelling Sensible Party care about catching the Troublemakers is because they made them look RIDICULOUS!' Tiberius ranted, very loudly.

A face peered out of a nearby workshop. Cordelia met Delilah Canemaker's anxious gaze and remembered that the last time the Makers had quarrelled badly, Delilah – then just nine years old – had ended up abandoned in a workhouse.

'BUT THEY'RE MAKING US *REAL* MAKERS LOOK BAD!' Ignatius bawled.

Delilah twitched anxiously. Even though she was now a fully grown adult, squabbling among the Makers made her very uneasy.

Uncle Tiberius opened his mouth to yell again –

'STOP!' Cordelia roared.

She grabbed a fistful of Hush Buttons from Mrs Cloakmaker's basket and threw them in the air. The Great Chamber was suddenly so quiet that everyone could hear the thrum of buttons landing on the floor.

'We mustn't argue with each other!' Cordelia whispered.

Vera and Violet Glovemaker and their brothers Buster and Bernard, along with Hop and Tick Watchmaker, Charity Cloakmaker, Goose and Sam all nodded sombrely. It had been this group of Makers – the children – who had put aside their families' quarrels and become friends. They all knew how hard-won this precious friendship was.

'Make peace,' Cordelia demanded, staring fiercely at her uncle.

'All right,' Uncle Tiberius muttered. 'Sorry.'

'Yes – sorry,' Ignatius mumbled.

Hatmaker and Bootmaker stuck out their hands and shook. The painting of the Makers looked down on the scene, smiling.

'Now, we need to see if there are any ingredients on the clothes that might give clues about where they came from,' Cordelia said calmly.

One by one, the Makers pinned down the items Miss Prim had been wearing. They unpicked stitches, removed buttons and examined ribbons. Within the lining of the cape, they discovered dozens of mysterious wriggling bright-green seeds, along with several unidentifiable orange feathers in the bonnet, and a handful of fleshy red flower petals that no one could name tucked into the shoe. There were even a few strands of long, knotted hair twisted round the fingers of the gloves.

'But hair from *what*, I have no idea!' declared Mrs Glovemaker.

Cordelia ran to fetch a jar for the wriggling seeds. Once the lid was screwed on tight, everybody passed the jar round to peer at the seeds seething against the glass.

'I've never seen seeds like this in my life,' Uncle Tiberius admitted.

'Nor have I,' said Tyde Watchmaker. 'Where on earth do they come from?'

'My father will know,' Cordelia said confidently, taking the jar. 'He's sailed all over the world seeking ingredients; he's bound to have seen these somewhere.'

'We may not know where they are from, but I think we can all agree on where they should go,' Aunt Ariadne said sternly, pointing at the Menacing Cabinet.

Six keys were fetched from the six Maker workshops. One by one, each Maker family put their key into the matching lock and turned, until the heavy iron door of the Menacing Cabinet opened with an ominous creak. The dancing shoes that had been on the unfortunate feet of Sir Piers Oglethorne at the Winter Ball tried to escape, tapping frantically towards the light, but Goose pounced on them and hurled them back into the darkness. All of Miss Prim's magicked clothes were swept safely away with them.

It was a relief to hear the six locks click once more.

'I wonder what was on the watch,' Sam said, after Delilah Canemaker had turned her key in the final lock.

'Which watch?' Aunt Ariadne asked tensely.

'I forgot!' Cordelia cried. 'There was a pocket watch, too, that made Miss Prim go backwards.'

'Into the pond,' Goose added, his mouth twitching.

'Oh no!' Aunt Ariadne groaned. 'Come along, Tyde. We should go to the park and see if we can find it.'

'There's also a shoe somewhere in the undergrowth!' Goose called.

After gathering a Calming Cloak, Pacifying Hat and pair of Serene Slippers, Ariadne Hatmaker and all three Watchmakers hurried off to the park.

'Back to work, everyone!' Mrs Bootmaker instructed bossily.

All afternoon, the air of the Guildhall fizzed with something that tasted a bit like wickedness and smelled of old fireworks. It always did after the Menacing Cabinet had been opened.

Cordelia found it quite difficult to concentrate, with Uncle Tiberius grumbling under his breath about the Sensible Party as he curled Flinty Feathers around a hot poker.

'Uncle, don't forget Sir Piers's daughter was kidnapped by the Troublemakers from her boarding school,' she said gently. 'Sir Piers must be very –' She dropped the Whorl Ribbon she was holding. 'Prudence Oglethorne was kidnapped from – oh, *mon chapeau*!' she gasped. 'Why didn't I realize before?'

'Realize what?' Uncle Tiberius asked, but Cordelia sprang from the room, leaving the ribbon unspooling across the floor. She urgently beckoned Goose out of the Bootmaker workshop when his mother's back was turned, and towed him up to the hexagonal tower at the very top of the Guildhall.

The tower had, long ago, been a fitting room. When Sam had become an honorary Maker, the tower room had been transformed into a special workshop for the weaving of light. There were instruments to catch sunlight and sieves for starlight, cool pillars of moonbeams stacked in a dark cupboard and a great net to collect swathes of colour-changing dawn. The throng of Dulcet Fireflies, which could often be seen orbiting Sam's head, were currently hibernating in the rafters, a cluster of slow-throbbing light pulsing like a heartbeat.

But the most precious thing to be found in the tower was Sam's brother, Len Lightfinger.

Len had been sent away three years ago on a prison ship for the crime of stealing a chicken. Thanks to Cordelia, he had been pardoned and brought back to England some months ago. Len was a kind, bright-hearted lad, but quiet, haunted by his time on the penal colony. He could usually be found hidden away in the tower, whispering light to life in the stamens of flowers and carefully peeling the shine off apples to be used on boots.

The Hatmakers had welcomed Len into their home just as they had welcomed Sam: wholeheartedly and with good square meals. He and Sam had kept the Hatmakers entertained through the dark winter nights, weaving tales using flame and shadow. Great-aunt Petronella suspected that the Lightfinger siblings were, in fact, descendants of the ancient Lightbringer family, who had been famous far and wide as wondrous workers of light.

Today, Cordelia found them busy making candles that would fill a room with merry music, using the tuneful beeswax of Zebedee Bees.

'Hello, Len!' Cordelia panted, collapsing against the door frame.

Len was gently winding threads of melody on to bobbins, ready to be braided into candlewicks. He looked up, smiling.

'I told him about the trouble in the park!' Sam called over her shoulder, digging through a stack of clinking moonbeams.

Len ducked his head to the warbling threads again.

'I try 'n' stay outta trouble,' he murmured. 'You should too, Sam.'

'Cordeliawhyhaveyoumademerunupallthestairs?' Goose gasped, clambering up the final steps into the tower.

'I've just realized something!' Cordelia told him. 'Something I don't think is a coincidence.'

Sam, Goose and Len all looked at her curiously.

'Prudence Oglethorne was kidnapped from *Miss Prim's boarding school.*'

She was pleased to see expressions of amazement spread like the dawn across all three faces.

'The Troublemakers kidnapped Sir Piers's daughter, then attacked Sir Piers and the Sensible Party at the Winter Ball,' Cordelia said. 'Now they've attacked Miss Prim herself.'

'There *is* some kind of weird pattern there,' said Goose, nodding.

Sam darted to a shelf, riffled through some panes of sunlight wrapped in old newspapers, and pulled one down. She unwrapped the pane carefully and shook out the newspaper.

It was the front page of *The Rude Awakening*. This particular edition was from the morning after the Winter Ball. Across the entire front page was a large advertisement, with thick black words proclaiming,

WE ARE THE TROUBLEMAKERS!

WICKED AND TERRIBLE TROUBLE WILL BE VISITED UPON ALL WHO HAVE WRONGED US!

YOU WILL SUFFER TWICE AS MUCH AS YOU MADE US SUFFER!

THE WINTER BALL WAS ONLY THE BEGINNING.

Everyone stared at the strange proclamation.

'*All who have wronged us?*' Cordelia frowned. 'Does that mean . . . that the Troublemakers think that Sir Piers and Miss Prim caused them suffering somehow? And that's why they targeted them?'

'The more important question,' Len said quietly, 'is: who's next?'

CHAPTER 4

Her father wasn't home yet when she returned to Hatmaker House, so Cordelia put the jar of strange green seeds on the kitchen table and dashed upstairs.

'Supper in a few minutes!' Cook called after her.

Cordelia found Great-aunt Petronella up in her Alchemy Parlour, peering skywards through a lunar spyglass.

'There are waxing beams emanating this evening. An excellent fortifying ingredient and good for encouraging things. Come, Dilly, you're strong enough to move my chair over to the Moon Mortar.'

Cordelia shunted her great-aunt's chair across the parlour to the glowing Moon Mortar, which was smooth and shiny inside from years of having moondust crushed in it.

'I want to do something to comfort Delilah Canemaker,' Cordelia told her great-aunt. 'I think she's afraid of the

Makers falling apart again, like they did when she was a child.'

The ancient lady nodded. 'People are like trees,' she said. 'When you look at a tree's rings, you can see that even the mightiest oak still has a sapling inside it. It is the same with people. And sometimes when a storm shakes a great oak, the sapling within quivers, remembering the storms it survived when it was very small.'

Cordelia considered this idea thoughtfully.

'SUPPER TIME!' came a shout from downstairs.

Sam and Len piled into the Alchemy Parlour. Together, Cordelia and the Lightfingers carried Great-aunt Petronella down to the supper table.

Prospero was back late from the docks, striding in through the kitchen door when almost all of Cook's stargazy pie and mashed potatoes had been eaten and everyone was ready to move on to pudding.

'*Little Bear* is afloat!' Prospero announced.

Everyone round the table cheered this news as Cordelia leaped up to greet him. Even after months of having her father safely home, she still took every opportunity to give him the biggest bear hug she could manage.

'I'm surprised you weren't there to watch her go into the water,' Prospero said, sitting down at the table and tucking into the slice of pie Cook had saved for him.

'We meant to come!' Cordelia cried. 'But we got a bit distracted. You see –'

She looked around for the jar of seeds. They were not on the table where she had left them.

'Caramel custard starlight pudding!' Cook announced, placing a jiggling pudding in the middle of the table.

Cordelia jumped up to check the sideboard. 'Cook, where's –'

She broke off as she saw the empty jar by the pudding basin.

'Where's what, Dilly?' asked Cook, dishing spoonfuls of caramel custard into bowls. 'By the way, Sam, I thought that new starlight you brought home was a little strange!'

'I forgot ta give it to ya, Cook. I'm sorry,' Sam said, producing a glimmering handful of starlight from her pocket. 'It's here!'

She blew a bit of pocket fluff off it, and it gleamed innocently in her hand.

Cook frowned.

'If that's the starlight,' she said, pointing her spoon at it, 'then what was in the jar I used?'

Aunt Ariadne put her hand to her mouth. Cordelia felt her eyes widen as she realized exactly what had happened.

'Nobody touch the pudding!' Uncle Tiberius shrieked, leaping up to stand on his chair, as though there was a spider on the floor.

Cook dropped her spoon with a clatter and jumped back from the caramel custard as a small green seed wriggled up to the surface.

Uncle Tiberius gasped, eyes popping in alarm.

The seed shot through the air directly into his beard.

'ARGH!' Uncle Tiberius bellowed, batting himself in the face. 'EVERYBODY, SAVE YOURSELVES!' he wailed, losing his head and kicking the pudding on to the floor, where it smashed in a mess of broken china and oozing custard.

Cordelia saw several seeds pelt for cover under the table. She dived after them, smearing the custard into a slick on the flagstones.

'Here's one!' she yelped, trying to catch a seed between finger and thumb. It wriggled away from her as her hands slipped in the mess.

'How many were in the jar?' Prospero asked Cordelia, joining her on hands and knees under the table.

'About fifty!'

Prospero groaned.

They dodged out from under the table, just as Cook's rolling pin arced through the air and smacked on to the floor between them.

'This is so exciting!' Great-aunt Petronella cackled, banging her spoon against her bowl.

'We need to get Great-aunt P out of here!' Aunt Ariadne gasped.

Cordelia leaped for another seed, but went skidding into Len's legs and sent him crashing into the coal scuttle.

'SORRY!' she gasped.

'Everybody, stay calm!' Prospero barked, as though ordering the crew of a ship to remain level-headed during a hurricane.

'THERE'S ANOTHER!' Cook screamed, bringing her rolling pin down, missing the seed but smashing crockery as Sam gave chase, clambering over the table.

'Got one!' Prospero trapped a seed under a glass as it shot across the sideboard.

Cordelia skidded over to her father. The seed flung itself against the glass, whizzing in spirals. Prospero watched it with narrowed eyes.

'*Turbidus turbida*,' he muttered, tapping the glass.

For a moment, Cordelia thought her father was saying a spell. Then he went on: 'This is a seed from the Turbidus Vine. One of the most troublesome plants in the world.'

Around them, the Hatmakers, Lightfingers and Cook continued to yelp and rush around frantically. The seed hurled itself against the glass.

'QUIET!' Prospero roared.

Everyone fell silent.

'The plant responds to the sounds of chaos, so the louder you yell, the more troublesome it becomes,' he whispered. He turned back to Cordelia. 'These seeds are incredibly rare – where on earth did you get them?'

Cordelia explained in a quick whisper about what had happened in the park.

'It must have been the Troublemakers,' she concluded as softly as she could.

'Well, they've finally let slip a clue about where they're hiding,' Prospero murmured. 'You see, the Turbidus Vine only grows in one place: a mysterious island in the western Atlantic. It's a place full of Menacing Magic – a place so dangerous no sensible person would go there.'

'If there's one thing we know about the Troublemakers,' Cordelia said extremely quietly, 'it's that they really hate the concept of being sensible.'

'The vines, roots and seeds all cause immense turbulence. Even a single seed, as you can see, has the energy to stir up an enormous heap of trouble.'

Cordelia looked around. Her father was right: the kitchen, usually kept so orderly by Cook, was in turmoil. Chairs had been toppled; there were shards of broken china covering the floor and splats of pudding sliding in sticky blobs down the walls. The seeds had caused this chaos within a matter of minutes.

Prospero carefully slid a spatula under the glass, flipped it over and tipped the seed quickly back into the jar, clamping the lid on tight.

'I've got to go to Admiralty House right away,' he said. 'The Royal Navy have been waiting for a clue like this for months. They'll finally be able to go after the Troublemakers.'

Cordelia felt her pride in her father swell like a rising tide.

'Will you be able to tell the admirals exactly where to find them?' she asked.

'Not *exactly* where,' Prospero admitted. 'The island is uncharted; the Mapmakers made sure it didn't appear on any seafaring maps. But this seed is a signpost that will point the navy in the right direction – we know the nearest island is a rather lawless place called St Freerest.'

Cordelia remembered how the secret society of Mapmakers had used enchanted maps to hide magical places, so they could not be found without a secret key or special directions. It was usually to protect magical places from being plundered by humans, but this time the Mapmakers had hidden the island to protect humans from being harmed by Menacing Magic.

'This is a dangerous weapon,' Prospero whispered, holding the seed up to the light. 'Just a handful of these seeds flung at a person can cause them trouble for days – trouble sleeping, trouble concentrating, trouble balancing.'

Uncle Tiberius, either from the seed in his beard or from a dead faint, fell off his chair into the remains of the custard pudding.

'How do we stop the missing seeds making more chaos?' Aunt Ariadne asked, pulling Tiberius upright as Cordelia fetched the smelling salts. 'They could be anywhere in the house!'

'Keep as quiet as possible until we've caught them all. I just hope they don't take root,' Prospero said, pulling the kitchen door firmly closed as he swept his cloak around his shoulders. 'Whatever you do, try and keep them out of the Hatmaking Workshop, or they'll cause havoc with every hat we make!'

He strode from the house, tucking the jar safely into an inner pocket.

'We've got a lot of cleaning up to do,' Cook announced grimly, emerging from behind the vegetable rack, wearing a copper pot as a helmet.

Cordelia held the smelling salts under Uncle Tiberius's nose and he jerked awake with a yell.

'The Sensible Party will have a field day!' he wailed.

'Shhh!' Cordelia hissed.

But it was too late. Excited by the noise, several seeds banded together and catapulted the vegetable rack.

Parsnips and cabbages went flying. A cabbage thunked Uncle Tiberius in the head, knocking him into a puddle of custard.

CHAPTER 5

S peakers' Corner was buzzing, like a wasps' nest that's just been kicked.

Speakers' Corner was a place in Hyde Park where ideas – and people full of them – met to crash against each other like opposing tides. Cordelia, Goose and Sam usually enjoyed the lively debates held there about whether the earth was round or flat, but not today; today, the subject that had people so divided was the Makers.

A group of people with grave faces to match their grey clothes confronted a mob of brightly coloured characters in feathered hats and swooshing cloaks. The Sensible Party had last been seen in public dancing crazily before fleeing from Whistling Wasps at the Winter Ball, but today they were being their usual sober selves – and much less entertaining. Sir Giles Borington (who owned a paper named *The Boring Ton*), Archbishop Downer, Lord Carp, the Earl of Slough, the Royal Physician Doctor Leech and Lady Norma de Sneer all wore expressions like those carved on the stone faces of suffering saints in St Deplorus's Church on Rue Street.

Their leader, Sir Piers Oglethorne, wearing the most sour expression of all, clambered on to a soapbox and glowered down at the crowd.

'MAKERS!' he sneered.

Cheers rose from the brightly coloured section, while the grey mass of Sensibles around Sir Piers rumbled and muttered like thunderclouds.

'First they snatched my darling daughter Prudence out of her bed. Then they attacked the Sensible Party at the Winter Ball,' he brayed. 'Yesterday – the latest villainy in their long list of misdeeds – they set their wicked sights on an upstanding member of our society: headmistress Miss Amelia Prim!'

Cordelia could not help herself. 'That wasn't us!' she yelled. 'That was the Troublemakers!'

'I say EVERY MAKER IS A TROUBLEMAKER!' Sir Piers roared back.

The crowd curdled into cheers and boos.

'WE LOVE THE MAKERS!' a young man called Ferdinand Spouter cried, raising his Sunnyside Hat into the air.

'Even the king agrees this Troublemaking must be stopped!' Sir Piers bawled. 'He is offering a reward for the capture of the Troublemakers: the price of a king's ransom, or something of equivalent value! This will be awarded to whoever brings the pirates to justice and returns my Prudence to me!'

Things grew increasingly stormy as the heated shouts of the pro-Maker crowd clashed against the cold jeers of the Sensible Party. Then, sailing into the upswell, came a man so covered in glinting medals that Cordelia had to squint to look directly at him.

'By Dick Turpin's Buttoned Boots!' Goose breathed. 'It's Admiral Ransom!'

Admiral Ransom was the Royal Navy's most decorated officer. He carved a path through the crowd like a biblical figure cutting the sea in half, and lifted his hand, commanding silence the same way he commanded his ship: with absolute confidence and a chin so square it could have been an address in Bloomsbury.

'The Troublemakers are cunning and tricky, and dashed dangerous!' he thundered. 'These are the villains that kidnapped poor little Prudence Oglethorne!'

The admiral clapped Sir Piers on the shoulder, who looked pained at this reminder of his missing child.

'But last night I received an essential clue from Captain Hatmaker,' the admiral continued, his voice carrying easily over the spellbound crowd. 'It was exactly what I needed to sniff out the Troublemakers' trail.'

Cordelia glowed with pride.

'I've come to announce that today I'll be setting off to hunt down the Troublemakers!' the admiral boomed. 'And you can be certain I will defeat them! I promise you, Sir Piers, I will return your daughter to you!'

Speakers' Corner erupted with cheers.

'My ship, the *Invincible*, has room aboard for any young men who love their country!' declared Admiral Ransom. 'If you've got the guts and the gumption to fight pirates, lads, join me today!'

Goose gasped. Cordelia could see Admiral Ransom's medals reflected in his eyes. Before Cordelia or Sam could stop him, Goose surged forward along with a dozen other youths, clamouring to join the admiral.

'Heroes all!' the admiral proclaimed approvingly, slapping their backs as they jostled into line. At the very front, wearing a proud smile, was Ignatius Bootmaker.

Goose, being the smallest, was quickly elbowed out of the way by the other volunteers. He joined the end of the line, eagerly awaiting his slap on the back from the admiral. But when Admiral Ransom reached Goose, he let out a booming laugh.

'A plucky little sailor!' he said. 'You're too small for such a dangerous voyage, son! Come back in a few years' time when you've grown taller.'

Goose's face fell. 'But —'

Before Goose could argue, the admiral clapped him jovially on the back, sending him back into the crowd. 'Come on, lads! Off we go to glory!'

'Ig!' Goose called. 'Ig! I want to come too!'

But Ignatius did not hear his brother. He stood straight, deafened by the admiring cheers, his chest thrown out proudly.

Sir Piers whispered something into Admiral Ransom's ear, and the admiral nodded. 'We will return victorious!' he roared, saluting the crowd.

With that, he turned smartly on his heel and marched away, leading his band of new recruits, singing a rousing sea shanty about killing monsters and rescuing distressed ladies.

Goose returned to Cordelia and Sam, his face crumpled with disappointment. They consoled him with firm squeezes of his shoulders, which they knew couldn't compare to an admiral's approval but hoped would be of some comfort.

The crowd began to drift away, like clouds that have wrung out their rain.

But Sir Piers wasn't finished.

'Admiral Ransom may be on the trail of the Troublemakers at sea, but let us not forget the trouble much closer to home: trouble right here in London!' he began. 'Think of the utter havoc that will descend on us in a few days' time when the king makes Making legal again!'

People drifting away were drawn back in.

'If Making is made free for all, it will soon become a free-for-all!' Sir Piers warned. 'Frivolity and disaster in equal measure!'

'Making is in our history!' a woman in a pineapple-decorated bonnet declared.

'It belongs in the dark ages!' Lady de Sneer shot back.

'Making brings us joy!' someone in a butterfly cape called.

'Sensibleness is Britain's best quality!' Archbishop Downer intoned.

'Along with the ability to form orderly queues!' added Sir Giles Borington.

'MAKERS ARE DANGEROUS. ALL MAKING SHOULD BE BANNED!' Sir Piers exploded. 'I have found the key to make Britain *sensible* again! Rather than Making becoming legal, it should be STOPPED ALTOGETHER!'

The crowd seethed and hissed like the sea around dangerous rocks.

'What a bluster!' a cheerful voice cut through the din.

It was Master Ambrosius, wheeling his sweet-laden cart up to the crowd.

'What's going on here?' he asked, smiling. 'Sensible Party trying to ruin all the fun again?'

'Yes!' Cordelia confirmed.

The crowd was growing wilder. Constables wielding truncheons began prodding people. 'Break it up now! Move along!' But their voices were lost in the great churn and crash of hefty opinions being hurled.

'I hoped I'd find you today,' Master Ambrosius confessed to Cordelia and her friends, pulling out a cloth-covered basket from beneath his cart. 'Because my usual tester isn't here.'

He threw a resentful glance at the Sensible Party. Lady de Sneer was berating a young woman for smiling too brightly.

'Who's your usual tester?' Cordelia asked.

'I beg your pardon?' The sweetmaker turned distractedly back to the Hatmaker. 'Oh – my little sister. But she was sent away last year. To, er . . . finishing school.'

'What happens at finishing school?' Sam asked with round eyes.

Cordelia shrugged.

'I suppose you get . . . finished?' she guessed.

Checking around to make sure nobody was watching, Master Ambrosius drew back the cloth from his basket to reveal a trove of delicious-looking sweets.

'Not available to the general public until *after* the Maker Laws are changed on Tuesday,' he whispered, handing Cordelia a pink chunk of nougat. It melted in a bliss of deliciousness as she chewed.

'*Mon dieu! C'est délicieux!*' she cried, then clapped a hand to her mouth. '*Mais, monsieur, je parle un français parfait!*'

'It's Nougat Gaulois,' Master Ambrosius grinned. 'While you're eating it, you can speak perfect French. I'm working on something to help with speaking German, but so far I've only managed a slight Bavarian accent using sauerkraut.'

Cordelia swallowed the nougat. 'Brilliant,' she pronounced. 'And *très* delicious.'

Master Ambrosius beamed as he handed Sam a golden caramel, which she chewed carefully. As she did so, she began glowing as though she was wearing a cloak of sunshine.

'My fingers and toes are toasty warm!' she exclaimed.

'Cockle Caramel!' Master Ambrosius smiled. 'Excellent to chew while on winter walks. Made with sunshine.'

Still looking a little put out, Goose plunged his hand into the basket and pulled out a hard, shiny candy the colour of amber.

'That's a Scruple!' Master Ambrosius said. 'I must warn –'

Goose sucked it grumpily.

'What does it do?' he asked.

'It's a sort of trick sweet . . .'

Goose suddenly spat out the Scruple. 'UGH!' he yelped disgustedly. 'It's so bitter!'

Master Ambrosius chuckled. 'Ah, Goose! Scruples only taste bitter to someone with something on their con-science!' he teased. 'If you've done something dreadful, the sweet will taste dreadful and you'll be reminded of your naughtiness.'

'Have you done something bad, Goose?' Cordelia asked.

Goose looked suddenly alarmed.

'No!' he protested. 'Maybe it's because I tried to join the admiral?'

'What admiral?' Master Ambrosius asked, producing a hamper that was fastened with straps and buckles.

Cordelia jutted her chin up proudly as she said, 'We found a clue hidden in Miss Prim's clothes yesterday.'

'Did you *really*?' Master Ambrosius turned wide eyes to Cordelia.

'Troublemaking seeds! My father knew *exactly* where they were from, so he told Admiral Ransom, *and* he's going to stop the Troublemakers!'

The sweetmaker's fingers slipped on the fastenings and a small lilac candyfloss cloud nudged upwards, floating out of the hamper into the air.

'Aah, my Doggerel Floss!' Master Ambrosius snatched at it, but missed as it bobbed higher. 'It mustn't be seen!'

Cordelia realized from the expression on the sweetmaker's face – not to mention the fact that the candyfloss was airborne – that the lilac cloud was a magical invention that was decidedly illegal.

'I've got to get it back!' Master Ambrosius gasped, wading into the seething crowd.

Sam darted up a tree while Cordelia and Goose threw themselves into the forest of people. Luckily everyone in the crowd was too busy hurling insults at each other to look skywards.

'MAKERS FOREVER!' somebody screamed.

'ALL MAKERS ARE TROUBLEMAKERS!' riposted another.

Sam snatched at the lilac cloud while Master Ambrosius leaped desperately from below. Cordelia and Goose squeezed into the midst of the Sensible Party, following the cloud bobbing like flotsam above them. It tossed on the churning air . . . and sailed right into the face of Sir Piers Oglethorne.

His brays became suddenly muffled. Sam hung above the scene like an angel painted on a ceiling witnessing a dreadful happening below.

Sir Piers wiped scraps of lilac sugar from his face and crushed them in his fists.

'The Makers only make more trouble,' he uttered. 'They must be stopped before it's double!'

Master Ambrosius groaned in horror.

'What in good grief is wrong with my voice? I can't stop . . . rhyming! It's . . . not my – choice!' Sir Piers spluttered.

Sniggers rippled through the crowd. Cordelia's heart sank as Doctor Leech narrowed his eyes at the sticky lilac mess on Sir Piers's face.

'Some villain's made me speak in rhyme; arrest him for his wicked crime!' Sir Piers blustered, eyes bulging. 'This infamy gets worse and worse. THE MAKERS ARE A DREADFUL CURSE!'

'The sweetmaker!' Doctor Leech cried, pointing at Master Ambrosius, who stood frozen amid the laughing crowd. 'He's made an illegal sweet! Some sort of enchanted candy floss! The worst kind of frivolity imaginable!'

'Arrest him now! Do not delay! In prison he will rot and pay!' Sir Piers bawled.

The Sensible Party brayed their agreement. The constables shouldered their way through the crowd, while Sir Piers ordered, 'Take him now; he's done a crime! In the Clink he'll serve his time!'

Howling, Master Ambrosius was dragged away by the constables.

'No!' Cordelia yelled, seizing Sir Piers's arm. 'He didn't mean that to happen!'

'A crime's a crime, that's my last word,' Sir Piers thundered. 'And children should be seen, not heard!'

He shoved Cordelia. She tumbled backwards into the roiling crowd, and was caught in a push-pull of people. The crowd was rowdy and dangerous. Goose grabbed her and yanked her to safety just in time to see Master Ambrosius being bundled into a wagon.

'I'll get you free!' Cordelia screamed. 'I promise!'

The wagon trundled away down Park Lane, a single hand reaching out from between the bars.

Sam rushed up to them, clutching Master Ambrosius's hamper. 'It's full of incriminating sweets!' she gasped. 'Quick!'

They ran up Park Lane and dived behind a bush. Sam and Goose crammed handfuls of sweets into their pockets, while Cordelia tipped the nougat into her hat and pushed it on to her head. Then they threw the empty hamper into the bush.

'I don't fink anyone saw,' Sam gasped, looking back at the distant crowd. 'We should get outta here.'

Snatches of furious rhyme erupted from the squall of noise, as the clash at Speakers' Corner became a riot.

'You know, the last time we saw anything this bad in London, there was one man behind it . . .' Cordelia muttered.

Goose turned to her fearfully.

'But he's . . . He turned himself into . . . You don't think . . .' he uttered in a wobbling voice.

'We should at least check,' Cordelia said stoutly. 'That he's still where we left him.'

Sam nodded. 'Let's go.'

CHAPTER 6

They found Lord Witloof in a quiet corner of the British Museum, locked behind layers of rippled glass and wrought-iron bars. It was what was left of Lord Witloof, anyway: a gnarled lump of lead, with a label beneath that read:

PLUMBUM WITLOOFICUS

The metal was twisted, like a scream that had been made solid. The last time Cordelia had seen it, it had been smoking in the core of an evil machine designed to turn human souls into gold. Lord Witloof himself had invented the machine and discovered, too late, that his invention would turn a wicked soul into a less precious metal.

Prospero Hatmaker had quickly realized that Witloof's leaden soul was extremely dangerous: it could suck the magic out of a person with just the power of its wretched wail. He advised Parliament to lock it away in a dungeon deep beneath the Tower, but Sir Piers Oglethorne succeeded in persuading the other politicians that it was a valuable warning about the dangers of meddling with magic, and he insisted that it was housed in the British Museum for the public to see. Prospero, unwillingly, was forced to obey these instructions.

Before it could be safely put in the museum, Prospero and Great-aunt Petronella spent several days painstakingly constructing a cage of Pyre-Iron and Leechglass, to keep the terrible scream of the soul from sucking all the magic from the people who came to see it. Prospero had moved the soul into the museum at night, to make sure that if something went wrong, nobody would be hurt. Sir Piers himself had locked the cabinet that night, before taking the key to the prime minister, who kept it in a vault beneath Parliament.

Goose pressed his nose up to the glass beside Cordelia.

'Father says it's constantly screaming – the sound of Witloof's last thought – and anyone who hears it will lose their magic,' Cordelia croaked. 'The Leechglass and Pyre-Iron muffle the scream, but Father wore Tight-Lip Limpets in his ears *and* Muzzle-Wool Ear Muffs while he moved it.'

Goose shuddered and backed away.

'I wish they'd put it in a dungeon and thrown away the key,' he muttered.

Sam peered in on Cordelia's other side.

'At least we know Witloof definitely ain't the leader of the Troublemakers,' she said. 'C'mon – let's get outta here. It's creepy.'

They turned away from the glass case and set off through a gallery populated by ancient marble statues in various states of undress.

'We've *got* to find a way to rescue Master Ambrosius!' Cordelia burst out.

'He should be freed once Making's legal next week, shouldn't he?' Goose asked.

'I dunno,' Sam said dubiously. 'They do love punishing people. Sir Piers would want ta make an example outta him.'

Sam and her brother, Len, having been pickpockets on the streets of London, had lots of first-hand experience of the severity of the legal system. Cordelia and Goose considered them experts in the field.

Halfway down the gallery, Sam stopped, staring up at a large stone block with small pictures carved on it.

'Where's all this stuff from?' she asked. 'I thought this was the *British* Museum. This don't look British!'

Cordelia examined the statues.

'It's Egyptian, I think,' she said.

'Begged, borrowed or stolen, I wonder,' Sam mused with a professional air.

Before Cordelia could answer, they heard loud voices echoing through the next gallery.

'You're meant to be *quiet* in the museum!' Goose fretted.

The doors at the end of the gallery burst open and the king himself strode in.

Goose's mouth went wibbly as he realized he had just admonished the most powerful person in the land for being too noisy. But His Majesty had not heard. He was being followed by his daughter, Princess Georgina, and the royals were mid-argument.

'Is it too much to be obeyed in this one small matter?' King George blustered.

'Small matter?' the princess wailed. 'It's not a *small matter*, Father!'

It did not sound like the kind of argument that wanted an audience. Sam dived behind the Egyptian monolith and Goose tucked himself between the stone folds of a Roman's toga. Cordelia dodged round a statue of a grinning satyr embracing an unenthusiastic lady.

'Being disagreed with is *extremely disagreeable*!' the king complained.

A small, neat man hurried into the gallery behind the royals.

'Ah! Your Majesty!' the man panted, smoothing his wig as he bowed. 'I'm glad to have caught up with you. I am Mr Smirke, the museum curator. Might I direct your noble gaze to the hierogly—'

'We have the blasted Sensible Party on the royal back already, trying to get us to change our mind about the

Makers!' the king complained to Princess Georgina, ignoring Mr Smirke. 'The last thing we need is our own daughter rejecting the perfectly good betrothal we've arranged for her.'

'Why do you keep saying "us" and "we"?' the princess asked. 'Are you having another episode, Father?'

'IT'S THE ROYAL *"WE"*!' the king answered, exasperated.

'Well, the royal *me* doesn't want to be betrothed to Prince Hector!' Princess Georgina insisted.

Cordelia watched through the stone limbs of the statue as the king rounded on the princess.

'Why NOT?' the king groaned. 'He's a PRINCE! *Isn't that every girl's dream?*'

'I want to marry Sir Hugo!' Princess Georgina argued. 'I've asked you hundreds of times!'

'Not this again!' The king sighed, sinking on to a sarcophagus. 'You can't marry that actor: he's a commoner!' He grabbed a clay jar topped with an eagle's head and waggled it at his daughter.

'Ah, the ceremonial Jar of Horus, Your Majesty!' Mr Smirke's voice was edged with panic. 'A most interesting artefact! *Very* valuable!'

'You *will* be betrothed to Prince Hector of Bohemia, and I shall announce it in my speech to Parliament,' the king growled, once more ignoring the curator. 'It's an important military alliance. Parliament will be pleased, even if you are not. That is the last thing to be said on the matter!'

There followed a silence bursting with unsaid things. The air strained. Mr Smirke managed to ease the ancient jar out of the king's hand.

Cordelia heard the princess give one small, mournful squeak.

'Don't worry,' the king said consolingly. 'It'll be several years till you'll actually have to marry him. He should at least come up to your shoulder by then! Now, if you'll excuse us, we are going to look at those incredibly silly long-necked cows in the next gallery.'

With that, the king trotted off through the crowd of statues, pausing only to admire a carving of a young man playing chess in the nude.

Cordelia kept out of the way until the king had gone, his royal guards striding behind him, with the curator scampering after them. She peered out from her hiding place to see the princess sobbing into her hands. She could not leave her alone and heartbroken, surrounded by a staring audience of cold statues. Sam and Goose pulled faces, shaking their heads when she beckoned them, so she alone sidled cautiously into view.

'Your Highness?' she ventured.

The princess turned, blinking her red-rimmed eyes in surprise. 'Miss Hatmaker?'

Cordelia was about to bow and sweep off her hat gallantly, as she had seen her father do, but just in time she remembered that she had illegal nougat hidden under her hat, so she bobbed a curtsey instead.

'Are you quite well, Your Highness?' Cordelia asked. The answer was clearly *no*, but sometimes, Cordelia had observed, grown-ups asked each other questions with very obvious answers to pretend they hadn't noticed anything unusual. Aunt Ariadne called this 'being polite'.

'Not *quite* well,' the princess said, sniffing. 'Actually, decidedly *not* well. In fact, I feel horrible.'

Cordelia was glad the conversation had steered away from politeness to a firm foundation of fact.

'I don't want to marry Prince Hector!' the princess wailed.

Cordelia pulled out her handkerchief, which Great-aunt Petronella had hemmed with Cheering Cotton, and offered it to the princess, who took it and mopped her tears. But before Princess Georgina could begin to list her reasons for opposing the marriage, a long shadow appeared in the doorway. It belonged to a person who wore a crown and carried a sword that tapped the ground ominously.

'This is BORING!' the shadow lamented, stomping into the gallery.

Cordelia blinked as the owner of the shadow came into view. It was a boy, no taller than the princess's belly button, carrying a toy wooden sword.

'Prince Hector,' the princess muttered. 'My *betrothed*.'

Prince Hector made a face at Cordelia.

'Why is that commoner here?' the child demanded. 'Make her dance or take her away!'

Bohemian guards, dressed in fancy frills, jogged into the gallery and seized Cordelia by the arms. She felt her feet leave the ground.

'Put her down!' Princess Georgina ordered. 'That is my friend Miss Hatmaker!'

Prince Hector stuck his tongue out at Cordelia, who stared defiantly back, her feet still dangling.

'We have much better Makers in Bohemia,' Prince Hector announced, poking the guards with his sword until they dropped Cordelia.

'Ah! Your Highness!' Mr Smirke cried, scurrying back into the gallery. 'I've been instructed to dazzle you with the finest treasures that the British Museum has to offer! See! Our fossils! Behold these old Egyptian sarcophagi! Observe the winged statue of Pegasus!'

'Playtime!' Prince Hector yelled, tumbling across the gallery to a statue of a winged horse.

'I can't marry him!' the princess hissed as Cordelia dusted herself off. 'He's *six years old*! And besides –'

Her face melted into a sort of liquid look of longing.

'Sir Hugo,' she whispered. 'I want to marry *Sir Hugo*.'

Cordelia remembered how the actor, who had long been interested in Princess Georgina's royal personage, had finally caught her attention with a crumb of sunlight. Their romance had blossomed through the winter months. Sir Hugo had sent bouquets of Gladsome Roses to the princess, dedicated his performance as Romeo to her at the Theatre Royal, thrown himself in the path of Whistling Wasps at the Winter Ball to save her from their stings (and whistled his way through the role of Julius Caesar the entire following week). He had written his lady-love poems, sonnets and limericks, and even serenaded her from the shrubbery beneath her bedroom window, which had resulted in him being chased through the palace gardens by the pack of royal hounds. Cordelia suspected the princess had found this brush with death his most romantic gesture of all.

Now, a six-year-old prince with a wooden sword was the latest threat to their star-crossed romance.

Cordelia heard a yelp. Mr Smirke was wringing his hands in despair as Prince Hector swung from Pegasus's wing.

'Fly, horsey!' Prince Hector urged, beating the statue with his sword.

'Please desist, Your Highness!' Mr Smirke wheedled desperately. 'That's a priceless antique! Perhaps we could all move into the new wing? I think we'll find it most interesting!'

Cordelia saw Goose and Sam peering out from their hiding places as Mr Smirke ushered her, the prince and princess, and their guards through a door into a huge newly built gallery.

'Here!' Mr Smirke announced breezily, mopping his brow. 'Isn't it wonderful, Your Highnesses?'

The new wing had nothing in it except empty glass cabinets and vacant plinths. Cordelia looked quizzically at Mr Smirke, who planted himself firmly in front of the door that led back to the gallery of statues.

'An unnamed benefactor will soon fill this new wing of the museum,' Mr Smirke told her. 'He's collecting things from all around the world!'

Cordelia narrowed her eyes.

'Collecting?' she said.

Mr Smirke nodded.

'Isn't it really a sort of stealing?'

The curator puffed out his chest and said, 'It is heroic! And patriotic! And nationalist—'

'What's he collecting?' Cordelia interrupted.

'Treasure!'

Cordelia nodded sagely. 'It's always treasure.'

Mr Smirke sniffed, bustling off to try to interest Prince Hector in an enormous empty plinth. 'Our benefactor has promised us the head of a monster to go here,' Cordelia heard him say.

'WHY ISN'T THE MONSTER HEAD HERE NOW?' the little prince wailed.

Princess Georgina slumped wretchedly against an empty cabinet. 'I don't know what to do!' she groaned to Cordelia.

'My father announces our betrothal in Parliament in two days' time. Once it's official I'll never be able to get out of it – the Bohemians would take great offence. I have to change my father's mind before then!'

The princess grasped Cordelia's arm with a sudden fervent grip.

'*You* can make a mind-changing hat!' the princess whispered. 'A hat that will change my father's mind about the betrothal! And about Sir Hugo!'

'Mind-changing hats are Meddling Magic; they're not allowed . . .' Cordelia began.

'But they are *possible*?'

Cordelia nodded slowly.

'Then you will start work on it today!' the princess whispered.

Cordelia shook her head. 'No, I really –'

But the princess had fire in her eyes. 'It *must* be ready for my father to wear in Parliament on Tuesday! You're my last hope!'

Cordelia found herself caught in the irrebuttable grip of royal entitlement. Clearly, royals did not hear the word *no* when uttered by a – what was that word she had heard several times today? – 'commoner'.

Then she remembered she was face to face with a princess. It felt like a slightly inappropriate time to ask for Master Ambrosius to be freed, but it might be the only chance she would get.

She squirmed a little, as Aunt Ariadne's frown and Master Ambrosius's frightened face competed for attention in her head.

'Could you persuade your father to pardon Master Ambrosius, Your Highness?' she asked tentatively.

'If you change my father's mind for me, Miss Hatmaker, then of course I will!' the princess promised, eyes shining.

CHAPTER 7

It was rather hard to concentrate with Sir Hugo defying the stars every few minutes. He peered up at the misty night, shaking his fist whenever the heavens appeared.

'I defy thee!' he keened, fogging the window as he pressed his face to it. 'I bite my thumb at you!'

He bit his thumb a little too hard, then whimpered.

Cordelia had decided to make the mind-changing hat in the workshop at Hatmaker House, where she would only have to hide it from her family, and not every Maker in the Guildhall. She had not seen Goose or Sam on her way out of the museum. Cordelia felt this was for the best: following the princess's orders was risky, and the fewer people involved, the better. What her friends did not know, they could not get in trouble for.

However, she had found Sir Hugo in a gutter outside the museum, trying to glimpse his lady-love. When she told him the princess's plan (mainly to stop him singing a ballad), Sir Hugo had insisted on accompanying her home to Wimpole Street. She had agreed, thinking the actor's presence would provide a good explanation if anybody started asking questions: she could pretend the hat was a costume for his next play.

Cordelia stared around the Hatmaking Workshop at the vast array of magical ingredients, wondering how on earth she should begin.

'A *mind-changing* hat,' she muttered, frowning.

It had sounded so simple when the princess said it, but it would be tricky to make. Minds were amazing and deep: like caverns or mountains, full of hidden mysteries. Changing a mind would be a delicate and complex procedure. But she definitely could not ask anyone for advice, and there were no books with helpful instructions about how to make this sort of hat. Even her aunt's handwritten recipes did not yield any clues, because this kind of Making was strictly forbidden. Magic that changed minds or hearts was considered Meddling. It was almost as dangerous as Menacing Magic.

'But I'm doing a good thing!' Cordelia told herself. 'The king *should* change his mind about marrying his daughter off to a six-year-old prince – he's being horribly unfair!'

Cordelia tucked her hatpin into her hair, and decided she would have to rely on her Making instincts to create this particular hat. She had wildness in her wits and magic in her fingertips, after all, which always led her in the right direction.

She just needed to choose ingredients that would work together in harmony to change the king's mind without producing any unwanted side effects, such as unstoppable hopping. The hat would also need to be small enough to hide inside the king's crown, but very powerful.

She began by creating a sort of tiny weathervane, which she fitted into the dome of a miniature tricorn, adding Barter Buttons fixed with criss-cross stitches to the points. Then she hammered a piece of Oscillating Ore into an arrow.

Sir Hugo pranced around the room. 'Seeing my Georgina is like – like –' He grasped for a simile drastic enough to describe his feelings. 'Like staring directly at the sun! I must do it every day, lest I die!'

Cordelia did not think staring directly at the sun sounded good for a person's health. But she had never been in love, and perhaps such things felt necessary at such times.

As the sun was, at that time of the evening, not available to stare at, Sir Hugo fell back to defying the stars for the seventh time. Cordelia looked up from hammering.

'Can't you think of something else to defy?' she enquired.

Sir Hugo looked around.

'The moon?' he suggested. 'Perhaps the very air that I breathe!'

'I wouldn't defy that,' Cordelia advised. 'You need that.'

Sir Hugo grew quiet, thinking. Cordelia took the opportunity to fetch some Metamorphose Rose petals from a jar, unfurl a Sympathy Ribbon and cut lengths of Permutating Twine from a reel on the wall. She filched pieces of dawn and twilight from velvet-lined boxes in her great-aunt's Alchemy Parlour (while Great-aunt Petronella was asleep in her chair) and fixed them opposite each other on the weathervane with the twine. The Oscillating Ore arrow went on the front.

'I just need one last thing,' Cordelia mused, scouring the workshop shelves as Sir Hugo, tired of defying things, announced that he would inspire Cordelia's magic with a sorcery-stirring Shakespearean speech.

He leaped on to the window seat, and began chanting: 'Double, double –'

Cordelia spun round.

'What?' she gasped.

Sir Hugo hunched his back and pulled a frightening face.

'Double, double, toil and TROUBLE!' he gurned, pretending to stir an enormous pot.

Cordelia's mouth fell open.

'Why did you say that?' she asked.

Sir Hugo looked slightly miffed at being interrupted mid-monologue.

''Tis the famous weird sisters' chant from *Macbeth*,' he explained. 'They delight in creating all sorts of magical troubles!'

Cordelia barely paid attention as Sir Hugo continued with his monologue.

'Double, double, toil and *trouble*!' she whispered to herself. '*Double, double* . . . Maybe what I heard at the docks was the Troublemakers' secret code!'

It made a strange sort of sense. Smugglers must need a signal that was short and easy to recognize. She had heard the whisper – *double, double* – moments after someone had thrown a crate overboard, to be collected by someone swaddled in a cloak.

That was the night before the Troublemakers struck again – Miss Prim at the park! Cordelia thought. *If only I knew the name of that ship the cargo was pushed from, I could investigate the crew and find out who knows what!*

'I'll ask at the docks,' she murmured to herself, as she searched for one last ingredient to finish the hat properly. 'Admiral Ransom might have set out on the high seas but Sam, Goose and I can find the London Troublemaker!'

In a dusty jar on a high shelf, she finally found a Lenity Lodestone.

'Perfect!' she cried.

Half of the Lenity Lodestone went on the final prong of the weathervane, secured with the Sympathy Ribbon. The other half, also strung on a length of Sympathy Ribbon, she gave to Sir Hugo. As Sir Hugo strode around the workshop, holding the Lodestone, Cordelia held the tricorn above her head and watched the weathervane spin towards him wherever he went.

'It's going to work!' she whispered, as Sir Hugo pirouetted with glee. 'You just need to wear your half of the stone when we all go into Parliament to watch the king's speech.'

'I shall wear it over my heart,' Sir Hugo declared.

'The princess will have to find a way to hide the hat inside the king's crown. Keep the stone with you, and once I activate the hat with a snatch of dawn chorus, the king's mind will gravitate towards you with harmony and sympathy. The pieces of dawn and twilight will make him change his mind about you and the betrothal.'

Cordelia allowed herself a moment of self-congratulation: this was a particularly tricky hat she had managed to make, without any help at all.

Her smug moment was cut short when she heard her family clatter into the entrance hall. She quickly swept up all evidence of mind-changing ingredients, placing the jar of rose petals in its original position and reeling in the Permutating Twine. She managed to place the tricorn in a hatbox and then pile peacock feathers around it just as she heard footsteps on the landing.

'Hello, Dilly!' called Aunt Ariadne, peering into the workshop. 'What are you up to in here?'

'Nothing much!' Cordelia said breezily, hiding an offcut of Oscillating Ore with her foot. 'Just working on a hat for Sir Hugo's new play.'

'A new play, Sir Hugo?' Uncle Tiberius stumped into the workshop. 'What's it about?'

'It is called *The Odious Brat and the Noble Hero*!' Sir Hugo invented. 'A tale of a daring knight who rescues his princess from a tiny tyrant, wreaking vengeance on the princeling for his crime.'

Sir Hugo slashed an imaginary sword through the room, leaving a trail of (thankfully imaginary) carnage behind him. Uncle Tiberius chuckled as Sir Hugo bent double, visiting what Cordelia guessed was a violent comeuppance on a small person.

'Does the knight have any help?' Cordelia asked pointedly, raising her eyebrows. 'Or does he manage it all by himself?'

Sir Hugo flashed a diamond smile. 'He has help from a noble and brilliant lady,' he admitted, bowing deeply in Cordelia's direction. 'Without whom he would be utterly lost.'

He took his leave, the Lodestone necklace tucked safely into his shirt. Sauntering off down the street, the actor was twinkled upon by stars, at which – for the first time in months – he felt no need to bite his thumb.

Everybody had to speak softly in the kitchen. Cook had found Turbidus seeds in her pots and pans, loafing in her barrel of flour, idling in her rice and skulking among the jam tarts. She had captured twenty-three seeds so far, by variously trapping them with ladles and jelly moulds, clapping them between oven gloves and snapping the kettle lid over them, then tipping them into an old mustard jar in the Menacing Cabinet where they could cause no more mischief. There were still at least a dozen unaccounted for, but aside from the hearthrug tripping people up and the shop bell ringing when nobody was there, the Turbidus seeds had caused very little harm in Hatmaker House.

Cordelia sat down to supper feeling quite relaxed. There were fretful whispers about Master Ambrosius's arrest, but she knew that, thanks to her agreement with the princess, he would be released in a few days' time, the king would announce that Making was free for all, and that Princess Georgina was free to marry Sir Hugo. All would be well before Cordelia and her father set off in *Little Bear* next week.

Even though they had to do it quietly, everyone heartily cursed the Sensible Party and comforted themselves by inventing appalling hats they would like to make for the politicians to wear. A Wobble-Bottom Bicorn was the favourite.

Prospero reported, over pudding, that Admiral Ransom and his new recruits were setting sail on the evening tide that very night, in the Royal Navy's fastest ship, the *Invincible*. They were sailing straight for the island of St Freerest. From there, they would search the seas for the exact location of the Troublemakers' island hideout. Ignatius had looked smart in his new sailor's suit, Prospero told them, but Mrs Bootmaker had cried all the way to the docks.

Because everybody was downstairs eating supper, nobody noticed a small green seed inching along the workshop table.

Nobody saw it drop into the hatbox in which the Mind-Changing Tricorn had been hidden, and slink under the brim . . .

CHAPTER 8

Every Maker in London crowded into the gallery above Parliament, ready to cheer when the king announced that Making was, at long last, free for all.

Cordelia and Sam wove through chattering Makers to hug both sets of Glovemaker twins and squeeze Hop Watchmaker hello. Charity Cloakmaker was nattering happily to Tick, while Delilah Canemaker eagerly searched the throng below to spot canes she had made.

'Where's Goose?' Cordelia asked Mrs Bootmaker. She was desperate to tell him what she had learned from Sir Hugo about the words 'double, double' being suspiciously linked to causing 'toil and trouble'.

'Lucas is sulking,' Mrs Bootmaker sniffed. 'He's refusing to come out of his room as he wasn't allowed to go so foolishly to sea.'

Her eyes were red-rimmed. Cordelia immediately decided to make Cheering Caps for Mrs Bootmaker and Goose before *Little Bear* set sail next week. They would both need them.

Cordelia adjusted her shell necklace, which she had worn today because it contained a tiny portrait of her mother, and she wanted the memory of her mother to be part of this important day. Cordelia and the smiling portrait around her neck peered over the railing.

Beneath an ugly chandelier made of overwrought pewter, Parliament appeared to be two opposing walls of white wigs and pale faces. This group of well-educated men who decided everything for everybody seemed very ordinary to Cordelia. From one section of Parliament, the Sensible Party were throwing poisonous glances up at the Makers in the gallery. They had failed in their attempt to sway the king and were now shuffling resentfully, waiting to bray their dismay when Making was made available to all. Cordelia waved merrily at Doctor Leech, who scowled back so hard his eyebrows and moustache nearly met.

Lady de Sneer, being female and therefore deemed by Parliament unable to make important decisions, was the lone sour face in the gallery. Around her, the Makers were bright with excitement.

'A historic occasion!' Prospero grinned, shouldering his way through the crowd towards Cordelia.

She grinned back at her father. He had delayed stocking *Little Bear* with food and water that day, so that instead he could come and witness history being made. It had been two hundred and fifty years since the freedom to Make had belonged to everybody. It was time things returned to how they ought to be.

It was also time for a certain mind to be changed.

Cordelia had sent the Mind-Changing Tricorn to Princess Georgina the day before, tied securely in a box, complete with secret instructions. She hoped the princess had successfully hidden the small hat inside the king's sizeable crown.

Cordelia felt in her cloak pocket for the vial she had hidden there. It contained several notes of pure dawn birdsong, humming slightly under her fingers.

Good, she thought. *I'm ready.*

Sir Hugo, dressed in a regal ensemble of purple and gold, strode on to the gallery floor and planted himself in the middle of everyone. He looked ready to be wed to a princess right then and there. Cordelia caught his eye, and he tapped his chest significantly. From this, she understood that he had his half of the Lenity Lodestone under his frothy cravat. She nodded at him once.

Sir Hugo's ready too.

'What're ya up ta?' Sam asked, squinting at Cordelia.

Cordelia turned an innocent face to Sam; Sam's face was

vivid with suspicion. They stared at each other for a long moment.

'It's best you don't know,' Cordelia said eventually. 'But everything will be fine.'

Before Sam could launch a full investigation, trumpets sounded below, and a voice rose above the hubbub: 'Lords, ladies and gentlemen! Pray be upstanding for His Majesty King George! And Her Highness Princess Georgina!'

Every wig turned towards the door.

The royals were arriving.

First, several men staggered up the aisle carrying a large golden throne. They set it down in the centre, in front of the Speaker's chair, and the Speaker tried his best not to look peeved.

Then came the king himself, crown wedged on his head. He moved slowly, laden with heavy golden chains, as though he was some kind of valuable prisoner.

The princess appeared, tottering behind the king in a heavy dress. Her searching gaze found Cordelia and she gave a small smile. It was a smile of triumph.

The hat is in position. Sir Hugo is in place.

Cordelia returned the princess's smile. The king would soon change his mind. Then the princess would arrange for Master Ambrosius to be freed by royal decree.

The air bristled and hummed with pent-up energy. The speech that would change everything was about to begin.

The vial of birdsong quivered in Cordelia's fist as she worked her thumb under the lip of the cork. As the king got ready to speak, she popped the cork.

Several notes of dawn chorus rose through the room, arcing over the churn of voices like the first beam of sunlight.

The king twitched. He adjusted his crown to scratch under his wig and shook his head slightly, as though he was shaking a fly off his nose. This was a good sign: the birdsong had awoken the piece of dawn on the Mind-Changing Tricorn. Everything was going as planned.

'Today!' the king proclaimed. 'The freedom to Make —'

The Sensible Party seemed unable to help themselves; their simmering opinions bubbled up.

'Bah!'

'Boo!'

'*Foolhardy!*'

The king's crown quivered, and His Majesty tugged it firmly down on his head, glaring at the Sensible Party. Cordelia frowned. Nothing she had put into the hat should have caused it to *quiver* like that, even amid the bray of opposing voices. Her heart pounded as she quickly tried to figure out if she had made a miscalculation with the hat. *No, I'm sure it was absolutely all right —*

Suddenly the king snapped his head up to stare at Sir Hugo. The actor clapped his hand to his chest in surprise, arranging his face into an expression befitting a future prince, but the king just glowered at him.

Cordelia gripped the gallery railing so hard her knuckles shone white.

'THE FREEDOM TO MAKE –' the king repeated, louder.

The Sensible Party let out hisses and boos. The king snapped his head towards them. Some clamped their mouths shut, but Sir Piers bleated sourly, 'Shame!'

The king snapped his head back and forth between the Sensible Party and Sir Hugo like a weathervane in a high wind.

'MY MIND IS MADE UP!' he shouted. 'MY MIND IS MADE UP!'

Something had gone very wrong.

'Cor, what's goin' on?' Sam muttered.

'I – I don't know!' Cordelia admitted.

'I HAVE DECIDED,' the king went on, 'THAT MAKING – MAKING –'

'This is madness!' Sir Piers yelled.

'MAKING IS BANNED FOR *EVERYONE*!' the king roared. 'FOREVER AND EVER, AMEN!'

There was a second of shocked silence before an explosion of noise – horrified wails spiked with spiteful cheers. Cordelia saw, in a blur of confusion and dismay, the Makers staring at the scene below, as appalled as the chorus of a Greek tragedy.

'AND SIR PIERS IS PRIME MINISTER NOW!' the king yelled.

'You can't do that!' the Speaker of the House shrieked, sticking his head out from behind the throne.

'OH YES I CAN!' the king crowed. 'I'm the one with the shiniest hat!'

He seized the Speaker's gavel and banged it against his crown.

The crown tumbled to the floor in a dazzle of gold and diamonds – and a green tendril as thick as a snake slithered out of it.

The gasp from the crowd was like the sea sucking in before a tidal wave.

'A Turbidus Vine!' Prospero whispered.

'MAKER TROUBLE!' Sir Piers screeched, pointing dramatically at the crown.

Chaos erupted in the chamber.

'No!' Cordelia shook her head desperately. 'This wasn't supposed to –'

The vine whipped back and forth, seeking out its next victim. It snapped tightly around the king's ankle, and he fell like a tree. Politicians danced out of the way.

'The Makers did this!' Sir Piers claimed, as King George groaned on the floor. 'I've always said they have too much power! Now they've attacked the king himself – TREASON! CONSPIRACY!'

'*That wasn't us!*' Makers protested.

But the seething vine swelled before their eyes, tugging Cordelia's Mind-Changing Tricorn out from inside the crown.

The crowd gave a horrified hiss.

The vine had tangled itself in the delicate mechanism Cordelia had made. It looked like an evil device: a mess of metal snarled in creeper.

'I am prime minister now!' Sir Piers bellowed – he had already somehow wrested the wig off the ousted prime minister, who lay dazed on the floor behind him. 'ARREST THEM!'

The upswell of noise was deafening. Somebody seized the king's sceptre and swung it; someone else hurled the orb – it smashed through a window. Boots clattered up the gallery stairs as the guards came to arrest the Makers. All of them, innocent and confused, would be dragged off to the Tower and punished for treason they had not committed.

Cordelia could not let that happen.

She clambered up on to the ledge, clinging to a pillar for support. The chamber floor was dizzyingly far below.

'IT WAS ME!' she yelled, her lungs burning.

The noise bubbled away as every face turned towards Cordelia.

'Miss Hatmaker!' sneered Sir Piers. 'The girl who refuses to be quiet!'

'None of the other Makers knew!' she said as loudly as she could, swaying on jelly knees. 'I made that hat myself. But I didn't mean it to –'

'You ADMIT you committed this vile act?' Sir Piers interrupted.

She heard the soft wisp of her aunt's voice – *Cordelia, no!* – but she pushed it away. Princess Georgina's face blazed up at her with terrified eyes. What would the punishment be for the princess if she was revealed to be behind this conspiracy?

'I DID IT!' Cordelia insisted. 'I did it – alone.'

Cordelia saw Princess Georgina blink, tears spilling down her cheeks.

'You plotted to poison the king's mind with your Maker magic?'

'It wasn't a plot!' Cordelia replied. 'It was a – a plan.'

'BAH! TREASON IS TREASON, WHATEVER DISGUISE IT WEARS!' Sir Piers screamed. 'AND IT'S WEARING MAKER CLOTHES TODAY! ARREST THAT GIRL!'

Cordelia swung round to see every Maker in London close ranks around her.

'Let us past!' barked a guard, trying to push through.

But the Makers made themselves into a wall. Each Glovemaker balled their fists. The Watchmakers stood steadfast as though time itself could never move them. The

Cloakmakers spread their cloaks in a dense wall, as Mrs Bootmaker stamped her feet, bawling, '*You'll never take our Cordelia!*'

But Cordelia was trapped in the gallery: the only way out was crammed with guards and their forest of glinting weapons. They pressed forward, swords drawn. Makers shrieked as they were forced aside and a cold claw grabbed Cordelia's wrist.

'I've got her!' Lady de Sneer snarled.

A strong arm wrapped round Cordelia's waist.

'Dilly – hold on!'

It was her father, grasping her tight to his chest.

Her stomach swooped like a kite in a gale and she was dragged from Lady de Sneer's brittle clutches. The chandelier jerked and danced above her as Prospero grabbed it with one hand, swung and let go. They dropped like stones, landing together on the empty throne.

The tide of the room turned, a sea change that swirled around and crashed on Cordelia. Black and white capes and wigs lunged at her from every direction. And she was being dragged towards a plane of light, over velvet benches and through a cacophony of politicians as a frenzied faction of the Sensible Party came after them.

The light was jagged and sounded like glass. There was a hitch of heels and hopes – an airborne moment – then Cordelia fell heavily into a scrunch of green.

The chandelier jerked and danced above her as Prospero grabbed it with one hand, swung and let go.

'Come on!'

Her father pulled her out of the boxwood bush.

They were in the gardens of Parliament.

Prospero had hurled them both out of the window into the bushes. The golden orb that had shattered the window lay like a planet on the grass. Sounds of pandemonium blared through the broken window.

Her father pulled her in the opposite direction.

'We've got to run!'

CHAPTER 9

Prospero and Cordelia sprinted down an avenue of bay trees, gravel flying up from their heels, leaving astonished onlookers in gaping blurs behind them. They vaulted a wall and dashed down to Rivergate. Boatmen and their vessels were lined up along a jetty, ready to take paying passengers. Prospero thundered towards the boatman at the very end, pulling Cordelia behind him.

'Two to St Katharine's!' he gasped, hoisting Cordelia aboard. 'Quick as you can!'

Cordelia's legs, wobbly from the mad dash, folded under her and she sat down heavily in the boat as the boatman cast off.

A door burst open in the side of the distant Parliament building, disgorging yelling people. As the boatman turned to look, Prospero stumbled. The boatman whipped round to

90

catch him. After all, customers who fell overboard could not pay their fare.

'Steady, sir!' the boatman cried.

Within moments, a troupe of guards was running down to the riverside, weapons flashing silver.

'Ah, I've got my sea legs now!' Prospero laughed heartily, drowning the shouts that came from the shore. 'Off we go!'

With that, he pushed the boat firmly away from the jetty. Cordelia spread her velvet cloak wide in the stern, blocking the guards from the boatman's view as he pulled on the oars.

'Tide's with us!' Prospero announced loudly, making a show of leaning over to look at the purling water.

The Thames pulled at their vessel, but the guards were crowding on to the jetty now, thrusting boatmen out of their boats and piling in themselves.

'They're going to catch up!' Cordelia muttered anxiously. 'What do we *do*?'

'Courage, Dilly!' her father whispered.

He pulled a small bottle from an inner pocket, sealed with blue wax. With a *pop*, the stopper came out and Prospero poured its swirling contents into the river right behind their boat.

'A tiny measure of Hydra Typhoon,' he told her quietly. 'To help us along.'

The water immediately stirred and rippled, making waves that pushed the boat speedily out into the middle of the river.

They raced out amid the other boats and barges, the boatman marvelling at his own unexpected strength as they whipped past all other river traffic. Soon the guards were lost behind them.

But there was still a long way to go before they reached St Katharine Docks. Cordelia shuddered as they passed beneath Blackfriars Bridge. Her heart was starting to slow a little, and her mind was beginning to catch up to this new, desperate reality.

She had committed treason. She would have to flee. Were they on the run already? Was that the reason her father had directed the boatman to the docks? They could not return to Hatmaker House with the guards after them. She shivered, full of questions she couldn't ask in front of the boatman.

Even the weather had turned against her: the air was needled with sleet, and the light was fading fast. London became a murkish blur of shapes and lantern flames. On the riverbanks, carriages and horses thundered by in both directions. Before long, Cordelia saw the hulk of the Tower of London half submerged in the gloom. The blunt blade of Traitors' Tower transfixed her.

Prospero began to whistle a piercing sea shanty as they passed Traitors' Gate. A few minutes further downriver, he squeezed Cordelia's hand firmly. It was a signal: *Be ready*.

'Kindly let us off here, sir!' Prospero instructed the boatman.

The boatman pulled the oars up. 'In the middle of the river?'

'Indeed,' Prospero said cheerfully, flipping a gold coin to the gawping man. He whistled another tune and a looped rope floated down through the river mist towards them.

'Come along, Dilly!' Prospero said.

Cordelia jumped up. For the second time that day, her father's strong arm went firmly round her waist and – with a hitch and a gasp – she was sailing through the air.

CHAPTER 10

They landed on wooden planks with a thud. Cordelia scrambled to her feet, smelling pine timber and the tang of tar, and realized that she and Prospero had come aboard *Little Bear* in a rather unusual way.

A lantern flame flared, turning the evening drizzle into a pearly mist, and Cordelia saw the faces of two of *Little Bear*'s crew: the first mate, Melchior Brown, and Davey Fogg, the ship's engineer.

'Captain and Miss Hatmaker!' Melchior Brown cried, dropping the rope he had used to hoist the Hatmakers aboard. 'A surprising entrance, even for you!'

'Cast off, quiet and quick – no time to explain!' Prospero ordered. 'Who's aboard?' He strode to the wheel as the two men sprang away into the rigging.

'Just us. Jack went off somewhere – he's not back yet,'

Davey Fogg answered from halfway along the mainsail boom. 'Catch!'

Cordelia staggered as she caught a heavy coil of rope.

'Lay it on deck!'

'Jack's not aboard?' Prospero asked regretfully. 'We've got to go *now*.'

Little Bear creaked as Prospero turned the wheel.

'We're still moored,' Melchior Brown hissed. 'Miss, help me with the mooring ropes!'

Cordelia dashed to the rail and began untying the ropes attaching ship to shore. In the half-dark, she saw a glimmer zigzagging along the wharves. Seconds later, someone leaped on to the gangway, streaked across it in a blur of light, and splayed on to the deck.

'Sam!' Cordelia gasped.

'They're comin'!' Sam panted. 'I only beat 'em cos I put Lightning Light on my heels and ran quick as wildfire.'

Sam's boots glowed faintly.

'Who's coming?' Davey Fogg called from the mizzenmast.

'Look!' Cordelia yelped.

Dozens of lantern flames speckled the twilight, weaving through the docks.

'Melchior, cut the mooring ropes!' Prospero barked. 'Everyone else, raise the mainsail!'

In a flurry of quiet but frantic activity, everyone rushed to obey their orders. Melchior seized an axe.

'Cordelia Hatmaker!' came a shout from the shore. 'Surrender immediately!'

'Haul, on my count!' Prospero cried as Cordelia and Sam grabbed the heavy rope behind him. 'Two-SIX!'

They hauled – the rope tautened like a tendon.

'Two-SIX!'

Cordelia clenched her jaw, heaving mightily. The rope strained under the massive weight of the sail. Above them, the canvas inched upwards.

'Two-SIX!'

The mooring ropes splashed into the water as Melchior chopped them free.

'We demand you hand over Cordelia Hatmaker!'

'Two-SIX!'

They hauled again, muscles burning.

'Two-SIX! Two-SIX!'

Arms worked like pistons in a machine as the sail unfurled in a slow banner above them.

'THIS IS YOUR FINAL WARNING!' came a furious screech from the shore. Cordelia recognized the voice of Sir Piers Oglethorne, but barely heard it over the screaming of her muscles and the thunder of blood in her ears.

'Two-SIX!'

'BOARD THEM!'

A dark shape swung across the rift between boat and wharf. Prospero dashed into the middle of the deck to tear the shape out of the air, propelling it over the rail.

SPLOSH!

'We're FREE!' Melchior cried, chopping the last mooring rope.

The deck lurched. The gangway parted company with the wharf and fell with a *splash* into the water.

'OPEN FIRE!'

Pssst! Pssst! The night whispered fiercely at them.

'TAKE COVER!' Prospero yelled, pulling Cordelia down behind him. Musket fire bit the mast, bringing the nip and sting of splinters.

'She's a child!' he roared. 'For pity's sake!'

Cordelia peered, wide-eyed, over his shoulder to see musket flashes peppering the dark across a widening canyon of water.

Prospero dragged her behind him to the wheel. 'AND HOLD ON!'

The ship bucked as Prospero wrenched the wheel round. 'Pull that sail taut!' he yelled. 'We don't have enough wind!'

An idea hit Cordelia like a hurricane. She rushed across the steepening deck, slammed into Win's Weather Pantry and flung it open, fumbling among jostling bottles to seize a thick knotted Breeze String. She tugged the knot with her teeth – it sprang open. A whip-tongue of air cracked free, the mainsail snapped tight, and *Little Bear* leaped forward like a wild creature.

'STOP!'

But the shouts from the wharves were lost in the whistling wind.

'More of that, Dilly!' Prospero yelled.

Cordelia undid another knot and *Little Bear* burst on to the wide silk of the river. The wind bellied in the sail and *Little Bear* chased along the Thames. Sam, still holding white-knuckled on to the mainsail rope, grinned a shaky grin. The tide was turning like an upsurge of hope beneath their hull.

'Another, Dilly!' Prospero eased the wheel to guide *Little Bear* into the mid-stream. 'We're not safely away yet!'

She untied knot after knot, and wind and river carried them onwards.

Davey and Melchior raised the foresail as Cordelia peered over the stern, her hair flying around her, looking out for pursuers. But their ship was too quick to catch. The master shipwright had wagered that *Little Bear* would be the fastest ship of her kind, and he'd been right.

The bulky shapes of buildings subsided and the land around them became empty and flat. Stars salted the sky, and all that could be heard was the rush of the river and a choir of nightbirds in the marshes.

They were soon far beyond London.

Melchior struck flint to tinder, lighting lanterns to hang on bow and stern to avoid collisions with other ships.

'Go below to your cabin,' Prospero suggested to Cordelia and Sam. 'Get some sleep. We'll talk in the morning.'

But Cordelia's skin tingled and her stomach jumped at every noise. She would never be able to sleep. Sam stayed with her, grabbing her arm whenever the ship tilted.

They paced the deck, checking ropes, feeling for the wounds in the wood where musket balls had punctured the beautiful new ship. Davey found a musket-ball hole in his hat, inches above his left eye, and wiggled his finger through it like a worm through an apple.

Prospero kept his eyes fixed on the horizon and his hands clenched on the wheel.

That was how they sailed through the night.

Cordelia woke as dawn stroked fingers of light across her face. Sam slept beside her. Someone had covered them with a blue jacket that jingled with shiny buttons as she sat up.

England had come apart at the seams and splayed open into a sky-wide sea. The ship rode the cusp between river and ocean, nosing past great rocks upon which was perched a lighthouse.

'Rivermouth!' Cordelia whispered. Her breath came out in a cloud.

Her father stood at the wheel, face crumpled from lack of sleep but shoulders square with determination. Cordelia got the impression he had not moved all night. Melchior and Davey were slung in the low reaches of the rigging, watching the horizon.

Cordelia, limbs stiff with cold, tottered to the prow.

'We need to get beyond sight of land, Cordelia,' Prospero called. 'Let's have one more blast of wind to speed us out to sea.'

She tottered to the Weather Pantry, selected a large, straining Wind Bag and climbed up into the aft-rigging to open it. The wind burst out, fattening the sails with bellyfuls of air.

Little Bear nosed through the waves, leaving a frothing trail of white in the dark sea. Cordelia felt as though she was riding a slow comet blazing a trail away from the life she knew. England was soon far away on the horizon, a land made of paper floating on the ocean.

She rubbed sleep from her eyes and blinked. A different kind of celestial body was approaching. It was a pale bird, winging towards the ship.

'Agatha!' Cordelia cried, scrambling down the rigging as the bird descended in a graceful arc.

Agatha was a Quest Pigeon, raised from a newborn chick by Prospero, a bird so elementally connected to him that she could fly to find him anywhere in the world. By the time

Cordelia reached them, Agatha was cooing softly on Captain Hatmaker's shoulder as he extracted a scroll from a tiny bottle on the bird's leg.

Cordelia held her breath as her father unfurled it. He read it with a face like a closed door, then handed it silently to Cordelia. She recognized her aunt's elegant handwriting, but the words had been written in a hurry and the scroll had been rolled up before the ink had time to dry. Everything in the smudged, urgent words spoke of desperation.

> *Flee with Cordelia and do not return!*
> *She is wanted for treason.*
> *Is Sam with you? We are so worried!*
> *We love you always – Ariadne*

Only then, in the grey dawn, with Aunt Ariadne's familiar handwriting curled in her palm, did the chaos of yesterday begin to sink in.

Cordelia could not go home.

She was wanted for treason.

She would have to run for her life.

CHAPTER 11

Setting sail on a voyage with her father, into the wide promise of sea and sky, had always been Cordelia's dream. But she had never imagined it would come tangled with feelings of fear and regret.

Goose was left behind, and her family too, and she had not said goodbye to her friends, or thanked the brave Maker families who had closed ranks around her to save her from arrest. Even Hatmaker House had not had a proper goodbye: the books in the library and the Quest Pigeons and the fern that unfurled when she sang it lullabies.

It is one thing to leave your home on a great adventure; it's quite a different thing to flee, not knowing if you'll ever be able to return.

She was a fugitive now. On the run. *Wanted for treason.*

A heavy hand on her shoulder interrupted her thoughts.

'Cordelia.' Her father's voice was stern. 'The king's hat —
what on earth possessed you?'

'I can explain!' Cordelia cried. 'Princess Georgina wanted
me to change her father's mind about the betrothal, and she
promised that if I helped her, she'd free Master Ambrosius.'

'Your intentions might have been good, Cordelia, but you
committed treason. You made a Meddling hat and conspired
to put it on the king's head.'

Her father wore all the stern authority of the captain that he
was. His uniform buttons glared and his eyes were terrible
with disappointment. Cordelia suddenly couldn't look at him.

'*Turbidus turbida*,' he muttered. 'Trouble, trouble. That
plant certainly delivers what it promises.'

'I didn't put a Turbidus Vine in the king's hat!' Cordelia
said, raising her chin. 'It must have got in as a seed.'

'Trouble always begins as a seed,' Prospero said. 'And if we
do nothing about it, it will grow and grow.'

Cordelia wanted to say something — something to mend
things — but digging through her exhausted brain to unearth
the right words was like digging through mud.

'I've got to take you somewhere safe, Dilly,' her father
murmured, eyes roving the horizon. 'Somewhere the king's
men cannot reach you.'

Before Cordelia could find the words she was searching
for, her father barked, 'Melchior, take the wheel! I've got to
chart a course to St Freerest.'

With that, he strode across the deck and disappeared down the hatch, Agatha riding on his shoulder.

'St Freerest?' Cordelia repeated.

The name brought a thrill of danger. Hadn't her father called St Freerest a *lawless* place? Was that the sort of place she belonged now: a dangerous island full of criminals and outlaws?

She looked around, feeling all at sea. Which she was. Everything was moving beneath her feet – her home was not solid ground any more. It was made of wood and rope and canvas, shifting with every breath of wind, rolling on the waves.

Cordelia crept past Sam, who was still asleep, and went down the hatch after her father. She pushed open his cabin door to find him frowning over an old sea chart, Agatha peering curiously over his shoulder. Behind him, the wide windows looked over the sparkling sea.

'Father?' she began tentatively. 'Isn't St Freerest where Admiral Ransom's going?'

Prospero looked up. Cordelia lingered uncertainly in the doorway. Around them, the ship creaked and swayed.

'St Freerest is a republic,' Prospero explained. 'Nobody answers to any king there. So the admiral can't carry out the king's orders.'

A squeezing feeling of relief grew hotter behind Cordelia's eyes. She staggered into the cabin as the ship rolled, and her father caught her. He hugged her so tight she felt her bones creak and her heart grow its courage back.

His voice thrummed in his chest. 'Now, can you help me find St Freerest on this old map?' he asked.

Together, father and daughter examined the map. It was very old and hand-drawn in fading ink. Agatha hopped on to the map, strutting across the Bay of Biscay and out into the Atlantic. She pecked curiously at the Canary Islands.

Cordelia found tiny inked creatures patrolling the edges and curling words promising forgotten legends.

Here Be Sea Dragons
Tempest Chase
The Susurrating Squid
Ye Turbulent Seas

'Here's St Freerest!' Prospero said, pointing.

Cordelia leaned across to look. The island of St Freerest lay in the middle of the tropics, a tiny freckle in the western Atlantic, far from the shrugging shoulders of continents.

'About ten days' sailing on *Little Bear*,' Prospero said, 'with her Fleetwood hull and no cargo weighing her down, not to mention the Flocculent Cotton in her sails and the Wind Bags from the Weather Pantry.'

Cordelia squinted. There was a mark on the map near St Freerest. Peering closer, she saw it was a faded silvery triangle of swirling waves with a writhing Sea Dragon weaving in and out. In a circle around it, written like a spell, were the words: *Beware! The Island of Lost Souls!*

Cordelia's heart was beating faster.

'Look!' she gasped.

The Sea Dragon and the words seemed to have been drawn in unusual ink, possibly made of very faded purplish starlight.

Prospero frowned. 'I can't see anything,' he said.

'It's right *there*!' She showed her father.

But he shook his head. 'It just looks like blank parchment to me. What can you see?'

'It says *Beware! The Island of Lost Souls!*' she read. 'And there's some kind of monster.'

Prospero fetched a brass instrument and measured from Cordelia's finger to the island of St Freerest.

'Not five nautical miles between them!' He stared from his daughter to the map and back. 'Dilly, I think you might have found the Troublemakers' hideout!'

Cordelia remembered the legend he had told her as they'd searched for Turbidus seeds in the kitchen. 'You mean the island that doesn't appear on any maps?' she asked.

Her father nodded. 'It's exactly where the lost island is rumoured to be – five nautical miles south-west of St Freerest.'

Cordelia frowned. 'But . . . why can *I* see it?'

'Perhaps because you're a Troublemaker too, now?' her father suggested. 'I'm sure treason counts as trouble!'

Through the storm of emotions swirling round Cordelia's mind, an idea struck fast as lightning.

'If I'm ever to be allowed to return to England, I'll need to find some way of winning a royal pardon,' she whispered. 'If we get to the Troublemakers before the admiral, and defeat them *and* rescue Sir Piers's daughter, we can claim the reward! Sir Piers himself said it was the price of a king's ransom or something of equal value. A king's pardon's as valuable as a king's ransom.'

It would be difficult, perhaps even dangerous, but Cordelia knew that, together, she and her father had enough wildness in their wits and magic in their fingertips to outsmart hundreds of Troublemakers.

Prospero's lips twitched in a smile.

'You, littlest Hatmaker, always come up with the biggest ideas.'

Up on deck, the air was free and the sun climbed high. Cordelia was used to her horizon being hemmed in on all sides by London's buildings. But out on the open sea she watched clouds assemble themselves in the distance, then pour themselves away again in great sheets of rain.

Ahead lay the absolute hugeness of the Atlantic. Prospero set the course according to the compass: sou'-sou'-west. Miles and miles beyond the snout of *Little Bear*'s figurehead lay St Freerest.

'We'll take watches of four hours,' Prospero told his crew. 'It'll be a tough ten days' sailing. So sleep when you can.'

He and Davey took first watch. Cordelia and Sam helped them raise every remaining sail, then, when even the bowsprit jib swelled its belly in the wind, they went below with singing, burning muscles, to roll into their bunks and sleep.

They were roused four hours later, jumping up to deck as Prospero and Davey went below to rest. Melchior kept

Cordelia and Sam busy finding the best places to climb into the rigging and release the Wind Bags to maximum effect. Sea spray splashed up from the prow as *Little Bear* surged onwards. They took turns at the wheel, holding the course true to Prospero's compass.

Cordelia was so busy with the business of sailing that only when she stood at the wheel, eyeing the compass and feeling the surge of the ship held in her grasp, did it occur to her that perhaps going after a bunch of kidnapping, chaos-loving pirates might not be a good idea. Indeed, sailing directly into seas that an old map warned contained vicious sea monsters seemed especially reckless, even for a person who had recently committed treason and fled the country.

But as the sun made itself gaudy in the west, sinking into the sea in a glory of crimson and pink and orange, Cordelia forgot her misgivings.

The world is so beautiful; sometimes there aren't words for it, she thought. *That's when you just have to give yourself up to the beauty and become part of it.*

Stars appeared – secrets that had been there all along, kept by the sunlight. The night glittered with them. One came loose, streaking across the sky in a silver blaze. Sam pulled threads of starlight down, delicate as spiderwebs, and wove them into cats' cradles between her fingers.

Melchior took the wheel, sending Hatmaker and Lightfinger to make food in the galley.

'We'll take turns cooking,' he said, seeing Cordelia open her mouth to object to being sent to the kitchen.

Cordelia (slightly reluctantly) obeyed the order, thinking it would not be wise to stage a mutiny over cooking. She and Sam found a small bag of flour, sugar, eggs, six oranges and a box of salt ready on the countertop and made zested cakes for everyone, which they placed in the brick oven to bake. Half an hour later, with the galley smelling of fragrant orange, they turned out ten golden cakes on to a plate to cool.

They went to the captain's quarters, where a polished dining table stood in the window with twelve chairs around it – a reminder of how many crew were really needed to sail the ship. They laid five places at the table, quietly, so as not to disturb Prospero, who slept in the adjoining room.

When they returned to the galley, there were only nine cakes cooling on the plate. *Strange.*

'Davey?' Cordelia called. 'Melchior?'

Sam put her ear to the wall.

'Davey's still snoring,' she said. 'And Melchior's at the wheel.'

Cordelia frowned at the plate.

She checked the floor, in case the cake had rolled off the plate when the ship tilted in a wave. She held the lantern high, peering into the shadowy corners, but there was no sign of it.

'Crumbs!' Sam whispered, pointing. 'Somefing's eaten it!'

Crumbs were scattered along the worktop.

Cordelia's neck hair immediately prickled. 'Rats!'

But . . . why had the rats only taken *one* cake?

She and Sam followed a trail of crumbs along the galley floor. There was a creak down the dim corridor ahead of them and Cordelia clutched Sam. It must be a very large rat to cause floorboards to creak like that.

Sam flung open the door, thrusting the lantern into the dark.

'AAAAAAARGH!' came a terrified squeal from inside the cabin.

Cordelia and Sam gaped at the creature they had cornered.

Its eyes were round. It clutched a half-eaten cake and wore the kind of expression usually found on the faces of wild beasts with their legs in traps.

After making several astonished noises, Cordelia found a word:

'*GOOSE!*'

Goose beckoned them desperately into the empty cabin and shut the door quietly behind them.

Cordelia hissed, '*What on earth are you doing here?*'

'It was a mistake – sort of,' he explained. 'Yesterday afternoon, while you were all in Parliament, I sneaked aboard to put

some food in a little hidey-hole I'd found. Then I got surprised when I heard voices on deck, then musket fire! And I – I panicked and hid, and then we were moving! And now –'
Goose swayed as the ship tilted. 'Now we're at sea, aren't we?'

Cordelia nodded.

'Why were ya putting food in a hidey-hole?' Sam asked.

Goose looked shifty and Cordelia realized.

'This is why Master Ambrosius's Scruple sweet tasted so bitter to you!' she said, grinning. 'You *were* planning something naughty! You were planning to come with us, even though your mother forbade it!'

Goose's mouth twisted with guilt, but Cordelia was filled with a rush of gratitude: it was really Goose! With his familiar rumpled hair and anxious eyebrows! She flung her arms round him, finding him reassuringly solid.

'I'm so glad you're here!' she said into his shoulder. She could never feel like an outcast with Goose and Sam by her side.

'But you know what they do to stowaways on ships,' Goose muttered fearfully. 'Your father can't find out!'

'Can't find out what?' a voice rumbled in the corridor.

'Oh no!' Goose wailed. 'Hide me!'

But it was too late. The door swung open, revealing Captain Hatmaker.

'Lucas Bootmaker!' he thundered. 'A *STOWAWAY*!'

Goose jumped to attention. 'Aye, aye, Cap'n!'

The captain leaned into the room, eyes dancing in the lantern light.

'And what *do* we do with stowaways?' he asked.

Goose's voice came out as a series of mumbles and squeaks. Cordelia thought she heard the words *'walk the plank'* among the mumbles.

'Follow me,' Prospero ordered, turning smartly on his heel.

Goose briefly seemed to consider jumping out of the nearest porthole, but then stumbled after Prospero. Cordelia and Sam hurried behind them as Prospero marched through the ship, Goose scuttling in his wake.

Melchior Brown looked astonished as he saw an extra person emerge on to the deck.

'We have a stowaway, Melchior!' Captain Hatmaker announced.

Cordelia was ready to leap forward and defend Goose. But she suspected, from the twitch of his lips and the arch of his eyebrows, that her father was not quite as angry as he appeared.

Goose shuffled under the scrutiny of the captain and first mate.

'Are you the reason Jack Fortescue wasn't on board when we left London in a rush?' Melchior asked sternly. 'He lives aboard ship, so it was strange he wasn't there.'

'I – I gave Jack a new pair of boots that I made for him specially,' Goose admitted. 'Balancing Boots! But I . . . I wove them with Turn-About Laces, so he'd go in the wrong direction on his way home. But I didn't mean for him to get left behind! I – I only did it so I'd have a bit more time to hide my . . . my . . . stowaway supplies.'

Possibly to avoid the first mate's fierce glare, Goose grabbed a rope and began twisting it.

'I know all the knots – look! Jack taught me,' Goose gabbled, presenting Captain Hatmaker with an organized chaos of twisted rope: a perfect sheepshank knot. 'And I'm willing to scrub the decks and keep lookout in the crow's nest –'

'I'd set you ashore at the nearest English port if I could, Goose,' Captain Hatmaker growled. 'But it's too risky. We'd be arrested right away.'

As Goose's eyes grew large with confusion, Cordelia whispered to him, 'There's a lot to explain.'

'As it is, we're a very small crew,' Captain Hatmaker went on. 'And we could do with the extra pair of hands.'

Goose looked as though he barely dared to hope.

'So . . . you won't make me walk the plank?' he asked.

'Not today,' Prospero said, half smiling. 'But I *will* tell your mother.'

The breadth and depth of every ocean in the world would not be enough to protect Goose from his mother's fury, which was bound to be the kind of fury that could follow a person off the edge of any map into lands unknown. But he was soon too busy to worry about this. Before long, the Bootmaker was clambering up and down the rigging, carrying out the first mate's orders to light all the ship's lanterns.

'There's a lot to fit on the scroll I'll be sending home with Agatha,' Prospero said wryly, watching Goose dangle from the end of the yardarm as he lit the starboard lantern. '*Sam safe with us. Bootmaker stowaway discovered. Treason-committer in good health.* Quite the band of rebels and runaways we make, don't we? We'll be more notorious than the Troublemakers soon!'

While Prospero went below to try to squeeze all this information on to Agatha's tiny scroll, Cordelia woke Davey, who greeted Goose with a shout of laughter and a slap on the back.

The crew ate their orange cakes up on deck, wrapped in blankets against the chilly night air. As Cordelia watched Agatha winging away, a tiny silver shape disappearing into the dark, her heart twisted and her eyes stung. Agatha was journeying to somewhere Cordelia could not go: home to Hatmaker House, where the windows glowed at night and the house hummed with love.

Homesick tears spilled down her cheeks, but Davey Fogg ruffled her hair as Sam and Goose squeezed her tight.

Melchior Brown began to play his fiddle and suddenly *Little Bear* was a party travelling across the ocean. The bright thread of music weaving around the masts cheered Cordelia immensely. She, Sam, Goose and Davey Fogg danced a boisterous jig across the deck as Prospero watched from the wheel.

After several jigs and a hornpipe, the festivities were really underway. Cordelia felt such a party deserved a proper feast to go with it. She took a lantern and hurried down to the storage hold to gather victuals from the barrels there.

'Bring some grog!' Davey called after her.

But she found the storage hold empty. There was not a single barrel, sack or bottle: just the empty belly of the ship.

'There is no grog,' Cordelia announced, climbing back on deck.

Melchior's song slewed into discord as he stopped playing.

'N-no grog?' Davey Fogg gulped.

'Never mind,' Sam consoled. 'Fiddle music'll help pass the time!'

'Grog's the only thing that makes the fiddle music bearable!' Davey groaned.

'What supplies *are* in the hold?' Melchior asked, ignoring the slight against his musical ability.

'Absolutely none,' Cordelia had to admit. They would find out sooner or later – when they ate invisible porridge for breakfast tomorrow, followed by air pie for lunch. 'We've got another half a bag of flour, half a bag of sugar, a small barrel of dry biscuit, an ounce of salt and one last orange.'

'I hid three apples and some toffees in the capstan,' Goose volunteered, before adding sheepishly, 'My stowaway supplies.'

'I got some sweets in my pockets,' Sam added. 'Scruples and nougat . . .'

But sweets wouldn't keep them alive for ten days out on the ocean.

Prospero stepped down from the wheel.

'In all the chaos I forgot: the victuallers were due to arrive this morning with provisions for the ship. The holds are empty.'

In the sober silence that followed this statement, several rumbling stomachs could be heard.

'Who enjoys the taste of seaweed?' Melchior asked hopefully.

Nobody did.

'We can ration the food. We won't feast like kings, but we can survive on ship's biscuit and the fish we catch until we reach St Freerest,' Prospero announced. 'It's water that we can't live without – and thankfully there's a large water barrel on deck, right here! I filled it myself, two days ago!'

He strode over to it, held a tankard to the tap at the bottom and turned it. A tiny spurt of water came out before quickly trickling dry.

Prospero frowned.

Goose leaped forward with a wail. 'Look!'

Near the bottom of the water barrel was a perfectly round hole the exact size of a musket ball. Sam scrambled to the other side of the barrel.

'There's another one here! They shot right through it!'

Cordelia immediately felt the dry tug of thirst in her mouth. All around them water sloshed. Undrinkable salt water.

Prospero's frown deepened. 'This is quite a serious problem.'

CHAPTER 12

Cordelia spent a restless night in her bunk, tormented by dreams about empty deserts and dry wells, while all around the sound of sloshing water mocked her.

She woke with the sun, its unblinking eye peering through her porthole. Her lips were cracked.

On deck, Davey Fogg stood at the wheel, staring at the horizon. His face was grey as the dawn. Cordelia tried to ignore the scratch in her throat as she swallowed.

Goose slouched, sleepy-eyed, out of his cabin.

'Change of watch!' he said, yawning as he rang the bell.

Cordelia took over from Davey. It was her turn at the wheel, and Davey's turn to fall into his hammock and get some sleep.

As Davey passed the water barrel, he threw it a despairing look.

'We should fix it, in case we get any rain,' Cordelia said, mustering all her hope. 'Dowels and wax should do it. Goose, fetch a candle.'

'But the sun's coming up,' Goose pointed out sleepily. 'We don't need candles!'

'For the wax!'

With Melchior at the wheel, Cordelia and Goose soon had small plugs of wood and wax fixed firmly in the musket holes at the bottom of the water barrel. Hatmaker and Bootmaker stood back to inspect their work.

'It's watertight,' Goose said. 'But it doesn't look like rain.'

The sky was blue from horizon to horizon. Cordelia, however, was not looking at the horizon. She was looking at the Weather Pantry.

'Maybe not . . .' she said slowly. 'But we're *Makers*, aren't we?'

Cordelia, Goose and Sam (newly roused from her bunk) pushed the water barrel into the middle of the deck. Cordelia had raided the Weather Pantry and taken out a heavy Fog Bottle. ('Fog can be helpful if you need to hide,' Win Fairweather had said as she'd heaved the bottle on to the shelf. Cordelia, however, had other plans for it.) Goose and

Sam had laid dozens of Breeze Strings in a perfect circle round the barrel, and now stood poised for action.

Cordelia took a deep breath. 'Ready?'

They nodded.

She uncorked the Fog Bottle. A great mass of grey bellied out, swallowing Cordelia in a dense, wet blanket.

'GO!' she yelled, though her voice was muffled.

They undid strings as fast as they could, running around the patch of fog, pushing it back into itself with the breezes they unleashed, hemming it in with wind.

'Keep going!' Cordelia shouted to the others. 'It needs to be as tightly scrunched as possible!'

The fog grew thicker, denser, as it was squished inwards by the wind. It grumbled.

'It's working!' Cordelia cheered.

She stuck a hand into the fog and it came out covered in droplets. She licked her hand.

'Just a few more!' she cried over the whipping of winds coming from several directions.

The fog formed into a miniature tower of cloud, stacked over the empty barrel, stormy grey and getting darker. Cordelia, Goose and Sam closed in, untying more Breeze Strings to concentrate the cloud. It protested, uttering a deep grumble followed by a crack of lightning.

A drop of rain fell into the barrel.

'One last push!' Cordelia yelped, grabbing the final handful of Breeze Strings from the Weather Pantry.

They untied them in a crazed kind of dance, circling the barrel and yelling encouragement as the cloud they had made gave itself up to rain. Before long it was sprinkling, then splashing. It thrummed and drummed into the barrel. The water sloshed as the great body of fog poured itself out of the air.

Eventually the cloud tower thinned, and soon Cordelia could see the exhilarated faces of Sam and Goose through it, sparkling with dew. The cloud became a bobbing wisp of white above their heads, and dried up to nothing as the final raindrops fell.

The three children stared at each other over the top of the sloshing barrel.

'We did it!' cheered Goose.

Sam clapped her hands. 'It worked!'

'We're . . . *Rainmakers*!' said Cordelia, laughing.

The water was cool and tasted minerally and heathery, as though it had been gathered from a purple granite mountainside. Cordelia, Goose and Sam all agreed that it was the most refreshing drink they had ever had, while Melchior declared it 'better than grog'.

The barrel was about half full. They carefully covered it so the sun would not evaporate the liquid, and woke Prospero and Davey with cool tankards of fresh water.

Days passed in a sea-sprayed, wind-blown, sunny haze of hard sailing. Cordelia soon got used to the rotation of the watch, sleeping for a few hours and waking with the bell, before falling back into her bunk when the watch was done. The Weather Pantry was opened every day, and Wind Bags were released into the sails to keep *Little Bear* speeding on her course sou'-sou'-west.

Davey could not read a book, but he could read the bulges of clouds and the curls of waves like they were a secret kind of handwriting. Melchior, it turned out, spoke Boat. He taught Cordelia the language of *Little Bear*: how a certain groan in her bow meant the topsail needed to be reefed, or the creak of a rope told that they were a little too larboard of the wind.

Cordelia slept with pods of dolphins rushing under the ship, beneath her dreaming pillow. In the mornings, dolphins jumped through the bow waves, laughing, and she answered back with wild cackles of her own.

The skies changed as they headed south, growing more intensely blue by the day. Clouds further south were different from the clotted-cream English ones Cordelia knew – these clouds were rowdier, more capable of violence. They floated like despots across the sky, ready to lash rain or churn up thunder as they chose. The sunsets flooded the west with fire.

At night, Cordelia would climb up on to the figurehead of *Little Bear*, gripping the ridges of his fur under her fingers, and gaze out between his ears at a purple star twinkling above the horizon. It whispered a secret to her: too quiet to hear above the roaring waves, but somehow she understood it was a comforting kind of secret. She only needed to get closer to discover what it was. Every night the star called, and Cordelia climbed up to listen as its light caught in her chest.

The only slight inconvenience was that Cordelia found her dress increasingly annoying. It was not made for sailing, and she had already ripped several decorative ribbons off it. She envied everyone else's trousers, which were much more practical than skirts trimmed with lace, and was delighted when Davey presented her with a neatly sewn pair of canvas breeches.

'I made them out of spare Flocculent Cotton sailcloth,' he told her, as she bounded across the deck, legs finally free of petticoats. 'They'll put a spring in your step, right enough!'

To her delight, Cordelia found she could now jump high enough to reach the jib.

With great enjoyment, she cut her dress in half, separating skirt from bodice, then hemmed the bodice with Starlight

Twine to make a shirt that twinkled slightly at the edges. Using a bit of the discarded skirt, she sewed a patch pocket on the shirt (because the more pockets a person had, the better) and twirled in front of Sam and Goose, who were suitably impressed by her new suit.

In return for Davey's kindness, Cordelia mended the hole that had been shot in his hat, using a small patch of rainbow from the Weather Pantry.

'Thank you, young Hatmaker! It's *better* than new!' Davey chuckled.

'The only thing that would improve things,' Goose mused on the sixth day, picking fishbones out of his teeth, 'is something else to eat. I know the fish we're catching are different from the ones we caught further north, but they're still very *fishy*. I'd just like something different for a change.'

Melchior offered him some seaweed.

'Not that,' Goose clarified.

Luckily, they still had several clear inches of water left in the barrel. Once this barrel was empty, they would have to get to St Freerest as quickly as possible.

Captain Hatmaker rationed the water carefully, making sure everybody had their fair share. But, even so, the water was gone by the end of the seventh day.

At noon on the eighth day, Sam called two words from the crow's nest – 'Sail ho!' – prompting a squall of activity aboard *Little Bear*.

Everyone rushed to the prow to see a sail winking white on the eastern horizon.

'Friend or foe?' Melchior asked Captain Hatmaker, who squinted through a telescope.

'Any ship with a water barrel is a friend, if ya ask me!' Sam rasped.

'Run up the colours!' Captain Hatmaker ordered. 'We'll hail her!'

A heavy signal flag – a red X on a white background, meaning *I require assistance* – was dragged out of its crate and hoisted up the main mast. Then all they could do was wait, willing the ship to see their signal.

Far away and tiny, a square of colour jerked up through the rigging. Then the sails changed.

'She's coming!' Sam yelped triumphantly.

Soon the ship was close enough for Cordelia to see the scales on the mermaid figurehead and read the name *Splendora* painted on her prow.

'AHOY, CAPITANO!' Captain Hatmaker yelled. 'COME ALONGSIDE!'

Ropes were thrown between the two ships. *Little Bear* and *Splendora* bucked on the ocean swell, reined together after days of ranging freely over the ocean. A gangplank smacked down, forming a bridge from deck to deck, and Prospero, Cordelia, Goose and Sam wobbled across it.

'She's coming!'
Sam yelped triumphantly.

Dozens of faces grinned at them from the rigging. The *Splendora* was populated with whistling sailors, jaunty in their blue suits. Cordelia was amazed to see the captain, a small but splendid man in a white lace cape and big straw bicorn, stride across the deck to throw his arms round her father before kissing him on both cheeks.

'Prospero Hatmaker!' he roared delightedly. 'I heard you were sunk! And now here you are aboard a brand-new ship!'

'My old friend!' Prospero laughed. 'Capitano Boniface!'

'*Dio mio!*' the capitano exclaimed, looking more closely at Cordelia. 'Is this the little bundle?'

'Indeed it is!' Her father grinned, and Cordelia suddenly found herself clasped to the capitano's chest.

'Ah, *bambina*!' he exclaimed. 'I first met you as a very small bundle being rescued from a shipwreck!' He cupped her face in his hands. 'You were a *piccola creatura* wrapped in rags, carried in a hatbox!'

'It was Capitano Boniface who found us, Dilly,' Prospero explained, 'after the wreck that claimed your mother when you were a baby. He came across us floating on the ocean.'

Cordelia had always treasured that story. To meet its hero felt like meeting a character from a legend.

'You rescued us!' she said, her eyes wide.

'And it seems I'm rescuing you again!' Capitano Boniface winked. 'You signalled you're in distress?'

'We need water,' Cordelia told him. 'We're parched!'

'*Acqua!*' the capitano called, beckoning his sailors. '*Subito!*'

Sailors swung down from the rigging and soon produced glistening goblets of water for the thirsty Londoners. A barrel was swung across to Melchior and Davey on the deck of *Little Bear*. Davey prised the lid off it and dunked his entire head inside.

Everybody gurgled their gratitude through great gulps of water.

'But I cannot invite you aboard my ship and give you merely *water!*' the capitano cried, when everybody had drunk so much that their bellies sloshed. 'Makers from London! Makers of Hats!'

'And Boots!' Goose added.

'And Boots!' Capitano Boniface made a specific and flowery bow towards Goose's boots. 'We shall feast!'

After beckoning Melchior and Davey across to the *Splendora*, Capitano Boniface led them all to his splendid cabin. At his groaning table, they ate delicious Italian cakes and nougat, creamy cheeses and chewy, salty bread fragrant with rosemary. As the old friends caught up on all the news, Cordelia, Sam and Goose admired the treasures in the capitano's chests: creations of the famous Venetian Glassmakers. They found swirly marbles that sang, harmonizing when they struck each other, and musical wine goblets and delicate glass-blown lampshades that refracted candlelight into rainbow hues. There were also mountains of frothy lace bonnets, silk dresses and magnificent brocade cloaks.

'I was worried you'd been attacked when I saw your distress signal,' the capitano confessed. 'There's a dreadful gang of pirates sailing these waters. They're rumoured to have burned the sails of a frigate with sailors still in the rigging, just for fun, and blasted a sloop clean in two with their cannons after plundering all its treasure.'

Cordelia shuddered, imagining a gang of hulking, flint-eyed men with ruinous swords that tore courage to shreds.

'The Troublemakers, they call themselves,' Capitano Boniface said fearfully. 'They paint their name on the decks of the ships they destroy and leave the wreckage as a warning to others.'

Cordelia felt this warning resound in her very bones. The Troublemakers were much more dangerous than she had realized.

Goose frowned. 'But the Troublemakers just play tricks on people, don't they?' he piped up. 'They're not – not *evil*.'

The capitano shook his head.

'They are more than tricksters,' he said. 'They sink ships and take no prisoners. I saw the ruins of a ship they destroyed, barely two days' sailing north of here. It was still burning when we found it – the masts felled like a forest and the hull gutted. There wasn't a soul left alive.'

Silence hung heavy in the cabin. Although what Goose said had been true in London, Cordelia realized, out here, on the fierce and savage seas, the Troublemakers' villainy went unchecked. They clearly had a dangerous thirst for destruction.

And yet nobody had ever *seen* the Troublemakers. They slipped like shadows, quiet as cut-throats, wreaking havoc and attacking innocent people. That made them even more dangerous.

Perhaps by the time you *saw* a Troublemaker, it was too late.

Little Bear and *Splendora* parted as the westering sun turned the sea into shimmering gold.

'Look out for the Troublemakers!' the capitano advised, yelling over the widening gulf as the ships pulled away from each other (he had barely stopped talking since clapping eyes on Prospero). 'If you see a strange ship, catch the quickest wind you can and sail in the opposite direction! Get to St Freerest as fast as possible! We're slower than you so we'll be there in a few days!'

Little Bear, well stocked with water and provisions, plunged once more towards the setting sun, the west and adventure.

Little did her crew know what awaited them just over the horizon . . .

CHAPTER 13

The sun rose on a catastrophe.

On the wide stage of the sea before Cordelia, bleeding black smoke into the sky, was a burnt ship. Sails gaped open in the wrong places, like slashed bellies. The portholes were put-out eyes, the hull was cracked, splitting the ship's painted name – *Innocenze* – in half. The masts were broken like bones.

Cordelia desperately clanged the alarm bell and everyone stumbled up to the deck, blinking in horror at the floating wreck.

'She must have been attacked in the night,' Prospero said. 'Just as Capitano Boniface described.'

'AHOY!' Davey bellowed. 'ANYBODY THERE?'

The blackened ship was silent as *Little Bear* sailed closer. There was no sign of life. The drifting ship groaned in the caress of the sea as Prospero swung aboard to search for survivors.

'I want to come with you!' Cordelia demanded, trying to follow.

But Melchior and Davey held her back. It made her heart catch painfully to see her father sliding across the charred deck, calling through the smashed doors for survivors.

'Look!' Sam pointed.

Large and reckless, the word TROUBLEMAKERS had been scrawled in red paint across the deck.

'It was them all right,' Goose confirmed grimly.

Prospero looked so small standing on the sinking wreck of the ship as the sea began to creep up his shins that Cordelia could not help calling out: 'Come back!'

Only when her father was standing safely on the deck of *Little Bear* again did Melchior and Davey let Cordelia go.

'My guess is the cargo was plundered and the stores robbed,' Prospero told them. 'Then they set fire to the ship.'

'And the crew?' Sam's voice was small.

Prospero looked down at her soberly. 'Perhaps they took them all prisoner.'

'C-Capitano Boniface s-said the Troublemakers t-take no prisoners,' Goose pointed out.

Cordelia clapped a hand on Goose's shoulder.

'That's only because nobody's ever met a prisoner they've taken!' she said bracingly. 'Besides, he forgot about Prudence Oglethorne. They took *her* prisoner.'

This reminder of a kidnap victim did not seem to bring Goose much comfort.

'We make for St Freerest as fast as possible!' Prospero announced, scanning the horizon.

All the remaining Wind Bags were opened halfway up the rigging, and *Little Bear* surged onwards, leaving the wreck of the ruined ship sinking slowly into the deep dark blue. Cordelia watched it until it was a blur on the horizon.

'We'll stop them,' she whispered to the disappearing wreck. 'I promise.' She was more determined than ever to defeat the Troublemakers.

'We've sailed faster than news can travel, so St Freerest won't have had word yet of what happened in Parliament,' Prospero told his gathered crew. 'But the less notice we attract, the better. We should invent a disguise.'

'For ourselves?' Cordelia asked.

'Yes.' He nodded. 'And also a disguise for our ship.'

All day, as they sped across the sea, they busily prepared for *Little Bear*'s entry into port.

'She'll be registered as a London ship, so we'll have to change her name, as well as the figurehead,' Prospero told them.

The figurehead would have revealed them quickly by roaring into port as a small bear. They found some mops meant for swabbing the decks and fashioned a curly mane out of them. Sam (being the most confident climber) edged out on to the bowsprit to tie the mane in place, turning the bear into a lion.

'Name next,' Prospero said. 'Any ideas?'

'Lionheart!' Goose suggested, squaring his shoulders as he gazed at their new lion figurehead.

'Excellent!' Prospero cried. 'But let's make it French – throw them off the scent even more: *Coeur de Lion!*'

Cordelia was lowered over the edge of the ship on ropes, clutching a paintbrush made of trimmed Honeybadger whiskers to keep her hands steady. Davey had dipped the brush in Trigment paint to ensure the lines stayed sharp. As the waves rushed beneath her dangling feet, Cordelia changed *Little Bear* to *Coeur de Lion*.

At dusk, a promise appeared on the horizon in the form of a faint glimmer away to the south-west. The newly named *Coeur de Lion*, flying a French *Fleur-de-Lis* from her top-gallant, sped towards it.

As the sun went down in their eyes, Prospero called Cordelia to the wheel.

'Dilly,' he said seriously, 'these Troublemakers are dangerous.'

Cordelia jutted her chin out. 'I'm not scared, Father!'

The solemn line of Prospero's mouth twitched.

'But *I am* scared, littlest Hatmaker,' he said. 'I'm scared of losing you.'

Cordelia noticed that her father gripped the wheel so tightly she could see the fine bones of his hand standing out like the veins of a leaf.

'I have decided that when we get to St Freerest,' he went on steadily, 'I will leave you, Sam and Goose with a woman who runs a tavern there. You'll be safe –'

'NO! Don't leave me behind!' Cordelia burst out. 'I can fight! I'm strong!'

Prospero knelt on the deck, gripping Cordelia's shoulders.

'I know you're strong and capable, my brave girl,' he whispered. 'I know you'd fight for justice with your lion heart and your roaring spirit. But I want you to stay safe –'

Unhelpfully, Cordelia felt hot tears of frustration welling up in her eyes. She took a deep breath.

'It isn't fair to ask me to stand aside while you do all the rescuing,' she said slowly, determined to shut the tearful wobble out of her voice. 'Besides, *I'm* the only one who can see the island on the map!'

It was true. Everybody else aboard *Little Bear* had taken turns to stare directly at the place where Cordelia had found the Island of Lost Souls and nobody had been able to see anything other than blank parchment. But, despite this useful talent of Cordelia's, her father had made up his mind.

'Once I'm sure things are safe, I'll fetch you and we'll go back home together.'

Cordelia felt thunderclouds gathering behind her eyes as her father turned back to the horizon. He wanted her to be quiet and good and boring while he swashbuckled across the ocean on a great, hair-raising adventure. It was quite breathtakingly unfair. It had been her idea to take on the Troublemakers, her idea to rescue Prudence Oglethorne, and her idea to win a royal pardon. And now her father was going to make her hide while he did it all without her.

Cordelia was about to unleash a furious storm of protest when her father said quietly, never taking his eyes off the horizon, 'I've already lost the great love of my life to treachery at sea, Cordelia. I cannot lose you too.'

All Cordelia's fury fell still. Her mother had been lost at sea, and her father's grief was an ocean he would sail on all his life: sometimes rough, sometimes calm, but always deep, and dark at the bottom.

She felt the fingers of the wind on her cheek, soothing her. The stars came out to comfort the empty sky.

'We'll slip quietly into St Freerest under cover of darkness,' Prospero murmured. 'I suggest you get a few hours' sleep before we arrive.'

Obediently, Cordelia went down to her bunk to be rocked to sleep by a sea that took so much and kept so many souls for itself.

CHAPTER 14

St Freerest glittered in the night like stolen treasure.

Cordelia hugged the lion-disguised figurehead, leaning towards the lights of the town that had appeared like a miracle out of the dark. After the clean salt of sea air, the atmosphere swarmed with pungent smells as *Little Bear* sailed into the bay. Soon the anchor clanked down, hitting the seabed with a *thunk*.

They lowered a skiff over the side and Cordelia, Sam, Goose and Prospero made for shore, leaving Davey and Melchior guarding *Little Bear*. They wove between clinking fishing boats and vast oceangoers, heading for the jigsaw of jetties reaching out across the shallows.

Music and wild laughter spilled from taverns along the waterfront. Lanterns studded the dark like carbuncle rubies. Cordelia could see them shining in her friends' eyes as they grinned excitedly at each other.

They tied their boat to a jetty and the world swam as their legs struck solid ground.

'Whoa!' Goose yelped, putting his arms out to steady himself. Meanwhile, Cordelia clutched Sam, and they fell in a heap on the dusty planks.

'You'll get your land legs back soon!' said Prospero, laughing as he swayed a little himself. 'Just keep your knees bent.'

'*Wee!*' Goose answered loudly.

'You all right, Goose?' Cordelia asked, tipping sideways as she tried to stand up.

'I'm being French,' Goose told her covertly. '*Wee* means *yes*.'

Sam thrust her hands into her pockets, pulling out sticky blobs of Nougat Gaulois. 'We can use these!' she said, passing them round and cramming a particularly large chunk into her own mouth.

'We need to find the Kingless tavern,' Prospero announced, chewing. '*Et faire profil bas.*'

'*Je parle français, mais je ne comprends pas!*' Sam said, spreading her hands wide and shrugging.

Cordelia giggled, feeling giddy as she staggered down the jetty. After days of wide skies and distant horizons, the world was suddenly very close and loud. She stepped on to a new land. Her feet had never walked on earth that wasn't England before.

With an explosion of noise, fighting sailors spilled out of a waterfront tavern.

Prospero seized an ancient mariner reeling past and asked, '*Où est le* Kingless?'

The man pointed along the waterfront.

'*Par ici!*' Prospero told Cordelia, Sam and Goose, then beckoned them to follow, because they didn't understand French.

They hurried along the harbour, through rowdy singalongs and wrestling matches. Fish sizzled on open fires. They had to skip over a game of pavement dice that turned violent in seconds, as a player accused of cheating was seized by his opponent and, with a roar, hurled into the sea.

Staggering onwards through a street party, they were temporarily deafened by a racket blasting from a battered hornpipe and Cordelia was swung into a dance by a one-eyed sailor. Thumping tankards and the clash of swords created a wild tympanic rattle that shook her bones and made her teeth clack as she spun.

Prospero waded in to pull her out of the dance, towing her through a rowdy night market where sellers jostled, shaking fistfuls of peculiar fruits in their faces and yelling the prices of spices.

'World's strongest peg legs!' a marketeer bellowed, waving ornately carved wooden legs. 'Can't be splintered, chopped or stabbed! I've got peg legs for dancing, climbing, running, jumping and hopping. Made of Limber Timber!'

Cordelia noted that if she ever needed a wooden leg, this was the place to come.

'Read yer fortune, missy?' A figure lurched from the shadows. 'Price is one of yer front teeth!'

Cordelia shook her head. '*Non merci!*'

There were musical instruments for sale that played enchanting songs, spools of moon-bright ribbon and cloud-woven carpets, currant-studded honey cakes and piles of fruit she didn't recognize. Cordelia caught the sunshiny scent of pure joy and realized a woman was selling perfumes that smelled like feelings. Immediately after that, she passed beneath banners of silk kites, watching them change colour as they rippled in the wind.

She wanted to stop and look at everything, but her father pulled her onwards. Sam and Goose followed, hands clamped defensively over their mouths.

They emerged from the chaos of the night market to find the strangest building Cordelia had ever seen rearing above them. It was a teetering wooden tower, curved on one side like an old man hunched over the harbour.

'Eh?' Goose peered up at the building.

It had a familiar shape, but something about it was wrong. Cordelia tilted her head and realized that the entire building was half an enormous ship, turned on its end as though it was sinking straight into the rocks it was perched on. Ropes and lanterns hung off it. Windows and a door had been carved into the curved hull and a sign swinging above the door declared this establishment to be:

THE KINGLESS

'*Allons-y!*' said Prospero, pushing the door open. 'Keep your wits about you.'

Inside was an uproar. Some kind of brawl was going on, which Cordelia quickly realized was simply business as usual in this inn. A horde of sailors sang, banging tankards, while a woman in red trousers and a billowy shirt, hair piled high on her head like a silver crown, served grog sloshingly from behind a bar.

'Drink a gizzardful, you old sea snake!' she hurled at one customer. And at another: 'Get that down you, you barnacle-bottomed bilge-rat!'

Insults apparently came free with each drink.

Prospero shouldered his way towards the bar, through arm-wrestles and arguments and spiralling sea shanties with rude lyrics. Cordelia, Sam and Goose scampered in his wake, staring around. Above their heads, a chaos of pulleys and ropes was lost in the haze of drifting smoke.

'Captain Hatmaker!' the woman roared from behind the bar, throwing her arms up in delight and drenching a nearby sailor in ale. 'I heard you were at the bottom of the sea. I'm glad to see how very untrue the rumours were!'

'And *I* heard there was a duchess on St Freerest!' Prospero grinned. 'I'm glad to find this rumour *is* true!'

A duchess? thought Cordelia. She had certainly never come across any duchess quite like this one before.

'Give me news from London!' the Duchess demanded, filling several tankards at once and firing them across the bar to her customers. 'Tell me, is there still demand for chocolate beans or have the Sensible Party finally got their way and banned everything fun?'

'Not as far as I know,' Prospero said carefully.

The Duchess jerked her head to some crates piled behind the bar. 'I ask because I've got a shipment leaving for London tomorrow. All the great chocolate houses clamour for my beans: the Sargasso, the Celestial, the Mariana,' she reeled off proudly. 'Ah! Here comes the last of the cargo!'

A boy with curly hair and a crooked smile descended on a rope from the ceiling, carrying a sack. He unhooked his foot from the rope as he landed behind the bar.

'You're late! I was expecting you this morning,' the Duchess barked, banging bottles of grog on to the counter for some clamouring customers.

'Wind just changed.' The boy grinned, swinging the sack from his shoulder and staring curiously at the newcomers as he began to prise the lid from one of the crates.

The Duchess turned back to Prospero. 'So, what brings you to this lawless island?' she asked.

Prospero's eyes flicked to Cordelia.

'It's complicated,' he muttered, checking over his shoulder before drawing Cordelia forward. 'This is my daughter, Cordelia. She's wanted for treason.'

'Treason? Impressive!' said the Duchess.

The boy packing the crate whipped round to stare at Cordelia, and she tried her best to look like someone capable of daring acts of righteous rebellion.

'What do you know about the Troublemakers?' Prospero asked.

'The Troublemakers?' the Duchess repeated. 'We leave them well alone. What d'you want with them?'

'I need to find the Island of Lost Souls,' Prospero told her. He had to shout louder as a fight broke out in the crowd. Accordion music squeezed and strained as one bellowing mass of sailors pushed against another. 'I think that's where they're hiding.'

'The Island of Lost Souls doesn't exist,' the Duchess answered. 'It's nothing but dark rumours and shipwrecks swirling round the sea!'

Cordelia burst out: 'It's real! I've seen it on the map!'

The Duchess's eyes flashed curiously at her. 'Have you?' she asked. 'And how can that be?'

The horde of customers pummelling each other was causing the very walls of the inn to groan. As one side gained the upper hand, the whole room slewed sideways. Bottles of grog slid down the counter and the crowd staggered as the floor tilted like a see-saw.

'Don't worry!' the Duchess reassured Sam and Goose cheerfully, as they clung to the bar, tankards tumbling past them. 'It's quiet tonight. On rowdy nights, the boat rocks several times a minute!'

The crates behind the bar slipped, and Cordelia nipped round the counter to help the boy, who was squished against the wall as the floor landed at a drunken angle.

'Thanks!' the boy panted, edging out from behind the crates as Cordelia hauled them aside. 'I was almost a pancake there!'

There was something unusual about the boy. He spoke with perfect round vowels; his words were like plum cakes on a duke's tea table, but his clothes were scruffy and his hair quite wild.

Cordelia picked up the sack that had tumbled loose and her fingertips suddenly tingled. The boy snatched it back from her.

'Thanks again!' he said, stuffing it into the crate. 'Here – hold this.'

He shoved the wooden lid down and Cordelia saw the words ARTIFICE CHOCOLATE HOUSE, LONDON stamped upon it. She knelt on the lid to hold it in place as he hammered nails into the crate.

Behind them, Prospero leaned closer to the Duchess. 'I've got to get a crew together to hunt the Troublemakers,' he told her. 'Rescuing Prudence Oglethorne is the only way we can think of to win Cordelia a royal pardon. Cordelia made a Meddling hat and put it on the king's head. That's *high treason*!'

'Brilliant!' came a whisper.

Cordelia looked up to see the boy staring admiringly at her, a wonky smile on his thin face.

'Did you *really* do that?' he asked.

Cordelia tried to look modest but failed. Her mouth twitched into a shy grin.

'Yes, I did,' she admitted, before adding, 'It was quite easy, really.'

She watched the boy's eyes widen. 'Jolly good show!' he gushed, shaking her hand fervently. 'That might be the most piratical thing I've ever heard of, including the time the Duchess traded her de Sneer family silver for a shark's-tooth earring!'

'What?' Cordelia frowned. 'She's a de Sneer?'

She looked round. The Duchess was deep in conversation with Prospero. At the end of the bar, Sam and Goose were taking swigs from a bottle of grog and saying 'ARGH!' in an apparent effort to blend in.

'But de Sneers are baddies, aren't they?' Cordelia hissed, turning back to the boy. 'One of them's in the Sensible Party!'

'They're not all baddies,' he said. 'The Duchess and Master Ambrosius are good eggs.'

Cordelia felt her head spin. The swaying room didn't help.

'*Master Ambrosius* is a de Sneer too?' she spluttered.

Before the boy could reply, the Duchess swooped down on him. 'That's enough chinwagging from you!' she barked. 'Bedtime!'

She slipped a heavy hook under the boy's belt, unlooped a rope from the wall and let go, sending him flying upwards with a yell. Goose and Sam howled with laughter, pointing at the boy's flailing legs as he disappeared up into the rafters. But Cordelia gawked after him, unasked questions still burning on her tongue.

She turned to the Duchess, who was staring at her, her gaze as sharp as the shark's tooth that dangled from her ear.

Is she really a de Sneer?

'You saw the island on a map, did you?' the Duchess asked quietly.

Cordelia nodded. In a whirl of silk shirtsleeves, the Duchess turned to Prospero.

'The children can't go off with you to fight pirates!' she declared. 'Far too dangerous! They must stay safe with me. And we'll need to find you a crew of brave, strong heroes!'

She swept her bar clear of tankards and jumped up on to it, crocodile-skin boots suddenly level with Cordelia's eyes. She banged two tankards together and the clamour of the inn died down.

'WHO'S BRAVE ENOUGH TO JOIN CAPTAIN HATMAKER AND FIGHT SOME PIRATES?' the Duchess roared.

'WHO'S BRAVE ENOUGH TO JOIN CAPTAIN HATMAKER
AND FIGHT SOME PIRATES?' the Duchess roared.

A bloodthirsty cheer rose from the crowd. Cutlasses were thrust skywards, turning the room into a field of sharp silver wheat, ready to be reaped. Prospero seemed pleased: with the Duchess's help, he would easily gather a crew capable of defeating the Troublemakers. Cordelia tried to look glad, but she felt somewhat resentful. It seemed that her father wouldn't need her help after all.

'Aaah, yes!' The Duchess nodded approvingly at the fierce faces gurning up at her. 'We have only the bravest souls on St Freerest, don't we, lasses and lads?'

'YAAAR!'

'You lot aren't afraid of the terrible wave that swallows ships whole, are ya?' The Duchess grinned. 'Or that fearsome sea beast, longer than a warship, *with a flaming tail* – it doesn't frighten you!'

The bravery on several faces seemed to shrink, like sea anemones recoiling.

'*You're* not scared of the golloping seaweed or the treacherous rocks! *Or* the enchanted storms that twist ships up and break them into splinters!' the Duchess went on, striding up and down the bar.

Another roar rose, slightly paler than before.

'Or the man-eating flowers or the fire-eating birds! Or . . . the *Troublemakers*!'

At the Duchess's last word, the drinkers' wide grins disappeared.

'WHO'LL JOIN CAPTAIN HATMAKER?' the Duchess yelled.

This time the invitation was met with silence. Nobody seemed to have any roar left in them. Cordelia was amazed: had the Duchess deliberately frightened everyone off?

Prospero's face was a wry twist of frustration. 'Will *anybody* join me?' he asked the room.

Cutlasses wilted and were quietly sheathed. Nobody would meet his eye, let alone his request. Then –

'I will!' came a cry.

But it turned out to be Goose, getting unsteadily to his feet and waving his empty grog bottle. Behind him, Sam fell sideways trying to stand up.

The Duchess hopped down from the bar.

'Never mind,' she said consolingly, clapping Prospero on the back.

He raised an eyebrow as the Duchess busied herself at the bar.

'I'll try some other taverns,' he said resolutely.

'You might have more luck at the Urchin or the Comeuppance – they're full of mad-headed vagabonds,' offered the Duchess. 'But I think this lot need to sleep off the grog.' She indicated Sam and Goose, who were clutching each other's shoulders and slurring like they were wearing Sluggard Yarn hats.

'I'll come with you, Father!' Cordelia said, making her way to him. But the Duchess pulled a huge basket down from the ceiling, cutting her off.

'I think your friends will need help climbing into their hammocks!' she said, laughing. 'Besides, I don't think the Comeuppance is any place for a little girl!'

'But I want to –'

Prospero shook his head. 'The Duchess is right, Dilly. It's not safe for you to come with me,' he said, kissing her on top of her head. 'I promise I'll be back to say goodbye before we leave to fight the pirates.'

Cordelia barely had time to take an indignant in-breath before she was thrust into the basket by the Duchess, who tipped Goose and Sam in after her.

'Fourth door up!' the Duchess instructed. 'You'll find hammocks in there – sleep well!'

Before Cordelia could protest, the Duchess let go, sending the basket shooting up through the smoky air.

'THASS MAZING!' Sam marvelled glassily.

'WHEEEEEEEE!' Goose squealed, and was promptly sick.

CHAPTER 15

Cordelia did not sleep well.

For a start, Goose snored loudly in the next hammock all night long. Rude sea shanties reverberated through the floor until the small hours, and Sam appeared to be having a garrulous argument with her pillow.

When Cordelia did sleep, she had hectic dreams, sharp with sharks' teeth and flint-eyed stares.

She woke as the first light seeped through the window, her mind blazing with an urgent thought:

The Duchess is a de Sneer!

Cordelia eased the door open quietly and peered out. A dizzying drop below, several sailors lay sprawled on the sticky floor of the inn, fast asleep. Ropes and pulleys hung in the stale air. There was no sign of the Duchess.

Cordelia considered waking Sam and Goose, but they were now sleeping deeply, and she thought it would be best to find that boy from last night and question him as quietly as possible before the Duchess woke.

She scrutinized the system of pulleys and ropes dangling outside her door, recognizing the one with the heavy hook that had dragged the boy up to the rafters. It must be the way to his room.

She hooked herself to the rope and jumped. Ropes and pulleys rushed past her in a blur. She clapped a hand over her mouth to muffle a whoop of wild delight as she soared into the rafters like a bird.

The rope brought her to a stop beside a trapdoor in the ceiling.

'Hello . . . boy?' Cordelia whispered.

She scrambled out through the trapdoor and found herself on the roof of the Kingless. The roof curved away steeply beneath her feet, leaving a small platform jutting over a sheer drop, attached haphazardly to the building with ropes and struts.

A big white X was painted in the middle of the platform, and a brass lantern hung beside the kind of iron ring that was usually used for tying boats to jetties.

The boy wasn't here. This clearly wasn't his bedroom. But . . . the Duchess had sent him up here to bed, hadn't she?

Cordelia turned, looking for clues, and gasped as she saw the island of St Freerest spread out below her.

Along the harbour, a jumble of brightly painted buildings leaned against each other, as though trying to stay upright while full of grog. In the sparkling bay, an enormous ship was dropping anchor. Behind her, a green mountain rose out of the turquoise sea, and the sunrise colours of the island were so delicious that Cordelia felt her mouth water.

But she couldn't be distracted by beautiful views and sunrise-coloured clouds. She had questions to ask: she needed to find the boy.

'Where did he go?' she muttered.

This platform perched on the Kingless's roof seemed to be a lookout spot; a telescope pointed out across the water. Cordelia put her eye to the telescope and jumped in surprise.

In the perfect circle of the lens, she saw an island floating on the flat blue line of the sea.

She took her eye away from the instrument to squint in the direction it was pointing. On the horizon, she made out a faint shape.

Cordelia knew that there was only one other island near St Freerest on the map.

'The Island of Lost Souls!' she breathed. 'It must be!'

The mysterious isle had a tidal pull that caught in her chest. She thought she saw a friendly purple wink in the sky above it, fading in the rising light.

'Good morning, Cordelia.' A sharp voice cut through the balmy morning.

Cordelia whipped round. The Duchess stood by the trapdoor, eyes flashing like an eagle's.

'I – I just came up to see the view,' Cordelia explained, trying for a breezy, conversational tone.

The Duchess did not seem convinced. 'And what did you see through that telescope?' she enquired.

Cordelia paused, sensing a trap. 'Just the sea,' she lied.

Last night, the Duchess had said that the Island of Lost Souls didn't exist . . . But this telescope was trained on it. Something suspicious was going on.

The Duchess observed Cordelia narrowly, and Cordelia felt her belly button tremble.

'That boy told me you're a de Sneer!' she burst out.

The Duchess smiled in a way that was not reassuring. 'That boy is correct,' she said.

Cordelia found there was no space to back away, even though she wanted to put a safe distance between herself and that shark smile.

'I won't deny, the de Sneers have a family tradition of making things worse,' the Duchess went on. 'There is a long and illustrious history of my ancestors sneering at things. One is famed for scowling at Joan of Arc; another is depicted grimacing on the Bayeux Tapestry. It is said: *If a de Sneer curls his lip at you, you're bound to be on the right side of history.*'

'So you *are* a baddie!' Cordelia uttered, her voice fluttering like a flag in a breeze.

'Oh, child! The world is far more complicated than that!' The Duchess chuckled, her shark's-tooth earring jiggling. 'Sometimes good people do bad things for good reasons! Some *baddies* come dressed as heroes in smart uniforms. And the most dangerous pirates don't even look like pirates at all: they come in disguise, dressed as respectable gentlemen.'

Cordelia dug her nails into her palms obstinately.

'My father wears a *smart uniform*,' she growled. 'And he's trying to do something *good*: catch the Troublemakers! But you tried to stop him last night by scaring everyone off from joining him!'

The Duchess frowned, invoking the ancient lineage of grim expressions that she had inherited. Cordelia could feel the pressure of scrutiny from a de Sneer. There was something searing about her stare; it blistered.

'You're very observant,' the Duchess remarked. 'You see everything . . . including invisible islands on maps.'

Cordelia raised her chin defiantly. 'You know about the Island of Lost Souls,' she said. 'You lied to my father. You *do* know where it is; your telescope's pointing right at it. And now I know too!'

The Duchess raised one eyebrow, which was enough to cause Cordelia's elbows to quiver.

'Do you know whose ship that is, that's just dropped anchor

in the bay?' the Duchess asked, pointing across the water to the hulking galleon that loomed over the other ships.

The ship's figurehead, Cordelia saw, was a golden-haired knight wielding a shining lance, and a shield decorated with a blood-red cross.

'That's the *Invincible* – Admiral Ransom's warship,' the Duchess went on. 'I'm sure he would be most interested to hear about a treasonous fugitive on the run from British justice.'

'But he can't arrest –'

'For the right price, *somebody* could sell you out.'

The Duchess stared coldly at Cordelia.

'What exactly are you saying?' Cordelia asked, trying not to let the curl of the Duchess's lip affect her knees, which were getting a little wobbly.

'If tongues begin to wag about the English girl at the Kingless, rumour will reach the admiral in no time, and you'll be caught. You might even be delivered to him in a sack.'

'Alternatively . . . I could simply put you in a packing crate and ship you back to London with my other cargo,' the Duchess added thoughtfully. 'There's a boat leaving today, and I know a sailor on board who wouldn't ask too many questions.'

She took a step forward.

'But, of course, it's possible to buy people's silence too,' she whispered. 'And I'll name my price.'

Her stare was so fierce that Cordelia felt the fire of it weakening her muscles.

'Do not tell your father where to find the Island of Lost Souls,' the Duchess hissed. 'Give me your word.'

The Duchess's threat was clear: Cordelia had to keep the location of the island a secret, or the Duchess would make sure she was captured and dragged back to England.

Cordelia summoned all her strength to answer back.

'That's where the Troublemakers' hideout is!' she said. 'They're burning ships and terrorizing London – we've got to catch them!'

'No!' the Duchess cried, lunging for Cordelia.

But Cordelia's trousers were made of Flocculent Cotton. In one bound, she was across the platform. The Duchess sprang after her, but Cordelia flung herself through the trapdoor and slammed it shut, throwing the catch.

She swung on to the ropes as the Duchess hammered furiously at the trapdoor. Cordelia lurched through the air, unhitched a pulley and plunged several floors at once.

'WAKE UP!' Cordelia yelled, kicking the bedroom door open.

Goose and Sam's bleary faces appeared as they sat up in their hammocks.

'WE'VE GOT TO GO – NO TIME TO EXPLAIN!'

Luckily, they had fallen asleep in their clothes, so they were ready to go.

Cordelia, Sam and Goose piled into the basket and it plummeted. With barely time to catch their breath, they trampled across several snoring sailors and burst out of the front door. In the dusty street, they could hear the Duchess's voice fluttering like a red flag on the roof.

'Someone'll wake up soon enough and free her!' Cordelia panted. 'We've got to get back to *Little Bear*!'

CHAPTER 16

'Isn't this stealing?' Goose wheezed.

'Not if we return it,' Sam replied breathlessly. 'Then it's *borrowin'*.'

The children were furiously rowing a small 'borrowed' fishing boat across St Freerest's Bay.

'I'm wanted for treason!' Cordelia puffed, pulling on her oar. 'What's a little boat-borrowing when the king of England's after you?'

Little Bear lay asleep at anchor. Cordelia, Sam and Goose climbed up the ladder on to the deck and hurried below to the captain's cabin. They found Captain Hatmaker awake, poring over his maps.

'Dilly, Sam, Goose!' he cried. 'What are you doing here?'

Cordelia quickly gasped out what had happened on the roof: how the Duchess had threatened her because she had

seen the Island of Lost Souls through the telescope. Before
her father had time to take in all this information, Cordelia
turned to the map spread across his table. The Island of Lost
Souls shone brighter than ever on the parchment.

'You *must* see it!' she cried, pointing as Sam and Goose
stared blankly at the map. 'It's clear as day!'

Prospero was distracted by the more urgent problem at hand.

'I thought I could trust that duplicitous Duchess!' he
muttered. 'Now the admiral's here, she could tell him
everything.'

Prospero grimaced, striding to his window and staring at
the dark blot of the *Invincible* in the bay.

'Wake Melchior and Davey,' he ordered. 'We put to sea.'

Making a ship ready to set sail was a slow process, like waking
a giant.

After leaving the Kingless last night, Prospero had not
found a single soul on the island of St Freerest willing to go
after the Troublemakers. So they remained a crew of six. But
they knew the ropes, and they all worked quickly. Soon, the
sails came down to catch the wind and *Little Bear* leaned
towards the open sea.

Will the Duchess give us away? Cordelia wondered as they
surged out of the harbour.

They met the open water with a bump. The sea was dark and stirring.

'If there's a storm, at least it will buy us some time if the admiral decides to give chase,' Melchior said grimly.

'It's coming in from the south-west,' said Davey, squinting up into the clouds.

'We can go after the Troublemakers now!' Goose joined in excitedly. 'Cordelia saw their island – now we know exactly where to go!'

'Yeah!' Sam added. 'Where's the island, Cor?'

Cordelia pointed to the south-west. 'That way!'

But the sky was painting itself grey before their eyes. Frowning clouds clotted the horizon as the sea grew teeth, gnashing at *Little Bear* with strange serrated waves.

'There's something freakish about this sea,' Davey muttered. 'I don't like it.'

'We're not going *towards* the Troublemakers!' Prospero announced firmly. 'Not with you three children on board!'

'*Why?*' Goose wailed.

Prospero adjusted his captain's hat as the wind fretted and shoved.

'Because I promised in the note I sent home with Agatha that I would return you to your mother in one piece, Lucas Bootmaker,' Prospero said, fixing each of them with a stern look. 'And you, Sam Lightfinger, to your brother. And you, Cordelia, to the rest of the Hatmakers. I promised you would all be safe! You are *children* and these pirates are clearly extremely dangerous.'

Cordelia, Sam and Goose burst into a chorus of objections.

'But I saw the island!' Cordelia protested. 'I know exactly –'

'I am the *captain*!' Prospero had to raise his voice to be heard above the grinding waves and mutinous shouts. 'This is my ship! When on board, you go by my rules!'

Cordelia, Goose and Sam fell into a surly silence. The wind muttered around the mast.

'We'll sail round the island of St Freerest to the southern shore,' Prospero said. 'We've already got supplies aboard to last a week or so. We'll hide until –'

'*Hide!*' Cordelia burst out indignantly.

Her father was a seafaring hero! He had not *hidden* during any of the daring exploits he had told her about. But that was when she was safely sitting at the kitchen hearth and any danger lay leagues across the sea. Now they were on a tiny ship racing out into the open ocean, chased by a tempest.

Prospero clapped a hand to his head to stop his hat being snatched off by the wind. The sea roiled like a cauldron coming to the boil; water drew itself up into green hills, bore down like a landslide over the ship and crashed over the rail.

'No arguing!' Prospero bellowed, staggering sideways in the drenching drag of a wave. 'Storm's here! Get below!'

Cordelia, Sam and Goose stumbled below deck feeling very hard done by. They were soon distracted from their malcontent by the more urgent problem of seasickness. As they opened the door to Cordelia and Sam's cabin, the floor fell away, and they went skidding down the sudden steep slope and piled against the far wall.

'Argh!' Goose moaned, lunging for a bunk but missing as the ship pitched again.

It was like being in the belly of a beast. A beast with a terrible bellyache. The ship reeled yet again. Cordelia felt as though a mean fist had grabbed her guts and twisted. With each sickening lurch of the sea, her stomach climbed up her throat.

'I suddenly feel uncooked in the middle!' Goose moaned.

Cordelia crawled along the rocking floor to peer out of her porthole. The sea was disobeying all its usual rules and arranging itself at very alarming angles against the iron sky.

Sam groaned as *Little Bear* rolled on the ocean swell.

'When's it gonna stop?' she whimpered.

'Not for a while,' replied Cordelia. 'We're surrounded by sea!'

That is the problem with the sea: there is an awful lot of it, and when you're in the middle of it, it goes in every direction.

'I can't swim,' Sam admitted, fear clouding her eyes.

Cordelia's belly dropped as *Little Bear* plunged down a wave into a valley of moving water. She tumbled over Goose, who was lying flat on the floor and groaning.

A solid slab of sea slapped the porthole and she fell backwards. Sam dragged her into the bunk. As Cordelia swung with the motion of the ship, the sick feeling that gripped her belly loosened a little.

'I'm scared,' Sam whispered, trembling, as the ship tipped sideways.

Cordelia reached for her hand and squeezed it hard as *Little Bear* reared and pitched over the steep waves. A great creaking sounded around them as the very bones of the ship protested.

'Is *Little Bear* going ta break apart?' Sam asked.

'No,' Cordelia replied decisively. 'She's stout and strong and she'll weather worse storms than this.'

Sam smiled shakily. 'I've weathered worse too,' she said.

Hours later, the storm abated and the sun cracked through the clouds, dripping egg-yolk gold. Cordelia, Sam and Goose staggered up on to the sea-slick deck to gulp lungfuls of fresh, salty air.

'At least we haven't been blown too far!' Cordelia said, pointing at St Freerest silhouetted on the starboard horizon.

However, breaking away from the outline of the island and chasing the ragged hems of clouds, came a ship.

'Is that the admiral comin' after us?' Sam gasped.

'Can't be!' Davey answered from the rigging. 'He'd be sailing from St Freerest.'

Cordelia turned to squint at Davey. He was peering at the horizon off the port bow, at the distinct mountaintop of St Freerest. Cordelia swung round, staring at the island that she had assumed was St Freerest on the opposite horizon. It was clear: a jagged cut-out against the bright gold sky.

'That must be the Island of Lost Souls!' she exclaimed. 'Look!'

Everybody peered in the direction Cordelia was pointing.

'Where?' Goose asked.

Cordelia jabbed her finger at the jagged island.

'Right *there*!' she cried.

After the thunderous grey of the storm, the world was gilded and glaring. The sea was a sheet of hammered copper, and light struck up into her eyes. But even through the glare, the island was clearly there.

Why could nobody else see its dark shape? It was so clear it looked almost close enough to touch.

Sam was shaking her head, and for a moment Cordelia wondered if they had all ganged up on her for a strange kind of joke.

'Father, you can see the island now, can't you?' she asked. 'It's right there!'

Captain Hatmaker had his eye pressed to his telescope.

'I can't see an island, Dilly, but there's something strange about that ship,' he murmured.

Cordelia squinted at it. It skimmed across the glittering sea towards them, wearing the storm like coat-tails. There appeared to be silk kites flying from the rigging and a vine of huge poisonous-looking flowers twisting round the bowsprit. The sails flashed as though they were laced with quicksilver, and behind the vessel trailed several clouds, seemingly being towed on ropes. The air around the ship flared red with the wings of strange birds, and the water surging beneath the hull was *alive*. Cordelia peered closer and saw something strong and slippery weaving in and out of the water. It had a tail that flashed strangely, making the water bubble. Black waterspouts erupted from the ship's wake.

'What in the world . . .' Sam whispered.

Cordelia peered into the sunset. The figurehead rushing towards them over the ocean had horns and a wicked grin.

The ship surged closer and she could make out a single word, painted in curling gold letters on the prow:

Trouble

CHAPTER 17

'*ALL HANDS ON DECK!*' Prospero roared.

They did not need to go looking for trouble; *Trouble* had found them.

'Now's our chance to defeat the Troublemakers!' Cordelia cried.

'NO!' Prospero yelled, charging to the wheel. 'WE FLEE! COME ABOUT!'

'*I want to fight!*' Cordelia yelled back, throwing open the Weather Pantry doors.

'Don't you *dare* disobey me, Cordelia Hatmaker!' Prospero barked. 'You, Sam and Goose – get below NOW! STAY SAFE!'

He wrenched the wheel round, and the ship slewed sideways. Jars of weather tumbled on to Cordelia as she hit the deck. Anger at her father exploded in her chest.

'*You're a coward!*' she screamed. 'LET ME FIGHT!'

Her father's face betrayed terror and pain as he wrestled the wheel.

Davey rammed a wad of storm-cloud into the muzzle of the Thunderclap cannon.

'FIRE!' Melchior roared.

There was the sizzle of flame gobbling a fuse, then a *BOOM* shook their bones. *Little Bear*'s cannon was designed to *not* sink ships, only to scare off attackers. But it did not scare these pirates.

A chorus of blood-curdling howls rose from the enemy ship. Goosebumps erupted over Cordelia's skin. She grabbed rolling weather jars and flung them at the *Trouble*.

Lightning cracked like a whip between the ships. A twister went spiralling across the sea, causing a waterspout that nudged the *Trouble* off course. But the ship cut through the water, correcting its course and surging forward with unnatural speed.

Cordelia saw the flash of cutlasses on the enemy deck, grinning faces and bared teeth. Figures scurried like rats up the rigging. Something was hurled through the sky trailing a silver rope: a large brown thing the size of a mop head. It landed with a thud at Cordelia's feet. For a moment she thought it was merely a hairy splat of seaweed. But it quickly picked itself up, scuttling on eight legs. It was a nightmarish creature, made of sharp angles and shiny eyes.

'WHAT IS THAT?' Goose shrieked, as it ran across the deck.

Davey dived for it, but the creature scuttled up the mast, the silver rope snaking behind it.

'IT'S A HUGE SPIDER!' Goose answered his own horrified question.

They were slowing down. *Little Bear* bucked like a wild horse that did not want to be harnessed, and Cordelia realized what the spider was doing: its web, thick as a cable, had joined the ships, mast to mast.

'STOP THAT SPIDER!' she yelled, scrambling after it.

But the spider sprang back to the *Trouble*, unspooling a second thread behind it and lashing the ships firmly together.

Prospero leaped down from the wheel, drawing his sword and slashing at the webs. But his sword bounced off: the spider's thread was uncuttable.

The crew of *Little Bear* looked at each other. In that instant they all understood: it was useless to try to flee.

They would have to fight.

'Cordelia, Sam, Goose!' Captain Hatmaker barked. '*I order you to hide!*'

But Cordelia disobeyed the captain. She hurled jars wildly at the *Trouble* and a commotion of weather happened all at once: mist, thunder, hail and snow. Howls erupted from the Troublemakers as they were engulfed, their ghastly ship swallowed by the miniature storm.

However, as the last of the weather – the final, failed weapon – evaporated, the Troublemakers reappeared, grinning, through the mist.

In unison, the pirates stuffed their fingers in their ears. Before Cordelia could wonder why, someone uttered a high shriek, and a screech of scarlet parrots descended from the crow's nest, wheeling through the air. The birds' screams immobilized everybody on *Little Bear*'s deck.

Petrifying Parrots! Cordelia thought frantically, her mind the only part of her that could move. These birds were highly Menacing: their screech could stop a person in their tracks, while their feathers stunned whatever they touched.

As the parrots wheeled away across the sea, Cordelia's bones loosened and her joints came unstuck. She looked around desperately for a weapon she could swing. But the iron mouths of cannons bristled from the *Trouble*'s hull.

BOOM!

Cordelia found herself swallowed up by thick purple smoke.

Puzzling Fug, she vaguely thought as she turned round slowly, trying to remember who she went and why she was. *No, that's not right. The questions is: where am why and how is me?*

Something was going strange. She just couldn't puzzle out what was wit.

A storm of war cries happened somewhere beyond the reach of her confusion, and as the fug cleared, so did her mind. Dark shapes wielding sharp knives were swinging aboard *Little Bear*, ragged nightmares sliding through the haze, using the spiderweb cables to swing aboard. The deck shuddered as their boots thudded down.

The Troublemakers were a gang of grinning villains, jagged and cackling. They loomed, terrifying, above the children.

Cordelia, Goose and Sam stumbled together, clutching each other, weaponless.

'What do we do?' Sam whimpered.

Before Cordelia could answer, a shape shot through the sky, bowling Sam over. To her other side, Goose splayed on to the deck, felled by a barrage of tiny grey cannonballs. As two wild-eyed pirates lunged for Cordelia, a silver-bladed saviour whirled between them: Prospero Hatmaker furiously clashing blades.

Cordelia turned to search for a weapon – anything she could use to help her father fight – and saw Melchior get swallowed by a large column of water spinning furiously across the deck.

Cordelia darted forward to help him, but fell over Davey, who was struggling through a moving mudslide. It trapped his ankles together, sticking him to the deck.

Davey pushed her out of the way. 'Don't let it get you too!' he gasped.

Kicking a tendril of clinging mud off her foot, Cordelia crawled across the deck, to find Sam stuck to the planks with glowing gobs of sticky goo. Sam's eyes were shut tight, and she moaned as though she was suffering a nightmare.

Cordelia shook her desperately. 'Sam! Wake up!' she begged.

Right beside Sam lay a boulder. It groaned and shifted.

'Goose! Is that you?'

It was indeed Goose, covered with hundreds of stony grey creatures with pincers that clung to his clothes and skin. He was so heavy with them he couldn't move.

'GOOSE!'

But there was no time to help. A smirking pirate with wild hair and glinting eyes was coming after her.

She dodged under his arms, rushing to help her father – Prospero was their only hope. He was now fighting two pirates at once. One had flashing knives that slashed and stabbed; the other was covered from head to toe in shaggy black seaweed.

To Cordelia's horror, the seaweed surged off the pirate, spiralling round her father and trapping his arms and legs in writhing slime.

'NO!' Cordelia yelled, scrambling to help him.

But she skidded to a stop as a terrifying figure smashed on to the deck in front of her.

This pirate wore boots like destruction and a hat like a thundercloud. Her clothes were stitched together with venom and revenge. Crackles of lightning sparked from her buttons, and her silver cutlass shone with bitterness.

She towered above Cordelia.

'I am Thorn Lawless!' she growled. 'Pirate queen and leader of the Troublemakers.'

For a moment, Cordelia was awestruck by Thorn Lawless's sheer awfulness. Then a weather jar rolled across the deck into her hand. It contained a crackling dagger of lightning! Cordelia flung it at the pirate, but Thorn Lawless was faster than lightning. Her sword flashed, and the lightning zigzagged away into the rigging.

'Don't play with fire, girl,' the pirate queen sneered.

Now weaponless, Cordelia only had her mettle left with which to defend herself. She leaped to her feet, squared her shoulders and said, 'I'm not afraid of you!'

It was a lie. Her knees were shaking.

All around her, infesting the deck of her beloved ship, the Troublemakers burst into laughter.

'She's brave!'

'A bold girl!'

'I told you she would be!'

'DILLY, RUN!' her father roared.

Cordelia turned and fled. She careered across the deck and scrabbled up the mizzenmast, out of reach of the pirates' snatching hands.

'IT'S YOU WE'VE COME FOR!' the pirate queen roared in her blood-and-thunder voice. 'CORDELIA HATMAKER!'

Cordelia was shocked to hear her own name in a pirate's mouth.

'Come with us and we'll leave your friends unharmed,' declared the pirate queen.

Cordelia clung to the mast, her mind tumbling over itself trying to understand. They had come for *her*? How did they even know who she was? How had they known where to find her?

At the bottom of the mast, the Troublemakers circled like hungry hyenas.

'*Come along – come with us, Cordelia!*' a sing-song voice, rough and nightmarish, sang gleefully.

'You'll leave the crew and the ship unharmed?' Cordelia called, her mind racing. 'They'll be free to sail away if I come with you?'

'Don't believe them!' Goose's yells were muffled. 'They're *PIRATES*!'

Cordelia's attention was caught by a shout from her father. Black tentacles of seaweed had wrapped all around him. His sword had been pulled from his hand, and his legs were lashed to the rigging. Worse, though, was the fact that the rigging was now crawling with flames.

'Cordelia!' he cried out, his eyes bright with despair as a tentacle snaked over his mouth. 'Save yourself!'

Cordelia dizzily cast about for something – anything – that might help her save everyone aboard *Little Bear*. But there was nothing. The only thing she could do was escape on the borrowed rowing boat they had tied to the stern, which had bobbed along behind them valiantly through the storm. She looked across at it . . . If she was quick, she could reach it and get away –

'Come with us, Hatmaker!' Thorn Lawless called. 'We asked you politely!'

'No, you didn't!' Cordelia shouted. 'If you think that was polite, you have absolutely *no* manners!'

'Well, if you won't come, we'll have to do this the . . . definitely impolite way,' Thorn's voice drifted up to her.

Cordelia hugged the smooth mast of *Little Bear*. She pressed her nose to it. It smelled of the forests where the ship had grown as Fleetwood Trees. If she didn't sacrifice herself, this ship and the people she loved most in the world would be swallowed whole by the hungry sea, sent down into the dark amid fire and destruction.

But she *could* save them. It just meant *not* saving herself.

Cordelia slowly slid down the mast. As her feet hit the deck, Thorn Lawless's craggy hand closed over her arm.

The pirate queen's eyes blazed triumphantly. Amid the Troublemakers' victory howls, Cordelia heard her father sob, half choked in the grip of seaweed.

'What about your side of the bargain?' Cordelia demanded. 'You said you'd free the crew and promise not to sink this ship! You've got to put out the fire!'

In answer, the pirate queen whistled a strange, high-pitched whistle. A shadow moved through the sky, swarming towards *Little Bear*.

'W-what's that?' Cordelia stammered.

'My side of the bargain.' Thorn Lawless grinned at Cordelia, then dragged her across the deck.

Cordelia stared in horror at the shadow.

'NO!' She leaped forward, wrenching herself free, only to be stopped by the sharp point of a cutlass at her throat.

'Little Maker, we had an agreement,' Thorn Lawless hissed.

With a savage shove, the pirate queen pushed her. Cordelia lost her balance, staggered backwards and fell, flailing, over the side of the ship. Her belly left her, her voice unspooled, her legs went over her head, and she plummeted towards the sea.

Mid-air, there was a pull on her shoulders, her legs, her hair. It was as though the air was made of water and she was caught in an outgoing tide: a tide that was impossible to fight. She was tumbling – tumbling and rolling, but not falling – riding a tongue of air that was slurping her in.

She saw a blue blur of sea and a jumble of matchstick masts and a smear of molten sky. She was being pulled towards the *Trouble*! There was the yawning mouth of an enormous flower – its throat splodged with purple – growing closer.

FLUMP!

She landed in the wide leathery mouth and slipped down its throat.

CHAPTER 18

Cordelia was disgorged from the slippery innards of the Troublemakers' giant flesh-eating flower. She sprawled on to the deck of the *Trouble*, sticky with nectar and caked in thick yellow pollen.

Around her, the barnacled boots of pirates thudded down as they swung aboard their ship. There were triumphant crows and jeers. A sea-bitten pirate with his beard on fire lurched forward.

'Hello, missy!' he taunted. 'Welcome aboard the *Trouble*!'

Cordelia scrambled to her feet, sparks from the pirate's beard peppering her skin. Villains leered from every direction, all jagged teeth and seaweed-matted hair, eyes glinting with wickedness. Cordelia glared at the circle of ferocious faces surrounding her. Her heart pounded and her belly clenched, but she summoned her courage like she was calling a creature from the deep.

'You didn't keep your side of the bargain!' she growled. 'Let me *go*!'

The Troublemakers erupted into harsh laughter.

The *Trouble* jerked forward with sudden speed and Cordelia fell to her knees. She shot through the pirates' legs, scrambling on slippery hands and knees to see *Little Bear* listing in the water, mainsail aflame. Her father was still trapped in the rigging, struggling in the grip of the dark seaweed, unable to save himself.

'FATHER! SAM! GOOSE!'

Vulture-like birds circled the ship. Cordelia recognized them from a picture in a book she had seen. Their shrug-shoulder wings and sharp red beaks were unmistakable: Sun Eaters. She cried out as the first one swooped.

'NO!'

She readied to throw herself into the sea, determined to swim back and rescue them all, but she found herself being dragged backwards across the deck. She came to a stop at the pointed red toes of Thorn Lawless's boots and looked up into the fierce face of the pirate queen, whose eyes blazed with fire.

'Don't try to escape,' Thorn warned, her voice like thunder far out to sea. 'Or I'll throw you to the Sea Dragon!'

'Let me get back to my ship!' Cordelia demanded, scrambling to her feet. 'NOW!'

Thorn leaned down so she was nose to nose with Cordelia. 'You're coming with us,' she growled.

Cordelia dodged round the pirate queen, but she was immediately seized and pushed against a mast.

'*No!*' she wailed. 'They need my help! Please!'

She fought hard against pirates far stronger than her. But her arms became sticky and slow. Someone was wrapping a Clinging Silk rope round her with quick, light hands, lashing her to the mast.

'All hands to the sails!' Thorn roared. 'Sun's setting!'

Cordelia struggled wildly as the pirates dispersed, the rope getting tighter. She glanced down to see that it was not a person tying her up but a hairy spider the size of a dinner plate, wrapping its glistening cord round and round her.

'GET OFF ME!' Cordelia screamed.

The spider scuttled away up the mast to crouch at the end of a yardarm, all eight eyes shining gold in the fast-approaching sunset. Cordelia desperately tried to tear herself free, but the clinging silk was impossibly strong.

'LET ME GO!' she yelled.

'Quiet, Hatmaker!' Thorn Lawless snapped. 'Or that spider will web your mouth shut for you.'

Cordelia swallowed her screams, and they boiled in her belly. She dared not make a sound; she could only watch, helpless, as the ship rushed along. The *Trouble* was being towed by a massive sea creature, its slippery body straining through waves that were thick with weeds. The beast seemed to be black and shiny, like living tar, the water seething around it.

Cordelia was aware of the Troublemakers crouched in the rigging, could feel their eyes peering down at her. But her own eyes were drawn like a magnet to the chilling sight ahead. Between the sunset-drenched blaze of sky and sea, a jagged black mass crouched on the ocean.

'The Island of Lost Souls,' she whispered.

She knew that once she was there, she would be unfindable. Nobody else had seen the island; her father and friends couldn't even see it on the map! They would never be able to reach it.

Her heart fluttered in her chest like a trapped bird and her frightened voice clawed up her throat, trying to escape in a scream. She fought it back down, struggling helplessly against the web that bound her.

The sun was sinking quickly now, like last hopes about to be drowned. The island was almost upon them. Wails were borne on the wind, crushed between the grinding waves; waterspouts twisted up from the seething sea like conjuring tricks, towering above the *Trouble*.

They surged past a rock that spiked through the water, black waves crashing against it. A ridge of ship-wrecker rocks curved away across the weed-choked sea. Beyond, the ridge of the island rose, like a giant craggy spine hunched against the sky.

A huge skeletal archway, dripping spikes, reared from the water, the sunset blazing through it as though it was a mouth breathing fire.

'Lightpath!' a voice cried in the rigging.

The ship surged along a molten-gold path cast on the black sea, speeding towards the archway.

The pirates all howled triumphantly as the *Trouble* passed beneath the enormous arch. Cordelia realized the white spikes dripping in a line from it were massive fangs.

They sailed into the yawning jaws of a monstrous skeleton.

CHAPTER 19

The skull curved way above the ship's tallest mast, high as a cathedral dome, empty eye sockets staring at the sky. The *Trouble* surged out of the skull into a wide bay, flat and dark blue in the dusk.

The last ray of the sun flashed across the sky, green and strange. It signalled the sealing of Cordelia's fate.

The anchor was dropped.

Cordelia, still tied to the mast, craned her neck to see a beach, bone-white in the rising moon. Shrieks echoed from the shadowy jungle beyond. The island reared above, forbidding in the half-dark, a jagged silhouette against the purpling sky. A single star appeared directly above its highest ridge, a cold fiery eye.

Cordelia thrust her chin in the air as Thorn stalked up to her. With a whisper of steel, the pirate drew her curved cutlass.

Cordelia's whole body shivered like a Jiggle Fruit quivering on a branch, even though she was trying very hard to be still. Suddenly she folded on to the deck as her knees gave way. Thorn had cut her loose.

One of Thorn's red boots poked her with its sharp toe.

'Bring the Maker.'

The boots tramped away. Rough hands grabbed Cordelia. Before she could find words to voice her indignance, she was upended into a large sack.

Several minutes later, she was tipped out of the sack on to the sand. She could feel magic all around her; the air crackled and fizzed with it. Her fingers, which could detect even the quietest magic, tingled so much it was painful, like she had pins and needles. The island was positively violent with magic.

She scrambled to her feet to find the Troublemakers staring at her, the rustling jungle black behind them. She counted eight of them in total, including their pirate-queen leader.

Show them no fear, she told herself sternly. *They probably eat fear for pudding.*

Thorn Lawless prowled forward, a hand poised on her cutlass hilt and her eyes dancing with malice.

'A real Maker,' she said menacingly. 'We've finally got ourselves one.'

'My father will rescue me and defeat you all!' Cordelia growled.

Thorn bared her teeth. 'Your father can search and search until he's a grey-haired old man, but he'll never get here.'

Cordelia knew this to be true. The fact settled like a stone in her stomach and she clenched her fists.

'You lied to me!' she shouted. 'You said they'd go free if I gave myself up!'

She was dizzy with fear for everyone aboard *Little Bear*.

'Quit your bellyaching!' Thorn spat. 'You're ours now, Maker.'

A wild-haired pirate stepped forward. 'Miss Hatmaker, please excuse our ferocious captain,' he said, his voice plummy beneath the gravelly rasp created by years at sea. 'What she *means* to say is: you're our *guest* now.'

Cordelia hesitated for a moment, thrown by this unexpected behaviour from such a fearsome villain. 'Guest?' she repeated. 'Guests aren't carried about in sacks – I'm not your *guest*!'

'Fine then, you're our prisoner,' Thorn snapped. 'Have it your way!'

'That isn't *my* way!' Cordelia objected.

Thorn's hand clamped on her cutlass, but the wild-haired pirate stepped between her and Cordelia.

'Perhaps you'd feel better if you were properly introduced, Miss Hatmaker?' he suggested smoothly. 'As you know, we are the Troublemakers, notorious pirates of the high seas and infamous creators of chaos in London on *several* occasions. You've heard of the disaster at the Winter Ball and the St James's Park fiasco?'

'I witnessed both of those,' Cordelia said through gritted teeth.

'Excellent!' The pirate smiled at her. 'We'll have lots of questions, I'm sure.'

He was behaving as though they had all happened to meet during an afternoon stroll down the Avenue. His smile, Cordelia thought – despite his terrifying jagged teeth – was meant to be polite.

'Introductions!' he insisted. 'You already know Thorn Lawless, our fearsome leader and pirate queen.'

In the interest of not being skewered by a sword, Cordelia decided it might be best to play along with this bizarre display of good manners. She wondered, seeing as Thorn had been introduced as a *queen*, if she was expected to curtsey. Thorn Lawless's hat *was* strangely crown-like, with twisting fingers of scarlet coral spiking up from it, studded with dozens of rough barnacles. A sea urchin made a black-spiked rosette, holding a ribbon of slimy seaweed on the brim.

Cordelia settled on a dignified nod to the pirate queen.

The wild-haired pirate walked down the line of the Troublemakers, his blazing torch throwing ugly shadows that made the pirates even more frightening. They were a band of rogues, each ghastlier than the last, all wearing gnarly tricorns decorated with spiky grey barnacles to match their leader's.

'This is Annie Stoneheart, Vinegar Jim and Bad Tabitha.'

Glaring, looming and alarmingly moustached in turn.

'Smokestack Doogray, Billy Bones and Shelly.'

Smokestack Doogray's beard had recently been on fire – it wreathed him in smoke, making him look like a chimney pot. He'd been the one to 'welcome' Cordelia aboard the *Trouble*. Billy Bones had a very unnerving grin, rather like an enthusiastic axe-murderer. Eyes were the only part of Shelly that were visible. The rest of her was covered in seashells, and perched on her head was an enormous conch, large as an admiral's bicorn but gnarly with barnacles.

'Oh, I almost forgot to introduce myself!' said the wild-haired pirate with a grin. 'I'm Never.'

'You're never what?' Cordelia asked.

'That's my name. My name is Never.'

'Why?' Cordelia demanded.

A forbidding expression suddenly closed over Never's face. His eyes glowed red in the lantern flame.

'Cos I'm *Never* going back,' he said darkly.

Cordelia stared. She thought she recognized something about him – perhaps the way his wind-blown hair curled around his ears, or the slightly wonky line of his mouth.

'Where do I know you from?' she asked.

'Nowhere!' Never growled.

'Never from Nowhere.' Cordelia couldn't help raising her eyebrows, but she thought it best not to press the question. Instead, she glared at the Troublemakers, trying to look fearless.

Fifteen eyes leered back (Smokestack wore an eyepatch). These were the ship wreckers and the soul sinkers, the terror spreaders and the chaos makers. What did this dangerous band of villains plan to do to her?

Cordelia stood, chin up, waiting for Thorn to growl a fate-sealing order.

'You caused such trouble in Parliament!' Annie Stoneheart said, a little admiringly.

Cordelia's belly swooped. 'How do you know about what happened in Parliament?' she gasped. 'That news hasn't even officially reached St Freerest yet.'

The other pirates nudged Annie, muttering, 'Shut up, *shut up*.'

'Where did you hear it?' Cordelia had to raise her voice to be heard. 'From the Duchess?'

The pirates fell silent.

'You won't tell me?' she asked loudly. She was surprised to find such a fierce voice within her as she stared up at these terrifying pirates. Defiance and fear were having an arm-wrestle somewhere in her ribcage. Defiance won.

'You've done dreadful things!' she growled. 'You terrorize London! You burn ships and leave no survivors! You hurt innocent people and – and you kidnapped poor Prudence Oglethorne!'

'*Arrr!*' a pirate howled triumphantly. 'OUR REPUTATION IS FEARSOME!'

The pirate queen, blazing with rage, pushed her face right into Cordelia's. Her words sizzled with hatred.

'Piers Oglethorne will never see his daughter again!' she hissed. 'That snivelling wretch Prudence is gone and she's never coming back! And if you're not careful, Hatmaker, the same will be true for you. The Sea Dragon is always hungry!'

Thorn seized Cordelia's arm in a barnacle-rough hand and plunged into the jungle.

It was all Cordelia could do to stay on her feet as she was dragged through the undergrowth. Howls and jungle shrieks sent shudders across her skin, and the scraping of a million insects grated on her very bones. Her fingers were on fire with all the magic she could feel.

The pirates marched after her, following through the dark like nightmares come to life. She glimpsed their faces, terrible in the torchlight.

Was she going to be fed to a ravenous creature right now?

Thorn pulled her into a clearing and Cordelia stumbled to a stop, trying to catch her breath. Strangely, there was a small rowing boat lying nearby on the jungle floor. Without warning, Cordelia was thrown into it. The boat bucked beneath her and she was dragged upwards through thrashing vines. The boat rocked violently, nearly tipping her out, as she twisted to look over the edge.

Cordelia let out a mewl of shock, rearing back. She was high, high in the air, and the height did something strange to her guts: she felt them shrink with fear. Faces looked up from the jungle floor far below.

'Sleep well!' Thorn's voice drifted up mockingly. 'We're such kind hosts that we've even supplied a nightdress for you!'

Cordelia gritted her teeth as the pirate queen and her fellow Troublemakers pushed their way back through the jungle, laughing.

So, she was going to be left in this boat all night long. She took several deep breaths, reminding herself that at least she wasn't about to be something's supper.

Cordelia could see vines attached to the bow and stern, silver lines in the starlight stretching away into the dark. The boat trembled with her slightest movement as she inched along until she could lie down. It was lined inside with spongy moss, which was surprisingly comfortable. She carefully laid her head on the mossy pillow.

That was when she saw, directly above her, almost near enough to touch, a purplish star shining beyond the treetops. It was the star she had gazed at between the wooden ears of *Little Bear*. The star that had been summoning her.

It hung serenely in the sky, exactly where it was meant to be. It calmed her with whispers of safety. She felt her belly unclench slightly, and she tentatively stretched out her hands. A cloth was folded neatly on the mossy boat bottom.

Cordelia unfolded it.

It was a frilly white nightdress.

As Cordelia held it up, she saw a name embroidered on the front, picked out in silver:

Prudence

CHAPTER 20

The next morning, Cordelia woke with a knot of worry in her stomach.

She sat bolt upright, causing her boat-prison to lurch sickeningly, but the fear coursing blackly through her was not for herself but the crew of *Little Bear*.

How could she have been such a fool? Goose's desperate cry – '*Don't believe them! They're PIRATES!*' – echoed in her head and she cursed her own stupidity.

Her sacrifice hadn't saved *Little Bear*. The last thing she had seen was the flaming sails being attacked by vicious Sun Eaters. She was sick with worry for her father, for Goose and Sam and Melchior and Davey, and bitter with blame for herself. Her thoughts swirled darkly downwards.

As her mind spiralled, the air began to thrum with wingbeats. A flock of indigo birds descended upon her through the green leaves, and Cordelia felt the dark thoughts being pulled gently out of her. She looked up, trying to see the creatures clearly, but they flashed away like fish, quick and shy, and swam off through the air, carrying Cordelia's dark mood with them.

Cordelia's gaze followed them as they disappeared beyond the trees.

She had never seen creatures like these before. Half-bird half-fish, swimming through human thoughts, breathing them like air, tasting a mood before easing it gently away.

'*I don't know!*'

A voice came from somewhere in the trees. And it was not the gravelly voice of a sea-bitten pirate. It was young and musical.

A *girl's* voice.

'*I said*, I don't know!'

There it was again!

She turned, trying to figure out where it had come from, and realized that her boat-prison was hanging near an old shipwreck, also suspended high in the air by rope-like vines. She had not seen it by the light of the stars, but in the morning rays it loomed huge among the ancient trees.

Cordelia stared in amazement. The ship was not intact – it had been broken apart and spread through the jungle. Living bridges made of vines strung between decks, linking up a dozen different bits of ship. Ladders and stairways reached across the air, between curved pieces of hull and broken-open cabins accessed by webs of rigging. There was even a mast, topped with a crow's nest, that poked out above the canopy. Everything swayed gently in the greenish light of the jungle, giving the curious impression that the wreck was rolling in the tides at the bottom of the sea.

If Cordelia had had to give this sprawling structure a name, she would have called it a treehouse. But that hardly seemed to do it justice.

'*Because I can't!*'

It was the girl's voice again! Coming from somewhere within the bizarre treetop maze of vines and decks, mid-air staircases and rigging.

Cordelia remembered she had been using the white nightdress, with the name *Prudence* embroidered on it, as a blanket. With a shudder, she recalled the story about how Prudence Oglethorne was kidnapped – she had been snatched from her bed, the word *Troublemakers* scrawled on the wall. This must be the very nightdress that Prudence had been wearing when she was kidnapped!

She heard the girl's voice again in the trees.

'PRUDENCE!' Cordelia yelled. 'PRUDENCE, IS THAT YOU?'

The girl's voice abruptly stopped, as though someone had clapped a hand over her mouth.

'I'M CORDELIA HATMAKER!' Cordelia shouted. 'THEY'VE GOT ME PRISONER TOO!'

She stopped herself from adding: '*I'm going to rescue you and get us off this island!*' because she thought it would be best not to alert the pirates to her plan.

Prudence's voice was replaced with the harsh growls of pirates.

Prudence must be scared. Well then, Cordelia would have to be brave enough for both of them.

The suspended shipwreck shuddered as someone stomped along it and the grinning faces of Bad Tabitha and Billy Bones poked through portholes in the nearest hull. They looked just as terrifying in daylight as they had by torchlight.

'Good morning!' Bad Tabitha growled.

'Sleep well?' Billy Bones enquired.

'Not really,' Cordelia answered pertly.

Her belly clenched as the little wooden boat suddenly lurched. The pirates were dragging her towards them using a grappling hook on the end of a rope.

When she got close enough, they pulled her out of the boat. The deck rolled beneath her feet as the pirates marched her along the platform. It was strangely like being aboard a ship bobbing on the ocean. But when Cordelia looked over the rail, there was no sparkling blue sea – just a shock of air and a deadly drop.

Cordelia was forced to scramble up a ladder, tooth-squeakingly high, and clamber through a wonky cabin crowded with thick branches. She kept a sharp lookout for Prudence, but saw no sign of her until they edged along a swinging vine bridge past a large-windowed cabin.

The entire back end of a ship – the captain's cabin – was held in the arms of a particularly tall tree. Heavy curtains behind the diamond-paned windows twitched as Cordelia went past.

'Prudence?' Cordelia called.

Billy Bones whirled round, widening his eyes.

'I warn ya!' he growled. 'Don't bandy that name about! You'll be thrown to the Sea Dragon!'

Cordelia thrust up her chin defiantly but shut her mouth.

Prudence is in there! she thought.

If she attempted a wild dash to Prudence's cabin, she would be caught before she could get there and probably thrown to the Sea Dragon.

I'll cause a distraction somehow and come back, Cordelia promised herself.

They led her through the treehouse, along bridges and branches, to a polished mahogany dining table hanging in mid-air amid the jungle leaves. It looked as though it had been stolen from the captain's cabin of a treasure galleon. Vines held fancy chairs all round it, dangling like swings.

Several Troublemakers were already at the table, drumming their fingers and rattling the silver cutlery. Cordelia (though she would *never* have admitted it out loud) was relieved that Thorn Lawless was nowhere to be seen.

'BREAKFAST!' the pirate called Never announced, appearing at the top of a nearby mast that poked through the very top of the jungle canopy. He was carefully carrying a small crate in his arms. The Troublemakers cheered his arrival in a rather bloodthirsty manner.

They must keep their food in the crow's nest, Cordelia thought. *Strange! Perhaps that's the only place it's safe from some ravenous island-dwelling beast.*

She felt the pirates' eyes on her as she was hoisted on to a chair, and glared along the table at them all. Acting fierce was the only way Cordelia could make sure she kept on feeling brave.

'Hello!' Annie Stoneheart rasped.

Shelly waved.

'Good morning, Miss Hatmaker,' Never growled, setting the crate down on the table.

'You're all monsters,' Cordelia growled back.

Being rude to pirates was probably not recommended for anybody who wished to survive in their company for long. But every time she looked at their flint eyes and craggy faces, she thought of how they had broken their promise to let *Little Bear* sail away safely, and a hot surge of anger leaped straight from her belly right out of her mouth in the form of blistering words.

'Where's my father's ship, you villains?' she demanded.

'*Little Bear* is safely anchored at St Freerest again,' Never muttered.

'Why should I believe you?' Cordelia said witheringly.

Never ignored both Cordelia's words and her glare. 'Watermelon!' he announced, rolling several stripy green cannonballs down the table.

They were set upon by pirates and hacked to pieces within seconds. Never salvaged some shards of the pink fruit and handed them to Cordelia on a battered silver plate.

'For *mademoiselle*,' he said.

Cordelia flashed her most poisonous look at him. But her belly grumbled hungrily, so she ate.

The pirates munched the watermelons down to the rind and held a competition to see how far they could spit the pips.

'Now we've all eaten some fruit,' Never said, plunging his hand back into the crate, 'it's time for . . . CAKE!'

The pirates burst into excited yowls as Never began throwing cakes to them.

'CAKE!'

'*CAKE!*'

'CAAAKE!'

Smokestack, Billy Bones and Annie Stoneheart fought over one, which ended up a mess of crumbs that nobody got to eat. Bad Tabitha stuffed three in her mouth at once, then Vinegar Jim clapped his hands on to her cheeks, spraying cake everywhere. Shelly systematically ate her way through a pile, undisturbed by the others.

When presented with cake, the Troublemakers seemed more like feral cats than battle-hardened buccaneers. But perhaps that was what happened after years of having the sea as your mother and fret winds for a father: perhaps a fully grown adult became a wild child.

Never placed the last cake on Cordelia's plate.

'Eat up,' he advised. 'You'll need your energy today.'

'Why?' Cordelia asked suspiciously. 'What are you going to do to me?'

Never grinned a flesh-eating kind of grin.

'Thorn has a plan,' he said.

Though Cordelia barely dared admit it to herself, she was terrified of Thorn Lawless. She felt the place where the pirate queen had grasped her arm last night. It was tender and raw, as though her skin had been scorched.

'If you're not going to eat that, I think Shelly would like it,' Never added.

Shelly's eyes blinked out from her clinking shell armour, staring fixedly at Cordelia's plate.

Cordelia studied the cake. It was studded with currants and glistening with honey. She frowned. She thought she had seen cakes like this for sale in the marketplace on St Freerest.

A barnacle-knuckled hand flashed under her nose and the cake disappeared beneath Shelly's conch bicorn. Billy Bones licked crumbs off the table as Bad Tabitha gnawed on a watermelon rind.

'Well, that's the end of breakfast!' Never announced. 'Come on, everyone – it's time for . . .' He slid his eyes sideways at Cordelia. 'Time for *you know what!*'

The Troublemakers roared. The dining table swung violently as the pirates left breakfast in a howling pack, racing away across a long vine-rope bridge. Never and Smokestack were soon the only ones remaining.

'Come along, Miss Hatmaker,' said Never.

'What is *you know what*?' she demanded, her voice stronger than her trembling knees.

'You'll soon see,' Never taunted. 'You're the . . . *guest of honour.*'

Never turned and followed the other Troublemakers. When Cordelia hesitated, Smokestack took her by the shoulders and marched her along the vine-rope bridge, which swung from side to side with every step they took.

Cordelia conjured disasters in her mind. Would they force her to walk the plank off the edge of the treehouse? Feed her to the Sea Dragon? Take her fingernails and teeth and toes, and use them to make some terrible piece of trouble?

Thorn had kept calling her *Maker*. But she had said it like a kind of curse word.

They came to a stop on a wide deck where a ship's wheel creaked as it turned in the breeze. The Troublemakers waited beside a heavy curtain of vines covered with flowers that snarled like hungry mouths.

Was she going to be sacrificed to the vines? Would those gnashing flowers devour her?

There was no way she could escape: Smokestack blocked the bridge behind her and there was a sheer drop on either side of the platform.

She decided to face her fate with her head held high.

Never strode to the vines and carefully drew them aside. Beyond was a piece of wreckage that had once been the stern of a ship. But there was no dreadful piratical torture chamber to be seen.

Instead, heaps of fancy clothes were strewn everywhere.

'This is our workshop!' Never announced.

Cordelia blinked.

A *workshop*?

It was nothing like the workshop at Hatmaker House, which was full of magical ingredients stacked neatly on shelves, and kept strictly spick and span. This place was a mess of clothes and chaos.

But, Cordelia realized as she peered closer, it was clearly a place where magical things were made. And not just any magic. She stepped forward and picked up a cloak that was stitched with tiny green beads –

'*Turbidus turbida!*' she whispered. 'This is where you make the Trouble Clothes!'

The cloak wriggled. She dropped it quickly, remembering how the last Trouble Cloak she touched had swirled her round like she was caught in a tornado.

Never cleared his throat.

'Do you like it?' he asked.

Cordelia was so surprised by the question that she forgot to be frightened. She turned to the pirates to find their faces hopeful beneath the broad brims of their hats.

'I – I mean, in your expert opinion,' Never went on haltingly, 'as a Maker from the London Guildhall itself. Is our workshop . . . good?'

Cordelia hesitated. The word *good* seemed a strange one for these pirates to care about. 'It's very –'

'HAH!'

With a swoosh and a thud, Thorn Lawless landed on the deck in front of her.

'*The London Guildhall itself,*' Thorn parroted Never in a spiky, high voice. 'All those Makers poncing around making Good-Manners Hats and Well-Behaved Boots and Uptight Timepieces. We're *pirates*! We don't need a Maker's approval!'

She poked Cordelia in the chest.

'But, Thorn, it was your idea to –' Annie Stoneheart began.

'QUIET, ANNIE!' Thorn roared.

Annie Stoneheart's mouth clapped shut like a clam.

Cordelia, on the other hand, opened her mouth to object to the claim that any Maker would bother making Well-Behaved Boots (the very idea would have Goose up in arms).

Thorn turned to Cordelia. 'We kidnapped you –'

'Invited!' Never interjected.

'Because you're useful to us.' Thorn ignored Never, bearing down on Cordelia and shoving her backwards.

'I'll never do anything to help you!' Cordelia declared.

Thorn pushed her again. 'Then we'll throw you to the Sea Dragon.'

Cordelia felt the end of the deck beneath her heels. One more step back and she would plunge over the edge.

Thorn's eyes blazed.

'You're going to teach us Making.'

The Troublemakers wanted Cordelia to be their *teacher*.

This band of dangerous, sea-bitten pirates wanted *her* to teach them the secrets of Making.

This explained why they had come aboard *Little Bear* asking for her by name: they had planned to kidnap her for this purpose. Though it still did not explain how they knew about the trouble she had caused in Parliament.

With a jolt, Cordelia realized Thorn was glaring at her, apparently waiting for her to respond.

'But – but you already know how to make crazily dangerous things!' Cordelia pointed out, as a glove frilled with what looked like poisonous fungi crawled on its fingers across the deck of its own accord. 'You've terrified the whole of London with your Menacing Magic!'

Thorn grabbed Cordelia's collar and pushed her face much too close to Cordelia's, something the Hatmaker heartily wished the pirate queen would stop doing. Cordelia could see her craggy teeth and smell seaweed in her matted hair.

'You know secrets of Making that we don't know,' Thorn hissed. 'You'll teach them to us. But if I catch a whiff of *sneakery* from you, Maker, you'll be clapped in irons! And then you'll be thrown to the Sea Dragon!'

Cordelia had absolutely no intention of being thrown to the Sea Dragon. What she *did* intend to do was rescue Prudence Oglethorne and then make a daring escape. She wasn't exactly sure *how* to do this yet, but, for now, simply '*some*how' would have to suffice as a plan.

Thorn pointed her cutlass, directing Cordelia to a workbench.

'Teach!' she commanded.

Cordelia straightened her back (and her collar too), and raised her eyes to meet Thorn's glare.

'I can't teach with you shouting all the time,' she said.

I just need to wait for a chance to get into that cabin, she thought, turning towards the workbench. *Then I can talk to Prudence and come up with a rescue plan.*

She would not be able to rescue anybody if she was in the belly of a sea monster, however. The only way she could bide her time and look for clues would be if she agreed to teach the Troublemakers . . .

'Don't worry.' Annie Stoneheart leaned down conspiratorially as she took a seat at the bench. 'She can't clap you in irons. We don't *have* any irons.'

Cordelia shot a curious look at Annie, who winked back.

It was quite a daunting sight: eight pirates sitting in a line on the workshop floor, watching her expectantly. There had been a scuffle over the workbench when it was discovered that not everybody could fit there at once. A vote had been called; the floor was accordingly chosen as equal for all.

Thorn sat grimly in the middle, her cutlass laid over her knees.

'In case I need to slash any clothes in half,' she growled. 'Things can get out of hand quickly in this workshop.'

'Try not to slash anything in half when somebody is wearing it,' Cordelia advised.

Thorn merely glowered in reply.

'Chaos and destruction aren't my areas of expertise,' Cordelia said crisply, observing the gnarly and menacing faces staring up at her. 'Most Makers concentrate on creating things to *help* people, not to frighten them. But I suppose you want to learn more Troublemaking techniques?'

There was silence.

Thorn turned her intense glare on Never.

'Well . . . no,' Never said, seemingly pressured into talking by the power of Thorn's stare. 'Not exactly.'

Thorn continued to glare at Never, who went on haltingly: 'We – we want to . . . we want to learn . . . other things . . .'

'Wrecking?' Cordelia suggested. 'Laying waste? Ruination?'

'NO!' Thorn exploded.

The pirate queen swung her cutlass, and Cordelia jumped as it sank into the workbench, rather too near her hand.

Never gave a nervous cough. 'Actually, we want to learn to Make . . .'

He looked round at the others.

'Barn-Dancing Boots!' Billy Bones piped up.

'Gladhand Gloves!' Annie Stoneheart yelled.

'Quick-Step Slippers!' added Bad Tabitha.

The air was filled with voices yelling suggestions. Cordelia was astonished. These grim and grisly pirates wanted to make bright, positive creations. The pirates who destroyed ships and left no survivors wanted to create dancing boots? And Gladhand Gloves? It seemed almost grotesque.

Shelly was flapping her arms, apparently miming some kind of Cavorting Cloak. The Troublemakers' faces became wild with excitement.

'A Good-Memories Beret!' Smokestack croaked as Cordelia held up her hands for silence.

'And you, Thorn Lawless?' Cordelia asked. 'What do you want to Make?'

For a moment, Cordelia was afraid that the pirate (who had remained tight-lipped as the Troublemakers around her erupted with enthusiastic suggestions) might seize her cutlass again, and threaten to slash her in two.

'A Compassion Cap,' Thorn muttered. Her hard voice was lace-edged with longing.

She glared around as if daring anybody to laugh. Nobody did.

Cordelia barely dared breathe.

She also barely dared ask herself the question *WHY? Why* did this notorious pirate, who took every opportunity to growl and threaten, want to create such a soft and gentle piece of clothing?

But even though the question bounced around her mind, it did not cross her lips. Instead, she said, 'A Compassion Cap. All right. That can be done.'

Before Cordelia would allow them to begin Making, she instructed the pirates to tidy their workshop. She remembered Aunt Ariadne telling her, '*An untidy workshop makes for unruly magic!*'

If they were going to make untroublesome clothes, they would need to clear all traces of Trouble away.

Cordelia made Billy Bones sweep every Turbidus seed off the edge of the platform. Shelly rounded up a troupe of pecking shells while Jim emptied a jar full of mischievous wind out at a safe distance, and Never shook some poisonous-looking caterpillars off reels of ribbon.

When Cordelia was sure there weren't any (very) dangerous ingredients left lying about, she inspected the workshop properly. She could see attempts at a ribboning table and a collection of needles made from twigs, as well as cup-shaped leaves that held heaps of pollen, and piles of knobbly pearl buttons that looked handmade.

She found fancy cloaks in a corner, threaded with gold. These clearly had not been made on the island. They must have been plundered from the last unfortunate ship the Troublemakers had robbed. Perhaps they had belonged on the ruined ship she had seen floating past *Little Bear*.

She picked up a hat decorated with strange inky crystals and shimmering lizard scales. It positively fizzed with wickedness, making her fingers burn.

'Ouch!' she cried.

'Give me that!' Thorn snatched the hat and threw it over the edge of the treehouse. Thinking it best not to annoy the pirate queen, particularly at such a high altitude, Cordelia backed away.

When the workshop was tidy and the tables clear, the Troublemakers sat back down in a row, staring at her expectantly.

'The first lesson: do any of you know about Makers having magic in their fingertips?' Cordelia began.

This question was met with blank stares.

Cordelia held out her hands.

'A Maker's fingers should be brimming with magic,' she explained, wiggling her fingers. 'The magic inside you comes from your heart and head and belly, and it travels right through the tips of your fingers. So your hands do your heart's work, to change the world for the better.'

'Isn't there any other way?' a gruff voice growled from the end of the row.

It was Thorn.

Cordelia hesitated, but there was only one true answer to this question.

'No,' she said finally. 'Your magic connects to the magical ingredients you use, and they work together, like a compass and the North Pole. So, without the right intention in your fingertips, you'll never be able to make the magic you want to.'

She thought she heard a growl from the pirate queen.

'You can do it!' she encouraged hastily. 'Everybody, hold out your hands!'

A line of gnarly hands stretched towards Cordelia.

'Now try to connect to the magic in your fingertips!'

The Troublemakers gurned and strained, as though they were trying to squeeze lightning bolts out of the ends of their fingers.

'ARGH!'

'YAAARRR!'

'GRRRR!'

'Good!' Cordelia called. 'Now, try to put that magic into Making!'

The pirates set to work, scowling in concentration as they added all sorts of ingredients to cloaks and gloves and hats and boots. To Cordelia's surprise, it was clear that every Troublemaker had strong Maker instincts and talent. She could tell by the way they reached for the right ingredients without stopping to think. But even though they chose the best ingredients, everything they made seemed to cause more mischief than they intended.

Bad Tabitha's Quick-Step Slippers carried her around so fast she became a dizzy blur, unable to stop, while Vinegar Jim's glistering seaweed Capering Cape swallowed him up like a tongue-twister come to life.

Never bashfully refused to try on his Happy-Thoughts Hat, but merely holding it made him burst into manic cackling laughter that turned him red in the face.

Annie Stoneheart's Gladhand Gloves clapped so hard that she lost control of her arms and pushed Shelly off the edge of the deck. Luckily, Shelly was caught by criss-crossing vines that bounced her back on to the treehouse, where she continued covering a cloak in conch shells as though nothing unusual had happened.

Smokestack's Good-Memories Beret made him babble the rudest stories he could think of, while Billy Bones's Barn-Dancing Boots sent him stomping on everybody's toes.

The Troublemakers clearly had powerful magic in their fingertips, but it was a runaway-horse kind of magic, wild and unpredictable, galloping madly.

Cordelia fled from Billy's stamping feet towards Thorn Lawless, who was hunched over a table at the end of the deck.

'What?' Thorn snapped.

Cordelia had avoided the pirate queen up until now; Thorn's mutters as she worked suggested far-off thunder coming closer. She held a hat in her fists, staring as though she was trying to set it on fire with her eyes.

'How is the Compassion Cap coming along?' Cordelia enquired in a delicate tone of voice with which one might ask a dragon what she was planning to set fire to next.

Thorn shot Cordelia a look, the way some people shoot flaming arrows at their enemies.

Cordelia tried again. 'What ingredients are you going to add?'

Thorn didn't answer, so Cordelia took another step forward to look at the selection of ingredients laid out on the table beside her. There were soft pale feathers, lacy spiderwebs, golden stamens of flowers and some morning dew collected in a shell. Cordelia could not help gasping at this beautiful collection.

'These are amazing!' she exclaimed.

Thorn glowered but in what Cordelia suspected might be a pleased way.

'The web's from a white spider that lives here. I found the feathers lining an empty nest, and the stamens are from flowers that grow by the lagoon. The morning dew is in a shell I liked,' the Troublemaker told the Hatmaker gruffly.

Cordelia was impressed. She did not recognize any of these ingredients, but when she ran her fingers over them with the gentlest touch, she felt immediately how powerfully magical they were.

'How did you know these ingredients would all work for a Compassion Cap?' she asked.

Thorn shrugged. 'I don't know . . . I just felt they'd work best.'

'All right, I think you should add them to the hat,' Cordelia told her. 'Remember to keep your magic in your fingertips!'

She watched as Thorn carefully tucked feathers into gaps in the stitching, wound the stamens round the crown, fixed them with the spiderweb and sprinkled the whole creation with morning dew.

The pirate queen placed the hat on the table and stared at it.

'Are you going to try it on?' Cordelia suggested.

'No!' Thorn pulled her tricorn down firmly over her ears. 'You try it!'

She thrust the Compassion Cap at Cordelia. Every Troublemaker turned to her, looking curious and a little worried.

Cordelia really did not want to put it on. But a prickly temper was rising around Thorn like a fast-growing briar patch. Remembering that the Sea Dragon was always hungry, Cordelia reluctantly pulled on the cap.

Thorn watched with narrowed eyes.

Cordelia felt kindness and sympathy and compassion flitting around her mind like butterflies. Amazement was rising like the sun inside her head. Understanding dawned on her like a clear day. It was wonderful, a breath of goodwill, fresh as spring.

Of course! Thorn just wants to be – to be – to – be –

Thunder interrupted the sunrise. Tumult clashed in the sky of her mind. All was storm and fury. Cordelia was consumed by a red rage of hatred. She seized the workbench – meaning to launch it at Thorn –

Never lunged for her.

Suddenly Cordelia's mind cleared.

Never had torn the Compassion Cap off her head.

THUD!

Cordelia dropped the workbench. It was extremely heavy. Only the cap had given her the strength to lift it.

Everyone stood in shocked silence, staring at Cordelia.

Thorn glowered furiously.

'I – I don't understand,' Cordelia stammered, her hands shaking as she stared at the Compassion Cap in Never's trembling hands. 'The ingredients you picked were good. How did the hat go so horribly wrong . . . ?'

She gingerly took the cap from Never, to inspect Thorn's work. But Thorn grabbed her cutlass, yelling, 'ALL I CAN MAKE IS TROUBLE!'

For a terrible second, Cordelia feared she was going to be slashed in half and fed to the Sea Dragon as the main course as well as dessert. But Thorn's sword flashed down and suddenly the Compassion Cap was in two pieces on the workshop floor.

'THE LESSON IS OVER!' the pirate queen yelled.

The Troublemakers scattered, fleeing up trees and down ladders. Several simply jumped over the edge of the treehouse and were caught by vines and carried to the ground.

Cordelia took her chance and fled.

CHAPTER 22

Cordelia hared across a rocking deck, scrambled down two ladders and up a staircase hanging in mid-air.

She could almost feel the deadly swish of the pirate queen's blade, the chomp of the Sea Dragon's jaws. If she was caught . . . But she couldn't worry about that now: *now* was her chance to talk to Prudence!

She stumbled past the dining table, still covered with mess from breakfast, trying to remember the way back to the cabin where she had seen the curtain twitch.

Cordelia picked her way along a horizontal ladder, swung on a rope across a gap between decks and skidded on to a high platform.

There!

The cabin lay ahead: Prudence's prison.

She glanced over her shoulder to check she was not being followed. The Troublemakers' shouts had faded, and the jungle was still and green all around her.

Cordelia edged across the trembling web of vines that led to the prison door.

To her surprise, the door was not locked. She pushed it open slowly, hoping it wouldn't creak.

The cabin was very dark. Cordelia could not see a thing.

'Prudence?' she whispered.

There was no reply. Prudence must be crouched somewhere in frightened silence.

'I'm a friend,' Cordelia said gently. 'My name is Cordelia Hatmaker.'

Still no reply.

Cordelia felt her way into the room and bumped into something soft.

'Oof! Sorry!' she gasped. But the soft thing rustled like blankets, and she realized she had bumped against a bed.

'Prudence, where are you?' she called, pushing herself upright and blundering on through the dark room. 'I'm here to rescue you! I've got a sort of plan!'

She felt cloth under her hand and pulled. The cabin flooded with light as a curtain drew back.

The word TROUBLEMAKER had been carved in huge, reckless letters across the wall. Like a threat.

Apart from a four-poster bed and a rocking chair, the cabin

was empty. Prudence was not there. But earlier Cordelia had seen a twitch at the window and heard a girl's voice. She *must* be somewhere close.

Cordelia threw the window open. 'Prudence Oglethorne!' she called across the treehouse. '*Where are you?*'

There was no reply except the laughing call of some wild bird.

Cordelia turned back to the room. On the wall opposite, she noticed scraps of paper pinned to the wall with inch-long thorns driven into the wood. On one scrap, a single word was scrawled:

MARIANA

Was this somebody else the Troublemakers planned to kidnap?

Beside a tattered map of London, riddled with more thorns, other names were scrawled. A list of victims?

Cordelia peered closer. *Arcana, Celestial, Sargasso.*

No – she realized with a jolt – these were names of famous London chocolate houses! Mariana was not a person but a chocolate house: a gilded parlour on Air Street. This must be the Troublemakers' next plan: they were going to attack the chocolate houses!

'What are you doing?' a voice snarled.

Cordelia yelped and swung round.

A hulking, wild-haired figure stood in the doorway: Never. He lunged at her.

'If Thorn finds you in here, even Shelly won't be able to stop you getting thrown to the Sea Dragon!' the pirate growled, dragging her to the door, before freezing. Someone was tramping along the treehouse, like thunder approaching.

'Thorn's coming!' Never gasped.

He quickly shut the door and towed Cordelia across to the window. He pulled the curtains shut, hiding them, and pushed his craggy face close to Cordelia.

'Don't make a sound!' he warned.

Cordelia's heart pounded as she heard the door squeak open. The floorboards shook as the pirate queen stomped into the cabin. Muttered words sizzled through the air like bad spells.

Never edged towards the open window, beckoning Cordelia. She sidled towards him, careful not to disturb the curtains. He pressed a rough finger to his lips, widening his eyes in warning. Then he took Cordelia by the arms, lifted her on to the windowsill – and pushed.

CHAPTER 23

Cordelia plummeted towards the jungle floor. She didn't have time to scream. She'd left her voice behind, along with her wits, and she was falling, falling to certain death.

Then all of a sudden she was swooping up, sailing high into the air again, defying gravity, with a strong arm clasped round her middle.

Not an arm. A thick green vine, rippling like a muscle.

As she burst through the green canopy of the jungle, the vine unclenched from her waist and flung her over the treetops.

This seemed a perfectly reasonable time to scream.

'AAAAARGH!' Cordelia screamed.

The world was a hurtling green blur –

– and she was falling – tumbling beneath the leaves – crashing through thin air – down, down towards the bone-breaking ground . . .

With a soul-jangling jolt, another vine snapped tight round her leg and dragged her upwards through the branches. She kicked helplessly as she was whirled back into the wide-sky world above the treetops. The crow's nest, sticking out of the jungle canopy, spun past.

'Put me DOWN!' she shouted desperately. 'Please!'

The vine stiffened and slowed, loosening its grip.

Her leg slipped.

'No!' Cordelia yelped – now dangling upside down above a hundred-foot drop, held only by one ankle. 'Put me down *on the crow's nest*!' she corrected quickly. 'Please!'

The vine obeyed.

Cordelia's entire body trembled as she pressed her cheek to the reassuringly solid wooden planks. She raised her eyes, muttered a shaky 'Thank you' to the vine and gasped: she recognized those green leaves bristling with mischief!

It was the same kind of vine that had come curling out of the king's crown in Parliament.

'*Turbidus turbida!*' she whispered fearfully.

A vine like that had dragged her into this wretched mess in the first place.

She wrapped her fingers round the rough planks of the crow's nest, hoping the vine wouldn't suddenly come lashing back to fling her off her perch.

'Please don't hurt me,' she murmured, and she watched with wide eyes as the vine retreated into the green canopy.

When she felt it was safe, she sat up, and her breath was taken away for the third time that morning. From up above the stirring canopy of the jungle, she could see the entire island, surrounded by sparkling waves, laid out around her like a living map.

The skull they had sailed through at sunset had a jumble of white rocks humped up to form shoulder-like hills behind it. A ridge of green jungle rose above the boulders. Cordelia was perched on the crow's nest halfway along this ridge. Higher up, the crest of the island hunched against the blue sky before tailing off into a curving breakwater of rocks that reached across the sea to meet the dripping fangs of the skull.

In the turquoise bay encircled by the rocks, the *Trouble* floated at anchor. The sea beyond was dark and choppy. A shape on the horizon, caught between the blues of sky and sea, drew Cordelia's eye.

'St Freerest!'

From up here, the island didn't look very far away – she felt she could have reached out to pick it up in her fingers. But she knew it was five nautical miles in the distance. Definitely not close enough to reach. Definitely not close enough to swim.

She searched the ocean. There was no sign of *Little Bear*; no white sails could be seen between this island and that one. Had her father somehow managed to steer his ship to safety and return to port at St Freerest as Never had said? She stared at the fathomless water stretching to every horizon and dared not think about the other place *Little Bear* could have gone: the ocean-deep place.

Cordelia clambered to her feet, turning full circle to scour the open waters, and nearly fell off the crow's nest in surprise. Floating silently in the air just behind her was a hole-ridden rowing boat with a barnacled bottom and sails made of colourful silk, moored to the very top of the mast. She touched the old weather-worn hull. It seemed to be made of Ebullient Oak, and the bright patchwork sails appeared to be stitched-together kites that changed colour as they rippled in the breeze.

Kites like these were for sale in the marketplace at St Freerest.

Then Cordelia noticed the heavy iron ring that the boat was tied to, and the brass lantern right beside it. She had seen an identical brass lantern beside an iron mooring ring on the platform perched atop the Kingless, where the Duchess had her telescope trained on the Island of Lost Souls.

It couldn't be a coincidence.

Was the platform on the Kingless roof a landing jetty for this airborne boat?

It would be pure insanity to sail this contraption across the air. Though if anyone was mad enough to do it, it would be the Troublemakers.

Cordelia stared across the waters to St Freerest.

'This could be my escape route!' she whispered.

She felt slightly seasick at the thought of sailing this tiny floating boat across the sky. The Troublemakers might be crazy enough to do it – but was she?

She pulled the mooring rope experimentally, wishing that Goose was with her. He knew all about sailing – and it couldn't be so different sailing a boat in the sky from sailing it in the sea. Either way, you had to catch the right wind and hope you didn't sink. But Goose wasn't here. And the only way she would see him again – and Sam and her father – was if she somehow escaped the wicked Troublemakers and their island filled with violent magic.

This thought was enough to make Cordelia climb halfway into the boat. She had one leg over the gunwale before she remembered that if she was ever to see the other people she loved again – the Hatmakers at Hatmaker House, and her friends at the Guildhall – she couldn't just escape by herself. She would have to rescue Prudence too, and bring her back to safety.

She slipped down the ladder into the green world beneath the canopy. She moved quickly and quietly through the Troublemakers' treehouse, through lace veils of tree ferns and curtains of vines, peering into cabins that had been turned into bedrooms with mossy blankets on the hammocks. There was no sign of Prudence anywhere, and eventually she reached the ship's prow, which stuck out of the treetops above the sandy beach.

From her vantage point, she spied Never peering into the jungle with a concerned frown on his face. He loped towards Cordelia, calling, '*There* you are!' and beckoning her down to the ground.

Cordelia glanced at a vine rippling towards her from a nearby tree.

'Please will you put me on the beach?' she asked. 'If you would be so kind.'

The vine flicked out a tendril, tripping Cordelia. It caught her neatly as she stumbled and – after a swooping nosedive moment – set her gently on the sand.

'Terribly sorry I pushed you out of the window,' said Never as he dusted her down. 'Thorn's very private about her cabin, so it was a choice between going *out* of the window or *into* the Sea Dragon. But I knew the vines would catch you – and they'd put you down as soon as you asked them politely.'

'My father told me they're Turbidus Vines,' Cordelia said. 'They cause nothing but trouble. You could have killed me!'

'Oh, is *that* what they're called?' Never asked airily, apparently choosing to ignore Cordelia's anger. 'We don't know the official names of anything here, all except – look! Here comes one now!'

Never pointed at a creature waddling on to the beach, out of the jungle. It was a shaggy grey bird that came up to Cordelia's waist. It had little wings, a big round body and splayed orange feet that shuffled across the soft sand towards her. It tilted its bulbous beak sideways, then turned small, inquisitive eyes on the Hatmaker and uttered a soft honk.

Cordelia had never seen a bird like it. It seemed so polite, poised curiously on the shore, that she felt as though she had just stumbled into its drawing room. She had an absurd urge to curtsey.

'Who are you?' she asked.

She half expected the bird to answer. But it was Never who spoke.

'This is a dodo,' he said.

Cordelia's mouth fell open.

'But dodos – aren't dodos all – all gone?' she spluttered. 'Extinct?'

Never shook his head. 'No, though most of the world believes they are. They've all disappeared from their natural habitat. We think maybe the last dodos in the world live here.'

Cordelia stretched her hand out towards the bird. She could feel its specific magic in the air, like nothing else she had ever encountered. It was a bright power, but she felt a tinge of melancholy within it. The bird nudged her hand gently, the feathers on its head flashing like a butterfly's wings in the sunlight.

'Such a magical creature,' she murmured.

'Their dropped tail feathers have powerful forgetting properties,' Never told her. 'And we found out their eyelashes are good ingredients for obscuring things. But we mostly leave them be. They have a colony on Shoulder Beach.'

The dodo waddled off, taking its magic with it but leaving its spell behind. Cordelia gazed after it in wonder.

'Come on,' Never said, interrupting her spellbound moment. 'We should make ourselves scarce for a little while. Give Thorn a bit of time to – uh – lose a few prickles.'

The dodo's forgetting magic had hazed the morning air. As it cleared, Cordelia remembered her plan: she had to find Prudence and then take the first chance they could, to escape across the sky. She would have to search the island.

She narrowed her eyes at Never, deciding to try a direct approach.

'Where's Prudence?' she asked. 'I know she's here somewhere; I heard her voice earlier. I just want to talk to her.'

Never's face closed like a door.

'If Thorn hears you asking for Prudence, there's no telling what she'll do,' he muttered. 'We like you. We want to keep you as our teacher –'

'You mean you want to keep me as your *prisoner*!' Cordelia snapped, clenching her fists.

'*Invited guest!*' Never insisted, a pained look on his face. 'Don't go looking for Prudence – I'm *dead serious*. And Thorn'll be *deadlier* serious. So don't.'

He strode away along the beach, calling over his shoulder, 'Whether you're our guest or our prisoner, I must insist you come with me.'

Reluctantly, Cordelia followed him.

The first person they found was Shelly. On a rocky promontory splaying into the shallows of the bay, she was crouched beside a rockpool.

'She loves listening to the seahorses,' Never said quietly as they approached. 'We think she's trying to learn their songs.'

The rockpools were alive with creatures Cordelia had never seen before. Peering into one was like opening a watery treasure chest bursting with jewels. Silver-scroll shells winked beneath the surface and a dozen tiny seahorses, with tails like curved fiddleheads, rollicked among the dancing seaweed. Their song rippled the water. Shelly was, very quietly, humming along.

Carefully, Shelly reached into the rockpool and plucked a silver-scroll shell no bigger than her little finger. She held it out to Cordelia, eyes wide and meaningful.

'She wants you to have it,' Never said, translating the meaningful look. 'We call them Secret-Keepers. They're very special. If you put a secret into it, it'll only come out when you want it to.'

Shelly tipped the Secret-Keeper into Cordelia's hand and nodded solemnly.

The Secret-Keeper hummed. It had a shining mystery to it.

'Thank you,' Cordelia murmured. 'It's a very special gift.'

She tucked the silver shell safely inside her shirt pocket.

'You escaped Thorn's rage!' came a yell. 'We hoped you would!'

Bad Tabitha and Annie Stoneheart were clambering across the rocks towards them.

'We're *so* glad we kidnapped you.' Annie grinned. 'We're going to learn so much Making!'

'Remember we don't say *kidnapped*, Annie,' said Never, gently admonishing her.

'There's magic in my fingertips!' Tabitha wiggled her hands as Shelly thrust her fingers confidently into the air.

'You're a brilliant teacher, miss!' Annie confirmed.

'Hear, hear!' Never added.

'I think you have more to teach me than I can teach you,' Cordelia said. 'I've never been anywhere as magical as this – can you show me more of the island? I want to see *everything*.'

The pirates positively glowed with pride and Cordelia felt momentarily terrible. She was only flattering them to make sure they showed her every secret place on the island – so she could find Prudence and escape.

'Let's show her Tablecloth Glade!' Tabitha burst out.

The Troublemakers surged away up the rocks, beckoning her towards the jungle. As Cordelia followed, Never fell into step beside her.

'I can teach you about this island if you like,' he offered gruffly.

Cordelia looked sideways at him. His craggy face, with lines so deep they looked like ravines in a rock, had taken on a bashful kind of enthusiasm. There was something beneath his frightening facade, beyond his fierce appearance, that she couldn't put her finger on.

Her fingers tingled as the powerful magic of the island swirled around them.

'We believe that every living thing on this island is endangered,' Never began. 'Some – like the dodo – are even thought to be extinct. The tiniest insects, the trees and the flowers and the fish swimming in the bay are all refugees. Since we arrived here a few months ago, we haven't found a single thing that any of us recognize, except the dodo because Billy saw one in a book once. Soulhaven is the last refuge of hundreds of species that human beings have hunted almost off the face of the earth.'

'But my father told me this place is called the Island of Lost Souls – not Soulhaven – and it's full of dangerous Menacing Magic,' Cordelia said slowly. 'It's hidden to protect people from it.'

Even as she spoke, she realized that the Mapmakers' cleverness had outsmarted even Prospero Hatmaker. The dark rumours of Menacing Magic her father had told her about must have been Mapmakers from centuries past creating a clever web of protection around the island, designed to frighten greedy people away.

'*You* are endangered, Cordelia,' Never said. 'Or you'd never have been able to see this island on that map, or spot us from St Freerest. Only a hunted creature can find this place. We think it's something to do with the Lost Star. Not everyone can see its light, but those who can, follow it over the ocean to safety. We think this island has been a haven for endangered creatures for thousands of years, called here by the same star that called us.'

'That purpleish star that hangs right above the ridge, you mean?' Cordelia asked. 'I've seen it! I climbed out to the figurehead every night to watch it from *Little Bear*. I felt like it was – was calling me.'

Never nodded. 'That's because you're being hunted. By the same people who are after us. The Sensible Party.'

'The Sensible Party are only after you because you attacked them first,' Cordelia pointed out. 'Those crazy boots and hats at the Winter Ball, the attack in St James's Park –'

'It's a bit more complicated than that, actually,' Never interrupted.

'I climbed out to the figurehead every night to watch it from Little Bear. I felt like it was – was calling me.'

Cordelia expected him to explain, but he maintained a glowering silence as they approached the bottom of an enormous sweeping staircase made of huge knobbly white boulders.

'These rocks are strange,' she said, frowning.

'They're vertebrae,' Never told her.

Cordelia stopped to stare.

'This entire island is made of the skeleton of a prehistoric Sea Dragon,' continued Never. 'We think it might be an ancient ancestor of our own Sea Dragon.'

Never turned to point back the way they had come, and Cordelia saw that the rocks they'd just clambered up were not a random jumble of boulders. In fact, they made the shape of an enormous reptilian foot, half buried in the white sand. Rockpools glistened between the long ridges of foot bones, and the toes were shaggy with seaweed, claws crusted with barnacles. A creature with a foot this huge must have been enormous – probably as long as the City of London from end to end. It could have swallowed the Tower and drunk the Thames.

Cordelia gaped dizzily, until Never pulled her onwards. 'Up the tail!'

The white rocks became narrower as they went further into the jungle. An arch of green leaves closed over them and soon they were scaling large boulders that led steadily uphill in a smooth sweeping curve. A rushing river splashed and tumbled beside them in a deep green gully. Each boulder was as tall as Cordelia, so the pirates had to haul her up, helped by vines.

Cordelia had to whisper the words that echoed through her mind, because they seemed too incredible to speak aloud: 'We're climbing up a spine!'

CHAPTER 24

As Cordelia and the pirates made their way up the gully, climbing a spine that was thousands of years old, Cordelia noticed more and more plants and animals, insects and birds that she had never seen before.

She imagined the slow congregation of endangered species arriving at this island over the past thousand years: from plant and animal kingdoms alike, seeking refuge on the bones of an ancient creature. She pictured seeds floating through the night; birds drawn across the sky, following the purple wink of the star like thread following a needle. She imagined trees, the marrow of their wood humming with desire to be safe from the bite of the axe; and the urgent flick of insect wings in the starlight as they flitted for safety.

All had come here for sanctuary.

Cordelia ran her hands over rough tree trunks and smooth rocks, stroked strange flower petals and the iridescent shells of beetles, and she realized she had been wrong about the island. When she'd first arrived, she had felt violent magic all around her. The place had been an assault on her sensitive magical senses.

Now she understood: there had been so many new magical things crowding in on her that she'd been overwhelmed, like listening to seven thousand symphonies at once.

She tuned her ear to the quiet music of a single flower. It sang its magic, a tender song of hope in darkness.

'Those flowers glow at night,' Never said, watching her as she cupped the blossom gently in her hand. 'D'you know what they're called?'

Cordelia shook her head.

'I don't know their name,' she said. 'But I can tell they're very precious.'

Further up the gully, on what Annie proudly told Cordelia was a prehistoric leg bone, they found Billy Bones and Vinegar Jim racing tumbling shrubs along the high white rock, speeding close to the edge and roaring with laughter.

'Come down!' Tabitha yelled. 'We're showing our teacher the island!'

As Billy and Jim clambered down from the leg bone, Cordelia watched several snails with orange shells the size of carriage wheels inch slowly upwards past them, leaving bright trails.

'D'you know what tree that is?' Annie asked, pointing up to a majestic tree taller than a cathedral spire, with branches like wide-open arms and bright green, heart-shaped leaves.

Cordelia did not recognize the leaves or the bark, but she carefully laid her hands on the tree trunk. Hope surged through her palms with the sonorous power of whale song.

She *did* recognize this magic! But it was like recognizing a song she'd once heard somebody humming, except now it was being played by a full orchestra.

Cordelia remembered – when she was very small, one quiet afternoon in the Alchemy Parlour – her Great-aunt Petronella unwinding her silver hair and handing Cordelia her ancient wooden hatpin. As her hand closed over it, Cordelia had felt a thread of faint hope humming in her hand.

'This is made from a branch of the last Soulhope Tree,' Great-aunt Petronella had told her. 'When I was a young girl, that last Soulhope Tree was felled in the Ashdown Forest: the king had it cut down for his warship. On hearing this terrible news, my father went to try to save some seeds from the fallen tree. He begged the king for just *one* pod, but the king laughed at him and threw him a bare broken branch. My father turned that slim stick of Soulhope wood into a hatpin for me, because hope is the most important thing to keep in your head. Soulhope Trees could grow higher than any tree in the world, because they had the deepest roots.

They should *never* be cut down or burned. When the king's warship caught fire in the channel, his men despaired, and that is how the war was lost.'

Cordelia pressed her forehead to the vast trunk, thinking of her great-aunt, and whispered, 'There *is* one still living. If I ever get home, I'll have to tell her.'

She turned from the tree, wiping hopeful tears from her eyes, to find the pirates looking at her curiously.

'It's a Soulhope Tree,' she sniffed, smiling. 'Your island is extremely magical.'

'It's not *our* island,' Jim corrected her. 'It doesn't belong to us; we belong to it.'

Before Cordelia could quite grasp this logic, the pirates pulled her through a narrow tunnel in the bone-rock to emerge in a wide forest glade that appeared to be draped with giant lace tablecloths. The tablecloths were each as wide as a galleon's sails, swagged above her head. They hung in intricate patterns from all the trees, with frilly white rosettes in their centres.

'This is Tablecloth Glade,' Tabitha announced.

With a jolt in her belly, Cordelia realized that the white rosettes in the middles of the huge tablecloths were spiders. And the tablecloths were, in fact, enormous spiderwebs.

Cordelia staggered backwards as a spider the size of a dinner plate descended silently on a thread of web, to peer at her with eight eyes.

'They won't hurt you,' Never told her. 'The worst they'll do is try to decorate you.'

He indicated Billy, who giggled and wriggled as a white spider spun an elaborate silken cape around his shoulders.

Cordelia studied the creature as it worked. Its legs were covered in snowy hairs and its eight bright eyes frilled with corkscrew ringlets. It was somehow neat and flamboyant at the same time, its legs busy and clever, its movements quick and trim.

They found Smokestack sitting on a boulder halfway up the glade. His grey hair had been embellished with an ornate hat made entirely of spider silk.

'Thought we'd find you here, Smokestack!' Tabitha called.

'I just love to sit here and watch them spin,' he said with a contented sigh. 'They make yarns of such beauty; I don't know how I could ever spin a yarn to match theirs.'

'Maybe our teacher will teach you?' Jim suggested.

But the teacher in question hardly heard this suggestion. Cordelia watched as Shelly carefully laid some frilly flowers on a rock. Several spiders scuttled enthusiastically down from their webs and began eating the dripping nectar.

Cordelia was reminded of her father. He always gave thank-you gifts to nature when collecting ingredients and never took more than was needed. Prospero Hatmaker believed that nature deserved the utmost gentleness and respect. Rivers should always be called by name, clouds should be bowed to (whatever mood they were in), birds should be addressed *Sir* or *My Lady*, and even trails of ants snaking across pavements should be given right of way.

He would love this island, Cordelia thought. Every leaf and petal contained enchantment, every bird call was a song of wonder, every insect a living glyph of mystery. Every breath of air carried magic on it.

'We should show her the lagoon,' whispered Annie.

With sudden enthusiastic howls of 'LAGOON!' the Troublemakers surged away up the white-veiled glade.

The lagoon was a deep, still pool surrounded by flowers that glowed like fallen stars. A waterfall tumbled down over smooth white vertebrate rocks at one end. Huge lilac boulders lay half submerged and vines trailed into the water, which was so clear Cordelia could see the bottom, shining brightly.

'It's solid silver down there. We think it's from centuries of moonlight falling on the ancient Sea Dragon's pelvis bones,' Never said. 'We call it Moonstruck Lagoon.'

The Troublemakers had already shed most of their clothes and were huddled together holding a whispered conference in the shallows. Shelly nudged the others as Cordelia approached. They turned, smiling shiftily, all looking rather absurd in their underclothes and enormous barnacled hats.

'Why don't you take your hats off?' Cordelia asked.

The wildness in her wits was telling her something was wrong.

Then, out of the corner of her eye, she saw a figure flash through the trees above the waterfall.

It was a girl, running fast.

This was no pirate; this person was too small. It must be –

'*PRUDENCE!*' Cordelia yelled.

Startled eyes flashed before the girl turned and fled.

Without even removing her boots, Cordelia dived into the lagoon, taking the most direct route in pursuit.

Never dived after her but she was too quick for him.

She splashed through the water, pirates bellowing at her to stop, and scrambled up the knobbly stones of the waterfall.

'Prudence!' she panted. 'Wait! I'm a friend! *Wait!*'

At the top, she sloshed along the shallow river to find footprints – child-sized ones – that led through the deep mud of the opposite bank, into the glade beyond.

She could hear crashing in the jungle ahead of her. She shouldered her way through dense shrubs and pushed aside curtains of vines.

'Prudence!'

Cordelia stumbled into a small glade and skidded to a stop.

Thorn Lawless stood in the yawning mouth of a cave, on the verge of being swallowed whole by the darkness. The pirate queen wore a mean grin.

'She's in there, isn't she!' Cordelia panted. 'You're keeping her in that cave! *Prudence!*'

Thorn hurled a sharp laugh at Cordelia, like a knife. 'You want to look for Prudence in the Belly? Go ahead!'

Thorn stood aside and Cordelia was suddenly wary. This was too easy – the way some traps are too easy.

She walked slowly towards the yawning mouth and saw that the cave had once been the hollow ribcage of the prehistoric Sea Dragon. The huge struts of its ribs, arching above her, were overgrown with vines. The dripping deep-green air smelled of ancient secrets and primordial time.

Cordelia stood on the threshold, poised between the light and the dark.

'Prudence?' she whispered.

The only answer was a soft snicker from Thorn.

Cordelia stepped into the underworld.

As her eyes grew accustomed to the dark, she began to see wonders in it.

Crystals in the cave glowed; stalagmites like galaxies stretched up from the floor. Luminous rocks bulged on the ceiling like planets blooming in a night sky. It was extraordinarily strange and beautiful.

But she couldn't get distracted. That was what Thorn wanted. *Where had Prudence gone?*

Cordelia noticed the tingle in her fingertips. There was something powerfully magic close by; she could feel it throbbing in the still air. It was something troubled and heavy – jagged enough to cut herself on – just out of reach.

She looked over her shoulder at Thorn, whose eyes flashed, daring her to brave it, to venture further in.

Suddenly a thought struck Cordelia.

In fact, her fingers knew before her brain did.

She took three quick steps, reached up and knocked the pirate queen's hat off.

CHAPTER 25

'**N**O!'

Thorn Lawless's face changed. It was like the tide rolling sand smooth on a beach.

Thorn's craggy features softened and grew youthful. Without her hat, she was barely older than Cordelia. Even her teeth became less jagged, though her growl was just as deadly as before and her eyes blazed.

She might be younger, but she was still as dangerous as wildfire.

'I'll make you sorry now, Maker!' Thorn snarled, and tackled Cordelia in a tangle of hair and fists and fury.

Cordelia hit the ground, fighting, and managed to shove the girl off her. She scrambled, panting, to her feet, her mind whirling. Thorn Lawless had been in disguise all this time! She was really —

'Prudence Oglethorne,' Cordelia whispered. 'It's *you*!'

Thorn's claim that Prudence was not dead but would never be seen again now made perfect sense. Because Thorn *was* Prudence.

'You've discovered my secret,' she hissed, voice harsh even though it had lost its gravelly rasp. 'Pity you'll never get off this island to tell everybody how clever you've been.'

'Pru–' Cordelia began.

'Don't call me that!' Thorn interrupted viciously. 'That's not my name any more! My friends have always called me Thorn. It's the only part of my real name that I like: Ogle*thorn*e. And now I'm an outlaw, *Lawless* is my surname.'

Cordelia nodded. 'All right – Thorn. Your father is worried about you! He thinks you've been –'

'My father!' Thorn's scornful bark didn't match the sudden fear in her eyes. 'My father has only ever worried that I'll bring disgrace on the family! He can't find me. He – he *mustn't*.'

Cordelia shook her head, sure there were pieces missing from this puzzle. 'But your father is the one who wants you to be found – when you were kidnapped by the Trouble–' She hesitated, frowning. 'Were you *really* kidnapped by the Troublemakers? Or . . .'

Cordelia trailed off as Thorn stared at her with wildfire eyes.

'We're not that different, are we, Hatmaker?' Thorn murmured. 'There's just one thing that makes all the difference between us.'

Cordelia frowned. She could not guess what the one thing might be.

'Permission,' Thorn said, her voice quiet as a cut-throat's knife. 'You were born into a Maker family. You're talented at it but – more importantly – you're *allowed* to Make. I am not; I've never been allowed to Make. But I couldn't help myself. From the day I could crawl, to pick daisies from the lawn, I've been a Maker.'

Cordelia must have stared for a moment too long, because Thorn suddenly snapped, 'Rainbow! Dinner!'

The air became charged, the way it does before a lightning strike, and a piece of living darkness surged out of the cave.

It was as long as a warship, nose to tail, with jaws big enough to crunch the king's carriage. Its tail, flicking menacingly behind it, was a fiery fork large enough to spear the king's best horse. Cordelia had seen that tail flashing in the boiling water – this was the fearfully strong monster that had pulled the *Trouble* across the seas at lightning speed!

Leathery wings unfurled like black sails, and its eyes were dreadful dark pools, deep enough to drown in. It wore a jackanapes' grin as it stalked forward, claws clicking like scimitars on the rock.

The Sea Dragon.

Leathery wings unfurled like black sails, and its eyes were dreadful dark pools, deep enough to drown in.

Cordelia knew she should run — but she was caught in those terrible whirlpool eyes.

'Devour her!' Thorn demanded.

Cordelia had found out too much: she knew Thorn's secret and now she was going to be eaten.

The creature opened its jaws, revealing a row of glinting teeth, sharp as swords.

Cordelia couldn't move. She couldn't speak. She could only squeeze her eyes shut and hold her breath and think of her family, her father, her friends —

There was a hideous tearing sound: the sickening chomp and mash of jaws.

But Cordelia didn't *feel* like she was being eaten.

She opened one eye. A tangle of green guts was jiggling in front of her face.

She opened the other eye and realized they weren't guts at all.

The Sea Dragon was chomping Turbidus Vines with great relish. Apparently they were so delicious they were causing the Sea Dragon to change colour: its dark scales rippled from snout to tail, becoming a contented sort of lilac. Not the colour of imminent guzzling.

The Sea Dragon, entirely lilac now, swallowed its mouthful of vines, then nudged Cordelia aside with its wide snout to nibble a vine hanging behind her.

This nudge was enough to send the feeling surging back to Cordelia's legs. She bounded away to the edge of the clearing —

ready to flee into the jungle if the Sea Dragon changed its mind about eating her.

She heard Thorn mutter resentfully to the Sea Dragon: 'Whoever heard of a vegetarian sea monster?'

'A *vegetarian*!' Cordelia burst out indignantly, whirling round. 'You've threatened me with being eaten at least a dozen times!'

'You're braver than I thought you'd be,' Thorn observed. 'You didn't even cry. Impressive for a wishy-washy *Maker*.'

'I thought you said *you* were a Maker,' countered Cordelia.

Thorn looked sharply at her. But the Sea Dragon turned its giant head to the pirate queen and gazed at her benignly, its scales changing from lilac to a friendly pink.

Cordelia was amazed as she took in the scaly creature that was turning rosy from its ridged snout to its splayed claws and flickering tail. It was indeed shaped like a miniature version of the island. Perhaps what Never had said was true: it was a descendant of the creature whose bones began this island. But that wasn't the most wondrous thing about it. The Sea Dragon seemed to be encouraging Thorn to talk.

But what followed was a long moment of silence. Thorn's face became a strange mixture of sun and cloud, like the sky deciding whether to storm.

'I *am* a Maker. Or . . . I *was*,' she whispered eventually. 'I made all sorts of treasures, using things I found growing in the garden, or dusty scraps of light that gathered in corners around the house. Birds shed feathers for me, and I'd make bits of ribbon from grass and find special pearls dropped from ladies' dresses. I made such wonderful things. I felt like I had magic living in my hands.'

The Sea Dragon arced its huge body round Thorn as she gazed at her palms. Its scales rippled from pink to red, giving her strength.

'But my father told me that Making was not allowed,' Thorn murmured. 'He said: *Oglethornes are respectable! We don't dabble in criminal magic!* One day he found all my treasures hidden in a chest in the attic and burned them. He – he made me watch. It made the most horrible smoke that filled the whole room . . .'

Cordelia shuddered; she knew too well the hopeless, acrid stink of burnt magic.

'I thought if he would just understand how important Making was to me that he'd let me carry on. Making was in my soul; I couldn't help it. Stopping would have been like snuffing out the sun.'

Thorn stared defiantly at Cordelia, as though daring her to say otherwise. Cordelia returned her stare steadily, waiting for her to go on.

'So, I set to work secretly making my father an Understanding Hat,' Thorn continued. 'I gathered long sticky grass and corkscrew-shaped twigs and Moon Phlox flowers that I thought would help increase his understanding. I even got indigo-coloured conches when we went to the seaside. It took months, and all the while I was pretending to have forgotten Making and be an obedient daughter and a good girl.'

The Sea Dragon's red scales rippled, turning forget-me-not blue, the colour of good memories.

Cordelia was silently impressed. It sounded as though Thorn had gathered Grasping Grass, Drift Twigs and Conscious Conches without even knowing what they were. But each of those ingredients was perfect for a hat to help a person understand something. Thorn clearly had a natural talent for Making.

'The night I finally finished the hat, my father was home practising a speech he was going to give to Parliament. My mother died when I was a baby, so it was just him and me in that big, dark house. I carried the hat down to the drawing room and asked him just to put it on for a minute while I explained what Making meant to me.'

Thorn held her hands up, imagining a hat balanced there. Cordelia could almost see an ingenious, madcap confection of woven grass and twigs and creamy yellow Moon Phlox flowers dotted among the shining nuggets of Conscious Conches.

Thorn snatched at the empty air, as though something was being torn from her.

'But Father wouldn't listen! He grabbed the hat and stamped on it. Shells shattered, twigs snapped. My

Understanding Hat that I'd taken months to make was ruined in moments. Father threw it on the fire.'

The Sea Dragon raised its head to Thorn's outstretched hands. Its scales glowed peach and creamy, the colour of rain clouds at sunrise, a comforting presence.

'As my hat burned, Father screamed at me. Making was dangerous, he said, and it must be stopped by any means necessary. He locked me in my room and sent for Doctor Leech.'

Cordelia found she was digging her nails into her hands, her heart breaking like the shells that had been crushed beneath Sir Piers's boots.

Thorn sighed. 'The doctor said there was a place I could be sent: a place that took wayward children and turned them good. It was an old castle, perched on Gaunthead Cliffs: Miss Prim's Academy for the Improvement of Small Minds. They took me there that night.'

'But Miss Prim's Academy . . . it's just a finishing school, isn't it?' Cordelia asked.

Thorn snorted angrily. 'My father *pretended* it was a finishing school, and told people I was learning how to embroider and curtsey and make mildly interesting small talk. But it's not a school; it's a prison. A prison for children who were born Makers but who aren't allowed to use their magical gifts. I met other kids there who'd also been sent there to be "cured" of their rebellious magical tendencies. Lots of them were the children of people my father had persuaded to join the Sensible

Party: powerful people terrified of the shame their wayward children might bring on their families.

'Miss Prim might look like a neat, sweet little china doll, but she's as heartless as one too. Anything that encouraged imagination was banned. All rebellion was punished. We were allowed an excursion to St James's Park, but only so that our parents could come and check how well behaved and obedient we were becoming.'

Cordelia remembered those rows of solemn children marching through the park in their dark grey uniforms, their noses pointing straight ahead. She, Sam and Goose had always been awestruck, watching such impeccable behaviour. But she realized now that what they had actually been witnessing was prisoners on display. She remembered how, when Miss Prim was overcome by the Trouble Clothes, her pupils had fallen back in frightened silence. They must have been terrified of being punished for laughing, or even blamed for the clothes themselves.

'The attack on Miss Prim in St James's Park – was that revenge?' Cordelia asked. 'You made those clothes and somehow sent them to her . . . all for revenge?'

In answer, Thorn held up her hands. Her palms were striped with shimmering white lines as though she was holding slivers of moonbeam.

'Miss Prim used a cane made of Malwood to hit our hands if we made anything magical. It hurt horribly and left us with a feeling of shame long after she stopped. But I didn't care. Nothing and nobody could stop me Making.

'I'd make hats from dried leaves that blew into the yard, or pebbles I found on the ground. I got countless strikes and lost track of my scars. Some kids lost the light in their eyes – when that happened, they were considered "cured", and they were allowed to go home. But I didn't. I checked my eyes every night in the dark window reflection. I knew that if I kept my light I could keep Making, no matter how many times Miss Prim used the Malwood cane on me.'

The light in Thorn's eyes blazed.

'I carved the word *Troublemaker* beside my bed. So I'd see it every morning and be reminded to fight another day.'

The Sea Dragon gazed at the pirate queen steadily, its tail rippling, as she turned a tortured face to her palms. Cordelia looked at the pale scars, the marks left from the Malwood cane.

'I refused to let go of my Making, but Miss Prim's cruelty changed it,' Thorn muttered. 'It got noxious inside me somehow. And now . . . I'm cursed. The word I carved beside my bed came true. Now I can only make one thing, whether I want to or not. Now I can only make trouble.'

Cordelia could see the curse in Thorn's eyes: it was in the particular way they blazed. Some fires warm the soul; some burn with destruction. Thorn's eyes flickered with sparks that could start an inferno.

A moment later, fire and water clashed as tears welled up in Thorn's eyes.

Great-aunt Petronella had once taught Cordelia that each individual teardrop has its own unique magical properties. Tears can comfort broken hearts or speak feelings when words won't come; tears have the strength to restore hope and seal promises. *That is why some people are so frightened of shedding them*, Great-aunt Petronella had said, *because tears contain the power to change everything*.

Thorn closed her eyes and several precious magical tears rolled down her cheeks.

Before she had even realized what she was doing, Cordelia quickly pulled out the Secret-Keeper Shell from inside her pocket. She held it up to catch a single teardrop dripping from Thorn's chin.

Thorn dashed her hands angrily over her face, wiping the remaining tears away as Cordelia tucked the Secret-Keeper, brimming with the shimmering tear, safely back into her pocket.

'How did you escape Miss Prim's?' she asked quietly.

'Sometimes, when you realize nobody else is going to rescue you, you have to do it yourself,' Thorn said grimly.

Cordelia had to admit that this was excellent logic.

'So . . . you definitely weren't kidnapped,' she said.

'No.' Thorn shook her head. 'I suppose Father preferred to tell everyone I was a victim of kidnapping rather than a runaway. He believes girls are much less disgraceful if they're victims not vagabonds, and a girl with her own opinions is a dangerous person.'

The curse bloomed like wildfire across her face again.

'I'm going to make sure I get revenge on everyone who's hurt me!' she vowed. '*Everyone!*'

She strode away into the jungle. The Sea Dragon turned iron grey and headbutted Cordelia firmly after her.

'Wait!' Cordelia cried, speeding after the pirate queen. 'Thorn! Revenge is *not* how you break a curse!'

Thorn grabbed her hat out of a spiky shrub and whipped round, ramming it on to her head. Her face got craggier, like barnacles growing on rocks at lightning speed.

'My father told me I should be like a flower. *Like a rose without a thorn*,' she growled. 'Girls are always being told not to be sharp or spiky. They tell us it's our duty to be pretty and sweet. Because the truth is, we're easier to control that way, aren't we? But I'd rather be a thorn in my father's side than a rose in his buttonhole.'

Before Cordelia could respond, Thorn gave a sharp whistle. Vines snatched Hatmaker and Troublemaker off the ground, dragging them upwards and flinging them through the trees.

The air was knocked from Cordelia's lungs as she was dropped on to the treehouse deck. Before she could get her breath back, Thorn had stalked across the bridge into her cabin and slammed the door.

'Thorn, please listen!' Cordelia yelled, scrambling to her feet. But the door was firmly shut.

'She didn't feed you to Rainbow!' came Never's voice from behind her. 'That's such good news!'

Cordelia turned to see the rest of the pirates arriving on the deck, looking surprised to see her still uneaten.

'It's not that she didn't *try*,' Cordelia told them drily. 'But it turns out I'm not the most appealing snack for the Sea

Dragon, after all. Not enough leaves on me and too many bones.'

Cordelia scrutinized the Troublemakers in their huge pirate hats laden with craggy barnacles.

'Are you . . .' she began shrewdly, stepping forward.

The Troublemakers took a step back, crowding closer together.

'Are we what?' Never asked defensively.

'You *are*!'

'*What?*'

'Wearing disguises,' Cordelia said. 'I know Thorn's secret . . . or should I say *Prudence's* secret?'

Several Troublemakers hushed her, frantically but silently, casting anxious glances towards Thorn's cabin.

But Thorn's voice drifted from the window. 'It's true. The Maker knows.'

Never's eyes widened, and he pulled the pirates into a huddle.

Cordelia watched with her eyebrows raised. She heard mutterings coming from the huddle. A minute later, they turned back to her, shuffling into a line.

Never looked at them all, and solemnly nodded. Then simultaneously the Troublemakers reached up to remove their hats.

Never, Annie, Tabitha, Jim and Billy all changed.

Without their hats, the Troublemakers were revealed to be children.

'What a RELIEF!' Billy sighed, scratching his head. 'Those Rockface Barnacles are so *itchy*! They're the reason I'm always saying "*AAAARGH!*"'

Billy, it turned out, was a round-faced boy of about ten.

Annie and Tabitha were even younger, their smiles much less frightening now they had shed their disguises. Jim was still looming, but in a much less cadaverous way. He loomed only the way gangly twelve-year-old boys, who have grown a lot in a short space of time, tend to do.

It was hard for Cordelia to tell if Shelly's face had changed, because all that could be seen of her were her eyes. She was still covered with shells and blinking silently.

Only Smokestack remained old. His eyes twinkled in his lined face as he smiled at Cordelia.

'So, you know our secret,' Never said. 'This is who we really are.'

Cordelia turned to Never, recognizing his lopsided smile at once.

'You're the boy I met at the Kingless!' she cried.

Never nodded. 'That was me,' he admitted.

A sparkling constellation of understanding came together in Cordelia's mind.

'And you decided to kidnap me because I told you *myself* that treason was easy!' Cordelia gasped.

Never had the good grace to look slightly shamefaced.

'Kidnapping isn't something we'd like to get a reputation for,' he muttered. 'It was *really* meant to be more of a polite invitation –'

'Everyone in London already thinks you're kidnappers,' Cordelia told him. 'They believe a wicked band of pirates called the Troublemakers kidnapped –' here, she wisely dropped her voice to a whisper to continue – '*Prudence Oglethorne*. And you're keeping her prisoner.'

'We're not kidnappers!' Tabitha burst out. 'We're *escapers* and *survivors*!'

'We are,' Never said, looking at Cordelia defiantly. 'And actually I don't really care if the whole of London thinks we're man-eating crocodiles. We had to save ourselves from Miss Prim's prison.'

'Wait – you were *all* at Miss Prim's?' Cordelia asked. 'Then how come only Prudence was reported kidnapped?'

There had been no news of other pupils going missing from the school. No word on the London streets nor in any newspapers about more kidnappings.

'Miss Prim probably hated admitting that even a single prisoner had escaped!' Tabitha said wryly. 'But she could probably keep the rest of us escapers quiet because it was a secret we'd been sent there anyway.'

'They probably had to say Thorn was kidnapped because "escaped" would have raised too many questions!' Never pointed out. 'Lots of Miss Prim's prisoners are the children of important politicians and noblemen who don't want their reputations ruined by the scandal of having their children's illegal Making skills revealed.'

'My real name's William Borington,' Billy Bones admitted. 'My father runs the *Boring Ton* newspaper. And Jim is really James Leech: his father's the one who sent most of us to Miss Prim to be "cured".'

Cordelia stared at Jim. 'Doctor Leech is your father?'

Jim nodded glumly.

'Annie and I are really the Ladies Annette and Tabitha of Slough,' Tabitha explained. 'Our father's the Earl of Slough.'

'And my father's Lord Carp,' Never added ruefully. 'He says, *Lords don't learn trades, especially illegal ones.* I was never allowed to Make. Now I'm *never* going back.'

'All your parents are in the Sensible Party!' Cordelia realized.

She remembered the line-up of unsmiling politicians at Speakers' Corner. There could not have been a greater contrast between those grim grown-ups and this ragtag bunch of scruffy children standing before her now, bright-eyed and rebellious, their hearts blazing with defiance and their fingers full of magic.

'And who is Shelly?' Cordelia asked.

The Troublemakers grew quiet as they turned to Shelly, clinking in her crustacean armour.

'Shelly's the reason we escaped,' a voice came from behind Cordelia.

Thorn appeared in the doorway to her cabin. She had taken her hat off again, and her face looked strangely vulnerable in its youth.

'One evening, months after my father left me in Miss Prim's cold courtyard, I heard the sound of his carriage over the cobbles outside,' Thorn said. 'I thought – I hoped – he was there to take me away from the prison. When he and Miss Prim went into her parlour, I sneaked along to listen in at the keyhole.

'When I heard what my father was saying to Miss Prim, I realized he wasn't there to take me home at all. He was telling her about something he'd heard in Parliament: one of the Guildhall Makers had reported to the politicians about this very dangerous thing: a bit of metal that had the power to destroy magic –'

'That was Father!' Cordelia interrupted. 'Back in September he told them about the soul lead that Lord Witloof turned himself into. It's in the British Museum now, under lock and key. But if its special cage is opened, it's really dangerous –'

Thorn nodded grimly.

'I could tell from the sound of my father's voice he was excited,' she continued. 'He said the key to a Sensible Britain was within his reach – the thing was being moved that night and he'd have access for an hour or two at most. He thought it was a way to stamp out magic, once and for all. To drain magic from all ingredients . . . and . . . a way to drain the magic out of people too.'

Cordelia remembered her father telling *her* the same thing, months ago. But Prospero Hatmaker hadn't been excited about this dark power; he had been extremely grave.

'My father said he needed someone to experiment on, to make sure it would work,' Thorn continued. 'He said he wanted to be sure it was safe before he tried it on – on me. So he needed a child with strong magic, like mine . . .'

Cordelia went cold. Such a wicked thing could not be true.

'Shelly was wild and wayward and rebellious and boisterous when she arrived at Miss Prim's,' Thorn went on through gritted teeth. 'She'd run around turning cartwheels among the geese when we paraded in the park. She'd make flower crowns out of weeds, woven with hope and strength, and kept nettle leaves in her shoes to give herself clever defences. She pulled faces at Miss Prim behind her back and sang funny songs about clouds. She was small but fierce and funny and full of defiance.'

Cordelia looked at the person blinking mildly at her, covered in shells. It was hard to believe this was the same person Thorn had just described.

'The day my father came to see Miss Prim, Shelly had got in trouble for making rude noises whenever Miss Prim opened her mouth during prayers, and she'd been locked in the castle dungeon since morning. I think Miss Prim was delighted at the opportunity to finally subdue the wild child: Shelly was so defiant that not even the Malwood cane had worked on her. I rushed into the parlour and begged Father not to take Shelly away. But he wouldn't listen.'

Thorn clenched her fists.

'I tried to stop them taking her – I fought like a wild thing – but Father and Miss Prim were too strong. They locked me in the dungeon and took Shelly away.' Thorn swallowed. 'I don't know exactly what happened to her – but –'

'I do,' Cordelia croaked. 'My father told me: anyone who hears the scream of the leaden soul is drained of their magic.'

She turned to Shelly. 'Sir Piers unlocked the case, didn't he?' she asked. 'You heard the sound that thing makes, didn't you, Shelly?'

Shelly slowly nodded.

CHAPTER 27

Thorn clamped an arm around Shelly's shoulders, her face grey as a lost cloud.

'Miss Prim only let me out of the dungeon when my father brought Shelly back the next morning. They carried her inside and put her to bed. She was nothing but a huddled lump under a blanket, hardly moving, barely breathing.'

Cordelia's insides were frozen, as though she had swallowed too many snowcakes.

'I think my father feared he'd gone too far. I think he thought it might've killed Shelly,' Thorn went on. 'He must have been afraid because he didn't take me away that day. He said he'd wait to see if Shelly got better or worse over the next few weeks. Perhaps he worried it was like a cut that bleeds you slowly dry, and when all the magic is gone, you die.'

The Troublemakers all huddled round Shelly protectively, patting her gently on her shells. The scene went blurry, and Cordelia realized she had tears in her eyes.

'*Is* Shelly going to die?' she whispered.

'No,' Never assured her. 'After several weeks, she started slowly improving.'

'But that was when we knew they'd be coming for us next, to stamp out our magic,' Thorn said grimly. 'We had to get out of Miss Prim's somehow. On the next trip to the park, I managed to get away from Miss Prim for a minute to explain to Master Ambrosius what had happened. He used to come to the park every day in case his sister was on parade, but he hadn't seen her for weeks. He made some –'

'Wait, wait, what?' Cordelia frowned. 'Master Ambrosius the sweetmaker? What does he have to do with all this?'

This question provoked a cloudburst of explanations. All the Troublemakers began talking at once.

'Master Ambrosius is Shelly's brother!'

'He helped us escape!'

'He made Slumberous sweets disguised as liquorice, and gave them to Thorn to slip to Prim!'

'Salted liquorice is the only kind of sweet that Prim eats because it's so disgusting!'

'Prim says *liquorice tastes of the bitterness of indulgence* –'

'Thorn spilled the sweets at dinner – well, she pretended –'

'Then Miss Prim ate them –'

'And fell asleep in her mashed potatoes!'

'Then we climbed out of the window on knotted bedsheets and met Master Ambrosius below the castle walls –'

'We had to make a sling for Shelly cos back then she was too weak to walk –'

Cordelia held up her hands, feeling positively drenched in information, and Never stepped in.

'We thought we'd be going to live with Master Ambrosius,' he explained. 'But he said it wasn't safe for us in England. Sooner or later our parents would find us, and we'd be right back where we started.'

'And he really is a de Sneer?' Cordelia asked, remembering her shock when Never had said this at the Kingless.

Never nodded. 'He is – but he's a good person.'

'He was heartbroken to see his sister so . . . *dulled*,' Thorn muttered. 'But it made him more determined to save us – and even more determined to help us with our revenge. He'd arranged for us to go to his aunt on an island far away – the Duchess – and he'd found an old sailor with a ship that could get us across the Atlantic. The sailor and his ship were waiting in the bay.'

The Troublemakers turned to regard Smokestack.

'*You're* the old sailor!' Cordelia gasped.

'I was glad of the company.' Smokestack smiled. 'I'd joined the navy as a young lad but left when I'd seen enough cruelty from the admirals to last a lifetime. I became a fisherman. It's a lonely life at sea, though, with nobody to listen to my yarns. When this pack of kids tumbled aboard my ship one stormy night, calling themselves the Troublemakers, I welcomed them with hot tea and buttered toast.'

'And bedtime stories!' Annie added.

'We set sail that night – we had to get away before Miss Prim woke up,' Never told Cordelia. 'We patched up Smokestack's boat with magical repairs and renamed it the *Trouble*. We set a course for St Freerest, and as we sailed south we realized we were travelling towards a star we'd never seen before, over the western ocean.'

Cordelia nodded, remembering the beckoning whisper of the star she had seen between *Little Bear*'s ears on her own voyage.

'When we arrived at St Freerest, the Duchess took us in. She was happy to have us all to stay with her at the Kingless, where she could keep us safe. We were there for a while, making plans for revenge.'

'But it was Shelly who brought us to the island. She was like a hermit crab, curled up and hiding for most of the voyage. But when we got to St Freerest, she kept wandering on to the beach and staring longingly out across the sea towards an island we could see like a ghostly shape on the horizon, right underneath that star. Shelly wouldn't speak; she wouldn't sing. No magical things sparked in her hands. But she could feel the pull of the island, like a tide. Though the Duchess didn't want us to leave her protection, she knew we had to go. She suspected it was the only way Shelly might ever get better.'

'The star led us safely through the rocks,' said Annie, 'through the gigantic jaws. And since we got here, Shelly's been slowly coming out of her shell again.'

'And it's been the perfect base to wage our war on the Sensible Party,' Thorn growled. 'So many ingredients here that we can turn into trouble. And so many passing ships to steal things from.'

'We rob ships of their fine goods, turn them into Trouble Clothes and send them back to London!' Billy crowed.

Cordelia gave a start. 'I've just worked out your smuggling route!' she cried. 'You get the Trouble Clothes to the Duchess, and she packs them in crates of cocoa beans – I helped you pack one! – and she puts them on ships back to London, to be picked up by Master Ambrosius, who makes sure they reach their intended victims!'

The crate she had helped Never to pack had been destined for the Artifice Chocolate House. *Artifice* was another word for *trick*.

'The Artifice Chocolate House doesn't exist!' Cordelia whispered. 'And I *saw* a crate get pushed off the back of a ship arriving in London. That was the other end of the route! And it happened the day before Miss Prim went berserk in the park.'

'The Tornado Cloak was my idea!' Tabitha yelled gleefully.

'And the Belch Bonnet was me!' Billy grinned.

'I used my own hair to stitch the Troublemaking seeds to her gloves.' Thorn grinned wolfishly. 'It's the best kind of revenge: tailor-made for the victim.'

That word again. It hung like a sword above their heads.

'*Revenge*,' Cordelia said quietly. 'Surely you can do something better than that with all your talent?'

'Prim's cruelty turned my talent inside out,' Thorn spat. 'I told you: everything I make turns to trouble. So we're sending the trouble back to the people who did this to us.'

'But Master Ambrosius has been arrested,' Cordelia told them soberly. 'So whatever you're planning next – something in the chocolate houses, by the looks of it –'

The moment the words left her lips, she realized she had put a foot wrong.

Thorn's eyes narrowed.

'How do you know what I'm planning next?' she hissed. 'Have you been sneaking into my cabin, Maker?'

Cordelia saw no point in denying the truth.

'Yes, I have,' she said. 'You've all been through something absolutely terrible, but spreading more terror won't help mend things.'

Thorn clutched Cordelia's arm, and the Hatmaker jolted as though she'd had a brush with an electric eel.

'I'm not good for anything else,' Thorn hissed. 'Revenge is what I'm made for. And we're going to keep stealing clothes and keep smuggling them into London until Trouble overruns the city! Though *nothing* we can do will ever be bad enough to pay them back for what they did to Shelly.'

Thorn's face was aflame. Cordelia was suddenly reminded of the last ship the Troublemakers had attacked. It had been set ablaze and sunk, not a soul left aboard.

These children had been changed by the cruelty they had suffered. Like creatures that had been inhumanely treated, they themselves had become inhuman and vicious.

She shuddered, remembering the chilling warning of Capitano Boniface: *They sink ships and take no prisoners.*

'And now you're one of us!' cackled Tabitha. 'I wonder what your pirate name will be?'

'I'm not one of you!' Cordelia gasped, pulling away from Thorn. 'You're the reason I'm an outlaw! The Turbidus seeds –'

'No, Cordelia Hatmaker.' Thorn smiled. '*You're* the reason you're an outlaw. *You* put a magical hat on the king's head, not us. You're a born Troublemaker.'

Cordelia shook her head, not wanting Thorn's words to be true.

'I'll *never* do the things you do!' she shouted. 'You do terrible things!'

The Troublemakers looked wounded at this.

'But you can help us with our revenge!' Never said.

'I won't!' Cordelia shouted, backing away. 'Making is meant to make lives better. It should never be a weapon! I won't teach you another thing. Not unless you stop your attacks. I won't teach *any* of you!'

A mutter rumbled round the circle of Troublemakers. The atmosphere turned darker.

Cordelia could not stand by while they burned ships and flooded London with destructive, dangerous clothes.

'Revenge isn't a good enough reason to do anything,' she said. 'No matter what's happened to you. If you want to break your curse, Thorn, you have to make something better than destruction, no matter how hard it is.'

Thorn's eyes narrowed.

'You're either with us or against us, Hatmaker,' she snarled, prowling forward.

Hatmaker and Troublemaker stood nose to nose, so close that Cordelia could see the flint-and-tinder sparks in the Troublemaker's eyes and the place where the curse smouldered in her soul.

'It has to stop,' Cordelia insisted.

'So, you're against us,' Thorn whispered. 'Remember, this was your choice.'

'What are you going to do?' Cordelia challenged Thorn defiantly. 'You can't feed me to the Sea Dragon – I know that's an empty threat.'

Thorn threw a meaningful look to one of her crew. 'Fetch the hat we made for this emergency.'

'Aye, aye, Cap'n!'

'Now, now, Captain,' a wise old voice began. 'Perhaps a little pondering needs to be done –'

'Your pondering takes ages, Smokestack!' Thorn roared. 'SEIZE THE PRISONER!'

Cordelia's arms were grabbed. She struggled, but Billy and Jim had her fast. The deck juddered as someone ran.

'WAIT!' Cordelia yelled. 'What are you doing?'

She twisted round to see Never hurrying back along the treehouse, carrying a dark blue tricorn. It was the colour of oblivion, studded with barnacles and fringed with dodo feathers.

Never had said that dodo feathers were good for forgetting.

'NO!' Cordelia screamed, struggling as the hat was borne towards her. 'I'm Cordelia Hatmaker! I'm Dilly! I'm the littlest Hatmaker! Father! Goose! Sam! I'm –'

'I'm sorry,' Never whispered.

The hat came down like banishment on her head.

CHAPTER 28

The Troublemakers' attack on *Little Bear* had left the ship in a bad state. If it hadn't been for the flock of birds descending on them right afterwards, *Little Bear* and her crew would have gone to the bottom of the sea.

The birds had swallowed the fire engulfing the sails. But still they were left in tatters. A crossbeam had been pulled down by the twisting waterspout, sticky ropes of spiderweb were tangled in the rigging, and the sea monster towing the *Trouble* had scarred the hull with its flaming tail. *Little Bear* wheezed and groaned as water seeped in through the damaged wood.

The moment Prospero, Sam, Goose, Melchior and Davey were freed, they ran to the rails. The birds that had rescued them streamed overhead, disappearing into the wink of the sunset.

Somewhere out there, very close but impossible to find, was the island where Cordelia had been taken.

'CORDELIA!' Prospero roared over the empty ocean. 'CORDELIA!'

They caught a little wind in their ragged sails and turned back for the only land in sight: St Freerest. Goose and Sam worked alongside the captain and the crew through the night, hauling up buckets of water from the hold and plugging the leaks that sprang through the damaged hull.

They dropped anchor off St Freerest at first light. Across the bay, the hulking form of the *Invincible* became slowly visible. Beyond, the Kingless towered at a rakish angle above the jumble of the port.

Prospero went ashore straight away, to seek out workmen and supplies to mend the ship. However, he got nothing but shrugged shoulders and furtive glances and returned to *Little Bear* empty-handed.

'The Duchess wouldn't even answer her door,' Prospero growled, striding across the deck. 'I think she's told everyone on St Freerest not to give us any help. She's desperate to stop us getting to that island.'

They lowered Davey over the rail on a rope to inspect the burn in *Little Bear*'s hull.

'She needs patching and tarring,' Davey called. 'She won't be seaworthy for a week, probably longer!'

'We'll fix *Little Bear* ourselves, even if we have to work all day and night for as long as it takes!' Prospero said. 'And then – as soon as she's seaworthy again – I'll think of a way to get to the island. There's *got* to be a way!'

He set to work mending *Little Bear*'s hull, swearing loudly in French if any sailors in the dark blue suits of the Royal Navy rowed past looking curious. He worked with heartbroken fury. The few moments he stopped, to wolf down food, he spent scrutinizing the place on the map where Cordelia had seen the Island of Lost Souls. He stared so hard he seemed likely to make a hole in the parchment with his eyes.

Goose and Sam clambered through the rigging, untangling spiderweb from rope. From up there, they could see the Duchess at the door of the Kingless, gazing out at them.

'If only there was a way we could make her tell us where the island is,' Sam said, scowling at the Duchess.

'We could go to my brother, Ignatius!' Goose suggested suddenly, turning to stare at the *Invincible*. 'Ig's aboard the admiral's ship! We could tell him we know where the pirates are, explain about Cor–'

'We're in disguise and we need to keep it that way, Goose!' Prospero barked. 'We've just got to hope the Duchess doesn't turn us in to the admiral. We'd be fools to turn ourselves in.'

Goose looked a little stung. He tugged sullenly at a spiderweb and got it wrapped stickily round his arm. He winced as he pulled it off.

The sun tracked across the sky, watching with an unblinking eye as the crew of *Little Bear* worked relentlessly. At high noon, the *Splendora* sailed into the bay.

'We mustn't communicate with Capitano Boniface,' Prospero instructed the crew as they watched the ship drop anchor. 'I'll go to him after nightfall and explain.'

They ducked their heads, working through the day and deep into the night, until even the stars looked tired. When Sam and Goose could do no more, they fell, aching, into their beds.

Sam gathered the energy to whisper, 'There's gotta be a way ta get to that island.'

And Goose whispered back, 'We might have to take matters into our own . . .'

But they were both asleep before he could finish his sentence.

The next morning, when Sam and Goose put their ears to the captain's door, they heard desperate mutterings coming from behind it. They softly knocked on the door and Prospero opened it, haggard and red-eyed.

'We brought you some tea,' Sam said, holding up a steaming teapot.

They could see the cabin was a mess. Papers were strewn everywhere.

'I can't find a single map with that cursed island on it,' Prospero croaked. 'I've half a mind to kidnap the Duchess, damn the admiral, and —'

Prospero froze, mid-sentence.

'The admiral . . .' he murmured. '*He's* looking for them too . . .'

He strode to the window, staring out at the hulking *Invincible* floating like a fortress in the middle of the bay.

'That island's hidden within shrouds of magic,' he muttered. 'But what if . . .'

Goose and Sam stood in the doorway, watching as Prospero dived for his treasure chest, throwing maps and instruments aside as he feverishly searched for something.

They set the teapot on a map of the Antilles and backed slowly out of the room. Clearly, the captain had taken leave of his senses, driven to distraction by grief and worry.

'We've gotta *do* somefing!' Sam whispered.

'I agree!' Goose said firmly. 'Where shall we start?'

Sam and Goose left a note pinned on the ship's wheel. At Goose's behest, it began and ended with apologies, but the middle was full of conviction (though no details, so Prospero could not follow them). Then they slipped away on the little rowing boat.

This time when they stepped ashore, they found the port of St Freerest sullen and tense. Instead of raucous mariners carousing in the streets, there were blue-suited sailors everywhere, hammering up posters that said:

WANTED: THE TROUBLEMAKERS
REWARD: The Price of a King's Ransom
(or something of equal value)

Scrawled in red across the bottom of every poster were the words:

ALSO WANTED: CORDELIA HATMAKER
FOR THE CRIME OF HIGH TREASON!

The words shone like fresh blood. They saw a sailor carrying a bucket of red paint, going from poster to poster, adding those words by hand. Red paint dripped down the walls, dotting the dusty ground.

Sam and Goose stared in horror, seeing Cordelia's name repeated in red like a curse. They slipped through the marketplace to the Kingless, following the drops of red paint like breadcrumbs.

There was even a poster plastered across the Kingless door. They were careful not to get red paint on their knuckles as they knocked.

The Duchess answered, saw their faces and immediately tried to slam the door. Sam stuck a foot in the doorway so she couldn't close it.

'We want to know how to find the Island of Lost Souls,' Goose demanded.

'I can't help you,' the Duchess hissed through the crack. 'It's impossible to get to unless you can see it.'

'*You* can see it, can't you?' Sam said.

'You can take us there!' Goose added. 'Please!'

'Go away and don't come back!' the Duchess told them in a fierce whisper. 'The admiral's already asking too many questions. Don't you dare breathe a *word* about the island to him or I'll –'

Her eyes suddenly grew wide and angry as she saw the poster pasted across her door. She ripped it down, tore it in half and hurled the pieces into the street.

With that, she kicked Sam's foot out of the way and slammed the door. They heard the lock click.

'We could hammer on it until she comes out again?' Goose suggested.

But Sam glanced around, shaking her head.

'The admiral's sailors are everywhere,' she said, eyeing a knot of navy-blue sailors milling around the quiet market stalls.

Sam and Goose slipped back along the harbour, careful to avoid any sailors in navy. They stared at the new ships that had recently arrived. Alongside the *Splendora*, they saw a British ship that had come from London yesterday, bringing news.

The market vendors gossiped as they set up their stalls for the day.

'Britain sounds grim!' one observed cheerfully.

'Making banned for all!' a lady hanging up windchimes tinkled. 'And that dreadful Sir Piers the new prime minister!'

'Wouldn't like to be a Maker now!' a watermelon seller added.

Goose and Sam stared at each other in dismay.

CHAPTER 29

L ondon was, indeed, a very grim and gloomy place. One of the gloomiest places of all was Hatmaker House.

The day after the disaster in Parliament, Sir Piers had arrived in Wimpole Street, bringing a small army of soldiers with him.

'Take everything magical,' he instructed. 'By order of the king.'

He watched as soldiers threw hats into sacks, swept magical ingredients off the shelves and smashed the special instruments used to spool starlight. Great-aunt Petronella fought ferociously over her Astroscope, Aunt Ariadne pleaded with the soldiers to leave the library books, and Uncle Tiberius refused to relinquish his silver stitching needles. But the soldiers were merciless. They took Cook's spurtle, saying it looked too much like a magic wand to be an innocent porridge-stirrer, and tore off Len's jacket because it was patched with moonlight. Even the rooftop glasshouse was emptied, the plants rustling their leaves longingly back towards home as they were piled on a cart.

'You brutes!' Aunt Ariadne exclaimed, chasing the last soldier on to the pavement, where Uncle Tiberius was wrestling over some ribbons as Great-aunt Petronella jabbed a soldier with her old wooden hatpin. Defeated, Uncle Tiberius fell heavily to the ground, ribbons torn from his fingers, and Sir Piers smiled the triumphant smile of a man with the law on his side.

'If you dare to even stitch a single spell into a handkerchief, you'll be taken away too!' he warned, stomping on a Storm Nautilus Conch attempting to scuttle back inside. 'These magical ingredients are illegal; they are going to be dealt with.'

The cart piled high with the Hatmakers' precious magical ingredients and tools rumbled away down the street. Great-aunt Petronella turned her hatpin on Sir Piers instead, but he prised it out of her hand and snapped it in half.

Then he leaned down, pushing his face horribly close to the ancient lady's, and hissed, '*You* will be dealt with too, soon enough.'

He dropped the broken pieces of the hatpin on the ground and left.

The Hatmakers stood on the pavement, staring in shock at the window of their once-beautiful shop. All the hatstands had been robbed of their hats. Some bald hatstands rolled on the floor, like heads that had recently been chopped off.

They crept inside to find every magical ingredient gone. It was as though a magic-eating beast had come and devoured its way greedily through Hatmaker House, leaving nothing but silent shadows behind.

Uncle Tiberius discovered Len Lightfinger hiding under the stairs, clutching a bottle of Sam's Sunset Nectar, and could only coax him out with Cook's last sunlight pie and the solemn promise that the soldiers were gone.

The Hatmakers soon realized that, although the house seemed empty of magic, there *were* several tiny magical objects remaining. The Turbidus seeds that had escaped from Cook's pudding, to slip into cracks between floorboards and nestle into the ashes of the magical fireplace in the workshop, had also escaped the soldiers' notice. But all the chaos and hullabaloo had stirred the seeds awake. Silently they sprouted and began to grow . . .

Vines curled round the bannisters and snaked across doorways. They crept down corridors and invited themselves into rooms, spiralling round door handles, surging across the floors and up the walls.

The Hatmakers snipped, pruned, hacked, yelped and yelled, but nothing stopped the vines growing. They watched in horror as the vines ran riot, terrified that Sir Piers would return and accuse them of making illegal magic.

When Mrs Bootmaker came tramping into Hatmaker House the next day, cursing Sir Piers like he was mud on her boots, she ran into a jungle.

'What on earth is going on here?' Nigella Bootmaker shrieked.

Uncle Tiberius hushed her.

'The more noise we make, the faster they grow!' he explained in a whisper.

He ushered her into the shop, which was the only room left that the vines had not invaded, and where everyone was sheltering.

'It's the only place we can be in peace,' Tiberius told her, wrestling the door closed as a vine tried to barge in. 'I can't even sleep in my bedroom – a vine tried to pick my nose at two o'clock in the morning!'

'We've tried everything, but we don't know how to stop them growing!' Aunt Ariadne added under her breath.

Hatmaker House groaned as a vine surged across the landing above them. A root appeared, thrusting its way down through the ceiling, crumbling the plaster.

'They're destroying our home!' Uncle Tiberius wailed, then clapped a hand over his mouth as the root wiggled excitedly towards the noise.

'Why have you got mittens sewn to your sleeves?' Mrs Bootmaker asked Uncle Tiberius curiously. Tiberius Hatmaker did, indeed, have a pair of woollen mittens stitched clumsily to his cuffs, covering his hands entirely.

'To stop myself Making,' Tiberius admitted miserably. 'I find myself Making without even thinking about it. These muffle the magic in my hands a bit – though I did set fire to them earlier.'

He held up his hands, like two large paws, to show Nigella the scorch marks at the fingertips.

'I make my bed every morning, you see,' he explained. 'I suppose I make it a bit magically. The mittens caught fire while I was plumping the pillows.'

Mrs Bootmaker shook her head, observing Cook attempting to roast sausages over a candle flame and Great-aunt Petronella crooning softly to a frazzled-looking Quest Pigeon she had saved from the soldiers, which was nesting in a hat on her lap. Len was curled up on an empty shelf, blowing motes of dust through a shaft of sunlight.

'You'll all come and live at Bootmaker Mansion,' Mrs Bootmaker said decisively. 'Sir Piers has taken all our ingredients away too, so there's plenty of room for everyone, and no blasted vines! Come along – I won't take no for an answer!'

She almost clapped her hands briskly, then thought better of it, and instead opened the shop door quietly.

But there was a person framed in the doorway, his fist raised, about to pummel on the door.

It was Sir Hugo Gushforth.

'I am forced to perform *The Sorrowful Tale of St Enoch* over and over again!' the actor wailed. 'It's the worst play I've ever done. My costume is a *brown cassock*, and the dialogue doesn't even rhyme, because *Prime Minister* Oglethorne considers rhyming too frivolous!'

Everyone hushed him, as they bustled out on to the pavement, with Len and Uncle Tiberius carrying Great-aunt Petronella in her chair.

'I'm so sorry, Sir Hugo,' Aunt Ariadne whispered. 'I hear they've shut all the chocolate houses too. The Sensible Party are determined to make everybody miserable.'

'I know Making's banned, but can't you make me just the smallest little hat?' the actor wheedled. 'A hat*let*, perhaps? To go under my awful monk's hood?'

'We cannot,' Aunt Ariadne told him. 'All our magical ingredients have been confiscated. And even if we had any left, we couldn't Make – it's far too risky!'

'Alas!' the actor wailed. 'Cordelia would have done it!'

Aunt Ariadne's eyebrows betrayed worry, hurt and grief in one frown.

'Cordelia has done several things of which I cannot entirely approve,' she said heavily.

They shut the door on the empty Hatmakers' shop and hurried off down Wimpole Street, past closed chocolate houses and dark shops, through a terribly glum London.

CHAPTER 30

Dagger Dauntless was having an excellent day.

She swung out of her bunk at sunrise, went for a swim in the lagoon with the other Troublemakers, ate some cake for breakfast, spent a little time leaping happily from the treehouse deck and being caught by the vines, and then went with the other pirates to collect ingredients from all over the island.

She could not remember what any of the ingredients were for, but she contented herself with collecting the shiniest shells and the sweetest-smelling blossoms. She shimmied up palm trees and waded into the shallows, eventually tramping back to the treehouse with her pockets full of shells, heavy-scented flowers and curling fronds of rainbow seaweed, her fingers tingling strangely.

At the treehouse, their captain sat hunched over a table, scowling at a half-finished hat.

'What madcap piratical thing are we doing next?' Dagger asked one of the pirates, whose name escaped her just at that moment.

The wild-haired pirate smiled at her.

'Making!' he said. 'Can you teach me how to sew memories into cloak hems?'

'I don't think so!' Dagger said. 'Why on earth should I know how to do that?'

The pirates all stared at Dagger with something that looked like concern – though Dagger was not quite sure that's what it would be called.

'Can you teach me how to weave happiness into hat ribbons?' a moustachioed pirate asked.

'Or moonlight into bootlaces?'

'Or stitch gratitude into glove seams?'

Dagger Dauntless scratched her head, dislodging her smart blue hat for a moment.

Making . . .

A pirate helpfully pushed her blue hat firmly back on to her head, securing the buckled chinstrap firmly. Dagger smiled blankly at them all.

'I don't think so!' she said cheerfully. 'I don't know anything like that!'

The captain snorted.

'Not much use to us then, are you?' she sneered, throwing a half-finished hat over the edge of the treehouse.

Dagger peered over the edge to see a large pile of discarded clothes in a heap on the jungle floor.

'That's a silly waste!' she pointed out.

Some of the other pirates made faces at her, miming silence. She saw the captain's face redden.

'They're all rubbish!' the captain yelled, leaping up and slashing a cloak in two with her cutlass. 'It's these useless clothes! We need to plunder ourselves some new ones! What ships are leaving St Freerest today?'

'A handsome one full of Venetian treasures, according to the whispers,' the wild-haired pirate supplied helpfully. 'The *Splendora*.'

'What say you, Troublemakers?' the pirate queen demanded, glaring around at the other pirates. 'Shall we take the *Splendora*'s treasures?'

They erupted into cheers.

Finding cheering in a bloodthirsty manner to be quite appealing, Dagger joined in.

The sails of the *Trouble* were raised, and the Sea Dragon was lassoed. Soon, the ship was surging out of the tailbone bay through the jagged white arch, with a rope straining into the water in front of them.

Dagger clambered into the rigging, forgot what all the

knots were for, and climbed back down again. She stood at the prow, admiring the jester figurehead with his three-pointed hat grinning into the teeth of the wind.

Dagger Dauntless and the jester had several things in common. Neither knew where they had come from or where they were going; they were both stuck on the ship whether they liked it or not; and both smiled woodenly at the oncoming adventure.

Dagger felt the wind in her hair and the captain's eyes on her back. She waved uncertainly at the captain, who scowled in reply.

The wind pushed up the brim of her navy-blue tricorn and she tugged it thoughtfully. A fellow Troublemaker wedged it firmly back on to her head and tightened the chin buckle.

The hat was a comfort to her; it fitted snugly. But the more firmly it was pushed down and buckled on, the more certain Dagger felt that something important was trying to emerge from the very middle of her head, like a seedling trying to find the light.

Before she could wonder about this strange little sprout in the blank blue of her brain, the captain – Thorn Lawless, her name was! – spun the wheel and howled.

'Swords at the ready!' Thorn called out.

'AAARGH!' came the chorused reply as a silver forest of blades were stabbed skywards.

'Fiercest battle faces ready?' the pirate queen cried.

'YAAAARGH!'

Dagger howled, a wild cry that made her soul roar.

'She's in our sights!' a bearded pirate yelled, pointing from halfway up the rigging.

Dagger ran to the rail and saw a beautiful ship on the horizon.

The ship seemed familiar to Dagger. Or perhaps it was familiar in the way all ships are, with her sleek wooden hull and her puffy white sails and a Venetian flag flying from the topgallant.

'The *Splendora* will be ours!' Thorn Lawless cried. 'TROUBLEMAKERS, ATTACK!'

'We're doing the right thing, aren't we?' Goose asked Sam anxiously, boosting her into the crow's nest.

'Goose, this was your idea!' Sam pulled him up behind her and curled to one side, to make space for him. 'It's a great plan,' she added reassuringly. Then she continued, 'Well – maybe it's not a *great* plan, but it's the best plan we have.'

Goose nodded nervously.

Standing forlornly on the dock at St Freerest and wondering how on earth to begin rescuing Cordelia, Goose had realized that the *Splendora*, bursting with valuable cargo, would be an enticing prospect for the Troublemakers. When the coast was clear, they had sneaked aboard and climbed up to the crow's nest. They reckoned Capitano Boniface did not seem likely to make stowaways walk the plank.

Now, as the tide turned, they listened as the ship woke below them.

They heard the cheerful voice of Capitano Boniface, the busy patter of a dozen sailors and the clank of the anchor. The *Splendora* met the open ocean with the wind singing in her sails and her hull rushing through the waves. The ship spoke a language to join sea and sky: a vessel between two deep blues.

St Freerest slowly became a green speck on the horizon.

'How long till we show our faces?' Sam muttered to Goose a little while later. It was getting uncomfortable folded up in the crow's nest, crouched to make sure nobody saw their heads poking up above the rail.

'Long enough so they don't turn round and take us back,' Goose said.

'All right.' Sam nodded. 'After sunset.'

It would be hours before the sun set. Indeed, it climbed higher, blazing down on them, and Goose began to wish he had thought to bring water and food.

'What if the Troublemakers *don't* come after this ship?' Sam asked Goose.

'Then I suppose we'll just have to go wherever the *Splendora*'s going, turn round and go back –'

A cry from the rigging interrupted them.

'EHI DELLA NAVE!'

'I think that means "sail sighted"!' Goose was triumphant. 'Must be the *Trouble*!'

He was immediately visited by a feeling of unease. They peered out from the crow's nest to see a ship coming straight for them, in full sail.

Sam groaned. It was not the *Trouble*. It was Admiral Ransom's ship, the *Invincible*, surging towards them with all the shiny purpose of a knight rescuing a damsel in distress.

'The Troublemakers'll never come after us with the biggest ship in the Royal Navy hanging around!' Goose moaned.

The *Invincible* ran up flags, a series of chequers, crosses and colours conveying a message.

'Stop . . . urgent . . .' Goose translated. 'Pirates nearby. Oh *no*! We're being *saved* from the pirates before we can even be *attacked* by them!'

Sam rolled her eyes.

'Heroes,' she tutted. 'Always getting in the way.'

The *Invincible* sheered through the waves, hatches opening in its side as it turned broadside. A hundred cannons emerged from the dark belly, pointing directly at the *Splendora*. The shouts from the naval crew sharpened and soured.

Another flag ran up the *Invincible*'s rigging.

This one meant 'Surrender'!

There was a shocked silence. For a moment only the wind could be heard, whistling in surprise through the rigging.

'I don't fink they're here to save us after all,' Sam muttered.

Alarmed murmurs rose from the *Splendora*'s crew.

Goose shook his head, frowning at the dark blue machinery of men's elbows and arms working on the cannons in the belly of the *Invincible*.

'They can't be going to fire on us,' he said. 'That would be an act of piracy! This is Admiral Ransom; he's a hero of the Royal . . .'

The words died on his lips as he saw the sparks of fuses being lit.

A *BOOM* shook their bones. Solid gobs of thunder bowled across the deck beneath them, knocking all the crew sideways.

The *Splendora*'s hull burst open.

BOOM – BOOM – BOOM –

The air ruptured around them as the crow's nest spiralled in the sky.

'Whadda we do?' Sam cried, digging her nails into the mast.

'We're safer up here!' Goose yelled. 'If we just sta-ay-ay –'

Before he could utter another word, there was a terrible screech of tearing wood and the world came loose.

'HOLD ON!' Sam cried.

She and Goose clung to the crow's nest. The sea rushed up to meet them as the mast fell like the great tree it had once been.

They slammed to a stop, barely an arm's length above the water.

The mast was sticking out, horizontal, over the ocean like a broken limb. Sam and Goose clung to it, their world turned sideways.

The ocean churned darkly, tasting their legs like a ravening creature, and Sam's fingers slipped in panic.

'I can't swim!' she whimpered.

The waves undulated hungrily beneath them.

'It's all right,' Goose panted, grabbing her. 'Come on!'

They inched along the mast towards the ship –

BOOM!

Further chaos broke out aboard the *Splendora*. Another volley of solid thunder made matchsticks of the deck. The air stung with splinters. Sails were aflame in horrifying banners of fire.

Sam peered over Goose's shoulder to see Capitano Boniface dragging a snow-white flag from a chest.

'WE SURRENDER!' he cried, waving at the *Invincible* like a drowning man. 'HOLD YOUR FIRE!'

A cannonball caught him in the stomach. In a blur, Capitano Boniface went over the side of the ship.

Goose and Sam stared in horror at the boiling crater in the sea where the capitano had fallen. They screamed his name, trying to call him back from his fate. But Capitano Boniface did not reappear above the surface and the water closed over.

'He – he's –' Goose croaked. He couldn't say the word.

The mast squealed. It was uprooting itself from the ship. 'QUICK!' Sam cried.

They scrambled over the smashed railing to safety. But the moment they set foot on the deck, they realized nowhere on the *Splendora* was safe. A swarm of navy-blue sailors swung across the sky, boarding the ship with cutlasses drawn. The crew of the *Splendora* were quickly overcome by the admiral's men. They were caught in iron chains and hurled into the sea, disappearing beneath the waves after their capitano.

Goose and Sam fled, scrambling over ruined rigging and under falling crossbeams. But they reached the dead end of the stern and there was nowhere further to flee.

They ducked for cover and peered over the bulwark. Admiral Ransom stood on the prow of the *Invincible*, directing the attack. He was terrible in his spotless finery, his medals flashing fearsome in the flames. The *Invincible* was a calm reflection of the devastated *Splendora*, separated only by a narrow chasm of sea.

'Find the cargo!' the admiral called across the water. 'I want every valuable chest brought aboard my ship!'

Sam and Goose watched in helpless horror as English sailors carried dozens of chests over to the admiral, who counted every one that came aboard. The *Splendora* was being robbed of her riches.

Admiral Ransom yelled orders to a sailor, who began daubing a word across the deck in paint as red as blood. It was the same scarlet word Sam and Goose had seen on the burnt carcass of the ruined ship *Innocenze*: TROUBLEMAKERS.

'*He's* the one raiding the ships!' Goose spluttered in disbelief, craning to stare at his treacherous hero. 'And he's framing the Troublemakers for it all!'

'Very professional system,' Sam said grimly.

The admiral jerked round, his terrible glare locking on Sam and Goose.

'There's two hiding back there!' he yelled, pointing. 'Kill them!'

A pair of sailors in navy-blue suits charged towards the stern.

'Quick!' Sam gasped, pulling Goose backwards.

But there was nowhere left to run. They whirled round, ready to fight as the sailors closed in —

'*Ig!*' Goose yelled.

One of the sailors skidded to a stop, astonished horror warping his face.

'Goose!' he gaped. '*Goose?*'

It was Ignatius Bootmaker, swamped in the dark blue uniform of the Royal Navy.

The Bootmaker brothers stared at each other. Then the second sailor lunged for Goose, swishing his blade.

'NO!' Ignatius bellowed.

He launched himself at his crew mate, who came crashing down, his cutlass slashing a deadly stripe in the air barely a hair's breadth from Goose's chest. Ignatius wrestled the sailor to the deck, fighting for the cutlass.

With a tearing *creeeeeeeeak* above them, the mizzenmast came loose.

Sam kicked the cutlass – it spun away across the deck and scythed into the sea.

There was a swoosh of flame and falling timber as the mast came down between Goose and his brother.

'JUMP SHIP!' Ignatius bellowed, struggling mightily to subdue his crew mate. 'It's your only hope! I can't keep him back!'

Goose turned to Sam.

'I can't swim!' Sam mewled, terror in her eyes.

'It'll be all right,' Goose promised, taking her hand and squeezing it tight. 'We go on three. One –'

'Two –'

'THREE!'

CHAPTER 32

The Troublemakers' cutlasses fell, along with their faces.
They had approached the distant *Splendora* with the same relish as scrumpers sneaking through an apple orchard with eyes on a ripe round fruit. However, as they stole closer, they glimpsed the flash of fire, heard the report of cannons and saw the tallest mast fall into the sea.

'Someone else got to her first!' gasped Dagger Dauntless.

By the time the Troublemakers reached the ship, ready to make the trouble they were famous for, the *Splendora* was a smouldering wreck, half sunk in the churning waves. A distant ship was shrinking on the northern horizon.

Thorn Lawless cursed. 'The *Splendora* was full of fine Venetian lace! It would have been perfect for our next batch of Trouble! I was going to sew Turbidus seeds into the shawls and send them in time for Lady de Sneer's next tea party!'

'We should go aboard and see if there's anything left,' Never suggested. 'To scavenge.'

Thorn spat on the deck. 'PAH! Like vultures gathering scraps after the battle.'

The crew rallied round Thorn, making sympathetic piratical noises.

But Dagger Dauntless did not. She pushed her way through to the rail to gaze at the smouldering ship being rocked in a final lullaby by the sea. She stared at the charred deck, the shattered rigging, the cannon-scarred hull.

No survivors.

Then she saw a red word scrawled across the deck. It sent a cloud across the blank blue sky of her mind. She had seen this before: a name painted on a different sinking ship.

TROUBLEMAKERS

'*We* did this!' Dagger Dauntless cried, turning to the Troublemakers.

'How could we have done this?' Thorn sneered. 'We saw it happen!'

'But . . . but the Troublemakers are the ones r-responsible,' Dagger stammered. 'That's what everyone says . . .'

She trailed away uncertainly as Thorn fixed her with those fiery eyes.

'Who's *everyone*?' Thorn whispered. 'You don't know *anyone*, Dagger. Except us.'

'The Troublemakers are to blame . . .' Dagger insisted. 'Look!'

She pointed at the word, a red smear on the blackened deck. Several pirates muttered uneasily as they saw their own name on the ruined ship, like an artist's signature proudly scrawled across a picture of pure destruction.

Dagger's hat was beginning to make her head very hot. It was too heavy, crushing the thoughts trying to grow in her mind. She tried to pull it off, yanking at the buckle under her chin, but Thorn held it tight to her head.

'Are you with us or against us?' Thorn growled.

'With you,' Dagger said.

Thorn stared so hard that Dagger was sure she was trying to see her thoughts through her eyes.

Dagger looked back at the shipwreck, simply to escape the extreme discomfort of being stared at by someone with flames where their pupils should be.

She saw a movement in the water, near the stern. There was someone clinging to a piece of the shattered mast . . . No! There were two people.

'Survivors!' Dagger yelled, pointing. 'Floating on some wreckage!'

'Fish 'em out!' Never commanded.

Soon there were two human-sized sausages wrapped in sailcloth wriggling at the feet of the pirate queen.

She poked one with her toe and it called her a rude word.

The other one thrashed around, nearly wriggling itself right off the deck into the sea, but Thorn put her foot on it.

'We're getting into the business of kidnapping, aren't we?' Thorn Lawless grinned. 'Finally guilty of what we've always been accused of.'

'Lmm ooua sss!' the wordier sausage demanded.

'Turn 'em loose,' Thorn ordered. Then she added in a louder voice, 'ANY TROUBLE AND YOU CAN SKEWER 'EM!'

The Troublemakers unrolled their prisoners so quickly they were sent tumbling across the deck. The boy sat up indignantly, staring around, and the girl leaped to her feet at once, looking a little dizzy.

'It's them!' the boy yelped. 'My plan worked!'

Dagger frowned at them both. Fuzzy thoughts were forming on the horizon of her mind like clouds in vague shapes.

'What have ya done with Cordelia Hatmaker?' the girl demanded, staring fiercely up at the craggy form of Vinegar Jim.

Thorn Lawless let out a nasty laugh. Dagger joined in with the laughing, as it helped to chase the clouds out of her head. All around her, the Troublemakers snickered.

'Don't laugh at us, Troublemakers!' the boy said stoutly. 'We know you've got her somewhere. We demand to be taken to Cordelia *right this minute*!'

Dagger felt a strange prickle every time she heard the name Cordelia. It sounded like a good name – a bright, magical, valiant name. The kind of person it would be good to be.

She was about to ask these two children about the sort of person who belonged to a name like Cordelia, but, before she could, Thorn stalked up to them.

'Oh, I'll take you somewhere *right this minute*,' she sneered mockingly, flashing her dagger so it swam like a poisonous silver fish in front of the children's faces. 'The BILGE!'

The boy's face broke open into a growl that was mostly teeth, but the girl staggered sideways in fright, plunging her hands into her pockets as though she was trying to make herself as small as possible.

'N-not the bilge!' she cried.

In a cascade of shimmering drops, something showered from her pockets and spilled on to the deck.

'Oh NO!' she wailed. 'My *sweets*!'

The Troublemakers suddenly had diamonds in their eyes.

'SWEETS!' they roared.

The deck was a mad scramble of pirates as the Troublemakers lunged for the sweets. Dagger chased a skidding sweet across the planks. Skirmishes broke out as Troublemakers fought over the sweets and stuffed them into their mouths.

Dagger dived through a pirate's legs, trapped a sweet under her hand and held it up to the light. It was an amber nugget with an *S* etched into it.

She crammed it in her mouth. It tasted bland and blameless.

But around her the Troublemakers were making dreadful faces and groaning.

'UUUUGH!'

'SO BITTER!'

'IT'S A TRICK!'

'WE'VE BEEN POISONED!'

Dagger sucked her sweet curiously while her comrades clutched their throats and spat slimy nuggets on to the deck.

'I'VE BEEN A BAD BOY!' Never wailed.

'STEALING IS WRONG!' Tabitha wept. 'AND WE'VE DONE *SO MUCH STEALING*!'

'WE'VE MADE SUCH TROUBLE!' Jim moaned.

'STEALING AND ROBBING AND THIEVING!' Billy pounded his chest.

The Troublemakers were a-frenzy, clutching their faces in shame, bent double with remorse. Even Thorn Lawless's face was puckered, as though all the sharp things she had ever said were bitter in her mouth.

'AND LOOK WHAT WE DID TO CORDELIA!' Annie burst out.

Dagger swung round – that name again!

'*Where is she?*' Goose yelled.

'Take us to her now!' Sam demanded.

Goose and Sam – those were the names of the boy and the girl! But how did Dagger know that?

She could feel thoughts growing in her mind, trying to climb out of the dark. She peered at Goose and Sam, pulling the buckle under her chin, her hat getting heavier every second.

Goose and Sam stared back.

'Cor?' Sam whispered.

Dagger knew these two people in front of her – they were important. They were *very* important. *They were friends.*

The fire in Dagger's wits and the clammy coldness of the hat were fighting a fierce battle, lashed tight together. She was rejecting the forgetting; something erupted like an oak tree from the middle of her mind.

It grew, spreading its branches in a sudden sunlight of remembering. She could feel the hat coming apart on top of her head: it burst at the seams, feathers fell away, Rockface Barnacles tumbled in chunks around her shoulders.

'It's ME!' Dagger yelled. 'I'M CORDELIA HATMAKER!'

CHAPTER 33

Goose and Sam's expressions transformed into ones of disbelief as the hat fell in pieces from Cordelia's head.

She felt her face grow smooth as the hat, along with the last of the barnacles, fell to the deck. She kicked the remains of the tricorn overboard, sending them splashing into the sea.

'*Cor!*'

'It *is* you!'

Sam and Goose bounded forward, enveloping Cordelia in a hug so tight she could barely breathe.

'Is Father with you?' she asked, voice muffled. She broke out of the hug to peer anxiously into the sea around the sinking ship.

'He's safe, back on St Freerest,' Sam assured her.

'You looked so . . . craggy!' Goose touched Cordelia's cheek with a tentative finger.

Sam grinned. 'Quite a scary pirate you make!'

'It's the hats — some kind of barnacle,' Cordelia began explaining. But she quickly became distracted; the sweet in her mouth was turning horribly bitter. With her memories returning like birds in a great murmuration, a recollection of something bad also darted into her mind. Guilt twisted her stomach. *London. All that trouble!*

She spat the sweet out, but it had left a nasty taste in her mouth.

'Scruples!' said Sam, smiling. 'I had them in my pocket! Who'd have thought somefing so small would defeat the dreaded Troublemakers?'

Scattered on the deck around them, Troublemakers lay clawing at their tongues and wailing. Smokestack had plunged his head into a barrel, and self-pitying moans were bubbling up through the water. Only Shelly was unaffected, sucking a sweet as she peered curiously at her crew mates.

Their hats had all fallen off in the chaos, and Cordelia saw her friends' eyes widen as they realized the Troublemakers were children.

'There's a lot to explain,' she said. Then, no longer able to stand the horrid taste on her tongue, she burst out, 'I should never have made that Mind-Changing Tricorn for the king! It's *my* fault things went wrong!'

The acrid taste of bitter truths was still on her tongue, so she went on: 'I knew it was wrong and I did it anyway! And the king was going to declare Making free for all, but then I made that Meddling hat and changed *too much* of his mind! I ruined everything!'

The tears that spilled down Cordelia's cheeks were so full of remorse that the nasty taste in her mouth faded away.

Goose handed her his handkerchief stoically.

'And the Troublemakers have done bad things too,' she sniffed. 'It's complicated –'

'But *they're* not the ones who did the *really* bad things!' Goose interrupted. 'It wasn't the Troublemakers ransacking ships and burning them – it was Admiral Ransom!'

Sam and Goose told her how the *Invincible* had ambushed the *Splendora* and the British navy had plundered the ship. Goose's eyes flashed with anger as he recounted how Ignatius had obeyed the admiral's violent orders.

Cordelia was appalled. Admiral Ransom, hero to swooning youths all over the country, upright champion of the British navy, was nothing more than a treacherous thief in a shiny-buttoned suit.

'The Duchess was right,' Cordelia muttered ruefully. 'Sometimes the most dangerous pirates don't even look like pirates at all: they come in disguise, dressed as respectable gentlemen.'

Sam's foot was suddenly seized by Vinegar Jim, who was writhing on the deck.

'How do I stop it tasting so horrible?' he wailed.

'Ya start by saying yer sorry fer the fings ya did!' Sam instructed, shaking her ankle free. 'Like kidnapping Cordelia?'

Jim subsided into mutters, in which the word *sorry* could be frequently heard. Only Thorn lay quiet, clenched on the deck, her mouth a stubborn line as the other Troublemakers' repentant cries of *sorry* rumbled around them.

'I'm sorrier than them all,' Cordelia whispered. 'How can I ever make amends?'

'We'll find a way ta fix it,' Sam said, patting her on the back.

Cordelia nodded; she needed to put it right.

'We have to send word to London about the admiral!' she declared. 'Even if it gives away where I am. We should set a course for St Freerest, so we can –'

'Oh no we shouldn't,' Thorn Lawless growled, squinting up at them. She was still clearly suffering from the effects of the Scruple. 'We're not going to risk getting captured. Next thing we know, we'll be dragged back to Miss Prim.'

'I said I'm *never* going back, remember?' Never added, unfurling himself painfully. 'That's the whole point of my name.'

'But it's the right thing to do!' said Cordelia.

Thorn shrugged. 'I don't care about doing the right thing.'

Uttering this sentence seemed to cause the pirate queen's mouth to sour. She grimaced, spat on the deck and dragged herself over to the wheel.

'Troublemakers, back to the island!' she ordered.

Cordelia wanted to wrest the ship's wheel away from Thorn. But she knew better than to challenge the pirate queen when her mouth was already a twist of bitterness as she scowled at the horizon. Instead, Cordelia led Sam and Goose along to the bow, and explained everything she had learned over the past few days to her increasingly astonished friends.

By the time they had sailed through the skull into the turquoise bay of Soulhaven, Goose and Sam knew the whole strange history of the Troublemakers and the truth about Prudence Oglethorne. They'd even made tentative friends with Shelly.

Cordelia had not wanted to risk being made to walk the plank out to sea, but when the anchor was dropped in the bay, she took her chance to begin a mutiny.

'Listen, Troublemakers!' she cried, climbing up the rigging so she could see them all clearly. 'I need to make amends!'

She was met with a sea of blank stares.

'A mends?' Annie repeated. 'What's a *mends*?'

'It means making things better,' Goose explained. 'Mending things.'

'Aah . . . mends,' Billy said, nodding wisely.

Thorn stood with folded arms, shaking her head. But Cordelia would not be beaten so easily. She knew what she needed to do. Even if it meant being arrested. Even if it meant being locked up in Traitors' Tower.

'I broke the law and I got Making completely banned in Britain. I need to go and face the consequences of what I did, and try to make things better,' she said. 'It's not enough to just send word about the admiral. I need to go back home myself and try my hardest to set things right.'

Thorn opened her mouth to argue, but a noise of objection was already coming from someone else.

'Errr . . . Cordelia . . .' Goose began. 'I don't think you realize how bad things are in London.'

Cordelia turned to her friends. They wore expressions like wet clothes hung on a washing line in the rain: dreary and hopeless.

'How bad is it?' she asked.

'There were ships bringing news,' Sam said. 'With Sir Piers officially the prime minister –'

'He's locked up the Guildhall and taken all the Makers' ingredients,' cut in Goose. 'He's even shut the chocolate houses –'

'Fings are *bad*,' added Sam.

'They're even worse than you realize,' Cordelia whispered. 'Sir Piers has a terrible power in his hands.'

Her eyes were drawn to Shelly, the girl who used to sing with magic before Sir Piers drained it from her.

That man was in charge now.

Cordelia remembered the words he had uttered at Speakers' Corner.

I have found the key to make Britain sensible again.

Those words made horrible sense now: he was going to make Britain sensible by getting rid of all magic – permanently.

And Cordelia's own actions had made him prime minister. He was now in possession of the key to the cage that contained Witloof's scream. He had his hands on an extremely dangerous weapon.

'He has the power to drain the magic out of people,' she explained. 'It's probably only a matter of time before Sir Piers starts draining magic from the Makers. He wants to make everyone sensible *forever*!'

As Goose and Sam gasped, Cordelia's eyes met Thorn's.

'Please let me go,' she begged. 'Sir Piers has *got* to be stopped before it's too late. And we're the only people who know what he's capable of.'

'If my father's in charge, it's – it's nothing but *foolish stupidity* for you to go back,' Thorn hissed. 'Look what he did to Shelly!'

'He wants to do that to everyone,' Cordelia replied. 'He's *got* to be stopped.'

'You're ridiculous,' Thorn sneered. 'No magic is strong enough to fight the power he has now.'

'It takes magic to change the world,' Cordelia said, determined to make Thorn see. 'And *we* are the best magical ingredients we have. Our most powerful magic isn't found in feathers or ribbons or petals or stones: it's in our hearts! I need to take my magic to London and use it to make things better. Please! I've got to try!'

Shelly shuffled across the deck to stand beside Cordelia, Sam and Goose.

'Come back here, Shelly!' Thorn barked.

'I think she agrees with them,' Never said quietly.

Faces turned like sunflowers to Cordelia. Some of the other Troublemakers were wavering.

'I'm the captain, and it's up to me to keep you safe!' Thorn declared, striding across the deck to place herself opposite Cordelia, with the Troublemakers caught between them. 'If we let this Hatmaker off the island, she'll blab, and we'll get caught by the admiral!'

Cordelia opened her mouth to argue, but Thorn shouted over her. 'Besides, why should we care what happens to people back home?'

She held up her hands, shining with the pearly scars from the Malwood cane. Her crew's expressions turned dark as the scars flashed in the sun.

'Never forget – this is how they punished us for Making!' Thorn cried. 'We owe them nothing except revenge!'

The Troublemakers agitated, like thunder's opening rumbles.

'AND –' Thorn grinned bitterly across at Cordelia, Sam and Goose – 'now we've captured *three* Makers to be our teachers!'

The Troublemakers roared triumphantly.

'No!' Cordelia cried.

But her voice was drowned in the storm of feet pounding across the deck. Thorn's eyes were triumphant as every Troublemaker rushed over to her side.

'Let's go ashore to make our own magic!' Thorn roared, and her crew cheered again.

Cordelia, Sam and Goose could only watch as the pirates surged away in a howling pack to the dinghy. The pirate queen drew her cutlass and pointed to it.

'Go ashore, you three,' she ordered. 'I'll be watching you, so don't try to sneak off the island. There'll be no mutiny while I'm captain.'

CHAPTER 34

The next day, Cordelia, Sam and Goose loitered on the beach.

They had sneaked out of the mossy hammocks in the tiny cabin they had been given, and stolen up to the crow's nest early that morning, only to find the sky-sailing boat gone and Tabitha waiting for them.

'We thought you'd try to take the wind-dinghy,' Tabitha said with a grin. 'But Never left for St Freerest at first light, to take a message to the Duchess, to pass on to your father that you're all safe.'

Cordelia was taken aback by this thoughtfulness.

'And Thorn posted me here last night to tell you – what exactly was her message?' Tabitha frowned as she tried to remember it word for word. '*Nice try, Makers, but do you think I'm stupider than a sea-urchin sandwich?*'

Deciding it would be wise not to answer that rhetorical question, Cordelia, Goose and Sam retreated.

'We've got to get to St Freerest somehow,' Cordelia muttered as they descended the mast.

Down on the beach, they eyed the *Trouble*, which lay at anchor in the bay. They, in turn, were being eyed by Billy Bones. Billy lurked behind a palm tree a little way along the beach, smiling shiftily whenever they saw him peering out from behind it.

Thorn had set a watch on the three Makers. Clearly, the pirate queen was determined to cut off every means of escape.

'We can't steer the *Trouble* out of the skull by ourselves,' Goose mused. 'We'd need a crew of at least six experienced sailors.'

'Then first we've got to persuade the most experienced sailor of the lot,' Cordelia said. 'I think I know where we'll find him.'

They found Smokestack exactly where Cordelia expected him to be: sitting on his favourite rock in Tablecloth Glade.

He wore an exalted expression and an elaborate lace-web tiara.

'I don't know how they spin such beauty,' he murmured happily, watching a spider turn a twig into a web-spiralled wand. 'It's miraculous.'

'Smokestack, we were wondering –' Cordelia began.

'Thorn told me you'd ask,' the old pirate interrupted her. 'But you'll never persuade me to sail away with you. When those children first came aboard my ship, their faces were full of a hunger I can't describe. And I saw that hunger slowly fade as we sailed towards this island. I'll never give up on those kids. Not even Thorn.'

He smiled kindly, and Cordelia knew he would never budge. Rather than being frustrated or angry, she was surprised to find that she felt glad. This old pirate, sitting on the rock, quietly watching a magical creature spinning its web, was a sort of craggy guardian angel for the Troublemakers. She was glad they had him.

Smokestack had been so kind to the Troublemakers that, in spite of her difficult relationship with Thorn, Cordelia wanted to give the old man a gift.

She coaxed a spider over to her, took the end of its delicate thread and began to wind it round her hands.

'I know you've got a lot of stories to tell, Smokestack,' she murmured. 'I think these spiders can help you spin your tales into yarn. Tell them your stories as they spin and they'll entwine them into their silk. That way, you can turn your lovely long stories into all sorts of knitted creations.'

Smokestack took the thread from Cordelia. 'Well, where do I start? Ah! The year was 1722 –'

The children walked away up the glade, leaving Smokestack chatting happily to the spider.

'We're running out of escape options,' Cordelia muttered to Sam and Goose as they reached the lagoon.

Before either Sam or Goose could respond, Annie caught up with them.

'Thorn says it's time for lessons. And the choice is between coming along to the workshop quietly or being rolled there by a fungus puffball.'

Looking at the sinister orange puffball trundling after Annie like a strange sort of dog, Cordelia, Sam and Goose decided to go along quietly.

However, when they got to the workshop, Cordelia was not quiet at all.

'Don't you want people to know the truth?' she demanded, striding through the vine curtains as they parted and ignoring the flowers snapping at her. 'Admiral Ransom is doing terrible things and making it look like it's *you* who's doing them!'

'Good!' Thorn sneered, stabbing her needle into the glove she was working on. 'We *want* people to be afraid of what we're capable of.'

'What about the children you left behind at Miss Prim's?' Cordelia added.

Around the workshop, the other Troublemakers shifted uncomfortably, magical ingredients wilting sadly in their hands.

'They had the chance to come with us,' Thorn muttered. 'Not my fault they didn't.'

Her mouth puckered. She was still tasting the bitterness of her regrets, awakened by the Scruples.

'And what about stopping Sir Piers?' Cordelia insisted.

Thorn's expression hardened.

'We're making him feel our wrath,' she snapped.

Cordelia had run out of reasonable reasons.

'What's the point of trying to learn about Making if everything you create makes you unhappy because you can't make it right?' she burst out. '*And* you're giving the Sensibles more reasons to clamp down on magic. You're not making your father feel your wrath; you're playing straight into his hands!'

Thorn dropped the glove she was stitching, and it leaped up and pinched her hard on the nose. She clapped a hand to her face, kicking the glove over the side of the treehouse.

'And you hate everything you create!' Cordelia yelled, her frustration boiling. 'That entire pile of clothes was made by you!'

Sure enough, a huge heap of discarded clothes lay beneath the workshop on the jungle floor, a mess of silk and satin and lace and magic, all tossed furiously over the side by the pirate queen.

For a moment, Cordelia thought Thorn would send her over the edge of the treehouse too. The rage on Thorn's face grew tighter and tighter, ready to explode.

That was when Never walked in.

'Hello!' he said cheerily. Then his face fell, looking from Cordelia to Thorn. 'Oh. What's going on here? Thorn?'

Without answering, Thorn whirled round and ran away into the treehouse. Cordelia thought she heard a sob as the pirate queen disappeared.

'I think she's worried about Rainbow,' Never muttered. 'He's been behaving strangely these last few days.'

Cordelia ignored the squirm of guilt in her belly.

'What's the news from St Freerest?' she asked. 'Did you tell the Duchess about Admiral Ransom's treachery? Will she tell my father?'

Never shook his head.

'She can't,' he said. 'Your father's missing.'

Cordelia's mouth dropped open in shock.

'Why – where –' she began helplessly.

'I told the Duchess everything. She was keeping watch on your father through her telescope at the Kingless . . . *Little Bear* is still anchored in the bay, with two crew working on her. But Captain Hatmaker's gone.'

Cordelia reeled. 'Gone? Just . . . gone?'

Never nodded. 'Last seen yesterday,' he confirmed.

Cordelia backed away from Never, shaking her head. Where could he be? Had he left of his own accord, or been taken prisoner? Was he trying to get to her, or was he on a ship back to England already? How – *why* – had he disappeared? There must be some reason, but trying to decipher it was confusing – troubling –

'Look out!'

Cordelia stepped on to air and went over the edge of the treehouse.

'COR!'

The vines caught her in mid-air, in a dizzy spin of green leaves.

'Please put me down on the ground,' she whispered to them, and they set her gently among the ferns.

'I'm all right!' she called up, seeing Sam and Goose's shocked faces peering over the edge of the deck high above. 'I – I've just got to think for a bit. Going for a walk.'

Cordelia wandered through the jungle. She waded through ferns that reached consoling fronds towards her, noticed lantern flowers flicker into light as she went past, splashed silver water from the lagoon on to her face, and was favoured by a fluttering visitation from a pale gold moth that spiralled comfortingly round her head in the green twilight.

She didn't think she had a destination in mind, until she arrived at the base of the Soulhope Tree, and she realized that she had made her way through the jungle, yearning to lay her hands on its humming bark.

She had never been in greater need of hope.

With her hands pressed against the sturdy trunk and hope surging back into the marrow of her bones, she realized – strangely – how lucky she was. She hoped desperately to be reunited with her father, but there was somebody else on this island who dreaded ever facing their own father again.

How lucky Cordelia was to love and rely upon someone so much that she felt that all the problems of the world would be solved if she could reach him. Thorn's world, on the other hand, would be destroyed if her own father ever reached her.

Cordelia found Thorn in the Belly Cave.

Rainbow lay in a languid S over the glowing gems in the middle of the cave. He was pale yellow, a sickly, worrisome colour.

Thorn crouched beside him, a hand on his heaving side. Cordelia had never seen her look so vulnerable as she anxiously checked the Sea Dragon's eyes and combed his whiskers with her fingers.

She hesitated at the cave entrance and Thorn's whole body tautened.

'Go away,' Thorn muttered. 'I've got nothing to say to you.'

But Cordelia did have something to say.

'I'm sorry,' she began, speaking to Thorn's hunched back. 'I didn't mean to be unkind about the things you make. It was wrong of me and I'm very sorry.'

'It's true, though.' Thorn's voice came out small. 'I can never make anything good any more. My hands are scarred.'

Thorn's back trembled, and she wrapped her arms around herself in a forlorn hug. Cordelia crouched down beside her.

'The power of Making starts in your heart, Thorn,' Cordelia told her. 'It's there waiting for you to be brave enough to find it.'

Troublemaker turned desolate eyes to Hatmaker.

'I don't know if I can. I've grown so many thorns around it,' she whispered.

Cordelia put a hand on Thorn's arm. 'You don't have to do it alone.'

She wondered if the Scruple sweets were still affecting Thorn; her mouth was a dam desperately trying to hold things in. The pirate queen glared at the Hatmaker for a long moment, and the feelings she seemed desperate to try to stop coming out of her mouth welled up in her eyes.

'I'm *sorry*!' Thorn burst out. 'I wish I could have protected every kid at Miss Prim's, but I couldn't make them come with us – they were too scared! And I can't let the others get hurt now. And I can't let *you* get hurt either. I'm only stopping you going back to London because I'm trying to protect you from my father, the way I couldn't protect Shelly –'

These words broke over them like a downpour after a scorching day.

'I'm sorry we kidnapped you and I'm sorry I was horrible to you! I hated you, because I was jealous. I wanted so desperately to be like you,' Thorn admitted. 'And I – I just want us to be *friends*!'

The word *friends* – *friends* – *friends* – echoed around the cave, returning to Cordelia and Thorn from every direction, like a good spell Thorn had cast on them.

Cordelia smiled at her. 'I'd like to be friends too.'

Thorn's mouth seemed – at last – to have been released from the bitter shrivel of the Scruples. She could finally smile back.

'And I understand now that you're trying to protect me,' Cordelia said gently. 'Thank you.'

These words seemed to cause a quiet magic somewhere within the pirate queen. She threw her arms round Cordelia.

For a moment, the Hatmaker was astonished, as Thorn Lawless hugged her with the same ferocity with which she did everything. Cordelia hugged her back, knowing she had made the fiercest of friends.

The light in the cave brightened as Rainbow suddenly glowed orange.

'What's happening to him?' Thorn cried, throwing herself down beside the Sea Dragon, who was rapidly turning purple. 'Is he dying?'

Cordelia watched in concern as the Sea Dragon writhed strangely, apparently performing some kind of painful dance. Rainbow was turning from indigo to black, changing into night like the sky. His wings flapped and his mouth opened, revealing winking fangs.

'What's wrong, Rainbow?' Thorn sobbed.

She threw her arms round the creature's scaly neck.

'Thorn, look!' Cordelia tugged her shoulder, pointing.

In the middle of the night-black coils of the Sea Dragon, a pale orb shone like a moon.

'He – he's laid an egg!' gasped Thorn.

Cordelia and Thorn stared in amazement at this startling miracle.

'That's why you were behaving so strangely!' Thorn breathed, stroking Rainbow gently on the head. 'You were getting ready to lay an egg! I – I suppose you're not a *he* after all – you're a *she*!'

Rainbow curled herself snugly round the egg and settled down with an expression of proud satisfaction on her ancient face. Around her, the gems studding the ceiling of the cave twinkled.

BOOM!

The air shuddered.

For a moment, Cordelia thought the egg was already hatching. But Thorn whirled round and clapped a hand over her mouth, pointing.

From the cave entrance, they could see out over the island and across the bay.

The sky had come together with the sea – it was causing a storm beyond the rocks. Lightning slashed across the murderous clouds.

A shining lance tore through the churning grey, and a golden-haired knight appeared, floating weirdly above the sea, before a blunt prow broke through the mist.

A hulking ship was sailing straight for Soulhaven.

Thorn's face suddenly wore the expression of the frightened child she had vowed never to be again.

The ship was the *Invincible*.

CHAPTER 35

Cordelia and Thorn bounded through the jungle, Turbidus Vines swooping them up off their feet so they ran on air.

They clattered on to the treehouse prow jutting from the jungle high over the beach to see the *Invincible* surge from the skeleton mouth into the bay. It was sundown and the sea was like a bloodbath, stained red.

'DOUBLE, DOUBLE!' Thorn roared, and the other Troublemakers came running.

'I – I thought this island was *impossible* to find unless you're being hunted!' Cordelia gasped. 'But Ransom's a *hunter*!'

Everyone converged on the deck in time to see the *Invincible* drop anchor with a crash. The *Trouble* bobbed like a toy ship beside the massive bulk of the naval galleon.

'What shall we do?' Never wailed. 'It's an invasion!'

'The admiral's terribly dangerous!' Goose cried.

'We need our hats!' Annie yelled. 'To make us look old and fierce!'

Before she could rush away to fetch hers, Thorn caught her arm.

'We don't need to pretend to be something we're not,' she said. 'No disguises. We fight as ourselves.'

A swarm of sailors poured from the *Invincible*, coming ashore in skiffs. Among them, glinting with medals, loomed Admiral Ransom.

A hundred sailors landed their boats on the sand.

The admiral stepped ashore with the ruthless swagger of a man coming to conquer.

'TROUBLEMAKERS!' the admiral boomed, striding up the beach. 'SURRENDER!'

Cordelia gripped the prow as the admiral glared up at them. He was terrible with medals, each a glinting memento of some frightful violence he had achieved.

'WE WILL NEVER SURRENDER!' Thorn bellowed.

'NEVER!' Cordelia yelled.

Their defiance was caught and amplified by the rebels around them.

'**NEVER!**' everybody roared in one voice.

In answer, the admiral raised his arm and let it drop.

BOOM!

The report of cannon fire echoed off the rocks.

A blast of smoke burst from the side of the *Invincible*.

The *Trouble* lurched in the water and dipped in a clumsy curtsey.

Smokestack arrived, puffing, on to the prow just in time to see the ship that had carried him over oceans sinking beneath the water. The jester figurehead was still grinning as though it was all a great joke.

In the shocked silence that followed, the admiral reached a hand into his jacket. Cordelia was sure he was going to produce some dreadful weapon –

Admiral Ransom pulled out a paper scroll.

'I have here a letter of marque,' he announced. 'Do any of you know what a letter of marque is?'

Cordelia didn't know, but Goose made a noise like bellows inflating.

'It's a licence giving you permission to commit – commit – PIRACY!' Goose blustered in disgust. 'On behalf of the British government.'

The admiral tilted his chin up to look at Goose.

'Exactly right!' He sneered, before turning to Thorn. 'This letter is from your father, Prudence.'

Cordelia saw Thorn shudder.

'He sent me to fetch you,' Admiral Ransom explained. 'And this letter gives me permission to do whatever is necessary to bring you home.'

'It wasn't *necessary* for you to sink all those ships!' Cordelia spat. 'And drown innocent crews!'

The admiral shrugged. '*I* deemed it necessary. And, according to this letter, I am allowed to keep all the riches I might happen to acquire on my mission to save Prudence Oglethorne.'

The smile he flashed was full of the kind of teeth that tear things apart.

'SHE DOESN'T NEED SAVING!' Tabitha screamed. 'SHE'S ALREADY SAVED HERSELF!'

Admiral Ransom raised an eyebrow.

'I have you cornered now, Prudence.' He smirked. 'And I will burn every inch of this island to get to you, if you make that necessary too.'

There was a tense silence; the space between navy and Troublemakers bristled with impending violence. Then a large round-bodied bird with stout wings and splayed feet shuffled on to the beach, blinking curiously at the shiny man towering on the sand.

'No!' Never groaned quietly. 'Dodo – *go away*!'

'*Hide*,' Cordelia urged the bird desperately.

But the dodo shuffled up to the admiral, tilting its head inquisitively at this strange glinting vision. He uttered a polite honk.

Cordelia's heart squeezed with fear for the fine-feathered creature peering innocently at the crushing might of the British navy.

The admiral pounced, snatching the bird by one leg, swinging it into the air. It honked frantically, flapping its short wings.

'NO!' Thorn cried.

'PUT THE DODO DOWN!' Cordelia demanded.

'*I will visit extinction upon this island!*' the admiral bellowed.

More dodos, alarmed by the distressed honks of their fellow, came bustling down the beach. Cordelia's nails bit into her palms as she turned to the others.

'We've *got* to stop him,' she gasped. 'He's going to destroy everything!'

'He has actual cannons that fire cannonballs!' Never protested. 'All we have are exploding coconuts and some vines!'

Cordelia was forced to agree that cannons were more dangerous than vines. But her eyes met Thorn's, which burned with righteous fire.

Thorn's hands clenched on Cordelia's shoulders.

'Look after them for me, Cordelia,' Thorn whispered.

And the pirate queen leaped over the side of the prow, into the arms of the vines, and was carried down to the beach.

'Thorn – WAIT!'

'*What're you doing?*'

The pirate queen landed on the sand in front of the admiral.

Thorn drew her sword – a stripe of silver through the air – and laid it at the admiral's feet.

*Thorn drew her sword – a stripe of silver through
the air – and laid it at the admiral's feet.*

'I surrender!' she declared, loudly and clearly. 'And now you have me, you don't have the right to wreak any more destruction. You have to leave the island immediately and take me with you – back to my father.'

Cordelia was dizzy with shock. She stared at Thorn – the girl who had only just become her friend – standing straight-backed in front of the towering admiral.

Thorn was giving herself up to save Soulhaven.

CHAPTER 36

Admiral Ransom signalled, and Thorn was seized by sailors and tied up in ropes.

'Very brave, Prudence,' the admiral drawled. 'And you've saved me a lot of unnecessary trouble.'

Cordelia and the Troublemakers watched, stunned, from the treehouse.

'I won't run!' Thorn declared as the ropes were knotted at her wrists. Her voice was steady, but, even from up in the treehouse, Cordelia could hear fear just under the surface of the words. 'You don't need to tie me up.'

The admiral tested the ropes.

'It's insurance, Prudence,' he explained. 'In case you change your mind.'

'I won't,' Thorn announced. 'I'm a girl of my word.'

A sailor ran forward carrying a sack and Admiral Ransom thrust the struggling dodo into it.

'Wh-what are you doing?' Thorn stammered, as the admiral tied the sack closed. 'You have to leave the island unharmed now that you've got me. You can't take that dodo!'

But the expression that stretched the admiral's face was cruel as he passed the wriggling sack to a sailor.

'There's an old mariner's myth that this island is home to a dreadful beast!' the admiral announced to his men. 'I want its head as a trophy!'

Cordelia was horrified. *He must mean the Sea Dragon!*

'I forgot to mention the other order your father gave me, Prudence,' the admiral continued, turning back to Thorn. 'The last thing Sir Piers said to me before I departed London was . . . *Kill all the other Troublemakers.*'

These words fell like an executioner's axe.

'NO!' Thorn screamed.

The admiral yelled, 'MEN, ATTACK!'

Ranks of sailors broke apart and stormed up the beach, producing ropes and nets and knives and sacks. Smoke exploded from their guns as they shot at the dodos. The birds scattered in a flurry of panic and feathers.

'NO!' Cordelia's voice was drowned in the yells of the Troublemakers and the squawks of frightened creatures.

Sailors swarmed beneath them, trying to get up to the

treehouse. More streamed into the jungle, swords slashing paths through the plants.

'The admiral lied!' Goose yelled.

'We've gotta save Thorn!' shouted Sam.

Cordelia turned to the Troublemakers – their faces blazed with outrage and fear, but she could see roaring courage alive in their eyes. Thorn had told Cordelia to look after them; they were her responsibility now. Cordelia turned to the youngest few.

'Annie, Billy, Tabitha – hide!' she ordered. 'You're too young to fight!'

Outrage exploded from all three.

'*NO!*'

'*We want to fight!*'

'*We've got to help!*'

Even Shelly shook her head in a hell-bent kind of way.

Cordelia felt frustration squeeze her from the inside out.

'You're *too young*!' she shouted at them. 'I'm trying to stop you getting hurt!'

Then she suddenly remembered her own furious objections to her father's order to hide: *I can fight! I'm strong!*

It was enough to change her mind.

'All right. But *promise me* you'll *be careful*!'

There was no more time to waste. Cordelia turned with a battle cry.

'TROUBLEMAKERS, ATTACK!'

With that, she launched herself into the vines.

The world was a blur of green and war screams – then Cordelia found herself set back down on the planks of the prow again. Around her, other Troublemakers were being firmly returned to the treehouse.

'No!' Cordelia panted. 'I need to get down to the beach!'

Below, sailors slashed and hacked, scrambling up the trees, trying to reach them. Thorn was being bundled into a rowing boat.

Cordelia threw herself at the Turbidus Vines. 'Take me down to the beach, please!' she gasped, in as polite a voice as she could muster.

But the vines replaced her firmly on the deck, catching the other Troublemakers and returning them all to the safety of the treehouse.

'I'm trying to help! I'm trying to save things!' Cordelia yelled. 'Please!'

She hurled herself into the vines again and again, but each time they caught her and set her back down.

'The vines are stopping us getting in harm's way!' Never panted, as he was returned to the deck beside Cordelia. 'They're trying to keep us safe!'

Indeed, thrashing and writhing around the trees, Turbidus Vines were smacking back sailors attempting to climb them. Men were knocked to the ground, grabbed and hurled, tumbled across the jungle floor. Bushes and fungus puffballs bowled through the trees, flattening sailors and pushing them down the beach into the sea. Sailors plunging through the jungle with armfuls of ripped-up flowers were knocked down and swept away.

The island was fighting the invaders.

But the sailors kept on coming. And they came with knives and guns.

The air exploded with acrid smoke around Cordelia's head.

'DUCK!' she screamed, pulling Tabitha and Jim to the deck beside her, flat on their bellies.

'We can't get down and they can't get up!' Sam cried.

'So let's chuck things at 'em!' Billy bellowed.

'To the workshop!' yelled Never.

Cordelia led the way, crawling across the treehouse, avoiding the crack and hiss of gunshots that exploded from below.

Sailors were heading in every direction. There were too many of them for the vines to stop their advance. Some, hacking footholds in the trees, were smacked back, but others surged onwards, deeper into the jungle, ripping up plants, snatching birds and butterflies out of the air.

The admiral sent a group of men ahead of him and carved his way through their wake. As they were taken out by tumbling shrubs and whipping vines, he ploughed forward, his drawn sword sharp for slaying. Cordelia spied his tall, wide figure stalking through the glade below.

'He's going to try to kill Rainbow!' Cordelia gasped. 'We've got to stop him!'

They reached the workshop and the Troublemakers seized every ingredient they could, pelting them at the sailors.

'Put trouble in your fingertips!' Cordelia instructed, hurling snapping shells at sailors hacking handholds in a tree trunk.

The Troublemakers rained chaos on to the heads of the invaders. Sailors cowered as they were met with a volley of chomping flowers and exploding coconuts. Vines thrashed and Sun Eaters divebombed them, sending them splaying in navy blurs to the ground.

The admiral was stopped in his tracks as several Petrifying Parrots landed on his hat. Tabitha took the opportunity to shower him with needling splinters of lightning. The parrots fled in a red blur and the admiral slashed furiously at the crackling air, but found he couldn't fight lightning with a sword.

'Somebody kill those Troublemakers!' Admiral Ransom roared, desperately hitting himself to extinguish the tiny lightning fires catching on his uniform. 'NOW!'

'We can't reach 'em, sir!' a sailor yelled, as his crew mates were hurled to the ground around him.

'Then do what we always do!' the admiral snapped. 'BURN EVERYTHING!'

'AYE, AYE!'

Cordelia emptied a sack of thunderclouds over the sailors, then hurled a Fungus-Glove that knocked the admiral's hat off. But the Troublemakers were running out of things to throw.

'What do we do when we're out of ingredients?' Smokestack panted.

Cordelia looked around for an answer and saw a blazing light coming down through the trees.

'It's Rainbow!' Never gasped.

The Sea Dragon was prowling down the hillside, swiping sailors aside with her tail. She was ready to defend her home, wearing the colours of righteous fury in her scales. As they saw her, sailors quailed.

'The – the beast of the island!'

'It's a monster!'

'RUN!'

The admiral stood like a rock as his crew rushed away. The Sea Dragon was fearsome to behold – the kind of sight that shrinks your guts and narrows your mind to a single point of pure fear. Her fangs flashed in the firelight as she roared at the admiral. Cordelia's belly blazed with something more ancient than pride, knowing they had this ferocious saviour on their side.

'FOUL BEAST!' the admiral yelled. But his voice was as pale as a surrender flag beneath the roaring fury of the Sea Dragon.

The Troublemakers marvelled as the Sea Dragon reared,

her wings bursting in a mighty banner from her back. She was poised, ready to strike. The admiral's sword drooped in his hand and he let out a whimper.

Then a terrible rending noise – like hope being ripped from a heart – tore through the jungle.

The Soulhope Tree crashed through the canopy, felled by the axes of sailors. Even Rainbow turned to look as birds fled their nests, screaming in distress.

The whole jungle grew darker.

'HA!'

Cordelia whirled round.

The world folded and failed as the Sea Dragon slumped to the jungle floor.

In the moment of distraction, the admiral had plunged his sword into Rainbow. The lights of her scales dimmed to darkness as the Sea Dragon's lifeless body crumpled at Admiral Ransom's feet.

'VICTORY IS MINE!' he gloated.

A crackle reached Cordelia's ears, sending a primal shudder through her soul.

The men were using what men have always used to subdue nature. It was fire, dancing a path of destruction through the jungle, licking at the trunks of the trees, gobbling plants in its greedy mouth.

The dreadful smell of burning hope twisted through the twilight.

And suddenly the island was overrun – sailors slashed through the greenery, uprooting ferns and ripping through glades, dragging the felled Soulhope Tree back to their ship. The Troublemakers stood, smothered by hopelessness, as the fire grew like a terrible symphony below them.

Cordelia looked around desperately.

Sailors were scrambling up to the treehouse now, hacking handholds in tree trunks and clambering up limp Turbidus Vines like ropes. The island was giving up the fight, its heart and soul both defeated.

Soon the treehouse would be swarmed by the enemy, who had orders to kill every Troublemaker.

'We've got to go!' Cordelia yelled. 'They're coming!'

They could not escape downwards, into the rising tide of fire and knives.

The treehouse shuddered as sailors thumped on to the decks.

'Go where?' Never wailed.

Cordelia had one idea left. She ran along the treehouse, yelling, 'Everyone, follow me!'

It was their only hope of escape; there was nowhere to go but up.

She skidded to a stop at the bottom of the mast and sent everyone scrambling up towards the crow's nest.

'Go on, missy!' Smokestack urged. 'I'll come last and cut off the rigging with my cutlass behind me.'

Cordelia threw herself upwards and Smokestack followed, sawing at the ropes below his feet to slow down the enemy.

It was crowded on the crow's nest. They could hear the shouts of sailors below, on their trail like bloodhounds on a scent.

'The wind-dinghy's our only escape route,' Cordelia panted. 'Everybody, in!'

Night was spreading like spilled ink across the sky. The lights of St Freerest glimmered distantly.

'I don't know if we'll get there with so many passengers,' Never hissed into Cordelia's ear as the Troublemakers climbed aboard. 'It's only built for one or two!'

The boat dipped as Sam and Goose swung themselves in beside the pirates.

'St Freerest isn't where I'm proposing we go,' Cordelia told him.

'Then where?'

'They're coming up!' Smokestack called. 'I'll hold 'em off!'

'I say we go back to London!' Cordelia told everyone.

'Back to London?' the Troublemakers gasped in disbelief.

'But how do we get to London?' Billy wailed. 'We've got no ship!'

Cordelia clapped a bracing hand on his shoulder.

'We *smuggle* ourselves.'

CHAPTER 37

'They're coming up the mast!'

Smokestack was the only passenger left to climb aboard.

'Hurry!' Cordelia reached out to pull him into the wind-dinghy.

But the old pirate did not take her hand. Instead, he unhooked the mooring rope. 'I'll fight these villains off!' he told her. 'Go!'

'Smokestack, NO!' Never called.

'I'd do anything for you Troublemakers,' Smokestack said with a smile, and let go of the rope.

A snarling sailor burst on to the crow's nest and Smokestack shoved the wind-dinghy, sending the Troublemakers plunging over the dark jungle. Cordelia whipped round to catch a final glimpse of Smokestack, valiantly fighting several sailors on the crow's nest behind them.

Never jerked the rudder and they bucked, lurching over the topmost branches of a jacaranda.

'I can't control it – too many aboard!' he gasped.

'Everyone, lean hard to starboard!' Goose instructed, throwing his weight across the vessel, pulling Shelly and Jim with him.

The sky boat swooped in an arc as the weight shifted, and then – in a soaring miracle like wind beneath wings – they were sailing through the air.

Far below, Cordelia saw the admiral emerge on to the beach, a pearl-white orb clutched in his hands: the Sea Dragon's egg! Cordelia clapped a hand over her mouth to stop herself from exclaiming in fury.

The Troublemakers slipped silently overhead, watching sailors load their boats with magical plunder from the island: piles of crystal wrenched from the bedrock, wriggling sacks and buckets of shells, nets crammed with insects and birds. Sun Eaters swirled through the sky, obscuring the Troublemakers from sight as they glided towards the towering masts of the *Invincible*.

Cordelia began to worry that the splash they would make landing in the water would alert the enemy to their location. She saw the admiral's cabin, the lit windows casting a bar of golden light across the darkening sea. A huge lantern hung from the stern on an iron frame.

'Steer for that!' she said, pointing.

'Hard to port!' Goose whispered.

Everyone leaned and the boat swerved.

'I've got it!'

Sam stretched across the air and grasped the lantern frame in one hand. Cordelia managed to grab Sam's ankles just before she slipped overboard, and suddenly the wind-dinghy and the *Invincible* were linked together, first by two girls, and then by the mooring rope.

Sam jemmied open a window, using a shard of moonbeam like a crowbar, and the Troublemakers piled into the admiral's private cabin.

It was full of stolen treasures: skulls were mounted on the walls alongside the stuffed heads of tusked creatures and splay-winged birds skewered through their hearts. There were chests overflowing with gold and jewels heaped against the walls.

'Blimey . . .' Sam muttered. 'He's been busy.'

Cordelia inspected the wide mahogany desk covered with maps and papers, as Never — last out of the wind-dinghy — unhitched the mooring rope, quietly tore the silk sail free and hopped through the window as the boat fell into the water and sank. He closed the window, leaving no sign that anyone had used it as an unconventional entrance into the *Invincible*.

'We've gotta find somewhere ta hide!' Sam whispered, peeking out of the door. 'Let's go – coast's clear!'

But a piece of paper on the desk caught Cordelia's eye. Beneath the words *FOR THE RANSOM WING* was a list of very rare magical creatures and plants.

'The Ransom Wing?' Cordelia muttered. 'What's that?'

One of the items on the list – *the head of a monster for plinth* – made her frown with faint recognition. But Shelly pulled her arm as the others milled anxiously by the door. There was no time to waste.

Cordelia, Goose, Sam and the Troublemakers slipped out of the admiral's cabin, crept along a low corridor and came across a ladder leading down. On the level below, they found themselves in a dark passageway striped with heavy cannons. The air was pungent with gunpowder.

Above, they heard the thud of boots, the bark of orders, and curse words being hurled like hand grenades.

Cordelia saw Never's teeth glint in the moonlight as he grinned.

'Thorn's aboard,' he said.

They quickly found another ladder leading down, down, down into the bowels of the ship. At the bottom, the walls curved in close, and it smelled of pitch dark and rotten water. They were almost at the bilge.

'There'll be a storage hold – here!' Goose hissed triumphantly, pulling open a trapdoor with a creak.

As Cordelia lowered herself gingerly through the dark hatch, Sam pulled a stick of moonlight out of her pocket and threw it down after her. By the cool glow of the moonlight, Cordelia saw a long, low space stretching the length of the ship, crammed with crates and stuffed with sacks. It would make a good hiding place.

So, while the admiral and his men dragged the plunder on to the *Invincible*, Cordelia, Sam, Goose and six Troublemakers bundled themselves below as illegal cargo.

The stowaways shut the trapdoor, huddled around the bar of moonlight and met each other's eyes in the pale silver glow.

'We should rescue Thorn now!' Annie declared gallantly.

But Cordelia shook her head. 'They'll know we're here if we do that,' she said. 'We'll have to wait and help her in London.'

'She's strong,' said Billy. 'She'll give the admiral hell all the way back.'

'Make yourselves comfortable,' Goose suggested, being the expert when it came to stowing away. 'We've got a long journey ahead of us.'

The sacks were full of fruits that had been ripped from vines by the sailors, so there was plenty to eat. And they discovered that, with a little clambering about on crates and some quiet rearranging of boxes, each could create a fairly comfortable bed for themselves.

Cordelia allocated everybody an emergency hiding place, making sure there were cracks between the crates to clamber into and sacks to cover themselves with, in case anybody came down to inspect this portion of the cargo. She had just finished conducting the first emergency hiding-place drill when they heard the anchor drag along the coral reef deep beneath them.

The *Invincible* was setting sail.

Cordelia wondered what was left of the island they were leaving behind. Her heart ached remembering the distressed wails of the birds and the screams of uprooted trees. The island had been devastated. Its great protector, the Sea Dragon – the descendant of the very creature whose bones had created the island – was dead. Thorn was captured and Smokestack had sacrificed himself so they could escape.

Cordelia lay on her own makeshift bunk in the utter dark, hoping she had made the right decision to bring them all aboard this ship.

They were in the belly of the beast now – and the beast was surging towards London. She heard the music of the sea humming through the hull as the *Invincible* picked up speed, racing out on to the vast plain of the ocean.

Cordelia did not need to open every chest to know that she and the Troublemakers were lying on a small mountain of the admiral's plunder. He must have sunk dozens of ships after collecting their treasures. And she'd seen the mysterious Ransom Wing list on the admiral's desk.

Her fingers tingled, but there was a sad throb in them too: these magical things had been torn cruelly from their rightful places.

Cordelia had a sudden memory of a wide white room full of empty plinths, and the curator Mr Smirke's pride in telling her: *An unnamed benefactor will soon fill this new wing of the museum. He's collecting things from all around the world!*

The dark, twisted scream of that evil metal lump – what remained of Witloof's soul – flashed into her head.

She *had* to rescue Thorn from that dreadful fate.

Suddenly Sam, who was on lookout beside the trapdoor, hissed, '*Hide!*'

Everyone slipped into their secret hidey-holes. Cordelia slid down the side of her crate, dragging a sack across the gap to hide herself. Was anybody visible – a toe, an elbow, a tuft of hair? She poked her head up to check, before Sam stuffed the moonlight under her hat and dived beneath a sack.

A moment later, the trapdoor latch snapped.

Cordelia saw a wedge of light widen across the ceiling as the trapdoor creaked open. Someone carrying a lantern was coming down. Through a chink between crates, she saw the dark blue of a sailor's cap.

The sailor dropped into the cargo hold, flashing the lantern around, casting light into the corners.

Cordelia held her breath. Had he heard voices? Had they been seen sneaking aboard? Was he coming to investigate?

To her horror, he took several deliberate steps in her direction. He paused again, as if listening hard.

Cordelia could hear her own heart beating far too loudly.

The sailor took another step – directly towards her. The lantern light cast a treacherous beam into her hiding place, like an accusing finger pointing her out.

She shrunk away from the light. But the sailor was reaching towards her! His hand grasped the sack above her and slowly peeled it aside.

Light blinded her as she was discovered.

CHAPTER 38

The sailor loomed over Cordelia, a terrifying silhouette poised like disaster above her, half blinding her with the lantern.

He reached into her hiding place to pull her out. As the light spilled on to his face, in a sudden dazzle of amazement, Cordelia found she was looking – through a large bushy beard – at her father.

Seconds later he disappeared beneath a storm of Troublemakers, furiously – but silently – wrestling him into submission.

'No, no!' Cordelia urged, pulling off her father's attackers. 'He's on *our* side!'

The whole scene played out as a frantic pantomime of silent gestures as Cordelia, Goose and Sam managed to drag Prospero out from under a squash of pirates.

'Hello, Dilly,' he whispered, pulling off the large false beard to reveal his face.

For several minutes, nobody could separate Cordelia from Captain Hatmaker.

'How did you find me?' she whispered into his shoulder.

Prospero opened his hand and Cordelia saw a half-shell nestled in his palm. A tiny golden compass arrow swung around inside it as his hand moved.

'This is the other half of your necklace, the one with your mother's portrait,' Prospero explained. 'I told you the heart is a compass, Dilly. You are my north.'

The golden arrow settled, pointing to Cordelia.

'I followed it to you,' he told her. 'Back on St Freerest, I realized the only way to find you was to get on the one ship that had a chance of defeating the Troublemakers. So I stole a sailor's uniform, made myself a disguise, and slipped aboard the *Invincible* when she returned to port amid rumours that the Troublemakers had just struck the *Splendora*.'

'That wasn't us!' Jim objected.

'It was the admiral,' Goose told Prospero.

Prospero pulled ruefully at his itchy sailor's collar.

'I know that now,' he said. 'I discovered the admiral's treachery much too late: only when his orders came to attack the island as I stood in his ranks on the beach. Before I knew the truth, I went to the wheel of the *Invincible* and set a course for the island according to my compass, telling the navigator

I'd seen a ship from the crow's nest. But I hadn't seen a ship. I knew that if there was one thing that might break through the shroud of the island, it was this.'

He held up the tiny shell compass.

'Love is the deepest and truest magic,' Prospero said. 'It will lead true through anything.'

But his face creased with sorrow.

'I had no idea that the island was a magical haven. I thought it was full of Menacing danger. And –' he looked around the Troublemakers – 'I thought you were all hardened pirates and wicked kidnappers. I did not know that you are, in truth, children. I set a course for Cordelia, thinking that the Troublemakers would get what they deserved while I finally rescued my daughter. When the admiral revealed his wretched intent, I meant to join you and help fight him, so I followed my compass. As I tried to climb into the treehouse, I was amazed that my compass suddenly told me you were rushing out across the bay towards the *Invincible*. I ran through the jungle and coaxed the waterfall to help put out the fire, then hurried back aboard the *Invincible* and followed my compass around deck. It told me I was right above you, so I came down here to investigate.'

Prospero turned sober eyes to the Troublemakers.

'I am terribly sorry for leading the admiral to your safe haven. I don't expect forgiveness for the destruction I unwittingly caused. It is a great loss to bear. I am so very, very sorry.'

'You made a mistake,' Never said. 'It's all right.'

'And we *did* kidnap your daughter,' Tabitha said fairly.

'You did,' Prospero agreed.

'She caused us a lot of trouble,' Never added with his wonky half-smile. 'But I'm glad we did it.'

Soon Prospero had to sneak back up to his duties on deck. The admiral, he told them (fixing his beard back on to his face), ran a tight ship, and if sailors did not keep to his strict schedule, they were punished with the cat-o'-nine-tails. Prospero could not risk drawing attention to himself, or he would be exposed as the intruder he truly was.

He told Goose that Ignatius had been thrown into the ship's prison as punishment for refusing to attack any more ships. Once back in London, Ignatius would be dishonourably discharged from the navy. Goose looked very proud when he heard this.

'The admiral thinks nobody who's been dishonourably discharged will be believed if they tell the truth about his terrible crimes,' Prospero added. 'But I think people will be very interested to hear Ig's side of the story . . .'

'But *how* are we going to tell people in London?' Cordelia whispered to her father as he grasped the trapdoor handle. 'It's so dangerous there – and Sir Piers is going to use Witloof's soul to drain the magic out of people. He's already done it once –'

Prospero followed her glance towards Shelly.

'Am I doing the right thing, taking them back?' Cordelia asked, turning a pained face to her father.

Prospero cupped his daughter's face in his hands.

'You taught me something about bravery the day you sacrificed yourself to save *Little Bear*,' he whispered. 'Sometimes you've got to go *towards* trouble.'

Prospero promised he would bring tankards of fresh water down every night when the watch changed.

Cordelia squeezed her father tight before he slipped away.

'Take care, littlest Hatmaker,' he murmured. He tapped his shell compass. 'I'll keep my eyes on you.'

The days passed in a dark rumble. The nights passed in much the same way.

They sneaked up on to the gun deck when they were sure it was safe, to gulp lungfuls of fresh air from the gunports and watch the iron-grey ocean surging past.

Cordelia became familiar with the different moods of the sea, and the way the air tasted of brine or seaweed or of the mistral wind. The air grew colder as they sailed northwards.

They amused themselves with very repetitive games of hide-and-seek and repaired their battle-torn clothes with Starlight Twine that Sam had beckoned down from the sky and spooled on her fingers, leaning out of a porthole at midnight. Goose rummaged through the chests and found some strong determined-feeling grasses that he used to replace the frayed laces on everybody's boots.

The admiral's treasures proved to be plentiful. He had clearly spent a lot of time and energy systematically stealing things from a wide array of people and places. Stored in the belly of the ship were crates and coffers, boxes and chests and sacks of stolen things. Cordelia and the Troublemakers were travelling back to London on a veritable dragon's hoard of magical artefacts, destined (Cordelia strongly suspected) for the new wing in the British Museum.

But it was not only this knowledge that caused her to frown as the ship rocked in the waves. It was the knowledge of the *other* thing residing deep in those marble halls . . .

Witloof's soul.

It was the most dangerous thing Cordelia had ever faced – far more dangerous than the man to whom it had once belonged. Because it had the power to drain magic from the hearts and hands of Makers and bleed enchanted objects of all their power.

When she was not privately wondering how she could possibly fight a man with such a weapon, Cordelia spent time teaching the Troublemakers simple stitches to catch happiness in the threads. They caused more frazzle than happiness in the first several dozen attempts, but Cordelia found that patience was a good teacher. Slowly, their fingers learned.

And Cordelia learned something too. There is such a thing as *good trouble*.

As they stitched, they also began to sew together a sort of plan . . .

CHAPTER 39

By the time the *Invincible* reached the English Channel (a fact that Prospero whispered through the trapdoor early one mist-edged morning), the plan had become a patchwork of outlandish ideas sewn together with a great deal of daring and a hint of hare-brained brilliance.

Soon they turned into the Thames, and the smell of London fog and April rain startled Cordelia with its damp familiarity. When the *Invincible* docked and the admiral's men came down to unload the cargo hold, they found everything as expected.

If some of the crates they hauled up on to the docks were heavier than they had been when they were loaded on to the ship, nobody noticed.

And nobody noticed the occasional eye peeping out from between the planks of the crates as they were piled on to carts and rumbled through the streets of London, up from the docks at Wapping and along Cheapside towards the British Museum . . .

'I feel a lot more seasick on land,' Goose grumbled. His face was squashed against the side of the crate. Sam, whose legs were folded at an uncomfortable angle, agreed queasily as the cart joggled over cobbles.

Cordelia looked at them both sideways. She had to look at them sideways because her whole self was sideways, wedged between the severed trunk of a palm tree and some slippery seaweed that had developed a terrible smell.

'It shouldn't be much further,' she told them. 'Listen! That's the clock at High Holborn!'

A number of dolorous clangs gloomily announced it was nine o'clock.

Cordelia twisted round to put her eye to a small knothole in the crate. Every Londoner was dressed in grey, with faces to match. They passed the Mercurial Chocolate House on Red Lion Street and saw it was boarded up.

The Sensible Party had got rid of everything fun.

Goose managed not to be sick as their crate was lifted off the cart and carried a jolting, twisty distance by two grunting men before finally being dumped on to a cold marble floor.

For a long time, they stayed very quiet, listening to the sounds of crates being shuffled in and set down all around them. Then they heard the whine and rumble of voices approaching.

'All delivered here to the new Ransom Wing!' came the cannon-boom voice of Admiral Ransom.

Then Cordelia recognized the drawl of Sir Piers Oglethorne himself.

'This must be kept secret, do I make myself clear, Smirke?' he said. 'Nobody else is to be allowed in until seven o'clock tomorrow night.'

'Yes indeed, sir!' came the reply, in a voice so oily you could slip on it. It was the museum curator, Mr Smirke.

'The grand opening of the Ransom Wing!' Admiral Ransom blared. 'A victorious return, with the head of a slayed beast, and the rescued girl alive and well.'

The voices arrived right beside the crate.

'In truth, your daughter was a nuisance all voyage long, Sir Piers: cursing me through the keyhole and singing loud songs when I was trying to sleep.'

They were so close it was possible to hear the hiss of Sir Piers's displeasure. Cordelia couldn't help grinning at this – Thorn had clearly not lost any of her spikes.

'Prudence must be subdued somehow until tomorrow evening,' Sir Piers said. 'I don't want her looking unhappy to be back; people would ask too many questions. I'll put her in the front row of the audience – along with all the Makers, who will be brought here by soldiers, to make sure nobody misses the special surprise I'll have waiting for them.'

'There's a lot of work to be done, Smirke!' the admiral bellowed. 'I've brought thousands of objects back and I want them all on display by tomorrow night.'

'You get the glory, Ransom, and I get the power,' Sir Piers said drily. 'Just as we agreed months ago.'

Smirke's simpers faded as he escorted them out, then their voices were snipped off like cut string as the door closed.

Cordelia listened for a long minute, then pushed the lid off the crate and poked her head up.

'*Double, double!*'

All over the Ransom Wing, heads popped up from crates as Troublemakers appeared one by one. Soon they were stretching their stiff limbs and staring around the huge gallery, with its high white walls and empty cabinets and plinths.

In the middle of the room, clenched like a grey fist and sealed inside a cage of glass and iron, was Witloof's soul. Its silent scream pulled them like an undertow, dragging their eyes into its dark gyre.

It would only become dangerous when Sir Piers opened its glass box, which had been expertly made to muffle its dreadful scream. But even now Cordelia shuddered at the dark pull it exerted. She didn't want the others to become frightened, so she quickly covered it with an empty sack.

There were a hundred crates and dozens of sacks waiting to be unpacked. The admiral had clearly gone about robbing with spectacular abandon.

Sam opened one chest to find that it contained dozens of crystal stalactites that had been sawn from the ceiling of the Belly Cave. They were dull and sad, having lost their glow when they'd been ripped from their rightful place. Goose upturned a sack, emptying shrivelled fungus puffballs on to the floor. Tabitha found a crate of glowing cocoons, and lantern flowers that had been ripped up by the roots.

The trunk of the Soulhope Tree lay across the floor like a slain giant.

As Cordelia touched the stolen treasures, a shocking sadness ran from the tips of her fingers right to her heart. These treasures had been carelessly torn from their homes and brought here, the spoils of ransack, reeking of ruin.

Then she noticed that one of the boxes was humming. Another clucked. A third jiggled and snuffled.

'Some are still alive!' she murmured.

There was a label pasted over one with the words FOR TAXIDERMY stamped across it.

Never joined her. As he read the label, his face became angrier than Cordelia had ever seen it.

'Typical of the Sensible Party – if anything's magical, lock it up and throw away the key,' he burst out. 'And if you can, kill it and stuff it! Make sure the light leaves its eyes!'

A wet nose snuffled between the planks of one of the boxes; a mournful honk came from another.

Cordelia opened the lid and an inquisitive face peered up at her.

'You survived!' she gasped. 'I'm so sorry you were captured!'

She lifted the dodo out of the crate. The bird was heavy in her arms, but it nudged her cheek in a friendly way.

'You must have been so lonely,' she said to it.

She looked across the pile of crates, humming and buzzing, clucking and snuffling. Dozens of creatures were trapped in boxes. According to the labels, they were destined to be –

'No visitors allowed in here!' an imperious voice rang across the room.

Cordelia swung round. Mr Smirke had returned – and he seemed likely to burst with indignance when he saw what Cordelia was holding.

'That beast is going to be killed and stuffed for the display!' he snapped. 'Put it back at once! You might damage it!'

'Damage it?' Goose spluttered. 'You're the one who's planning on *killing* the poor creature!'

The curator snapped his fingers, striding forward. But he had only taken a few paces when Cordelia squared up to him.

'There's only one beast in this room that's going to be stuffed and put on display,' she growled.

She felt thorny and furious.

Mr Smirke reared back and scurried for the door. But the Troublemakers had blocked the way out. When he opened his mouth to yell for help, Shelly promptly stuffed a gob of seaweed into it.

A few minutes later, Mr Smirke became the first object to go into one of the Ransom Wing display cabinets, with dodo feathers stuck in his hair and several large orange snails moving slowly across his forehead. He stared at himself with treacle-slowness.

'He's not very interesting as a display,' Sam observed. 'But at least he's outta the way.'

The dodo honked mournfully.

'He's not going to stuff you – don't worry, sir,' Cordelia assured the bird.

But she turned seriously to all the Troublemakers.

'Tomorrow night, Sir Piers is going to open the soul-lead cabinet and bleed the magic from everyone at the grand opening: every Maker in the country, and Thorn – and us too, if we're in this room to hear the scream.'

She had to be sure the Troublemakers knew exactly how dangerous things would get.

'Anyone who wants to can leave and hide until it's over,' Cordelia assured them. 'I'm going to stay and try to stop him.'

'I'm staying,' Goose added.

'Me too,' Sam said.

A chorus of determined nods and fierce growls told Cordelia that every Troublemaker would stay.

'What's the plan?' Never asked.

Cordelia surveyed the brave faces surrounding her.

'We Make Trouble.'

CHAPTER 40

The Ransom Wing was opened at precisely seven o'clock the next evening.

The doors appeared to open of their own accord, but a sharp-eyed observer would have noticed hair-fine spiderwebs stretching from the door handles up to the ceiling, where (almost invisible on the high walls) white eight-legged shapes twitched.

Sir Piers was pleased as he marched to the front row, steering his daughter ahead of him.

Smirke had done a good job: every plinth in the Ransom Wing boasted wild and dangerous-looking beasts, razor-beaked birds and gnarly plants, frozen in life-like attitudes. It was an excellent collection, a monument to the conquering power of the British navy.

A giant prehistoric tree trunk had been pulled upright and covered in vicious-looking flowers large enough to swallow a man. The body of a ghastly beast, longer than a warship, twisted around the walls. A plinth displayed its enormous snarling head beside its pearly egg.

Sir Piers shuddered. He *hated* magical things. He hated their glow, their spark, the unpredictable way they moved and shone and hummed. It made his paltry soul twitch with fury.

Everything magical in this museum would soon be firmly where it belonged: frozen in the past. Sir Piers looked to the cabinet in the middle of the room, currently covered by a red velvet curtain. It contained the key to finally ridding Britain of magic and making everyone permanently sensible.

He smiled down at his daughter. Soon she would be sensible too.

Thorn Lawless had become Prudence Oglethorne again. Her wild hair had been tamed and her shoulders were slumped. Nobody could know that beneath her grey cloak her hands had been bound to a Malwood cane that burned her skin with a shaming coldness, and she wore a necklace of hangman's rope to tie her tongue. She stood, like a statue that had been torn from a temple, with a face of stone.

The people shuffling into the gallery behind them saw a father smiling at his once-lost child, and marvelled that she had been rescued. They did not see the very real fear in her eyes.

Alongside the general public, Hatmakers, Bootmakers, Glovemakers, Watchmakers, Cloakmakers and the lone Canemaker all anxiously obeyed the soldiers who marched them in. It was a strange way to arrive at a party, being directed by stone-faced soldiers to stand beside a man who openly hated them.

Miss Prim trotted in, leading a straight line of her pupils, recognizable as prisoners by their frightened eyes. The Sensible Party stalked behind them, stern-faced.

King George, Princess Georgina and her betrothed, young Prince Hector, proceeded into the gallery, followed by courtiers and nobles. Surprisingly (as the Sensible Party hated all forms of creative expression), artists, musicians and actors had been invited to the opening too. They arrived eager to see the strange creatures that had been whispered about in London since the *Invincible* had docked. Prince Hector grinned with ghoulish appreciation at the snarling Sea Dragon's head on its plinth, while Princess Georgina gazed around forlornly.

The admiral himself, the source of many of the rumours swirling through the streets, strode in last. He looked satisfied with Smirke's work: after all, he too preferred everything dangerous around him to be dead and stuffed.

'Do not fear!' he announced, planting himself in front of the plinth on which the head of the Sea Dragon rested. 'This beast's egg requires powerful magic to hatch! But it will never hatch, because, as you can see, its mother is extinct!'

The admiral gazed around as a few people applauded the demise of the Sea Dragon.

'I saved the girl and killed the monster!' he roared, yanking Prudence Oglethorne to his side. 'And I rid us of the scourge of the Troublemakers! They're extinct now too!'

The crowd suddenly understood they were expected to cheer, and mustered some noise. A particularly sharp-eyed observer of the scene, watching through a small gap between flowers and branches, noticed that many among the crowd did *not* cheer.

'Every Maker in London's here,' the observer whispered.

Sir Piers Oglethorne – the new prime minister – stepped to the front of the crowd. He signalled to the soldiers to lock the doors.

'Tonight is *an historic* night!' he announced in his high voice. 'Tonight, Britain puts magic in the past and moves into a Sensible future! I have the key to finally make Britain Sensible again. And the Makers have a front-row seat to be part of this important change.'

Sir Piers turned a hostile smile on the Makers as he dragged the velvet curtain off the cabinet in the middle of the room. The Makers quailed as the frightening gnarl of Witloof's soul was unveiled.

The sharp-eyed observer, hidden amid flowers and branches, eased open a small box and released a flock of moths.

'Here is the key,' Sir Piers was saying, taking a small key from his pocket, 'to a Sensible Britain!'

The moths flitted like shadows across the gallery, drawn to the glowing lanterns. They feasted on the candle flames and one by one the lanterns winked out, until the only light came from the faint glow of the Sea Dragon's egg.

Sir Piers, trying to fit the small key into the cabinet lock, faltered as the Ransom Wing was plunged into darkness.

'What is going on?' his voice snapped through the gloom.

Cordelia heard the soft *pit-pit-pit* of thousands of tiny seeds falling.

'DOUBLE, DOUBLE!' she yelled.

In an instant, the whole room filled with light as Sam broke open a box of sunshine.

Scattered across the wide floor of the gallery, thousands of seeds wriggled in the sudden sunlight, bursting open and growing faster than a mind could think.

The entire gallery was transformed into a blooming meadow of poppies, flowering brightly all around the amazed crowd.

Even seeds that had fallen into the king's crown burst into bloom, and ones caught in wigs scrambled up to flower. People who had been wearing dark grey sensible clothes became moving meadows clad in tapestries of colour.

Cordelia saw all this as she parted a curtain of snapping flowers to clamber out along a high branch of the Soulhope Tree, overlooking the room.

'WELCOME TO THE PALACE OF STOLEN TREASURES!' she roared.

CHAPTER 41

'WHAT IS THIS MADNESS?' Sir Piers bellowed. 'WE DEMAND MAGIC BACK!' Cordelia cried, balancing on the branch as faces turned to her in astonishment. 'People of London – Makers, prisoners of Miss Prim – *everyone*! Sir Piers has a terrible weapon that he's about to use TO TAKE OUR MAGIC AWAY!'

Her lungs burned; her heart blazed.

'Come down here, you little brat!' Sir Piers screamed. 'I ordered the admiral to kill you all!'

'He didn't manage to kill any of us!' Cordelia told him defiantly. '*DOUBLE, DOUBLE!*'

All around the room, the frozen dioramas came alive. Troublemakers emerged from beneath the wings of huge birds, rustled out of grasses, rolled aside fungus puffballs and unfolded from corals. Annie shook off a multitude of musical

376

birds that swam away through the air in a blue fugue. Jim appeared atop a giant snail as it moved ponderously into sight, and Shelly uncurled from an enormous clam shell, rising like a sea goddess.

Exhibits awakened – vines stretched as though they had cramp from staying still too long. The dodo, who had been poised on a plinth, shook his tail and honked. Sun Eaters turned their heads imperiously, while flowers snapped their petals, crystals clinked, huge hermit crabs flashed lightning from their shells, butterflies flurried through the air and spiders uncurled their legs and scurried to work.

Sir Piers stared around in terror, cowering against the one plinth that showed no sign of life: the one holding the Sea Dragon's head. Wild magic was everywhere, bursting into chaos around him! The large pearly egg rolled on to the floor as birds arced overhead and giant spiders scuttled around him. He clutched the cold cabinet key in his sweaty hand.

The Troublemakers grinned at the gasping crowd below them. They had smeared shining nectar on to their skin and stuck feathers in their hair. Sam had an entire flock of dragonflies flexing their wings on her head, and Goose was completely covered in green succulent plants.

'We are the Troublemakers!' Never announced. 'And Prudence Oglethorne is our captain!'

Several people in the audience tried to flee, but a spider scuttled across the doorway, lacing the exit shut.

All around the room,
the frozen dioramas came alive.

Cordelia blew through an enormous trumpet-like flower, shivering the room into silence.

'We can't change your minds with magic!' she announced. 'I learned that lesson, and I'm sorry for the mistakes I made. Your Majesty, I should never have put a Meddling hat on your head.'

The king's eyes bulged in surprise as Cordelia gave him a deep bow from her perch on the tree. Princess Georgina blushed and shuffled beside him.

'Please, before Sir Piers unleashes his terrible weapon,' Cordelia continued, 'let us show you the magic we have, and allow it to *freely* change your minds.'

The king raised an eyebrow. Without waiting for royal permission, Cordelia cried, 'Welcome to the *least sensible party of the year!*'

Hearing the cue, the Troublemakers sprang into action.

There was an explosion of colour and joy and noise. Magic – something Londoners had been starved of – burst into exuberant mayhem around them.

Troublemakers led magical creatures to meet Londoners in a jubilant reunion of magic and humans. The guests tasted music blooming from bugle flowers as the air was bejewelled by a charm of hummingbirds. Vines raced across the floor, and flowers burst open like fireworks. Moss velveted a wall, while insects winked and buzzed through the air, leaving trails of bliss. Goose trailed ribbons of rainbow across the room, and the king himself played in a stream of bubbles being released by an enormous clam that was opening and closing like a musical box.

But amid the chaos of a crowd erupting with joy, Cordelia saw Thorn, standing as still as stone. Something was wrong with the pirate queen.

She scrambled down the branches of the Soulhope Tree and leaped to the floor, landing knee-deep in poppies. She waded across the mini meadow, hurrying through a swoosh of birds, under banners of spiderlace, over a highway of glowing snails and past a thrum of dazzling insects.

Cordelia shouldered through Miss Prim's pupils, who ran from their teacher as indigo birds descended upon her to feast on the horrible thoughts swirling around the headmistress's head. She bypassed Shelly and her army of scuttling knife-clawed crabs, who were busy rounding up several terrified members of the Sensible Party.

'Thorn!' Cordelia called, glimpsing her through a rumble of fungus puffballs. 'Come on!'

But Thorn didn't move. Cordelia *had* to get to her –

She dashed past Never, who was rolling politicians up in tumbling shrubs, and narrowly dodged the bellowing Admiral Ransom as he tripped over a snapping flower vine snaking round his ankles. Meanwhile, as Sam's sunlight faded, the moths that had devoured the candle flames closed themselves into glowing cocoons that hung from the ceiling like wild chandeliers.

Cordelia finally reached Thorn through the joyful frenzy of magic. But the magic itself could not reach Thorn.

The young Hatmaker grasped Thorn's hands and gasped in shock as she brushed against the Malwood cane and saw the necklace of hangman's rope. The Sensible Party and Miss Prim claimed to reject all forms of magic, but they were using it now to control Thorn!

Furiously Cordelia tugged the cane. A second later she reared back. The Malwood was full of grim, burning coldness. It must have been agonizing to Thorn, bound so tight to her hands.

'Thorn, can you hear me?' Cordelia whispered, peering into her eyes.

Exactly what Thorn had feared the most had happened to her: there was no light left in her eyes.

Tears spilled down Cordelia's cheeks and she dashed them away.

'I have to get this cane off you!'

She gritted her teeth. The Malwood hissed as Cordelia wrapped her hands around it. Somehow, the cane was weakening. Something on Cordelia's hands was splintering the wood.

'Tears!' Cordelia exclaimed. 'Of course, they're very powerful!'

The wood creaked, but it was still strong. And Cordelia remembered something that had lain forgotten for days. She stuck her hand into her pocket –

'YES!'

Miraculously, the Secret-Keeper that Shelly had given her had stayed tucked in her pocket all through her journey home.

She tipped the shell. A single tear glistened on the tip of her finger, bursting round and fat with powerful magic. It was the tear she had collected from Thorn, back on the island. A tear full of grief and hope and love.

Cordelia trickled the teardrop on to the Malwood cane. It slipped between Thorn's fingers and –

CRACK!

– snapped the Menacing wood in half.

Cordelia pulled the pieces apart, dropping them to the floor with a clatter. She dragged the frayed hangman's rope from Thorn's neck, looking for the fire that had always lived in her eyes.

'Thorn?' she whispered. 'Are you there?'

It was like calling somebody far away in the dark.

'Thorn!' she said again, this time louder.

But Thorn was staring in horror at something over Cordelia's shoulder.

Cordelia swung round and felt her heart drop.

Sir Piers was turning the key in the cabinet door.

CHAPTER 42

'NO!' Cordelia threw herself forward and closed her hands over Sir Piers's sinewy claw.

The key was already in the lock. One twist of his wrist was all it would take to unleash utter destruction. Cordelia pulled his hand back with all her might as he fought furiously to turn the key.

'Your – magic – is – about to – end – permanently!' he hissed.

Cordelia held on with all her might, as their hands shook in a death-grip struggle. But Sir Piers was too strong for her. He slowly turned the key.

'NO!' Cordelia screamed. 'SOMEBODY, HELP!'

The iron squealed as the lock slowly opened.

'Enjoy – your last – moments of – magic,' Sir Piers sneered. 'I'll be glad to get rid of mine too –'

His eyes blazed with destruction and Cordelia felt her fingers slip. In a hair's-breadth moment, the cabinet would spring open and her magic would be caught in a vortex and sucked away into the black hole –

She despaired.

Then another pair of hands grasped hers. Strong hands, in spite of their scars.

Thorn was beside Cordelia, eyes blazing brighter than ever.

'We can do it, Maker!' Thorn said, grimacing.

Sir Piers's eyes flashed with surprise. 'Prudence?'

'NOW!' cried Thorn.

With a huge effort, she and Cordelia twisted the key. The iron lock squealed, shunting back into place.

'NO!' Sir Piers raged.

Cordelia and Thorn yanked his hands away, pulling the key out of the lock.

The key somersaulted through the air, arcing across the room – and caught in the silver lacework of a spiderweb, high above their heads. It hung, suspended there, far out of reach.

Sir Piers's face was a snarl of fury. He lunged for Cordelia, but an eight-legged saviour sprang towards him and, in a froth of lace, lashed him to the plinth of the Sea Dragon.

Thorn walked up to him, wearing the most serene expression Cordelia had ever seen.

'You can't take away my magic, Father,' Thorn said softly. 'Magic is who I am. And you might never understand me, but I don't need you to understand me any more.'

Sir Piers opened his mouth to spit out a retort, but the spider promptly webbed his mouth shut.

Thorn gave a little trembling laugh, and a tear slipped down her cheek.

CRACK!

The air broke in half.

Thorn's tear had fallen on to the stone-hard shell of the Sea Dragon's egg, and it was hatching with a sound like musket fire.

CRA-CRA-CRACK!

Everybody in the gallery turned to see a white snout push its way through the shell. A face with the wisdom of an ancient mage and the innocence of a baby bird emerged. The creature stretched its wings – wings that were made for gliding across deep oceans, over underwater mountains and through glades of enchanted seagrass.

It was a tiny Sea Dragon, no bigger than a poodle from snout to tail, and white as a rainless cloud. It peered at the strange new world it had entered. The strange new world peered back.

'Evil beast!' the admiral bellowed, lurching out of a nest of snapping flowers that had surrounded him. 'I caused their extinction and I will NOT have that honour stolen from me!'

He brought his sword crashing down, but, acting on sheer instinct, Cordelia grabbed a broken branch of the Soulhope Tree and swung it upwards.

With a *clang*, the admiral's sword clashed against it.

Soulhope wood was strong, but it couldn't fight the sheer fury of the admiral. The branch strained.

Any moment it would break.

The tiny Sea Dragon mewled in distress.

'Remember your thorns, Cordelia!' Thorn yelled.

Cordelia finally knew what the pirate queen had meant: thorns protect the flowers. She needed her spikiness to defend the beautiful, gentle, helpless things in this room.

Cordelia bit the admiral's hand – he roared with pain. She kicked him in the codpiece – he doubled over gasping . . . Then, strengthened by the Soulhope wood surging strong as whale song through her hands, she shoved Admiral Ransom with such mighty fury that he flew backwards as though he had been kicked by a carthorse.

He lay splayed on the ground – and all his stolen treasure descended upon him.

There was a scramble of spiders, a quick slither of snakes, a rush of bushes, gnashing flowers, vengeful creatures and furious birds. When the frenzy was over, Admiral Ransom was snarling, trussed up in spiderwebs and vines, in a mess of moss on the floor. His medals had been pecked off by Sun Eaters, and his hat was covered in snail slime.

'You'll *never* hurt a Sea Dragon again!' Thorn declared.

To make very sure the admiral knew he was defeated, the dodo waddled up and pooed on his boot.

Cordelia turned to the crowd to see the king, who had paused in the act of being decorated by a spider.

'Admiral Ransom's the one who's been sinking ships and terrorizing the high seas!' Cordelia told him.

'Nonsense!' the admiral barked, working a hand stiffly into his jacket. 'This letter of marque proves it was all legal!'

As he managed to pull the scroll out, the baby Sea Dragon took its first staggering steps, tottering up to him curiously. It hiccupped, unleashing a tongue of flame that devoured the scroll in a heartbeat.

'Aaaah!' the admiral yelped, as his letter turned to ash in his hand.

'Without that letter, I'm afraid you're just a common thief and a treacherous ship-sinker, Ransom,' Prospero Hatmaker said, stepping through the crowd and pulling off his disguise. 'As young Ignatius Bootmaker here witnessed on your voyage.'

The crowd muttered and stirred like a wilding sea. Behind Prospero, Ignatius Bootmaker appeared, thin-cheeked and serious.

'You killed Capitano Boniface,' Prospero said heavily, 'a man of great kindness and heart. An honourable man to whom my daughter and I owe our lives.'

The admiral looked surprised. It seemed that kindness, honour and heart were unfamiliar qualities to him.

'And Admiral Ransom is not the only one who's been lying about their methods,' Prospero went on, turning to the room. 'Miss Prim –'

'She doesn't help young people *learn manners* at her school!' Jim interrupted.

'She bullies and frightens the magic out of children!' Annie declared.

'We ran away from her cruelty!' Billy added.

'Lies!' Miss Prim squealed, turning bulging eyes to her runaway pupils. 'Lies are *unbecoming*!'

However, Delilah Canemaker made her way through the crowd to pick up the broken pieces of Malwood cane.

'These were made by my father,' she announced, wincing as she held them up. 'I recognize his craftsmanship, his attention to the evil details. This is a highly Menacing cane – and using it is a crime. Terribly *unbecoming*, Miss Prim.'

Miss Prim's face was a guilty sneer.

The men who made all the rules stood in judgement: the king glared and the Sensible Party glowered.

'We came back to say that Making should belong to everyone!' Cordelia cried. 'It should be free and –'

'*Mmm – mm – MM-MMM!*' Sir Piers was clearly trying to say something furious from behind his spiderweb gag.

Cordelia reluctantly tore the gag from his mouth.

'Making is ILLEGAL!' Sir Piers spat. 'And I'm the prime minister!'

'Oh, but I've missed it *so much*!' the king burst out. 'It's extremely boring being sensible all the time. Sometimes a king needs a bit of magic in his life! Tonight, you Troublemakers have reminded me how important magic is.'

He said this with a cackling parrot perched on his crown and a rainbow-striped bumblebee attempting to harvest nectar from his nose.

'I've changed my mind of my own free will!' the king announced. 'Making is now officially free for all!'

'But, Your Maj—' Sir Piers began indignantly.

'And it's not very wise being *sensible* at the cost of everything else in life,' the king added, cutting off Sir Piers. 'No more being *sensible*!'

'This is NOT LEGAL!' Sir Piers exploded. 'All the pretty speeches in the world don't matter if you don't have the law on your side. Not even the *king* can just decide any more! It's up to the politicians, and *we* say it's illegal!'

Around the room, however, members of the Sensible Party scowled at Sir Piers, who was struggling like a furious fly in the spiderweb.

'You told us that if we joined you we'd get our children back safely,' Sir Giles Borington bleated.

'And I distinctly heard you say you'd ordered Admiral Ransom to kill them all!' Lord Carp barked.

'You should call a vote,' Never suggested. 'That's how we settle everything on the island.'

'It's the fairest way,' added Tabitha.

The Earl of Slough turned popping eyes on his daughter.

'Very well!' he blustered. 'We can't vote to change laws – that's got to be done in Parliament – but we CAN get rid of Sir Piers!'

Cordelia tensed. The Troublemakers had done all they could to change their minds – but had they done enough?

'All in favour of voting out Sir Piers – say AYE!' the Earl of Slough called out.

'AYE!'

'AYE!'

Even the Troublemakers themselves joined in.

AYE – AYE – *AYE!*

It was a landslide victory.

'That settles it!' announced the king. 'If I understand correctly the frankly ridiculous rules of British Parliament, I believe that Sir Piers is no longer prime minister!'

Scenes that nobody could describe as sensible erupted in the room. Joy never looks sensible – it is something much better than that.

'I DO get to decide something, though,' the king shouted over the din. 'Every Troublemaker is pardoned and forgiven and is off the treason list! That includes you, Cordelia Hatmaker. You're *most definitely* a Troublemaker!'

Cordelia and her fellow Troublemakers stared at each other in amazement, suddenly standing in the brave new light of their own freedom.

'And I've had quite enough of admirals and Prims,' King George added. 'Take the criminals away!'

Admiral Ransom and Miss Prim could only wail as they were led from the gallery by some guards.

'Silly that they can change everything with just a few words, isn't it?' Cordelia murmured, quite dazed.

Thorn grinned. 'Nothing sensible about that *at all*.'

CHAPTER 43

The Makers welcomed Cordelia, Goose and Sam back with delighted hearts and open arms. Uncle Tiberius sobbed so much that a flock of moths landed on his head, pulsing their wings in a comforting way.

Aunt Ariadne cradled Cordelia and Sam's faces in her hands and said their names again and again, as if they were magic words.

Great-aunt Petronella had no time for an official greeting because she was crooning over the white spiders, which she was calling Lacemakers, as she was decorated with an entire gown of silvery spider silk, her armchair transformed into a frost-laced throne.

Mrs Bootmaker could be heard declaring that Goose and Ignatius would never be allowed out of her sight again.

And Len was so glad to see Sam that he positively glowed and sunbeams shone from his fingers.

The Maker children – the Glovemakers, Watchmakers and Charity Cloakmaker – tore across the room to Cordelia, faces blazing with glee.

'You've saved us from being sensible!' they cried. 'Making's allowed again, thanks to you!'

'Well,' Cordelia admitted, 'it *was* my fault it got banned in the first place.'

'Sometimes you have to lose something to find it again,' Hop Watchmaker said wisely.

Amid the happy scenes, there were some more difficult ones. Not all the Troublemakers were hugged joyfully by their families.

When Sir Piers was freed from the spiderweb, he stalked up to Thorn (Prospero following him closely to be sure he didn't get near Witloof's soul).

'You are no daughter of mine,' he spat at Thorn.

Then he turned and marched out of the room, leaving an icy trail in the air behind him.

Two other members of the Sensible Party marched after him: Lady de Sneer swept out, casting a withering glance at her daughter, Shelly; Doctor Leech did no more than raise an eyebrow at his son, Jim, before leaving.

However, the rest of the Sensible Party remained, shuffling their feet and glancing shyly – almost nervously – at the Troublemakers, who stood with bashful pride in the midst of the best trouble they had ever made.

Lord Carp, whose wild hair matched Never's, shuffled up to his son.

'Quintus, I'm quite beside myself with remorse,' Lord Carp uttered. 'I – I sent you away to keep you safe from scandal.'

'The best way to keep me safe, Father,' Never said firmly, 'is to let me express who I am!'

Lord Carp launched into an apology, which Never put a stop to by flinging his arms around him.

'I am so sorry I sent you to Miss Prim!' Lord Carp snuffled into his son's shoulder.

Meanwhile, Sir Giles hugged his son, Billy, and the Earl of Slough wept as he held Annie and Tabitha in his arms.

Cordelia saw Jim gallantly teaching some of Miss Prim's now-liberated prisoners about the magic in their own fingertips, and Shelly sharing her shells with several awestruck children dressed in grey prison-stripes.

Cordelia picked her way across the flowery meadow towards Thorn.

'Hello, Maker,' said Cordelia.

'I *can* be a Maker now,' Thorn whispered. 'Now it's free . . . Now *I'm* free.'

'You already *are* a Maker,' Cordelia said, smiling at her. 'Look at this very excellent change you've made.'

The quiet mewling of a creature met their ears and they turned to see the tiny Sea Dragon staring forlornly up at the plinth where the head of its mother lay.

'I'm sorry your mother's been taken away from you much too soon, but I'll do my best to look after you,' Thorn murmured, crouching down and holding out a hand.

The Sea Dragon sniffed her fingertips, seeming to approve of what it found. It clambered across Thorn's shoulders and settled there, as though it was a long, white leathery scarf. If the scarf were magic, it would have been made of things to cause heart-gladness. Thorn glowed.

Not far away, Prince Hector swung on a Turbidus Vine.

'WHEEEE!' he squealed. 'Finally, some *fun*!'

Princess Georgina rolled her eyes at the child.

'He *is* a bit young for you,' the king admitted to Georgina. 'All right, betrothal's off! You can marry the commoner!'

Sir Hugo, who had become entangled in a runaway shrub as it bounced across the room, could be heard rapturously celebrating his imminent marriage to Princess Georgina. The princess chased after him, dived into the shrub, and they rolled happily around the room together, giggling poetry at one another.

'I quite like changing my mind – it's fun!' the king barked. 'Let's swap Tuesdays with Fridays and see how everyone likes that.'

'Sooner or later, Daddy, we'll have to involve the people in decisions like these.' Princess Georgina's voice tumbled past him from the rolling shrub. 'And we need to release Master Ambrosius right away!'

Prospero found Cordelia amid the wild, silly magical party.

'Hello, my little Troublemaker!' He grinned, pulling her into a bear hug.

Delighted to be with her father again, she showed him how to ask the Turbidus Vines politely to take them up to the ceiling.

'They're very helpful if you ask them nicely,' Cordelia told him.

He marvelled as the vines sprang them easily upwards. She plucked Sir Piers's iron cabinet key down from the spiderweb as though she was picking fruit from a tree.

'I'm going to turn this key into another bar for the cage, so that there's no key and no keyhole,' Prospero promised, tucking it into an inner pocket of his jacket. 'That way, the cage can *never* be opened. And we'll put it in a dark vault beneath the Tower of London, where nobody can reach it, to be extra safe.'

A plaintive honk called them back to the floor.

'Who's this?' Prospero laughed, looking down at the bossy bird snuffling at him as he landed.

'This is a dodo,' Cordelia told her father. 'I think he'd like to be taken back to his family on Soulhaven.'

Prospero nodded. 'No need to leave through the window this time, via the chandelier,' he said with a wink.

Cordelia remembered the last time she had caused trouble in public.

'We still *could* leave via chandelier,' she replied, smiling. 'It's much more fun than using doors.'

CHAPTER 44

M agic spread like sunrise across the whole country.
The grim grey clothes made mandatory by the
Sensible Party were quickly replaced with enchanted outfits
that shimmered and sparkled and glowed as everyone put on
their happiest apparel to welcome magic back. Faces changed
with the clothes: expressions became brighter and more
joyful. Singing could be heard in the streets.

In the explosion of enthusiasm that followed the restoration
of Maker magic, magical delight broke out everywhere.
This delight turned, in places, to chaos. There were reports
of some home-made Gambolling Garters running away
with their owner across Shortgrove Park, and of a High-
Spirits Hat (made by an enthusiastic dabbler using too
many Giddy Geraniums) floating with its owner over
Cambridge.

Dozens of similar incidents kept the Makers extremely busy rushing around the country fixing things. They would gasp out explanations about balancing ingredients and weighing principles – rules of Making that the public could be forgiven for having forgotten over the last two hundred and fifty years – before dashing off to rescue the next amateur cloakmaker who was being squeezed inside a cape made using too much Snug Grass.

When someone tinkered with the organ in St Paul's Cathedral so that it filled the entire dome with giant musical bubbles, and sets of furniture began fighting in the streets of Liverpool, and an entire nunnery in Hull came down with fire-breathing hiccups, nobody could deny that something had to be done.

The Maker families met with Parliament to discuss how they could manage the magic to stop it from running wild. Cordelia, inspired by her time teaching the Troublemakers on Soulhaven, made a very important suggestion.

So when Parliament voted again on magic being free for all, they made one important amendment . . .

Meanwhile, Cordelia, it turned out, did have an opportunity to make amends in London. She did so with the help of the newly hatched Sea Dragon, whom the Troublemakers had voted to name Flash, after the flash of fire it had hiccuped that had defeated the admiral.

Turbidus Vines had taken root in the city – in St James's Park, at Hatmaker House, and even stretching from floor to ceiling in Parliament. They had sprouted wherever trouble had happened, and quickly grown out of control.

The royal gardeners tried everything, but nothing they did could stop the Turbidus Vines growing. They'd tried cutting them back with shears, sharp knives, scissors and swords, but every time they trimmed, cut or slashed, the vines grew back with more feisty determination than ever.

A swathe of the park was now too dangerous to go near and the politicians had simply closed the door on Parliament and let the Turbidus Vines go wild. Meanwhile, leaves could be seen crowding at the windows of Hatmaker House. The building was bursting with vines, and there was no way to get rid of them. Even asking politely was, at this stage, too little too late.

However, it turned out, the only food that the baby Flash would eat was Turbidus Vines.

Cordelia discovered this when the tiny white dragon began munching on the vines that had taken root in the British Museum. As Flash ate, she grew. And as she grew, she began to change colour.

'I think perhaps the more they eat, the more colours they're able to make,' Cordelia mused, watching Flash gnaw through the roots in the floor of the museum and turn an appreciative shade of pink.

The next day, she and Thorn took Flash to St James's Park, where she enthusiastically ate her way through the dense jungle blocking the promenade. By the time the vines had been devoured, the Sea Dragon was larger than a wolfhound and could turn her scales an impressive array of greens, from soft sage to vibrant emerald.

By the end of the week, Flash had worked her way through all the vines crowding Hatmaker House, and managed scarlet, ruby and crimson, as well as royal blue.

After Flash sauntered out, glowing indigo and the size of a carthorse, the Hatmakers ventured back into their house. Cordelia was shocked to find the rafters of her beloved home groaning, the stone walls crumbling. Hatmaker House was in serious need of repair.

All the Makers converged on the building, bringing their tools and determination. Thankfully, the king had ordered the immediate return of their confiscated ingredients, so the Makers were able to patch up walls with strong starlight and repair roof beams with Soulhope wood taken from the felled tree that had once stood proud on Soulhaven. They even replaced broken roof tiles with some of Rainbow's scales. Although the noble Rainbow had died and her scales had fallen grey, when they were gently slotted into the roof of Hatmaker House they began to glow multiple colours again. Every time

Cordelia looked up at the roof patched with colour-changing scales, she was reminded of the beautiful Sea Dragon.

When Hatmaker House was finished, it had been fixed up with the love and care of all the Makers of London. This made the house more magical than ever, and walking within its walls felt like being cocooned in magic.

Next, Cordelia, Thorn and the Troublemakers took Flash into Parliament. She systematically chewed her way along the single vine that had begun as the seed in the infamous Mind-Changing Tricorn Cordelia had made for the king. Now the vine stretched from floor to ceiling. Flash turned purple as she finished it, and Cordelia felt she had finally made up for her naughty Meddling hat.

When the Guildhall was reopened, the Menacing Cabinet was found to have a tendril curling cheekily out from under its door. Thorn, who could no longer wear Flash draped around her shoulders because she was so big, led her through the doors of the Guildhall.

'These must be the last Turbidus Vines in London,' Cordelia told Thorn, saving some Turbidus seeds in an empty jar before the ravenous Sea Dragon could devour them. 'You'll need these seeds to grow new vines to feed Flash!'

Thorn turned to gaze up at the dome of the Guildhall's Great Chamber.

'The others are all safe now, either back with their families or living with Ambrosius,' she said.

Master Ambrosius – who, thanks to Princess Georgina's insistence, had been let out of the Clink an hour after the king had pardoned the Troublemakers – had immediately taken in Shelly, Jim and Thorn, whose parents had all refused to have 'dangerous Makers' under their roofs.

'But Flash is getting too big for Master Ambrosius's little house,' Thorn added.

Master Ambrosius had found the presence of a marvellous creature that changed colour at will to be highly useful in attracting customers to his newly reopened sweetshop. People bought Air-Walking Pralines and Carolling Caramels, Loftus Nougat and Whistling Candies, and stood with their noses pressed against the window, waiting for Flash to change colour. Indeed, although the other Makers' shops had all filled up with magical goods again, and the chocolate houses had all reopened to general delight, Master Ambrosius's Emporium was proving the most popular spot of the lot.

Sir Hugo had even admitted a bit of jealousy about how much attention Flash had attracted during her short stay in Piccadilly. Cordelia tried to persuade him that his idea of roping the creature into his latest exuberant version of *The Tempest* was not wise. 'She's a wild creature,' she had pointed out. 'She doesn't belong on the stage. She belongs in the ocean and in the jungle on the island . . .'

Thorn, Cordelia could instinctively feel, believed the same thing.

'She needs to go back to Soulhaven,' Thorn said, as they stood in the Great Chamber. 'That's where she belongs.'

Cordelia knew that Thorn wasn't just talking about the Sea Dragon. A lump rose in her throat at the thought of Thorn and Flash sailing away.

'We'll linger a little longer,' Thorn told Cordelia, seeing the Hatmaker's eyes brighten with tears. 'Besides, I need at least one more lesson from an actual Maker from the Guildhall . . .'

CHAPTER 45

It was the first day of school at the Guildhall.

A week ago, King George had officially declared (in a newly repaired Parliament) that magical Making was finally free for all. But it was under one condition: to ensure that the use of magical ingredients did not get completely out of hand, anybody who wanted to learn magical Making would have to do so at the new School of Making at the Guildhall.

In a very short space of time, the Guildhall had been transformed into a school. It was swept and tidied, dusted and polished. The magical ingredients that Sir Piers had confiscated were all put back in their rightful places.

Jars of shiny buttons stood on shelves, fat spools of ribbon were ready to be unfurled, and bottles of sunlight, feathers, shells, leaves and flowers all waited for the new pupils. The

Makers' workshops were rearranged into classrooms, with rows of desks set facing a workbench at the front.

Cordelia, Sam and Goose tiptoed across the Great Chamber, which now had tables with scales for weighing ingredients lining the walls and displays of the finest Maker clothes to inspire the new pupils.

Everything was still and silent. The doors of the new school had not yet been opened. The other Makers were milling about in the square outside the building, ready to welcome new pupils and usher them inside.

'It's strange, isn't it?' Goose said, his voice echoing around the high domed ceiling. 'It's belonged to just us for so long; now it's going to belong to everybody.'

Cordelia squeezed his hand.

'It *is* strange,' she agreed. 'But sharing is the best thing we can do with our magic.'

Goose nodded. 'I'm going to teach timid people to make Bossyboots,' he decided. 'To help them stand up for themselves.'

Sam chased a dust mote through a heavy shaft of sunlight.

'I fink Len and I will teach people how ta weave sunshine and shadow together,' she said.

'Those both sound like brilliant lessons!' Cordelia enthused, and Sam grinned.

They heard nearby St Auspice's bell chime nine.

'It's time!' Cordelia yelped.

They hurried through the velvet curtains into the front hall, just as the doors opened. A crowd of people came chattering excitedly into the new school.

First among them were a bunch of Troublemakers, cleaner and neater than they had been before, and no longer wearing piratical clothes, but still wearing piratical grins.

Thorn came afterwards, by herself, twisting her hands together uncertainly. Flash trotted behind her, shaking the floorboards beneath her scaly claws, wings brushing the top of the door frame.

Thorn paused, standing in the entrance to the new school. 'I – I don't know what I want to make,' she admitted.

'Have a look around,' Cordelia advised. 'And see what makes your fingertips tingle.'

After the Troublemakers came hundreds more potential students. It seemed that half of London had turned up to learn the secrets of the Makers. Cordelia and Goose greeted everyone, listening as they told them what they dreamed of creating. Then Hatmaker and Bootmaker directed them to the correct classrooms.

Prospero arrived soon after that, having spent the previous night carefully moving Witloof's soul in its protective glass prison through London to the darkest dungeon beneath the Tower of London. He had sealed the doorway with ironweb and made sure it was secure. From there, he had gone on to Miss Prim's Academy to collect a group of grey-clad children whose faces didn't look like they were familiar with the shape of hope. But Cordelia saw the light in their eyes come alive as they entered the magical building.

'They're the last of Miss Prim's prisoners,' Prospero whispered. 'Freed, but still frightened.'

'I fink I know what they need,' Sam said, appearing at Cordelia's shoulder. She led the children up to the Light-Catching Tower, to introduce them to the flickering gentle magic of her Dulcet Fireflies.

When Win Fairweather blew in through the door, announcing that she wanted to learn how to make a Breeze-Ruffled Cloak, Cordelia had news for her.

'You're needed on the roof!' she said, beaming. 'You're going to be a teacher — there's about a dozen people who want to learn Mist-Stitching! We made a weather-brewing workshop up there.'

'Oh, goodness me!' Win blustered. 'I've had my head in the clouds all week, Cordelia, quite literally! But I would be *honoured* to teach. Which way to the workshop?'

Meanwhile, Delilah Canemaker welcomed a boisterous bunch of young women who were all intent on creating Self-Expression Canes. They tumbled into her classroom, shouting with excitement about everything.

Master Ambrosius arrived next. He was being led by his little sister, Shelly, who was still covered from head to toe in her clinking shells.

The sweetmaker drew Cordelia aside to whisper, 'I know my sister has no magic left in her fingers – but could you let her have a go? I know she'll never be able to Make, but –'

His eyes had a desperate, pleading kind of heartbreak in them.

Cordelia reached into her pocket. When she, Sam and Goose had carried a bucket of the Essence of Magic to St James's Park early that morning, to water their magical apple tree, they had discovered the tiny tree boasting one plump, shiny golden apple. The tree seemed so proud of itself it practically swaggered in the breeze.

'Shelly has magic in her heart,' Cordelia told Master Ambrosius, pulling the golden apple out of her pocket and holding it out to Shelly. 'It might only have survived as a tiny sprout, but it's *got* to be there.'

She spoke more with hope than knowledge. Sometimes hope is the more important of the two.

Shelly took the apple solemnly and bit into it.

Nothing changed at once; that isn't how the biggest trees grow. It is the same with a person's magic. But as Shelly chewed and swallowed the golden apple she began to smile, and she took another bite, then another.

Uncle Tiberius and Aunt Ariadne were giving eager students a lesson in weighing the different qualities of buttons, and Great-aunt Petronella was sequestered in a dark room lit only by bars of moonbeams hanging from the ceiling. There, helped by a Lacemaker spider that seemed particularly fond of her, she showed curious pupils how to encourage Luminant Mushrooms to sprout.

When most of the pupils had disappeared into the classrooms and the entrance hall was empty, Cordelia turned to Shelly, who solemnly handed her the well-nibbled apple. Five shining seeds were nestled in the core.

'We'll go and plant these tomorrow and start growing an orchard,' Cordelia told her. 'Will you keep them safe for me until then?'

Shelly produced a Secret-Keeper Shell and tucked the five seeds safely into it.

A bright bell rang out through the Guildhall – Sun Chimes that the Watchmakers had hung in the Great Chamber's dome. Prospero appeared at the door to the Hatmaker workshop and called, 'Dilly, it's time for you to give your lesson!'

Feeling nervous and excited all at once, Cordelia led Shelly into the Hatmaking classroom and settled her at a desk.

Then Cordelia walked to the front of the class. The magic in her fingertips sparked.

Shining, expectant faces watched her from every desk. Some faces she recognized, many she did not. Thorn Lawless, she saw, was in the front row.

Cordelia took a deep breath.

'Welcome to the School of Making!' she announced, smiling around at the class. 'Let's begin!'

Epilogue

Months later, after Cordelia, Goose and Sam had waved off *Little Bear* as she sailed down the Thames carrying all the admiral's stolen treasure, squawking and fluttering and on its way home at last, Cordelia received a small package. It was wrapped in a hessian sack that smelled faintly of cocoa beans.

She undid the string and a silvery-white lace shawl slipped out of the sack, pooling on her bedroom floor.

'Lacemaker silk!'

As she picked it up, it hummed with words. It was as though the yarn itself had stories twisted into it that she could feel through her fingers. Cordelia wrapped the beautiful shawl round her shoulders, and suddenly saw, in her mind's eye, Thorn and Flash on the deck of *Little Bear*, approaching the familiar craggy outline of Soulhaven Island.

Cordelia saw Smokestack on the beach, walking with a limp, his arm in a spiderweb sling, his old face cracking into a delighted smile. She saw the wounds in the jungle where rocks had been torn away; she saw the scars from ripped-up plants and the severed trunk of the Soulhope Tree. But she also saw new shoots growing where the earth had been disturbed, the dodo waddling back to his colony, Lacemakers diligently repairing the gashes in their intricate webs, and the young Sea Dragon slipping curiously into the cosmic depths of the Belly Cave.

Cordelia laughed, whirling on the spot, feeling all the joy and beauty and stories of the island carried in the threads of the shawl.

She saw the ocean, the sky and the Guiding Star twinkling above.

She saw Thorn, her eyes shining with a bright, merry fire, before she disappeared into the wink of the sunset.

Captain Hatmaker's Secret Logbook of the Wondrous Creatures Discovered on Soulhaven

This is a highly confidential logbook of all the magical creatures, plants and minerals discovered on the island of Soulhaven. The island's location is strictly secret to protect the home of these rare, endangered magical beings.

(With very helpful additional notes by Thorn Lawless.)

Belly Gem – The crystals that formed over thousands of years in the Belly Cave of Soulhaven are quite extraordinary: their colours and swirling patterns range from bright pinks

to deepest blues and greens. They slowly move and change according to the emotional temperature around them. They should never have been taken from the Belly Cave by that horrible admiral. They're treasure that belongs in the earth.

Bombulant Coconut – The fruit of trees that have grown with their roots in Guzzle Mud and had their palm leaves rustled by Mischief Wind. The coconuts rumble as they grow, and when they hit the ground they explode. We fired these out of our cannons – they make such a brilliant BANG!

Canticle Seahorse – This tiny seahorse has a curling tail like a fiddle. They form choirs in rockpools and often sing chorales as they sway in the waves. Shelly learned all their songs and harmonizes with them beautifully.

Clod Worm – This appears to be a small grey rock, but is, in fact, a heavy round worm that slowly eats its way through igneous rock. These worms sometimes attach themselves to mammals, using their mouths like pincers, in the hopes that they will be carried to some new delicious rocks. Really useful for hampering enemies because the worms weigh them down.

Conquista Caterpillar – An orange caterpillar resembling a large, bushy moustache. It undulates in a hypnotic rhythm and, after forming a captivating cocoon, transforms into a dazzling Bamboozling Butterfly with markings like hypnotized eyes on its wings. In the fifteenth century, monks used the caterpillars' eggs to make purple ink for illuminated manuscripts. The popularity of this ink eventually led to the creatures being hunted to supposed extinction. We sent a box of eggs to Master Ambrosius and he hatched them and put the caterpillars on portraits of the Sensible Party hanging in the Royal Academy.

Cuddling Succulent – A bulbous, affectionate succulent that clings to everything it touches. Can become smothering if not kept in check. Very comfortable for pillows, but sometimes they stick to your face in the morning.

Devil's Toenail Oyster – A particularly gnarly-looking oyster that yields large knobbly pearls. If you put a speck of Guzzle Mud into an oyster, the pearl it makes will jump around of its own accord. You can play a kind of tiddlywinks with them.

Dodo – *Raphus cucullatus* – A large flightless bird from Mauritius, this incredibly friendly, gentle bird was hunted to extinction in the 1600s by Dutch sailors who landed on

the island. *Luckily some got away and escaped to Soulhaven. Their eyelashes and feathers are good for making people forget things.*

Earthstar – A pale mushroom that springs up where the light of the evening star touches the earth. *You have to collect them incredibly gently, otherwise they shrink away back into the ground.*

Featherlight Fern – This incredibly gentle, ancient plant's leaves capture sunlight and brush the light gently on to everything they touch, rather like a paintbrush that has been dipped in gold. *And by moonlight, they paint things silver.*

Gaudia Sea Ribbon – A multicoloured seaweed that forms dancing underwater forests beneath the waves. *It makes people dance as though they're underwater.*

Guiding Star – The light of this star can only be seen by those who are hunted. The pull of the Guiding Star is what brought all the magical creatures, plants and entities to Soulhaven. *It feels like it's whispering a secret and you have to get closer to find out what it is.*

Guzzle Mud – Mud that has formed a greedy habit of sucking in whatever it can. Dangerous in large quantities. It travels

across impermeable surfaces and tries to uproot whatever it finds. It's quite fun if you're in up to your ankles, but it gets less fun if you're in up to your knees. Having a Guzzle-Mud-ball fight is BRILLIANT. But it's really hard to clean out of your nostrils.

Halcyon Bugle – *Ajuga alcyonem* – A golden flower that creates music when the wind whistles through its petals. Halcyon Bugles grow upright on stalks, with the flowers blooming at slightly different heights, which allows different tones between each flower. In the thirteenth century, whole gardens were planted with Halcyon Bugle bushes, because their music was said to be good for the soul and encourage daydreaming. But during the witch trials of the seventeenth century, the notorious (and humourless) Witchfinder General Matthew Hopkins decided that the music was too beguiling and 'causeth a man to become enswamped by reckless fantasie' and so entire gardens were put to the flame. Some of the seeds must have been smuggled out by witches, though! They made it to Soulhaven and these flowers grow by Moonstruck Lagoon. Billy played lullabies on them, to send us off into lovely dreams.

Harlequin Bumbler – A rainbow-striped bumblebee that used to roam the high meadows of the Swiss Alps. Multicoloured because of its varied diet of different magical

flowers, it was hunted and used to dye ribbons. Jim once got stung by one and said he could taste colours.

House-Proud Hermit – This neat, fastidious crab takes care of its temporary home with care and pride. It once paraded on beaches for other creatures to admire it, but its beautifully polished shell proved too tempting for humans, who stole them by the handful. House-Proud Hermits have now retreated to the safety of Soulhaven. One of these tried to make a home in Shelly's ear. She let it stay there for a week until she found it a coconut to live in.

Icthy Fledge – Before they went into hiding on Soulhaven, these mood-eating birds were kept in aviaries by kings, who used them to detect deceptive behaviour or resentful feelings in the minds of their courtiers. These birds fly around people's heads and taste the moods they sense in the aura, and change colour according to the taste of that mood. Of course, this made a feeling of jealousy or hatred difficult to hide from a king. They used to always turn black whenever they flew around my head, but now they turn a hopeful kind of pink.

Jumping Jacaranda – An exuberant tree with purple leaves, highly ornamental but considered a pest in the garden

as it jumps from place to place, uprooting other plants as it goes. The wood of these trees can be used to create violins that play catchy and exciting songs. Even their purple leaves have rhythm. Most trees were cut down to make violins when they became the most popular instrument in the orchestra. We raced them across the island, but only Tabitha managed to stay on hers the whole way.

Lacemaker Spider – This large but gentle arachnid was captured and made to work creating lace ruffs. At the height of the ruff fashion in Elizabeth the First's time, whole colonies of Lacemakers were captive in factories, taken from their native silver birch forests. The last Lacemakers died out in Europe from being overworked in ruff factories, and were believed to be extinct by 1622. However, they survived and made a new home on Soulhaven. They spin incredibly intricate webs that resemble the finest filigree lace. They will decorate a whole person, given half a chance.

Lacewing Griffinfly – A giant turquoise dragonfly, the thrum of its wingbeats creates excitement in the air, leaving trails of joy behind it. Smokestack once followed one all the way along Tailbone Breakwater and swam after it across the bay.

Lantern Flower – This delicate flower hangs from a fine stem and flickers into light at dusk. Lantern Flowers glow particularly brightly if they sense a creature is lost. We planted them by our hammocks in case we woke up feeling lost at night.

Laughing Gull – These birds were driven to supposed extinction because their eggs, which invoke jollity when eaten as an omelette, were considered a delicacy during the medieval period. Jolly omelettes were popular among the monks of Normandy. But they flew away to Soulhaven, where nobody tried to make any omelettes.

Long, knotted hair from an unidentified creature – Mrs Glovemaker found long hairs from a creature knotted into the straw bonnet of Miss Prim's Trouble Clothes. We're not completely sure what creature they came from but the hairs were FULL of wicked intentions. Those were from my head.

Luxor Poppy – This yellow flower bursts into bloom when the first rays of the sun touch its petals. Once grown in enormous meadows in the Nile Delta, these flowers apparently died out because their seedpods were over-harvested by the Ancient Egyptians and eaten as a delicacy. They grow all over the top of Skull Rock on Soulhaven, so it looks like the island is sprouting a big blonde wig every sunrise.

Melodious Clam – A slow-growing clam that (if left to grow) eventually reaches a huge size. It absorbs sounds into its shell and creates melodies by playing these sound memories. The larger the clam grows, the more complex and tuneful the melodies become. *Annie taught it about farts, and its songs became much more sonorous and majestic.*

Mischief Wind – Tendrils of wind that cause particular mischief when unleashed. *The truth is, this wind (which we sewed into Miss Prin's Trouble Cape) was made of us whispering all the naughty things we'd ever done and every rude name we could think of.*

Nightjar Moth – A moth that feasts on small flames and transforms the light it eats into its glowing cocoon. When they emerge from the cocoon, their wings are blue (like the hottest part of a flame), slowly becoming pale gold and finally turning white, at which point they lay their eggs on the undersides of Lantern Flower leaves. Their presence brings great comfort, but these moths became endangered when humans began burning too much coal, the fires of which they could not digest properly. *Jim persuaded one to make its cocoon on his earlobe, so he'd look piratical with a gold dangly earring, but it was so hot it singed his hair and turned his ear pink.*

Noctius Seaweed – A black seaweed that undulates and twists, growing quickly across any surface it can attach itself to. Useful for tying up enemies, but Sun Eaters love it, so they peck the enemies free pretty quickly.

Pecking Whelk – A carnivorous sea snail, particularly belligerent if provoked. Watch your toes!

Petrifying Parrot – A large scarlet bird with feathers that can cause a person to stop in their tracks as if turned to stone. Even its shrieks briefly paralyse a person. The birds were hunted for their tail feathers, which were used on arrows. They're great for playing Grandma's Footsteps. They're also very useful when we're boarding an enemy ship, as long as we're wearing limpets in our ears.

Rockface Barnacles – Found growing on the primordial bones of ancient fossils, these barnacles are extremely rough and tough, causing any soft-skinned creature around them to develop a thick, craggy exterior. Once we discovered these, they made our disguise hats SO much better!

Sabre-wing Hummingbird – A graceful turquoise bird, so quick that it is usually visible only as a bright blur in the air. These beautiful creatures were hunted and their wings

used to make handles for daggers, because their amazing speed gave the dagger handler the ability to attack with swift (and deadly) precision. They're very gentle, though — it wasn't their fault they were made into daggers. We would NEVER do that! Shelly once got one to eat pollen out of her nostril.

Sea Dragon – An ancient mythical sea creature. Despite its fearsome reputation, stoked by superstitious sailors, it is actually very kind, and has been known to pull ships free from whirlpools and tow them to safety. Appearing on mariners' maps for centuries, spoken of only in the most fearful of whispers, the Sea Dragon was long believed to be pure myth, born of the wild imaginations of sea-drunk sailors. But it's as real as you and me.

Secret-Keeper Shell – A silver shell that has grown in swirls or scrolls around invisible eddies in the sea. Its delicate shell will safely hold a secret, whether it's a secret of whispered words, writing on a scroll of paper, a kiss or a wink. Or a teardrop.

Silver Skink Lizard – Known as Mirage Lizards, these reptiles shimmer dazzlingly in the sunlight, but are completely invisible in shadow. Their scales were used to make

camouflage armour, up until their last sighting in the time of Saladin. Beware! In the shadows, these lizards can trip you up.

Somnambulant Snail – This snail feasts on moonlight. The trail it leaves causes an instant moonstruck sleep full of strange dreams. Hunted from its native Moon Mountain, its translucent shell was used in pottery. We collected their snail-trail goo to fire from our cannons, but we had to wear gloves to stop it making us fall asleep. They grow fatter on the full moon and the biggest snail we found was taller than Shelly!

Soulhope Tree – An ancient species of tree, the tallest in the world, with heartwood that hums with deep-rooted hope. It has green heart-shaped leaves and seedpods that oscillate with optimism. Its wood is supple but very strong, and cannot be used to make attacking weapons but creates the strongest shields. The last Soulhope Tree was felled by Henry the Eighth to make his ill-fated warship, the *Mary Rose*. If you get a splinter from this tree, it leaves you feeling that everything will be all right.

Sun Eater – These vulture-like birds are often seen circling wildfires, and are hunted by humans because they are considered to be bad luck. However, these brave avians actually shepherd

distressed creatures to safety and they eat the flames from the wildfires. We always send them to help ships we pirate because they tidy up much better than we could. Their eggs are always warm: good for putting at the bottom of the hammock for toasty toes at night.

Tanglethatch Spider – A brown hairy spider that spins immensely strong unbreakable webs. In the Middle Ages, when archery was the main form of battle, these spiders were used for their webs; but because their webs were taken away to make archery strings, their homes were destroyed and they were easily caught and eaten by their main predators, Cain Wolves. They're very fun to play games with. One time, we attached a Bombulant Coconut to the end of a Tanglethatch Spider's web and played tennis with it. Annie tried to make one follow her around like a dog.

Toft Moss – A soft and lovely moss that quickly spreads across forest floors. It was over-harvested by humans to make tapestries and wall hangings in the medieval period. Also makes lovely soft spongy beds and grows over the floor to make cosy carpets. Never once made himself a whole jacket out of it, and Shelly wouldn't stop cuddling him all day.

Trundling Fungus – A highly inventive, bright orange shape-shifting fungus. Playful but tricky-tempered, it takes

many shapes and can grow both literally and metaphorically attached to people. Once it is attached, it becomes very loyal. Annie trained a puffball to be like a dog; it even sat on command.

Tumble Shrub – A rootless shrub that once roamed in enormous herds across the Serengeti, causing earth-thunder that drummed up courage in human hearts. However, these shrubs were chased into the ocean by poachers harvesting them for their speed-inducing leaves. Easiest way to climb a hill: dive into a tumble shrub going upwards – but keep your eyes AND mouth shut if you start feeling sick.

Turbidus Vine – *Turbidus turbida* – A tricksy, trouble-making vine that can cause mischief with its leaves, shoots and even its seeds. Very clever, extremely fast-growing and wickedly wily! You only need to ask politely and the vine is really very helpful. But if you're shouty or rude, the vine responds the same way! Sometimes people just need to learn some manners.

Twitching Honeycreeper – A particularly paranoid bird with a penchant for sweet treats, especially honey. If it is caught with its beak in a bee's nest, drinking the honey, it shrieks and jumps up and down, flashing its tail feathers and

carrying on furiously to cover its embarrassment. These birds used to steal the honey cakes that the Duchess sent us.

Venus Mantrap – The cerise-pink flowers grow on vines, snapping at each other as they grow. The largest flowers exist alone on their vines because they have eaten all the rest of their competition and are big enough to swallow a human whole (as their name suggests). However, contrary to their name, they cannot digest a human, so will spit it back out after tasting it. They create heavy golden pollen and shining nectar. The nectar is delicious on toast. We put small petals of this flower into Miss Prim's shoes.

New Creatures Discovered by the Proprietor of this Book

Acknowledgements

Writing a book is a bit like going on a long voyage over the high seas: it's an epic journey, full of adventures and surprises; the sailing is by turns rough and smooth; and the people who go with you make all the difference. Sometimes they even save you from sinking!

Alongside me on the wild adventure of writing *The Troublemakers*, I've been very lucky to have the best crew a pirate could ask for, and I want to express my earnest gratitude to them all with a resounding YARRRRR! THANK'EE, ME HEARTIES!

Nat Doherty, with her humour, kindness and wisdom, steered this book safely through storms; at times she took the wheel to stop me from sailing into the jaws of a kraken or going completely off the edge of the map.

Wendy Shakespeare with her all-round brilliance and eagle eye for details has made the book shipshape and seaworthy, from crow's nest to keel.

Jane Griffiths and Josh Benn have kept the book sailing merrily in the right direction, and have done the very important work of guiding the ship into port and safely lowering the anchor. And Sarah Hall, Petra Bryce and Louisa Hunter have expertly secured the metaphorical halyards!

Paola Escobar has created yet another gorgeous cover, a magnificent new map and enchanting illustrations. Emily Smyth's brilliant design skills have brought the book beautifully to life.

Charlotte Winstone, Michelle Nathan and the brilliant team in publicity and marketing at Puffin have championed the Makers books with swashbuckling spirit and verve!

My brilliant agent, Claire Wilson, and the wonderful Safae El-Ouahabi at RCW – two fearless and mighty heroes to have aboard ship – are ready at all hours to hoist the mainsail and go marauding in search of glory.

Simon Boughton and Kristin Allard at Norton YR took Cordelia and the Makers on their maiden voyage across the Atlantic, and for that adventure I will always be wildly grateful.

Thank you to the wonderful rabble of children's authors for all your generosity and camaraderie. It is endless fun being part of this brilliant band of swashbuckling storytellers! Especially Hana Tooke and Rosie Hudson: you are diamonds and your friendship will always be treasured. And special thank-yous go to Anna James, Catherine Doyle and Emma Carroll for your very kind and generous quotes.

ACKNOWLEDGEMENTS

Thank you to the crew of the beautiful *Blue Clipper* – Captain Chris, first mate Jack, engineer Mo, Chubbs the cook, sailors Emily, Zara, Gilles, Rich and Kat, and my fellow passengers Adele, Will, Elizabeth and Mark. I will never forget night-sailing round the Isle of Skye beneath the Northern Lights. And I will also never forget Mo's expression when I declared I was glad to be seasick because it would be great for my book.

Thank you to Mum and Dad, and family and friends, for your patience with my pirate voices and ship talk. And to my sister, Katie (to whom this book is dedicated), for going on adventures and stirring up trouble with me ever since we were big enough to go roving round DOSC together, barefoot and unsupervised.

And to Barney, the star by which I set my compass, for reading every draft and inspiring the name of Smokestack Doogray.

A wonderful thing about writing a book is that once it is finished, *that* is when the book's journey truly begins: the story goes out into the wide world to find its way into the hands of the people it will belong to – such as *you*, dear reader!

Finally, I would like to thank the wonderful booksellers who put books into the hands of young readers: you perform life-changing acts of true magic every day. I doff my piratical tricorn to you all!

Tamzin Merchant has been an actor since the age of seventeen. Her acting work has taken her around the world and on a journey through time. She has been a Tudor, a Victorian, a Jacobean, and has survived the Blitz and succumbed to pneumonia in Edwardian times. She's been an alien, a witch, a doomed queen, a feisty Scottish warrior and a rebellious high-society runaway.

Follow Tamzin on Twitter and Instagram
@tamzinmerchant
#TheHatmakers #The Mapmakers #TheTroublemakers